PETER M. BOURRET

OTHER BOOKS BY PETER M . BOURRET

THE PHYSICS OF WAR

LAND OF LOUD NOISES AND VACANT STARES

SNOWFLAKES FROM THE OTHER SIDE OF THE UNIVERSE

All titles are available online @ amazon.

Three Joss Sticks In The Rain

Peter M. Bourret

Three Joss Stick in the Rain
Copyright © 2016 Peter M Bourret

Printed by CreateSpace in the USA
Fiction / Vietnam War / PTSD / Buddhism
First Edition (October, 2016)
First Printing (October, 2016)
ISBN-10: 1516952278
ISBN-13: 978-1516952274
Cover design by Denham Clements
Sean Fonseca of MaverickWebMarketing.com

DEDICATION

With deep appreciation for his support and friendship, I am dedicating my first novel to Mike Fitz, a true friend for the past fifty-seven years. He has always been willing to truly listen when I needed to talk, which has helped me process my Nam experience. Not all combat vets are as fortunate as I have been to have someone who was always there for them. I am blessed to be best of friends with Mike, a compassionate person who has always been willing to truly listen. For me, this has been more valuable than a parade or sayings like *thank you for your service.* Actions do speak louder than words. I am truly blessed and fortunate to know him; he is a class act and as genuine as they come.

CONTENTS

ACKNOWLEDGMENTS

I'd like to offer a special thank you to the following people: Mary DeSantis and Cheryl Watters, my editors, for there insight and support; and a very special shout-out to my friend Denham Clements and to Sean Fonseca of MaverickWebMarketing.com for their combined talents and tireless work, which brought the cover design to fruition; additionally, Denham Clements for his keen observations and enthusiastic support; Bill Black for his feedback, encouragement and invaluable technical help; Melissa Stirton for her formatting assistance; Ann Reaban, and Morris and Sharon Barkan for their support and detailed and insightful observations; and my sister Mary Bourret, Michael Brewer, Vicki and Howie Hibbs, Erin Fitzgerald Jacobs, Wendy Newell, Carolyn Kittle, Mary Pat Sullivan, Nancy Curran, Linda Leighton, Carla Turner, Lynda Gibson, my son Jeremy Bourret, and Robert Lindsey, the group founder and primary administrator for *Vietnam War Book & Film Group* on Facebook for their steadfast encouragement.

Terry DeWald was gracious enough to connect me with Homer Marks, a member of the Tohono O'odham Nation who served as a Marine in Vietnam and was most generous with his time. My conversations with Homer Marks provided the basis for O'Brien's friend Baptisto Santos. Additionally, I am indebted to Cheryl, a friend from Richmond, Virginia, who provided first-hand information about her city, which helped me paint an accurate picture of the funeral route and the cemetery in the story. Pam Bourn, a friend from high school, introduced me to Conroe, Texas, which became the inspiration for the locale for several characters in my novel. I am truly grateful to be blessed with so many good people in my life. Finally, I would like to acknowledge a North Vietnamese officer, one whom I met on my second post-war trip back to Vietnam; he shared his belief about the significance of individual behavior in war: our behavior does not happen in a vacuum. His observation was the catalyst for the idea for my story. Had we met back in '68 rather than in 1999, we would have both tried to kill the other; fortunately, fate prevented that, and thus, we have a novel rather than a gravesite for one of us.

PREFACE

Three Joss Sticks in the Rain is much more than a war story, yet the Vietnam War, the 1968 Tết Offensive in particular, are key to the story's development. "the catechism of killing," a poem from *Land of Loud Noises and Vacant Stares*, my second book of poetry, succinctly sums up the comprehensive nature of war and its long and tenacious tentacles: *"war is deceptively simple / when the bullets are whizzing by / and shrapnel is racing for its finish line / war isn't complicated until you get home."*

As is always the case in any war, there are those who are killed and those who survive; no one leaves *their* war unscathed. War's demons can torment and destroy, yet for some there is redemption and growth for. Something as horrific as war has the potential to become a crucible for positive, personal growth. Whether Việt Cong or US Marine, war does not discriminate. War is greedy: not satisfied with stealing the lives of the young, it attacks the souls of the survivors as is the case in this story, narrated from the point of view of two young members of the Việt Cong, a brother and his sister, and two United States Marines, one an eighteen-year-old and the other a twenty-one-year-old who is on his second combat tour of duty. Because the story is not presented with an objective, omniscient narrator's perspective, the reader must rely solely on the subjective, and therefore skewed, nature of the perspectives of each of the four narrators. Because the reader must rely on the prism of the worldview of four very distinct characters, Shakespeare might aptly state, *"Ay, there's the rub."*

Some of the diction—racial slurs and foul language—might rightly be considered offensive for a variety of reasons. The use of such words enables the reader to view the world from the perspective of a particular character who might be bigoted, intolerant or angry. My goal was not to edit the typical diction of some young Marines living in 1968, thus being politically correct for an audience in 2016, but rather to allow the reader to listen in and experience the worldview of the characters, flaws and all.

An important clarification for the reader is that when I refer to *Charlie's sister*, I am referring to *Tuan's sister*, an eighteen-year-old South Vietnamese villager who is a pivotal character because of her relationships with the three other narrators. Her brother Tuan, who serves dual roles as narrator and character, is a member of the Viêt Cong, thus the reference to Charlie's sister, because *Charlie* is an abbreviated slang name for all Viêt Cong or VC based on the military's code name for the letter *C*, which is Charlie; a longer version is Victor Charlie, based on *VC. Charley*, an alternate spelling, is the name of one of the Marine companies.

I ask much of the reader in the arena of military terminology; therefore, I am providing a quick course in Vietnam War lingo: *the Nam* is Vietnam, more the experience than solely the geographic location; *Charlie* is the name American troops gave to the Viêt Cong, aka the Cong, but these South Vietnamese Communist forces referred to themselves as the NLF, or National Liberation Front, which was modeled after the Viêt Minh who defeated the French in 1954; the *NVA* are the North Vietnamese Army or the PAVN, the People's Army of Vietnam; the *ARVN* are the South Vietnamese Army (American allies); *gooks, dinks* and *slopes* are pejorative terms for the Vietnamese; *Uncle Ho* is Ho Chi Minh, the leader of North Vietnam; the *Têt Offensive* is the surprise attack by Communist forces (VC and NVA) throughout South Vietnam during the Têt holiday (Vietnamese New Year) at the end of January 1968; the *grunts* are American infantry; *corpsman* are Navy medics, beloved by the Marines because of their courage under fire; an *FO* is a forward observer who would call in 81 mm mortar or artillery fire missions on the enemy; *arty* is artillery, which fire various sizes of shells/rounds: 105 mm, 155 mm, 175 mm and 8 inch shells; *122s* are 122 mm NVA rockets with a range of five about miles; *81s* refers to 81 mm mortars, with a range of almost three miles; *HE* are High Explosive shells or rounds; *illum* are illumination rounds used to light up the night sky in a specific area; *PRC-25* is a field radio used to call in fire support or assistance; *FDC* (*Fire Direction Cent*er) is a bunker where the calculations for fire missions are created; a *topo map* is a topographical map used as reference by a forward observer to request a fire mission from the Fire Direction Center; a *klick* is 1,000 meters on a topo map; the *M14* rifle and the newer *M16* rifle are Americans assault rifles; the *AK-47* assault rifle is mainly used by the NVA but also by some VC; the *SKS* is a 7.62 mm rifle used by the VC; the *M60* is an American 7.62 mm machine gun with a cyclic rate of fire of 550 rounds per minute; the *RPD* is 7.62 mm machine gun used by the Communist forces; a *Chicom grenade* refers to a Viêt Cong or NVA grenade; a *Claymore mine* is an American anti-personnel device that fires a blast of pellets toward the enemy and is primarily used to prevent infiltration; *C rats* are C rations, carried on patrols and consist of several cans of food; *782 gear* is the military name for all of a Marine's equipment for the field; a *Marine squad* consists of 10 to 12 men; *spider holes* are camouflaged surface openings in a VC tunnel system that helped the VC fire and then disappear quickly; *R&R* is a 5-day break in which troops unwind outside the war zone; *KIA* stands for Killed In Action; *WIA* stands for Wounded In Action; *MIA* stands for Missing In Action; *AWOL* stands for Absent With Out Leave; *POW* stands for Prisoner Of War; *piasters* are Vietnamese currency; *Indian Country* and *Dodge City* are names given by Marines to dangerous locations in Vietnam with heavy concentrations of enemy forces; a *ville* is a rural village or hamlet, which, based on a French mapping system, frequently is followed by a number inside a set of parentheses, designating that the village is broken into various sections or annexes; *Dông Bích (1), Phuóc Ninh (7), An Nhon (1) and (2) and Phuóc Nhân (2)* are villes between seven and nine miles southwest of Da Nang; *Hill 10* is the battalion hill for the 1st Battalion, 7th Marine Regiment, 1st Marine Division, aka 1/7; *Hill 270* and *Charlie Ridge* are NVA strongholds 10 miles southwest of Da Nang, which is the second largest city in Vietnam and is the location of a large American airbase; the *Q16 Company* is a Viêt Cong company with a guerrilla cadre, or force, of approximately 100 that operates in the area of Hill 10; the *368 B Artillery Regiment* is a North Vietnamese 122 mm rocket regiment that operates in the area southwest of Hill 10; the *3/31st* is a North Vietnamese infantry battalion operating in the area southwest of Hill 10 and consists of about 400 soldiers; a *cadre* is a small military group trained for a particular purpose; the *Silver Star* is the second highest combat medal given for exemplary bravery above and beyond expectation; the *Purple Heart* is a medal given to those wounded or killed by hostile fire. Hopefully, I have clarified enough terminology to make my novel more understandable for those who did not serve in Vietnam. When in doubt, 'Google' any unfamiliar terms.

MAP OF DÔNG BÍCH (1) AREA

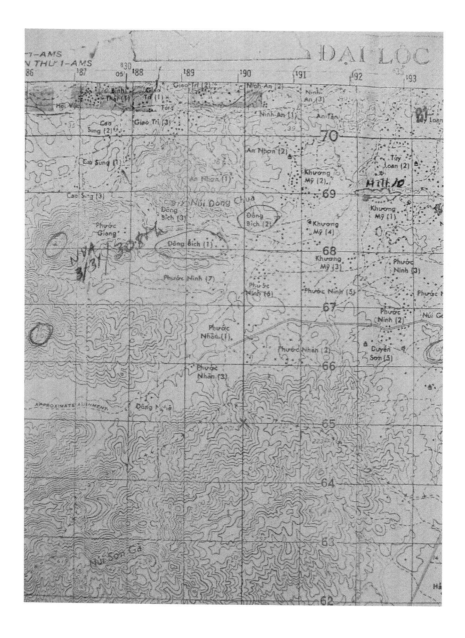

1

O'BRIEN
10 SEPTEMBER 2001
HOLY TRINITY MONASTERY, ST. DAVID, ARIZONA

An oasis of serenity—the only way to describe this place. Had someone back in '68 told me that I'd end up in St David, Arizona as a monk, well, I'd have told them they were nuts. My only concern back then was surviving the Tết Offensive and then getting out of the Nam alive by the summer of '68. From Marine forward observer to Benedictine monk—that's a stretch, but stranger things have happened. I have always taken the road less traveled, so I guess I shouldn't be surprised that my life has turned out the way it has. No regrets. Even the negatives have been my teachers, offering me profound lessons. Although not always pleasant, my journey has been perfect. Checking my ego at the door is the best lesson I have learned, but I kicked and screamed on the way to acceptance. Oh, the simplicity and the serenity of a life of *letting go.*

I am one with this place and its billowy clouds that slide slowly, silently across the powder-blue, early September skyscape; and the pair of hungry Harris's hawks with outstretched wings, floating effortlessly in the midday air, hovering above the mesquite bosque and then rocketing toward the pecan orchard and a cottontail rabbit, their unsuspecting lunch that is at the wrong end of the food chain; and the pond, a sanctuary for a family of ducks, and its carpet of lotus pads that cuddle up to the forest of reeds that hug the bank closest to the mesquite bosque; and the solitary bee, circling and then strafing the army of black ants that scurry across the desert's skin in search of a mesquite leaf; and I am one with the earth, hard and overgrown with desert weeds that don't know they are weeds. They checked their egos at the door.

A slight breeze cools the warm September air above me, and the ghosts of yesterday surround me, and I am at peace.

2

TUAN
12TH DAY OF THE TÉT OFFENSIVE
SOUTHEAST OF DÔNG BÍCH (1)

I was proud to be part of the National Liberation Front, a cadre helping in the defense of our land from the foreign invaders. We were certain that the Americans would eventually tire of their fight just as the French had, and the thirty-two of us who made up the Q16 Company's 2nd Platoon would help them to leave as corpses if that was what their leaders wanted for these young American Marines. They are such fools to fight for their corrupt leaders, just as the French soldiers who had to be sacrificed during their war until their leaders realized their war of aggression was impossible to win.

We have been so fortunate to have the great patriot Uncle Ho as our leader in our struggle to eventually have one Viêt Nam, not a South and a North. Sadly, many will have to die until the Americans finally realize the futility of their unjust American War.

The tree line was the perfect place, not for an ambush of the dozen American Marines who were approaching my village of Dông Bích, but for me to fire one perfectly-placed round from my prized weapon, a captured M14 rifle taken last summer after a successful ambush. The blood of six Marines had soaked into the red soil near the road leading to their firebase at Hill 10. Our brothers from the North had attacked the ARVN camp just east of the American Marines' base, which drew their reaction force into our ambush. We had outnumbered their force by two to one, and the darkness had been our friend.

But today, there will only be one shot. In the distance, walking along the rice paddy dike, the American Marines look so small. I will wait for the right moment when the afternoon air is calm and certainty is in my mind—the shot will be perfect and my tunnel escape will frustrate the Americans once again.

Four hundred meters away and moving closer. Because I am an excellent shot, one of the Marines will go home today. And a mother will shed her tears because her son foolishly decided to come to our land. This young American Marine's family will feel great sorrow—this I know because I also have felt such pain like so many of our fighters have.

Three hundred meters away. I must focus and concentrate the hatred that still burns in my heart for the Marines whose artillery killed my father last year. I know this pain all too well. When my sister and I were small children, the French stole our mother's life—they stole our lives. I was a little boy who wanted his mother, yet my tears could not bring her back to me and my little sister.

Two hundred meters away—an easy shot for me. The wind is picking up. Be patient. This shot must be perfect. My target will die for our father. Which one will die? The one at the back of the squad. When he falls dead in the rice paddy, the rest of the American Marines won't see him fall. They will only hear my rifle shot, and it will have the sound of an American rifle. I'll have a few more seconds to escape into the tunnel before they return rifle and machine-gun fire. And when their mortar barrage begins landing in the tree line, the explosions will kill banana trees and I'll be safe in our tunnel system. I'll be gone, and there'll be one more dead American Marine. It will be a good afternoon.

One hundred meters away. Gray and cloudy, the afternoon sky is watching. The air is calm. A slight smile crosses my face. I inhale a deep breath. Releasing it slowly, I squeeze the trigger.

3

SANDBURN
11 FEBRUARY 1968
8 MILES SOUTHWEST OF DA NANG

I hated that son of a bitch O'Brien. Mr. Two-Tours-in-the-Nam. Hell, he wasn't even a real grunt, just an FO for 81s. What's so damn special about a forward observer for mortars? Anybody can read a map and call in a fire mission. If a nigger like Webster could, I guess anybody could. I never understood why God decided to punish me by putting me in a squad with a nigger for a squad leader and that almighty Sergeant O'Brien as our FO. O'Brien was nothing more than a damn gook lover, and in 87 days, I'd be rid of both O'Brien and Corporal Webster. Then the fine colored folks back in Conroe, Texas could have his black ass back again. But I'd have to wait till the end of June before I'd rotate back to the World. I just didn't want to end up on the same flight home with that prick O'Brien. Never wanted to see that son of a bitch again if it could be helped.

I couldn't figure out why he got so pissed off when I took a whiz on the gook burial mound out by Phuóc Ninh (7). I needed to take a leak, and there were only dead gooks buried there. What was his problem anyway? Lucky for him that his buddy Chukut pulled him away. I would've kicked his ass and then gotten busted. I hated to have to admit it, but the Papago powwow boy was good for something besides humpin' a radio through this shithole.

Before saddling up just after sunrise, Webster put the word on us that the North Vietnamese of the 3/31st NVA battalion were in the area of Hill 270, which was about two and a half klicks west of where we were to set up our night ambush. Before setting our trap, we had to see if we could win the hearts and minds of the gooks at a sorry ass excuse for a hamlet called Dông Bích (1). We'd been out there before and heard the same, old, lame shit about the Việt Cong being numba ten, and, of course, they always said, "No VC, no VC" when we asked if Charlie had been visiting them at night. Of course, the Cong had been there. It was just a game.

I got so tired of those betel-nut smiles of those old, ugly-ass mamma-sans. How could we ever win the hearts and minds of the dinks if the corpsman couldn't even get 'em to use a toothbrush? They probably gave the toothbrushes to their Việt Cong buddies of the Q16 Company so they could use them for cleaning their weapons. I never understood why Doc Reyes wasted his time doing that kind of civic shit for the damn gooks. Maybe 'cause them beaners are all Catholics, and they get into all that love your neighbor bullshit. An eye for an eye, that's my goddamn religion.

Actually, Reyes wasn't bad for a taco bender since he gave me the stuff to clean up the case of clap I got on R&R and kinda forgot to put it in my medical records. I hated to admit it, but Doc Reyes and I actually had somethin' in common, but it sure as hell wasn't our neighborhoods. I was from Richmond, Virginia, a real city. I thought he was bullshitting me when he told me he was from Truth or Consequences, New Mexico. We were both stuck in the same cesspool, but that was it. You'd never catch me doin' any reminiscing in Truth or Consequences. You could put money on that, real money, not those gook piasters.

I was in the mood for some contact with Charlie, but they stayed clear of us in the morning when we patrolled through An Nhon (1) and (2). Gathering intelligence from the gooks in these villes was boring as hell, so I hoped we'd catch the North Vietnamese being careless like they'd been a week earlier when we ran into a platoon of regulars in broad daylight as they were ditty bopping out of Phuóc Nhân (2) at the base of Charlie Ridge. O'Brien called in some mortars and artillery from Hill 10 on them, but a couple of Phantom jets from Da Nang hit them hard with napalm. It was real nice.

Unfortunately, we hadn't had much daytime contact with the

NVA, much less the Cong, since then. I guess they didn't like what our jets did to them, so it made more sense that they'd come strolling out of the mountains at night to set up their rockets to blow the hell out of Da Nang, but we'd be sitting there waitin' for 'em. Even though O'Brien was an asshole, he could call in some serious fucking mortar and arty fire on the gooks. We could get a serious body count, genuine confirmed kills, not that 'blood trails' bullshit. Lots of dead dinks, and I'd piss on their dead asses.

In the early afternoon, we moved out from An Nhon (1) and headed southeast toward the edge of some rice paddies. There we found Dông Bích (2), dumb ass name and all. I never understood how the gooks came up with these weird-ass names for these villes or why they also had to have numbers added on. They all looked the same. Of course, O'Brien, Mr. Know-It-All, explained some lame bullshit about the French havin' somethin' to do with it. Give me a fucking break! Didn't O'Brien know the Frenchies live in France? Why the fuck would they give a damn about a bunch of villes in this part of the world?

Anyway, the nice thing about going there the way we did was that we avoided the paddies that were to the east of the ville. We had a lot of ground to cover before nightfall, so Webster didn't have our squad hang around in the ville too long. I'd love to be a fly on the wall of one of their hooches to hear what they said when we headed southwest for about one klick away from the rice paddies and towards Dông Bích (1), which was in the area where Webster said we'd set up the night ambush.

The North Vietnamese rocket boys wouldn't have much of a walk from Hill 270 down to this location, maybe two klicks or so. We were closer to their hill than our own, but we were within the range of our own 81s and arty. Mortars were nice, but I liked the damage a barrage of 105 mm artillery rounds does. Blows the shit out of a target real damn good.

Day patrols sucked because we usually had to be careful of all the booby traps that the Cong had everywhere, and night ambushes were a drag since sleepin' in the rain wasn't no damn fun. But after a while, I got used to it. Although the commies were trying to kick our ass with their offensive, there were two nice things about early February. First of all, it hadn't rained much, which was just fine with me. And the other thing was the Viêt Cong had cleared out a shit load of their booby traps so their NVA buddies from Up North could roam around at will.

Actually, there was a third good thing about February. We got four Fuckin' New Guys. Since our squad was down to five men, not counting Doc Reyes, or O'Brien and his radioman, we got a fresh supply of Fuckin' New Guys. Being at half strength was a drag, but having four cherries to look after wasn't much better.

Sometime in the mid afternoon, just as we were coming up on Dông Bích (1) from the east, a sniper cranked off a headshot from a tree line about a hundred meters south of us. The squad let loose and poured some serious shit his way. Since we had to save some of our ammo for our night ambush, Webster had O'Brien do his forward observer thing and call in a ten-round barrage of 81s. The damn gook was probably safe in some tunnel by the time mortar rounds from back at the hill started landing in the tree line. We never found nothing out there but a bunch of blown-to-hell trees. What else was new? Lucky for that sniper that O'Brien didn't call in a napalm air strike. That would've been cool, but we had to settle for ten rounds of mortar fire.

That gook was lucky all around; lucky shot for him but not for MacWhatever, MacSomethin'. Hell, he was MacFuckin' Dead. He was just a cherry, so I wasn't interested in being his buddy and finding out his name. The dude couldn't even get past his fourth shitty day in the Nam. The PFC stopped being a Fuckin' New Guy real quick and turned into a DMF, a Dead Mother Fucker, about the time the medevac chopper finally got here to fly his dead ass away. Reyes was a pretty good corpsman, but Mac had lost too much damn blood, and headshots aren't real good for your future. He didn't even get to go on R&R and get laid. Kind of a fucking drag, but at least I got some of his stuff.

A grunt can always use a couple extra magazines of ammo. Would've gotten more, but Webster made us give each of the cherries a couple of magazines. In a firefight they wouldn't need 'em since they'd be too scared to make use of the ammo they had. Webster should've given the extra ammo to people who knew what the fuck to do with it. At least I got his C-rats before that nigger started making us be all fair when we split up the dude's shit.

I did pretty good on the deal. Got a can of peaches and some smokes, not to mention one of his canteens, a full one, and a couple of grenades. I didn't have no use for his ham and motherfuckers—just not a lima bean fan—so I gave them to one of the Fuckin' New Guys, some farm boy from Iowa or some other boring-ass state like Nebraska. This dude was only on week number two in the Nam, so I gave him the ham and motherfuckers. Dumb shit that he was, he smiled and actually thanked me. When he gets zapped in a firefight, and I know he will, I hope he has some good C-rations on him. Peaches, that's what I hope he has.

When the medevac chopper finally showed up just outside of Dông Bích (1) to pick up Mac's dead ass, Webster was an asshole once again, maybe because he was still pissed at me for scrounging up Mac's stuff. The son of a bitch actually made me help lug that cherry's dead ass to the chopper. I had done plenty of that shit before, but it wasn't fair since he had three new dudes who should've done it. A lance corporal with almost nine months in the Nam shouldn't have to do that kinda shit.

To make matters worse, it was beginning to get cloudy, which meant we'd probably get rained on later, but at least we had our ponchos with us. Right after the medevac chopper took off for Da Nang, we saddled up and headed out towards Dông Bích (1), a hamlet surrounded by high ground on three sides. Northeast of that hamlet was the smaller ville of Dông Bích (2), which sat between paddies to the east and a mile-long ridgeline that was about 400 meters to the north of Dông Bích (1). Just south of the ville were two hills that were about 50 meters tall. To the west were the mountains, NVA turf.

There was an excellent chance the North Vietnamese would come visit us soon, but first, we had some business to take care of with the local VC, the good old Q16. We'd run into this gook company before, and we kicked ass and had took names each time. The sniper that had blown Mac away was probably from this outfit, so it seemed they hadn't gotten the message and needed us to teach 'em a lesson they wouldn't forget.

As we reached the western edge of Dông Bích (1), I spotted a dink bitch standing by a small pagoda about fifty meters to the north of the path that ran along the southern boundary of the ville. For a gook, she wasn't too bad looking, so I decided to make a little conversation with her. Since I was at the ass-end of the squad, I figured Webster wouldn't miss me. How long does it take to get a quick piece of ass, especially when you don't have to do no foreplay and romantic shit? Just wham bam, rocks off, and you're outta there. If the bitch didn't want to be cooperative, it would just take a little longer to let her know that she was wasting her damn time resistin' my charms. A man's got to do what a man's got to do. I knew the location of the night ambush site, which wasn't very far away, so I disappeared for some gook *boom-boom.*

As I got closer to her, she started lookin' real nervous, the way VC suspects always looked. She had to be a teenager, perky tits and all. They didn't sag the way they did on the old, ugly mamma-sans, but give her a few more years in this shithole and she'd look just as wrinkly and ugly as all the old gook bitches. I just hoped that chomping on betel nut hadn't messed up her teeth yet, but it would someday. The nice thing about getting laid out here in the bush was that I wouldn't have to waste a rubber on her. There was a pretty good chance she didn't have the clap like most of the whores in Da Nang. And if I was wrong 'cause she was putting out for the Cong, then good old Doc Reyes would take care of me.

There she stood, just a couple of feet away, looking like a typical gook chick with her long black hair and matching black pee jays. Up close her face wasn't as cute as it looked when I first spotted her. She looked like she had some acne scars or small pox or chicken pox, or some shit like that when she was a *babysan.* Actually, I wasn't too interested in how cute she was. Just needed to get some *boom-boom.*

I figured she didn't speak no English, so I stuck the barrel of my M16 on her right tit and pushed her back past her little pagoda. That was all the foreplay the bitch was gonna get out of me. A few feet behind the shrine was a clump of banana trees, which seemed like as good a place as any to fuck the shit out of her. But she liked her little pagoda a little too damn much and wouldn't move away from it, so I yelled, "Okay, if you don't want a little privacy in the banana trees, then I'll do you right here in front of all your fucking ancestors. And when I'm through, I'll shit on your goddamn burial mound, you slant-eyed, fuckin', gook bitch! *Didi!*"

She didn't move like I told her to. Instead, she got dumb and started screamin' all this gook gibberish. I didn't have no time for this bullshit, so I shoved her hard enough with my rifle to knock her to the ground. She started to sit up and scoot away from me, but I used the butt of my rifle to push her back down where I wanted her. She went from nervous to scared shitless real damn quick, and that was fine with me. Not thinking real good with my brain, I threw my helmet down next to her. She grabbed it and heaved it at me as hard as she could, but I dodged the flying helmet, which hit the backside of her family's pagoda. Without wasting any more time, I quickly leaned my M16 against the pagoda, but I didn't bother to take off my flak jacket or any of my gear since she wasn't being very cooperative.

Before I could pounce on her, two wrinkled up, old mamma-sans and a crowd of five or six skinny kids showed up. The kids stared, and the ugliest of the two old bitches started screaming all sorts of gook shit at me. I turned around and yelled, *"Didi!* Get the fuck out of here, you old hags!"

My piece of ass sat up and was crying and jabbering, and the old bitches just wouldn't shut the fuck up. "Okay, then you'll have to watch 'cause I'm gonna fuck this bitch!" One of the mamma-sans came at me, swinging her skinny-ass arms. She looked so stupid that I wanted to laugh. She wouldn't stop, so I grabbed the old bitch by the throat with my right hand to shut her up. The trick worked, but I had no use for her, so I shoved her ugly ass to the ground. She started sobbing and shit, but at least she knew I meant business. I didn't have no more time for her and the other gawkers, so I turned back toward my piece of ass.

Before I could drop my utility pants and give her a thrill, I heard a voice that I had learned to hate. I turned abruptly and saw O'Brien walking quickly towards me. He always seemed to have a serious look plastered on his dumb-ass face, but this time he was way past serious. Pissed off big time. He reminded me of the way my old man used to look when he'd kick my ass for lyin' to him. I knew O'Brien would give me some crap because he was one of those gentlemen types, so before he reached me, I tried to convince him that I was only havin' a little fun. I knew this line didn't work when he shouted, "Fuck you, Sandburn. Get your sorry ass back to the squad!"

His bullshit was getting old real quick, so I yelled back, "Go fuck yourself, you fuckin' gook lover!"

He responded by swinging his rifle at my head. The famous horizontal butt stroke that we had learned way back in boot camp would have knocked me out, but I was moving back when the butt of his rifle grazed me across the forehead. Before I could grab my M16 and make things fair, he aimed his weapon at my crotch and yelled, "I'll empty a full magazine into your balls. That should cure you, Fuck Head!"

Blood was streaming down my forehead as I put my helmet back on. O'Brien had the advantage and my head was throbbing, so I gave up my idea of getting laid in Dông Bích. Because it hurt too much to wear my helmet, I lugged it in my left hand. I reached over to the little pagoda, grabbed my rifle, and headed south toward the trail with O'Brien a few feet behind me. I don't think that he trusted me.

Once I reached the trail, I waited for him to catch up. Just before we began heading west on the path, I quickly lobbed a grenade back toward the pagoda. It was still standing, but it got messed up pretty good. All the dinks that had been standing around watching the show a couple of minutes earlier had dispersed, so none of them took any shrapnel. Amazingly, O'Brien got all bent out of shape when I laughed and said, "Wasn't trying to hurt no body. Just trying to scare 'em a little. Just having a little fun since you messed me up from gettin' a piece of ass."

He wasn't laughing. When he replied, "Sandburn, you're a genuine fucker," I knew we'd never be buddies, and I mean never. Fucking never.

4

CHARLIE'S SISTER
2ND WEEK OF THE YEAR OF THE MONKEY
DÔNG BÍCH (1)

I hated the French and the Americans equally, but when the American Marine tried to rape me, the scales of my hatred were tipped toward the Americans. Earlier in the afternoon, my older brother Tuan had killed an American Marine as one of their patrols approached our village of Dông Bích from the east. The Marines always took reprisals for such incidents, so I was not surprised when the American Marine tried to rape me. Neither was it unexpected to me when he hurled a hand grenade at the small shrine outside our hut. Like the French soldiers in the past, the Americans had done similar acts before to others in our village. These foreigners only knew how to disrespect us and our traditions. They are no more than savages who will be defeated.

We were certain that the Americans eventually would grow weary of their war, just as the French had, and they would return to their lives of ease and their luxurious homes in America, but first, many of their young men would have to die for their foolish and arrogant leaders. Someday there would be no puppet government and no foreign invaders in our beloved country. My hatred of the Americans could only be matched by my zeal and passion for our war of national liberation.

When I informed Tuan of the incident with the American Marine, he responded as an older brother might; he wanted to kill this Marine for attempting to dishonor me and for exhibiting great disrespect to our ancestors when he damaged our shrine. Yet, I also told him of another American Marine, one who acted very differently from the man who tried to dishonor me. This Marine wore a serious face, and he became enraged at the other Marine. When I told my brother that the American Marine with the serious expression prevented the rape from occurring because he hit the other man with his rifle, he seemed shocked at first but then laughed sarcastically. "It is good when enemy soldiers fight among themselves. This is more proof that our cause will succeed and the Americans will fail to subdue us."

My brother was very similar to the Marine with the solemn face. It had been many years since there had been a glow, a sparkle in his eyes. The French had killed that aspect of him when they made him a motherless small child, and the Americans made certain that this part of him remained buried when they killed our father with their artillery. They destroyed our family. I can only remember a few things from when I was four or five, but I can't remember him smiling with his eyes. It was all so long ago when we had both a father and a mother.

I understood the cause of Tuan's melancholy, but the source behind the American Marine's expression was a mystery for me. I knew only that he had saved me from being violated and dishonored by the other Marine and that he had also returned to the shrine shortly before sunset. He may have struck the other Marine as a reaction or simply because they were enemies, yet I could not fathom why he had chosen to return to our family's pagoda. Apparently, there was intention and thought in his action. Both men had left their patrol, one to rape me, the other to place an offering at our family shrine.

The sun was beginning to set when he arrived at the shrine. Kneeling on one knee, he reached into his rucksack and withdrew a can of food, which he placed at the base of the pagoda. Then he pulled from his pack what appeared to be several joss sticks, which he stuck in the soil in front of our shrine that had been damaged earlier in the afternoon by the other American. He lit the three joss sticks, and the aroma was most pleasing to me, yet I was baffled why he would do such an act of reverence. Just as he was standing up, random raindrops splattered haphazardly like miniature mortar explosions in the reddish soil of our village of Dông Bích.

When the Marine realized that the joss sticks would be soaked by what was becoming a steady downpour, he planted several branches round the three joss sticks and sheltered them from the rain with something that the Marines called a poncho. Having protected the burning incense sticks from being snuffed out, he abruptly turned away and began running back toward the path that ran through our village. He did not observe me as he ran past our hut.

I had seen it all, but he did not know that I had been watching. As usual, the Marines were unaware that they were being watched as they prepared for their ambush.

Erasing the final shades of dusk, a steady drizzle stretched on from early evening until shortly after midnight. It was at this time that the American Marines realized that the eyes of the Q16 Company had been watching them.

5

O'BRIEN
11 FEBRUARY 1968
BENCHMARK CACTUS

Unlike the rest of the men in the squad who referred to Corporal Izaiah Webster as Dictionary, Lance Corporal Trent Sandburn used an abbreviation of Webster's nickname but never to his squad leader's face. That wasn't Sandburn's style. He fought his personal wars the Việt Cong way, with guerrilla tactics.

Sandburn hated Webster for several reasons, and one of them was the color of his skin. As far as he was concerned, there were niggers, jungle bunnies, coons, niggras, coloreds, and if he felt like being warm-hearted and Sunday-go-to-meetin' Christian, he'd refer to Webster as a Negro, but that had been a one-time deal. Once out of earshot, Webster's identity was immediately abracadabraed back into a fuckin' nigger. The way I figured it, Sandburn, who didn't seem to like anyone, just used Webster's dark skin as an excuse. Sandburn wasn't a big fan of anyone—especially 'one of them people'—giving him orders, which is what a squad leader does for a living.

Webster, who planned on attending college after finishing his three-year hitch in the Marine Corps, wasn't yet familiar with the famous line, "the best laid plans of mice and men," but his ten months of staying alive had made him keenly aware that even the best plan could go awry. And he even used the word *awry* when he reminded us to be prepared for the unexpected. Unlike the other members of the squad, I had attended twelve years of Catholic school, so I knew how to use the word correctly, most of the time. Back in Conroe, Texas, Webster's grandmother would've been beaming her pearlies had she known that her grandson had taken her advice about learning one new word each day. 'Words are power', she'd always told him. He hadn't always listened to her, but his time in the Nam had changed him in so many ways, and some of them were good.

"Okay, Dictionary, what the fuck does *awry* mean?," asked Westlake, our M60 machine gunner.

Smiling, Webster replied, "Kinda interesting that you used *fuck.*"

Fuck, accompanied with a question mark as big as Montana, flashed like a neon sign in the minds of the three cherries, but none dared say the *huh* that was trying to break out. Westlake, who was the emperor of his own world, wasn't shy, just focused on his job. But every day, he hopped off his throne long enough to play the role of five-year-old. Asking questions when he was in school hadn't been one of his strengths, but he had learned to love two things in the Nam. Because Webster didn't give grades, Westlake was always first to blurt out a question about Webster's word for the day. Besides asking questions, Dave Westlake cherished his M60 machine gun and its lethal power. He loved asking questions about words because he bought into Webster's grandmother's line about words being power, but knowing all the words in the world wouldn't do him any good unless he rode the Silver Bird back to the World, minus the green body bag. His M60 would be his ticket out of the Nam, one way or another. "Interesting?" rolled out from an impatient Westlake. "What the hell is interesting about it?"

Dictionary knew he had little time remaining for his lesson, so he replied, "Listen up, and I'll put it in terms that we can relate to. If our ambush goes awry, then it got all fucked up and didn't go the way we planned."

While most of the squad nodded their helmets in unison, I smiled, and Sandburn muttered something that Webster chose to ignore. He'd have a chat with him in the morning, but first he knew he needed to make certain that the ambush didn't turn out like the example that he'd just offered. Tomorrow's word would be *success.*

Stretching for more than a klick along the southern boundary of the trail that eventually ran through Dông Bích (1) was a ridge with two high points. The hilltop directly south of the ville was a few meters shorter than the forty meter hill which was about four hundred meters west of the spot where Dông Bích (1) stopped being a ville. At the base of this hill, the narrow trail began winding slowly south; within one hundred meters, it arched toward the northwest. We would spring our trap on the NVA rocket boys as they moved east out of this saddle.

Most of the squad set up positions ten meters south of the path. When the NVA entered the area where the trail dipped, we would greet them with the blast of Claymore mines and a hail of automatic weapons' fire. While seven of us positioned ourselves tactically near the trail, Webster sent Baptisto Santos and Trent Sandburn approximately one hundred and fifty meters to the east to set up a listening post at the top of a hill that was thirty meters high at best. From the high ground, equipped with a radio and a night-vision scope, they could detect any enemy movement from the south or from our eastern flank, but they could also provide us with early warning if they spotted the NVA coming down the trail that lead to Dông Bích.

The final ingredient for our ambush was a second listening post located about twenty meters southwest of the main ambush group. Manned by Nellis and Hesse, they would not only protect our rear, they could also cover our western flank. During better times Webster would have sent different men to this listening post, but that option had been taken away because our squad was under strength due to an increase in casualties which we had sustained since the onset of the Communist offensive. During the previous week and a half, we had lost three experienced men, two as KIAs and one as a serious WIA, so Nellis, who was nine days short of going home, and Hesse, who was only on day number three in the Nam, set up their Claymores mines. Because I would be calling in mortar fire on the NVA, I crawled over to the listening post to verify their position. I didn't want to accidentally call mortars in on them, especially on Nellis who had a strong desire to become eight days short.

When I arrived there, Nellis, who had spent more time on R&R than the cherry had spent in the Nam, was turning Hesse's

Claymore mine around so it was pointed away from them. He wasn't interested in having all its pellets flying his way if he had to set it off. He had every right to chew out Hesse for his potentially fatal mistake, but he refrained from doing that since new guys don't know shit and, more importantly, it wasn't part of his nature; calling Hesse a fuck-up wouldn't have helped his karma, which he had been concerned with ever since I had met him when I started my second tour the previous summer.

Nellis had tried to enlighten me, but I wasn't too interested in Buddhist philosophy at the time. Several months back, Nellis asked my opinion about whether fate or karma ran our lives. I hadn't thought much about that, so I just replied, "Fate?" When he responded, "Yes and no," I knew he had been in college too long. Whether it would be karma or fate that would get us back to the World, I didn't care. None of us really had time for philosophical speculation since we were all scared, but there was a major difference between the Nellis and Hesse as they set up their listening post. Nellis had learned to leave the part of fear that gets in the way back at Hill 10, discarding it like it was a non-essential piece of 782 gear, an unnecessary piece of equipment, only a burden to lug into the bush. Maybe, if the Nam chose to smile on Erik Hesse, he would learn this trick too. By putting these two men together, Webster had created the perfect example of one of his recent words: *juxtaposition.*

Those of us who took up ambush positions about ten meters south of the trail waited patiently, huddling under ponchos that made the night bearable in a steady drizzle which seemed to make time crawl. Webster was in the center of our group, and I was to his right as were my radioman J. D. Ethridge, and another cherry, a kid named John Sartoretti who, unlike Tom MacAndrews, had a chance of making it through his fourth day in the Nam. On Webster's left were Doc Reyes, Westlake, and Jimmy Rappaport, a cherry from Iowa who had quickly learned how to feed a steady diet of ammo into Westlake's M60.

The rain played stop-and-go, so everyone continued to wear their ponchos. Unfortunately for me, I had given up this option back at the ville when I had used my poncho to protect the burning joss sticks from being doused earlier in the evening. The rain would eventually stop, but I'd remain soaked for the rest of the night. Being soaked was a drag, but it beat being dead. Two tours in the Nam gave me some perspective, but I was still wet and shivering as I waited patiently for the early morning to bring us the NVA.

Although our main ambush was located on the topo map at the coordinates of 883678, we would not use these numbers when referring to our location during any radio transmissions, but rather we would refer to our position as Cactus, which would mean nothing to the NVA or the VC. Having a predetermined benchmark made it possible for quick target calculations at the Fire Direction Center back on Hill 10. It also simplified my life as an FO when I needed to call in firing corrections quickly.

For us to achieve success, we needed everything to fall into place. I'm certain my third grade nun would've been happy to know that I was resorting to a prayer of petition, asking God to cut us some slack and let us survive. Having thought about the way I put my request, I realized that I'd put God in a genuine bind. If He granted my prayer, it would happen at the expense of the NVA. I knew the NVA were the bad guys, but I wasn't sure anymore about why I prayed or whether or not God was even interested in my night ambush. But maybe He was listening, and maybe He knew whether it would be karma or fate would get us out of the Nam alive

Bless me Father, for I am about to sin, and for my penance I will say one hell of a lot of rosaries, at least. Double Amen.

6

CHARLIE'S SISTER
AFTER THE AMBUSH
WEST OF DÔNG BÍCH (1)

After the firing ceased, I helped to gather the weapons and equipment from the eight American Marines that had died for their corrupt leaders. They were a tenacious enemy, but they died just the same, as must all enemies of the Revolution. Because they had fought with a strong determination, they left us very little ammunition to collect. They had moved through our village with the intention of ambushing our comrades from the North. As was typical, they chose the wrong trail for their ambush. Moving about eight hundred meters to the south of the American position, the Northerners swept past them with great stealth and, upon reaching Phuóc Ninh (7), veered north to set up their rockets, which they fired at the American airfield in Da Nang.

The American Marines were not only outflanked by elements of the People's Army, but they also became the target for an ambush by thirty-two courageous soldiers from our National Liberation Front's Q16 Company. The Americans were such fools to venture away from the safety of their own hill. Their jets could not save them. They have yet to learn that the land and the night have always been our allies. Once again, we have schooled our enemy in this lesson.

7

SANDBURN
12 FEBRUARY 1968
HILL 10

I was so beat on my ass from lugging that damn O'Brien outta there last night. The Captain cut me some slack. Even let me catch some Z's before he sent me down to S-2. Those guys were kinda pissed when I showed up late. Hell, I was so exhausted that I nodded out just before lunch and didn't make it to our beloved mess hall for their eats. As I was entering the S-2 tent, O'Brien was just finishing up his debriefing with the intelligence boys. He even tried to come up with a smile when he saw me. I still don't trust that guy, just the way you can't trust them gooks when they do their smilin' act.

I agreed whenever they asked about something that O'Brien had told them. I guess they assumed all sorts of stuff about what happened during the ambush. If it made me look good, I figured I'd just go along with it. What the hell. Because O'Brien had been knocked unconscious, they needed me to fill in the gaps. I told them how I put the good old fireman's carry to use when we escaped the VC ambush. The Lieutenant got all impressed with how we slipped by the NVA rocket battalion, but he wasn't too happy that we had lost the night-vision scope. Now Charlie could watch us at night. I let Santos take the fall for that since he was a POW somewhere in the mountains if he was lucky. Of course, I told him how happy I was when we finally ran into the reaction force that had been sent out to save our asses. But by the time we ran into them, there were only two asses that needed saving. We sure could've used the reaction force a little earlier, but what the hell, at least we ran into them. Continuing on to the ambush site would've been a waste of time. Everybody being dead and all. Plus the reaction force wasn't even a full squad. This damn commie offensive had taken a toll on the battalion. Probably would've gotten ambushed, and we would've been screwed royal. We'd had enough of that shit for one night, and damn, hauling O'Brien back to the hill just about wiped me out. Beat on my ass. I hoped the son of a bitch appreciated what I did for him. He owed me, and I really liked that. When the debriefing was finished, I kept the Lieutenant happy by giving him one of those correct salutes. I knew he wanted to smile, but officers, especially Lieutenants, couldn't afford to ever look pleased or happy. That was definitely against Marine Corps regulations.

Just before sunset, I went on bunker watch with a couple of Fuckin' New Guys. Of course, these FNGs didn't know shit about nothin', so I had to explain which way was up for these dumb motherfuckers. I even had to explain why two choppers landed out by Dông Bích earlier in the day, 'round about nine or ten to pick up the eight KIAs. Their eyes got all big. I think they were impressed that they were doin' bunker watch with one of the survivors of the ambush. I guess it wasn't that bad doin' bunker watch considering the alternative. At least I didn't have to be on a night ambush with their sorry asses. Of course, since I deserved to get some uninterrupted sleep, I took first watch, and they got stuck with the shitty watches.

Actually, the evening turned out pretty damn good except for the fact that I had to sleep in a bunker with a wetback and a damn colored guy. Just about when the sun was going down, I spotted what looked like a big-ass fire to our southwest, out in the direction of that fuckin' Dông Bích. I hoped I wasn't just having a good dream. It sure looked like some shit was going down in that goddamn ville. Those dink bastards deserved it for what the Cong did to us. It sure as hell looked like it was payback time for those assholes.

The cherries that I was stuck with had dumb-ass expressions plastered all over their faces. Me on the other hand, well, I had a shit-eating grin since I figured that the ville was gettin' lit up real good. The fire looked damn good at night, but I was a little pissed that I didn't get to go along and help kick some ass on the fuckin' dinks. I couldn't wait for bunker watch to be over so I could find out if our guys wasted that goddamn ville. Damn, I wanted to be out there so bad it hurt.

In the morning, I felt like a kid who can't wait to open presents on Christmas. Shortly after I got off bunker watch, the squads from Charley and Bravo Company began arriving back at the hill from their night ambushes. Bravo didn't send patrols to the southwest of our hill, so I knew it was some bad ass Charley Company grunts that built that beautiful bonfire. I'm glad my company got to do the ass kickin'. Marines take care of their own.

I was right. Dông Bích (1) had quickly been turned into Dông Bích (0). Fucking zero! That fire pretty much canceled the damn ville. The grunts torched the place just after sunset so the NVA and the Cong could check it out real easy. They didn't want them to miss the view of the bonfire. Those gook bastards deserved getting their sorry-ass hamlet torched since they had to have been in on the ambush. Hell, they were lucky that the grunts didn't waste them all. Eight guys in my squad with a bullet hole in the head. The fucking gooks went and executed most of the squad and that damn sniper blew away that FNG Mac earlier in the day, but that wasn't enough for those bastards. Word was them gooks cut Westlake's dick off. Fucking animals. Yeah, the Zippo treatment was just what that ville needed. My only regret was that me and my Zippo lighter missed out on payback on those motherfuckin' gooks. So much for their Year of the Monkey. The squad from Charley Company turned it into the Year of the Zippo Lighter.

8

O'BRIEN
14 FEBRUARY 1968
HILL 10

Valentine's Day, and all I had was a date with the doctor in the sickbay bunker. He checked the stitches from my bayonet wound. "A puncture wound would have done you in, Sergeant. You're lucky you just got sliced. Definitely lucky the guy at the other end of the rifle didn't kill you. These NVA usually don't miss. You're one fortunate Marine."

I could have clarified that the Viêt Cong had ambushed us, not the NVA who were the target of our ambush. Unable to muster up any enthusiasm in my voice, I just said, "Yeah, lucked out one more time." His eyes looked too tired to care that I hadn't bothered to say, "Sir" when I responded to his observation. The past few weeks had reminded him that he was a doctor first and a Naval officer second. I was in no mood for him to see things any other way.

After I thanked him, I headed over to Sandburn's tent at the west end of the hill. When I entered it, all I saw were empty cots with too many memories, so I headed up to my official home a little further east, a tent where two 81 mm mortar squads lived. I was usually in the bush calling in fire missions for these guys. I was like a salesman who drummed up business, and they delivered the goods. With this type of relationship, I only rarely saw them. Even when, on those few occasions, I was back on the hill during

25

the day, most of them were on working parties. It turned out to be a typical day. The tent was empty, which I liked.

Because I had light duty for the next couple of days, I had no responsibility until the evening when I did some gun watch. I was a good man to have around if there were a fire mission. Before becoming a Forward Observer, I had been a mortarman during the early part of my first tour. Being out there with the grunts was what I wanted from the start, but the folks in charge didn't care about my wishes until our battalion lost two FOs in one week. With these instant job openings, a desperate Lieutenant let me learn the hard way. Back during my first tour, I called in my first fire mission when our platoon, which was supposed to have about forty men but only had twenty-two, walked into an ambush by around a hundred and fifty, hard-core NVA regulars.

At first, our mortar barrages kept them at bay, but being outnumbered by about seven to one finally caught up with us, so 105s and 155s, the big guns, came to our rescue. I was scared shitless that I'd call in a bad fire mission, a friendly-fire mistake, but there were so many North Vietnamese that it was pretty hard for arty and mortars to miss them.

A few NVA broke through our perimeter, but they got to meet their ancestors, compliments of Marine bayonets. Then, the platoon's situation got hairy when close to one hundred NVA got within a few meters of what was left of the platoon's right flank. I even had to do a little hand-to-hand shit with an NVA soldier who was trying to stab my radio operator. Because they were so close, I had arty back off, so I used mortars instead because they were better suited for our close-quarters situation. It was scary calling in mortars almost on top of us. I definitely called in some serious shit on the NVA when I wasn't busy playing grunt in between my fire missions.

I don't think they thought I had the balls to call it in so close. God must have been listening to my prayers. A bunch of North Vietnamese soldiers got a chance to personally ask God why He hadn't listened to their prayers. What was left of their company broke off contact after a twenty-minute barrage. After that, I wasn't a cherry as an FO. Welcome to the Nam. But all that was a long time ago. The summer of '66 up at the DMZ was a long damn time ago, but that memory was still fresh.

I went on second watch just as Valentine's Day disappeared, at least in our part of the world. If the NVA were going to hit the hill with rockets or mortars, they typically did it during the midnight-to-two watch. That was commie SOP. Our book of Standing Operating Procedure was thick, but theirs, on the other hand, was quiet a bit thinner, yet they still had one. Part of me was hungry for a payback fire mission, but I wouldn't complain if the NVA stayed away. Charlie had other business to attend to, which meant that getting some sleep would be on my agenda.

At three in the morning, I was still awake. I lay in my cot, staring into the quite darkness. I kept replaying a scene from the last part of January, the time just before the Tét holiday and the ceasefire that fell through—big time. I had been over at Webster's tent talking with Nellis about his favorite subject—Asian philosophical thought. As he was spouting out words like the *Noble Eightfold Path* and *karma*, the sparkle in his eyes made it easy to tell that he loved having an audience that would actually listen and ask questions.

He never told me what kind of grades he had back in his university days, but he struck me as a man with an inquisitive mind. I only knew bits and pieces about him, one being that he had dropped out of college only one semester before graduation. He never went into any detail except that this pissed off his old man who was a retired Marine. Nellis was going to be the officer his father had never become, but then came Buddhism. So much for a career as an officer. He would have been a good officer, but he would have gotten killed just the same. It would have just been later on. He would have been buried with officer's bars rather than stripes. Good old fate.

Sandburn was also in the tent, and as usual he had interrupted our conversation. Nellis ignored him; I had less patience, but I was calm as I responded, "Fuck you. If we want to hear from you, Sandburn, we'll send you a personal invite."

Santos, whose cot was between Nellis's and Sandburn's, was caught in a No Man's Land of verbal abuse. He shut out his immediate world, concentrating instead on cleaning his 45. Because Santos was blocking a clear view of me, Sandburn leaned to his right and said, "Fuck the both of you."

Before Sandburn could continue, Santos, remaining intently

focused on his weapon, softly and carefully enunciated one word. "*Chukut.*"

"I didn't hear no one invite you into this conversation, powwow boy. Didn't anyone on the res teach you injuns how to talk in sentences? I doubt it."

"You don't have to be such an asshole. His name is Baptisto Santos…not powwow boy. You either watched too many Lone Ranger movies when you were a kid, or you're just a dick."

I didn't know why I wasted my time trying to reason with Sandburn. He and I had had never gotten along from the first time we had met. Fortunately, not everyone in the Nam was an asshole. I liked Santos for the same reason that I got along with Nellis; we both had a low-key approach to life.

We pretended that Sandburn didn't exist, ignoring him completely; eventually, he left the tent. Nellis referred to this technique as existential magic. With Sandburn's exit from the tent, we discovered that *chukut* meant owl. More importantly, Santos informed us that he had dreamed of an owl the previous night. In his dream, he watched from atop a hill as it pecked out the eyes of a squad of Marines. As he was telling us about how the sky was crying many tears as *chukut* flew away into the darkness, Sandburn, smoking a joint, re-entered the tent.

Interrupting, he repeated in a mocking tone some of what Santos had said. "Crying many tears…give me fucking a break."

Admonishing him in a soft but serious voice, Santos cautioned, "Our dreams must be taken seriously, especially when *chukut*, the owl, appears. This is a bad omen."

Sandburn found it impossible to resist snickering. "A wet dream…that's the only dream to be taken seriously. Well, maybe when you have a dream that's got some fuckin' NVA in it instead of some damn owl, that'll be a bad omen." He paused for a moment as a grin rolled across his face. He had one last salvo of stupidity left in him. "Santos, you really don't look like no Baptist to me. Aren't all you Papagos a bunch of Catholics…like the Mexicans? Yeah…perfect…I'm going to give you a better name. From now on, we'll call you *Chukut.*"

Sandburn grinned, but Santos just shook his head and muttered something indistinguishable. Maybe it was Papago for *fuck you*, but that was just my wishful thinking.

28

At four in the morning, unable to sleep, I lay there remembering Santos's dream, which felt too real. As the lazy, mid-February morning sun took its own good time to crawl over the horizon, the stitches in my side just waited for the doctor. Somewhere in the darkness, Baptisto Santos waited, or maybe the NVA had already put a bullet in his head. *Chukut*, the owl, knew.

9

CHARLIE'S SISTER
14 FEBRUARY 1968
Q16'S BASE CAMP

Several hours after our courageous fighters ambushed the American Marines, Khiem, my brother's friend, told me that Tuan had been killed. I no longer had a reason to remain in my village of Dông Bích, so I slipped away in the morning darkness and met up with the Q16 Company, a local Viêt Cong cadre. The Americans had robbed me of my brother. They were greedy; my father's death was not enough for them. I was so exhausted with so much death in my family. I wanted to scream when I heard the news, but my lips were frozen and my eyes only stared into nothingness, into yesterday, as I tried desperately to remember his gentle and reassuring voice. I carried a small photo of Tuan, now my only connection to my brother. The other members of the Q16 Company became my family, but I wanted Tuan back. The bullet that blew a hole in the back of his head hadn't cared one bit about me or my brother.

From our base camp in the mountains several miles west of Dông Bích, I could see my village burning shortly after sunset on the day Tuan was killed. I was learning to hate the Americans more than I ever thought I could. My mother, my father, my brother, my village. What more did they want? My anger was pushed aside as doubt began to creep into my mind and guilt gnawed at my tired heart like a hungry dog while I watched my village burn in the distance. Had I not told my brother about the Marine who had tried to rape me, the Q16 would not have ambushed the American Marines and Tuan would not have been killed. My village was burning because the American Marines wanted revenge. How many people died because I had not remained silent?

We needed to bury my brother, so the answers to my questions would have to wait for a time when I could afford the luxury of pondering. Although I was only eighteen, I knew that pondering never killed any enemies of the Revolution, and it wouldn't dig the hole for my brother's body. American patrols made it impossible to have a traditional funeral: a luxury for another time.

So, as the fog of my sorrow hung heavy, memories of my mother's funeral snuck in, and I settled for a child's remembrance, the images of her good-bye ceremony. It had seemed so strange that a chopstick had been laid between her teeth and a bit of rice and three coins had been put in her mouth. I hadn't liked it that we stopped bringing rice to the altar after forty-nine days. Customs were part of my father's life, but I was only a four-year-old girl who didn't want my mother to be hungry, but my father didn't know how to explain that she no longer needed food. Tuan simply told me that our mother wasn't hungry any more. When I was six, my father told me that the time for being sad was over, but I missed my mother even if I wasn't supposed to be sad any longer.

Because we were in the midst of our offensive against the Americans, we did not have the luxury of a funeral ceremony or burial rituals. We only had time to dig a hole to bury our dead, and sometimes we didn't.

10

TUAN
THE PRESENT
HEAVEN

The night I was killed, everything changed. Labels such as Buddhist and Viêt Cong became obsolete the instant the bullet tore through the back of my skull. To my parents, I was son Tuan. To my sister and my village, I was brother Tuan. To my National Liberation Front cadres, I was Sergeant Tuan, martyr in our war of liberation from the Americans and their puppets in Saigon. To my friend Khiem, I was a secret to be hidden. To the American Marines, I was a confirmed kill, one less Victor Charlie, a dead gook, something on which to drop the ace of spades.

On that rainy night at the beginning of Tết during the Year of the Monkey, I was freed from my anger at the Americans for killing my father the previous year. On that night, the lesson I learned was both my redemption and my death sentence, but that was so long ago, and time does not matter here; the beauty of my current life is that most of what mattered before I died is insignificant and irrelevant now. This place is about *being*. At some point, I will be reincarnated if I still have lessons to learn. For now, I must observe the remaining acts in a drama which was born on the last day of my other life as Tuan the Viêt Cong who decided to be Tuan the Buddhist, who decided to be compassionate, to just *be*.

32

11

SANDBURN
7 APRIL 1968
HILL 10

The Colonel, the full bird from regiment, gave me the Silver Star yesterday. He said that I made the Corps proud by my example of courage under fire. He kept going on about how unselfish I was because I'd put my own life second to bringing back a wounded Marine. He rambled on about the large VC and NVA forces that I had evaded when I carried the only other survivor of the ambush back to the hill.

I knew my old man would eat this stuff up when I got back to the World in a couple of months. Good shit for a resumé. That's what he'd say. Sounded good to me. If it would keep him off my ass, what the hell. I was positive he'd love the hero crap, but the Purple Heart that I got along with my Silver Star is what I was sure he'd love even more. Of course, I'd kinda forgot to tell the office at my debriefing and my old man that I got the Purple Heart for my head wound which I got when the asshole O'Brien hit me with his rifle butt. A good Virginian has got to be willing to shed a little blood for his country. The way I saw it, bleed just enough to get the goodies. Maybe my old man would be right. A few medals never hurt nobody's career, even in civilian life.

Back in February when the damn gooks kicked our ass, things didn't turn out too good for us, especially for the guys who got blown away. O'Brien went back to mortars and did his thing as a mortar Forward Observer with other squads of grunts, but I didn't have no squad to be in no more, so I had to stand a bunch of boring ass bunker watch until the platoon commander figured out what to do with me. Guess that wasn't too bad considering I had it better than Santos, being MIA and all.

Guard duty only lasted two days. Then I got assigned to another squad. They only had five dudes. Way undermanned. Tết was a real bitch. I think everything turned out for the best since I got to be the squad leader. The other five dudes weren't all cherries, but I had a shit load more time in the Nam than they did. It might not have mattered, but I heard that O'Brien talked to the Lieutenant and put in a good word for me. I figured that he owed me for finding him in the brush next to the trail and lugging his dumb ass out of there until the reaction force showed up.

Being unconscious and all, O'Brien didn't have no clue that I'd found him about a hundred meters outside the ambush site. What the fuck was he doin' there anyway? Probably got smart and was hauling ass outta there with them two VC hot on his trail, but I can't figure out how he ended up bein' unconscious. Also, it don't make no sense what happened to the guy that the one VC was carryin'. What the fuck. I was fairly wasted, so I'm not really sure about much except that if I hadn't brought his dumb ass back, the gooks would've found him. He definitely would've been as dead as all the other guys in the squad.

At least we got some payback when arty and mortars blew away a bunch of fucking gooks from the NVA rocket battalion that faked us out of our jock straps and snuck around us by going through Phuóc Ninh (7) instead of straight through Dông Bích (1) where we had expected catch 'em. Webster's brilliant ambush idea hadn't turned out to be too damn brilliant since the NVA pulled an end run on us while the Cong laid some serious shit on us. Nigger that he was, the gooks were able to outsmart his black ass. That made him dumber than the gooks. What our squad needed was a white man, and things would've turned out a whole hell of a lot better.

12

TUAN
THE PRESENT
HEAVEN

In the days before our offensive, I longed to see my sister. With our father and mother gone, we only had each other. Of course, the people of Dông Bích are like a family for her, but during the Tết holiday both our hearts were heavy. I ached for the days when our mother patiently prepared the salty *bánh chung*, a special treat signifying that the Tết Lunar New Year celebration was upon us. I missed those rice squares stuffed with *mung* beans and meat, but the child that I used to be ached for all the days which had been stolen from us by the French officer who interrogated our mother, and ultimately tore her out of our young lives.

The interrogator did not believe her when she denied that she was a member of the Việt Minh. She spoke the truth, but he was not in the mood for believing, so he made her suffer for three days before he crushed her skull with his boot. Just before my sixth birthday, our father, who only wanted to be a farmer, joined the Việt Minh to fight against the French, and he became my teacher. My sister remains heartbroken and sad, but I have no need for sadness because I am now with my parents. I hope that my sister, who is alone with her grief, finds peace soon. The journey is hers.

13

O'BRIEN
6 JULY 1968
LAX

In general, I always hated airports, but I cut LAX some slack this time since it was going to get my almost civilian ass home. Amazingly, I was alive. Way down inside I suppose that I was ecstatic about surviving my second tour in the Nam, but the crowds of here-to-there people, which I couldn't stand, would never know it, partly since they were too busy to notice anything, but mostly because I'd learned how not to let out the stuff that I had buried inside of me.

I made it out of the Nam—twice—because I'd figured out quickly that letting out my feelings was as stupid as lighting up a smoke on a night ambush. Emotions got in the way of survival. I wasn't dumb; I was alive, and I'd been lucky the night of the ambush. That night, my getting knocked unconscious was a stroke of good fortune since I woke up in the morning without a bullet hole in my head like most of the squad. That was the good news, but now I was standing in one more goddamn line, and I wasn't even on a Marine base, but at least I wasn't at the ass-end of the line or in a body bag waiting for the flight home on the Silver Bird.

So, how the hell did I end up on a plane to Vegas if I lived in Tucson? I'd have to wait a little longer to find out for sure. I was pretty smart in high school, that is, when I felt like it. All my

English teachers, nuns times four, had tried to convince me, unlike my algebra teacher Sister Mary Quite Contrary, that I "possessed" potential—translation: "Why the hell aren't you acing this class?" Their question definitely wasn't rhetorical. I knew I'd figure out this rhetorical question thing upon completion of a four-year tour of duty at the University of Arizona. I'd be moving up in the world; the Irish-American, Marine Corps Sergeant would become an English major. With a name like Michael O'Brien, I definitely wasn't a fan of the English who, after all, were responsible for God not being able to rest on the seventh day until He had invented the English so someone could organize His flowers, shrubs, and trees into perfectly manicured gardens; however, Sister Mary Metaphor, who had taught me how to dance with a semicolon without stepping on its toes, had made me a great fan of the English language. I loved the irony.

Somehow I'd managed to row past James Joyce who was sentence surfing in the stream of consciousness; a little digression never hurt anyone, except in the Nam, especially out by Phuóc Ninh and Dông Bích before the NVA began using the area as a corridor to their rocket sites. When the booby traps started disappearing several weeks before Tét, we knew the Cong weren't giving us a belated Christmas present. The NVA of the 368B Artillery Regiment, who were operating in our area, were carpet-bagger cousins of the Cong, so they weren't as familiar with the area. The VC, aka Victor Charlie, in the Q16 Company were homegrown commies; this was their turf, so they were in charge of booby traps and the NVA's 122 mm-rocket-boys were in charge of blowing the hell out of the the Phantom jets at the air base at Da Nang.

While the commie cousins were doing their damnedest to send me home early, my job was to go out on day patrols and night ambushes with the grunts of Charley Company and help send the NVA to their ancestors before they fired their rockets at Da Nang. The firepower of a squad of a dozen grunts could inflict damage, but my being an FO meant that I could not only call in 81 mm mortars but even artillery, the big guns like the 105s and 155s, on the NVA or the VC. Not unlike a corpsman, I was a good man to have around, but for very different reasons.

Because my top priority was to be available for my July flight date, I made damn sure that I didn't do any digressing in those days in late '67 when the Phuóc Ninh area was still Booby Trap City. If I wanted to survive my second tour, my jungle boots had to play a successful game of follow the leader, finding the friendly American footprints of the grunt in front of me. Digressing was one word that I left back at the hill.

14

O'BRIEN
7 JULY 1968
LAS VEGAS, NEVADA

Toward the end of my first tour in the Nam was the only time that being wounded had gotten me a free medevac chopper ride to the hospital. Nothing life threatening, just lots of small pieces of shrapnel in my leg. As usual, I had lucked out, just as was the case when Sandburn carried me out the night of the ambush near Dông Bích (1). It must have been almost a klick or more that he had to lug me before we met up with the reaction force that was sent out to save us. I really didn't like the idea of being indebted to Sandburn; as far as I was concerned, he was a son of a bitch, but he was the son of a bitch who saved my life. But this time was different; there was no medevac chopper—nor Sandburn to save me—in Las Vegas. Just me, so I owed myself a thank-you.

Before they could wheel me down the hotel hallway, they had to step between the bodies of the two men who lay very dead in the doorway of my room. Once in the hall, they set the stretcher down and rolled me away to the ambulance. I really didn't need the stretcher treatment, but I humored them since everybody has a proverbial book to go by. Head wounds always look worse than they are because of all the blood. I'd seen plenty of blood during my two tours in the Nam. Being quite drunk helped me not feel the pain much. The two KIAs back at the hotel room weren't very cooperative when it came to answering the cops' questions, and I was still too drunk to make much sense, so they cut me some slack and waited a couple of hours before they interrogated me.

My story seemed to make sense to them, probably because it was so chronological, so one-foot-in-front-of-the-other simple to understand. But for me, nothing that had happened in Las Vegas made much sense. There really wasn't much to say about the actual shooting—bang, bang and two dead guys—but they wanted to know about the events leading up to the shootout on the fifth floor of the hotel. It was their turf, so I took them on a stroll down memory lane.

"I'm just back from the Nam, and..."

I was unable to finish my first sentence because the detective who thought he was Sergeant Joe Friday's clone, the taller of the two detectives, interrupted me with a one-word question, "Army?"

Obviously, he had been asleep when his mother had taught him manners, so I resisted my urge to punch him in his been-out-of-shape-since-V-J-Day potbelly. Instead, I calmly replied, "Marines."

A pair of "Wows" dribbled in unison from their lips. Born at the wrong time to have experienced combat during any of the recent wars and thoroughly impressed by John Wayne in *Fighting Leathernecks*, they were drooling for a war story, but the sparkle in their eyes disappeared when I continued with my story, and these little kids became middle-aged detectives once again.

"I'm at LAX, ready to get a ticket for my flight back to Tucson to see my family for the first time in thirteen months. But I guess I wasn't quite ready for the family scene. For reasons that I don't understand, I hop a flight to Vegas. Once I find a casino that I like, I get a room so I can crash when I'm too drunk to gamble any more. I pay for it in advance since I figure that I'd used up all my luck in the Nam and won't have any money left for a room. Once I get all squared away, I head downstairs to the casino with a grand that I saved up in the Nam. About five months' wages in the good old war zone."

"You gotta be kiddin'. Not a lot a money to get shot at."

Both detectives shook their heads back and forth in disbelief.

"I never expected to get rich being a Marine, but I'm not in the Nam anymore. Anyway...roulette's my game, so somewhere around nine o'clock I get all comfortable at a table. Start off real conservative like, with red or black and odd or even bets. I'm winning, up a hundred bucks, but it's too damn boring for me, so with some help from my pal Jack Daniels, I get adventurous and start puttin' hundred dollar bets on the numbers. Before you know it, I'm a regular attraction. People are cheering when the ball hits my number. By this time, some blonde chick gets all friendly. Starts snuggling up to me. Hell, I know she ain't after me 'cause she's feelin' patriotic and wants to welcome the troops home. She's a gold digger, but I don't care."

Both detectives nodded their agreement and offered up a "Yeah" in unison.

I continued, "I'm on a roll, so I get real brave, actually I didn't really give a shit what happened at this point, and I pushed every stack of chips I had out to the space for the number *nine*. I figured it didn't matter if I lost, and if I won, well, it just meant...just like in the Nam, some guys just had their number called and some just lucked out. That's just the..."

The shorter and younger detective, whose glasses kept sliding down his nose, couldn't control his curiosity, so he asked, "Why'd you pick *nine*?"

"I picked *nine* for the nine Marines that got their number called one night back in February. See, back here in the World, I can lose it all and it doesn't really matter, so, what the fuck?"

"Whoa. That's some bad shit."

I replied in a monotone voice, "Just another day at the office, Nam-style."

What they learned about the Nam was not what they had expected, but I wasn't there to entertain them. As I continued to plow through the events of the previous night, the Las Vegas version of Dick Tracy and Sergeant Joe Friday nodded in unison more often than not. Although they seemed to be impressed at my gambling skills, I knew better. Sometimes you win and sometimes you don't. I had won over twenty thousand dollars, and I didn't care why. My blonde friend with a fine set of supple breasts and an ass worth gawking at wasn't concerned with the whys of my winning but with the actual winnings, stacks of crisp, smiling Andy Jacksons.

With gambling out of the way, Andy Jackson, Jack Daniels, Sergeant Michael O'Brien, and Jane Doe with her supple breasts and eye-candy ass left the noise and the neon of the casino for the privacy of my room on the fifth floor. Because Jack Daniels was in charge of my brain, I was thinking only in the southern hemisphere, so the prospects of getting laid made more sense than wasting valuable time going to the Casino's safe. My horniness and my sizable winnings headed to the elevator.

Much of my adventure was irrelevant to the investigation of the shootings, but the two detectives seemed to be enjoying themselves so I rambled on. But I neglected to tell them about the wettest, deepest French kiss that I'd experienced in more than a year. That elevator ride was great also, but Las Vegas' finest would never know about the details. With my hands occupied, a bag of money in one hand and a fifth of Jack Daniels in the other, I had to be satisfied with tongue wrestling. She, on the other hand, wasn't shy with her breasts, shoving them into my chest. For that matter, she threw every sexual body part available at my wiry body, which was ready to put up the white flag of surrender.

What I did offer up to these desert cops was that I didn't get laid because I threw my new friend out of my room. Of course, I forgot to let them in on the full story of how I went berserk when she asked me one question too many. When she saw a six-inch, diagonal scar just under my armpit, she asked, "Knife fight?"

Although Jack Daniels was running the show, I still felt uneasy with her question, but I responded, "Sorta. Some commie sliced me with his bayonet when I was in the Nam."

Before I could pull off my skivvies, she replied, "Vietnam...you've been to the war."

I wanted intercourse not an interview. Had I wanted a conversation, I would have found out her name. She was being too much of a Socrates for me. Like the almost empty bottle of bourbon on the nightstand, my patience was disappearing quickly. When she asked her last question, a really stupid one, I exploded. I don't think she liked my response when she asked, "Did you kill anybody?"

I shoved her off the bed. Looking up at me from the gold-colored carpet, she screamed, "You're fuckin' crazy!"

I was standing up, glaring down at her as she reached for her dress, which was lying on the floor near the bathroom door. "I just don't need this shit. Okay?"

She put on her dress as quickly as she had abandoned it earlier. For the first time in her twenty-two-year-old life, her first priority was not her hair, which looked like a rat's nest. The hell with the hair; escaping from the fifth-floor room of the psycho Nam vet was what made sense to her at that moment. What was his problem; she'd only asked an innocent question. Then, as she edged her way to the door, she dug herself in deeper when she kept repeating, "You're fuckin' crazy!"

I bolted toward her, grabbing her by the arms before she could open the door and escape to the safety of the hall. I slammed her once-desired body hard against the wall by the door. Her breasts were heaving, and she was trembling but not from sexual passion this time.

"You fuckin' bitch. How dare you ask me such shit? Didn't your fuckin' old lady ever teach you any goddamned manners!" With one final, "Fuck you, bitch!", I opened the door and shoved her into the hall. Falling to the floor, she peered up at me with hate dancing in her blood-shot eyes. She bid her final good-byes to me with a middle-finger salute as she stumbled down the hallway.

Although I'd won at the roulette wheel, flying to Las Vegas was proving to be a bad idea. Even a chug from my Jack Daniels bottle wasn't making her question go away. To make matters worse, the faces of the Fuckin' New Guys, four of them, and the five others kept flashing through my mind. Hesse, MacAndrews, and Sartoretti got the revolving door, Nam style. In country for less than a week. At least they didn't have to put up with the bullshit of the Nam. And farm boy Jimmy Rappaport showed up the day Tét began and didn't last more than two weeks. Picked the wrong time to show up. Hell, just about the whole squad had bad timing. One body bag during the daytime and eight KIAs that sorry-ass night. And we had no idea if Santos would survive being captured. Damn his owl dream.

I hated the early morning of February 12, 1968. I hated the

fuckin' rain and the goddamn gooks. When the medevac choppers flew the dead out the next day, six Marines and one kick-ass corpsman each had a single bullet hole in the head. And those VC bastards weren't even satisfied that Nellis' face had been blown away, so the motherfuckers had to fire their guarantee shot into his crotch. Angel "Doc" Reyes, the man with a heart of gold, was all business in the thick of it. He'd get to your wounded ass no matter how heavy the shit was coming in. How could they do that to a guy with a name like Angel? I didn't even want to think about the other guys. All I wanted was another swig of liquor, the perfect solution.

I had done two tours in the Nam, yet I still hadn't figured out the logic of survival. It seemed that the Grim Reaper really wasn't particular, just as long as he got somebody. Sandburn survived and carried me away from Đông Bích. In one night the Grim Reaper scooped up a bunch of cherries who didn't have a clue, and just to be a genuine prick, he put his hooks into Nellis who only had nine days left, but he let Lance Corporal Trent Sandburn, an asshole as big as his home state of Virginia, survive. It just didn't make sense.

Nothing made sense anymore. Where was the clarity of those long ago days when memorizing the catechism made life so simple, so black and white? There were too many shades of gray and too many shadows for me. I wanted to be a kid with a curfew and a guilty conscience for saying a cuss word or having an impure thought. I wanted calm, but there was none to be found, even with the help of Jack Daniels. Since the time machine for transport back to the 1950s was in the shop and unavailable, I decided to solve my problem the way we had in the Nam.

Within about an hour of throwing out the woman who had asked all the wrong questions, I became the proud owner a .357 Magnum and a box of ammo. I didn't intend to miss my target, so I only needed one round. Money was no object; I didn't want to bring any attention to my plan, so I bought an entire box of shells, but I didn't care who would inherit them or the .357. The number nine had brought me luck earlier in the evening. I had won it all for the nine men, but now the number *.357* would be my ticket to the place where dead grunts go. I just hoped they would let me in and wouldn't call me a coward. I hoped that God would forgive me; Jack Daniels had.

The time for thinking and hurting was over; it was lock-and-load time. I was the ultimate short-timer, and the cold steel of the barrel rested squarely on the sweaty skin of my soon-to-be-former right temple. Just as I placed my finger on the trigger, the door, which I had left unlocked, was flung open. Bursting through, two pistol-wielding men had almost finished screaming their instructions to me before I stole the odds away from them.

It was obvious that they wanted my cash. Had they been a few seconds more patient, allowing me to splatter my brains on the hotel room wall on the fifth floor of a second-rate casino, they could have inherited the leftover bullets and the cash, two items that I was certain my catechism had told me wouldn't be needed in the after life. I wasn't sure if impatience was one of the seven deadly sins, but their poor timing and greed would turn out to be deadly sins, for them.

When they burst through the doorway, I instinctively switched to autopilot. I was in 'the Nam' gear, so having been ambushed, I immediately shifted into survival mode. Swinging the .357 away from my right temple, I instinctively clutched the handle with both hands and squeezed off six rounds in the direction of the two would-be robbers who were in a free-fire zone.

Half my shots found their targets. The right side of the second man's face splattered on the wall in the hallway as the rest of his useless body slammed up against the wall and slid down, finally coming to rest on the gold carpet of the hallway floor. The point man on this gone-wrong ambush took two rounds in the torso area, one in the stomach and one in the chest. The force of the bullets flung him back, quickly draining his blood into the blotter that used to be a gold carpet. I was drunk, so three of my shots missed them, but the rounds that hit them canceled their scheme. They had successfully killed the wall behind me. The dust from the five holes in the plasterboard was still floating around like LA smog.

Having learned a final valuable yet now useless lesson, the would-be robbers waited patiently for the boys from the morgue to cart their sorry asses away. They hadn't failed completely; one round had grazed the right side of my temple on its way to the wall behind me. The blood streaming down the right side of my face made the wound appear more serious than it was. A week earlier, I would've gotten a Purple Heart out of this, but I was back in the World where they did things much differently.

Upon providing the detectives with my parents' Tucson address in case they had any further questions, I left them and the air conditioning of the hospital lounge for a short walk through the arid July heat to a taxi that would take me and my Andy Jacksons to the jet that would return me home to Tucson.

I left two content cops, a pair of inept former robbers, one pissed off lay that didn't happen, a .357 Magnum and an obsolete reason for using it, when I boarded the plane out of the detour city that had saved my life.

15

O'BRIEN
AUGUST 1968
WIOTA, IOWA

My mother had taught me two things well: guilt and manners. I chuckled, but not in front of my hosts, when they called it a heat wave. They and everyone else in Iowa took weather seriously, so I politely played along as they chatted about the sacred heat index and sang their we're-in-Purgatory blues. They dismissed the dry desert heat of my beloved Arizona as "no big deal" because it was only dry heat. I wasn't there to win them over to the belief that 110 degrees is hot as hell, whether or not it's dry. These farm folk had never been to Arizona; for that matter, they had never been to the Nam in the summer, where high temperatures and high humidity readings stuck together like Batman and Robin. It was just nervous weather talk, so using the I-need-a-smoke excuse, I politely excused myself from the kitchen table.

The sound of the storm door slamming behind me evaporated into the dusk air that sparkled with squadrons of fireflies. The western sky waited patiently, affording shutterbugs at least another hour to take that perfect picture of an Iowa sunset. I could have told them not to waste their 35mm film on a second-rate attraction. On the other hand, maybe those devotees of the Kodak Instamatic should click away; they took pictures not photographs, so it really didn't matter what they did. As for me, Iowa's plain-Jane summer sunsets didn't stand a chance of competing with those of Tucson and the Sonoran Desert.

I walked across the open porch and plopped myself into a green, metal lawn chair which wasn't especially comfortable, but that didn't matter. Like stop-and-go traffic at an intersection with an erratic traffic signal, a light breeze sporadically pushed by me as I sucked in every ounce of pleasure that the makers of my Camel cigarette managed to pack into it. With each drag off my cigarette, the tip glowed like a giant firefly from hell. Like the aimless Mississippi, the smoke from my almost dead cigarette floated across the porch and disappeared into what was left of twilight time. Unfortunately, the aroma from each puff of my Camel hitched a ride with the cloud-colored ribbon of smoke. Gone but not forgotten. Cigarettes and the Nam had a lot in common.

I took up the smoking habit during my first tour of duty in Vietnam back in '66 and '67. After a few close calls near the DMZ, I began smoking. Being hooked on my pack-a-day habit meant that my lungs usually got a thirty-minute reprieve between each cigarette. Someday I would quit my nasty habit but not tonight. Besides teaching me how to cope with anything, being in the Marine Corps had taught me four other things well: killing, surviving, cussing, and smoking. Back in the Nam, they were all quite useful for a variety of reasons, but now that I was a Fuckin' New Guy back in the World, I knew that several of these skills had to be abandoned.

Reinventing that good Catholic altar boy from the early sixties would prove even more difficult than routing the NVA from a mountain bunker complex. Surviving was useful even outside a combat zone, so I wouldn't trash that skill. For several reasons I knew I had to leave my killing skills back in the Nam. Serving time in prison was the obvious reason, but of course, there was a less apparent one: there weren't any Viêt Cong or NVA ditty bopping around the cornfields of southwestern Iowa. The cussing habit was so thoroughly ingrained in me after three years of practice that inappropriate language seemed to spurt out without me realizing it. Because my well-intentioned apology typically contained words like *shit* or *goddamn*, I quickly realized the hopelessness of my changing this habit any time soon. There would be thousands of people with ears burning and mouths agape before I would rid myself of this vestige of my life as a Marine. Finally, I was fairly certain I wouldn't be running in any marathons, so I couldn't come up with a good reason for abandoning smoking, my fourth bad habit. I liked the way a Camel cigarette—non-filtered of course—made me feel relaxed and in control of something…pleasure in this case.

I knew I needed to be in Iowa, taking care of business with the family of a fellow Marine. Being inside their farmhouse, sitting down to dinner, or *supper* as they liked to call it, made me want to double my smoking habit. They weren't smokers; they were Methodists. I was a Catholic with a bad habit but good manners, so I found myself lighting up another cigarette on a porch full of almost black silence. On autopilot, snapping my Zippo lighter shut, I slipped it into the right front pocket of my Levis. Hungry for the seductively rich flavor of a Camel, my lungs beamed a smile as I inhaled deeply.

As was the case in the Nam, I wasn't especially fond of feeling nervous. Back there, it just got in the way and could get a short-timer blown away easily. Getting killed wasn't the problem here in Iowa on this muggy night. I was becoming increasingly edgy as I wondered how this salt-of-the-earth family would respond to the things that I knew I had to tell them. It had been six months since they had buried their oldest child, and I'd be visiting his gravesite in the morning on my way out of town. They didn't need to revisit their sorrow, so why was I willing to tell them about that night during Tết when their lanky son Jimmy had become more than just another KIA statistic? He was their heartland hero, compliments of a burst of Việt Cong machine gunfire.

The last words from his trembling teenage lips, "God, don't let me fucking die. Where's my fuckin' mom? I want my mom," would need to be paraphrased, but his basic message would make it home to his mom. After a few more cigarettes of encouragement, I would tell his family that he said he loved them all. This version would be the one I'd use. After all, my mother had taught me manners before the Marine Corps got a hold of me.

"Tell 'em I'll miss 'em." That's what I told them. And they believed me, probably because they needed to.

After a six o'clock breakfast of ham, eggs, hash browns, coffee, and too much sad silence, I waved my good-bye to a mother, a father, a brother, and a sister who still asked their *whys* but wanted to believe that God had a purpose, but their Methodist faith didn't appear to make their grief hurt any less. Although Mr. Rappaport offered to drive me to the bus station, I passed on his offer. Hitchhiking had gotten me to Wiota, Iowa, and if bumming a ride didn't work, a long walk down a lonely country road would allow me time to reflect before my visit with an Iowa farm boy at his new home.

I was glad that their forever image of an eighteen-year-old Jimmy lacked the soundtrack of his gagging on the torrent of his too-young-to-die blood. Jimmy's screaming, the night's darkness, and the soup of blood and rain that soaked his once olive green utility shirt: these were my haunting images that I gladly didn't share. Like the bullet holes that tore through Jimmy, these images ripped through the kid that I used to be before becoming a Marine.

The Rappaport family evaporated in the distance. When I arrived at Jimmy Rappaport's grave, I stood speechless for several minutes, and then I saluted Jimmy with slow Marine Corps precision. "Semper Fi, brother." I turned and walked away, but the Rappaport family's sad eyes tagged along with me, even as I boarded the bus that would take me to another family. I wouldn't be quitting smoking any time soon.

16

O'BRIEN
AUGUST 1968
THE ROAD TO BUTLER, PENNSYLVANIA

The oceans of ready-for-harvest cornfields rushing by me on both sides didn't exist. The bald head of the man sleeping in the seat directly in front of me didn't exist. The stench of passenger sweat that roamed the bus didn't exist. The crying of the baby that irritated the other passengers who hadn't escaped to lala-land didn't exist. Resting on my right shoulder, the sixty-year-old head that was attached to a black wig which failed at its job of making someone's grandma appear to be forty didn't exist. Her flowery dress, like a tent covering six decades of saying 'yes' to food, didn't exist. Interstate 80, like a black asphalt ribbon stretching straight and true across a green Iowa, didn't exist. The highway signs that pointed to Ladora, Cedar Valley and Davenport didn't exist. Mark Twain's river, that offered proof that Iowa had to stop and Illinois had to begin, didn't exist. The junction of Illinois Routes 6 and 34 didn't exist. The city of Jolliet, the doorbell to Chicago, didn't exist.

With the sunset hanging patiently in the western sky, the Greyhound bus rolled on, but my thousand-yard stare saw none of this, only that last terrible moment of black silence just after the rain had stopped, just before the first explosion of a Chicom grenade. And the stillness died as abruptly as Private Hesse, who never realized that the grenade that landed next to him had been lobbed from behind his listening post. Nellis, the other man on the listening post and better known to the rest of the squad as Pops, would outlast Hesse as he had outlasted so many others during the past twelve months of his thirteen-month tour of duty.

The ambush ultimately went on without Hesse who absorbed most of the shrapnel from the grenade explosion, and thus had saved Pops' life. Hesse hadn't meant to, but that didn't matter to Nellis who desperately wanted to see his girlfriend from college and enjoy his twenty-fourth birthday back in the World. He intended to survive this night, but circumstances would be different for Hesse whose useless blood streamed from a dozen gashes in what had been the backside of his legs. The boot with his right foot was lost somewhere in the darkness and his screaming didn't matter; it was just something to do until he bled to death. Instinctively, Hesse began crawling through the mud in search of safety or maybe for his severed foot. The kid who too quickly became a KIA would never get the luxury of the thousand-yard stare. Instead, his dead eyes stared without purpose into the mud that had become his final pillow. Even Doc Reyes who crawled twenty meters from our main ambush site couldn't work the magic this time. In the morning Erik Hesse, no longer needing to send his first letter from the Nam, would get to go home to Butler, Pennsylvania, but not the way his mother had hoped for. The Marine Corps' gift of a Purple Heart and an American flag folded in a triangle would not be enough.

Nothing would be enough for me either. The bus, with its hodgepodge collection of passengers, was on the outskirts of the Windy City, but the only place that existed for me was the outskirts of Đông Bích (1). I wanted to find a liquor store when the bus would make its stop in Chicago, but I knew that all the fifths of booze in the world, like the Purple Heart and the flag they gave Hesse's mother, would not be enough.

After a two-hour layover in Chicago, I aimed myself back toward the bus that would take me to Pennsylvania and the Hesse family. Once on board, the aisle was helpful because it limited my swaying as I navigated my way back to my seat. Although I was taking the straight and narrow path, it definitely wasn't in the biblical sense. The old lady, who had mistaken my shoulder for her personal pillow, was my beacon, but she abandoned the seat next to me when she inhaled a whiff of the bourbon smell that I had brought back with me.

Although the bus was almost full of passengers, the seat to my right remained empty. Within a few minutes I was asleep, and the stretch of Interstate 80 that ran across Indiana and Ohio didn't exist, but the Pennsylvania border and a throbbing headache existed when I finally woke up. Shortly after leaving Ohio behind us, the bus bid farewell to Interstate 80 and headed south on Highway 79, the final leg of the journey for the Pittsburgh-bound passengers. With Butler, PA as my destination, I said good-bye to the vacant seat to my right and began walking east on Route 422.

As I began my twelve-mile trek, I pondered my upcoming visit to the family of Private Erik Hesse. How could my words help them? The answer, as elusive as the VC sniper that had killed MacAndrews outside Đông Bích (1) back in February, played hide-and-seek with me just as the Cong had from their tunnel system that night. Their spider holes had served them well in their goal of ambushing the ambushers. Their success had sent me down this road that would take me to one more family that got a hero although longing for one more son to carry on the family name, but the Chicom grenade lobbed into the silent blackness of a February night didn't care; it just exploded, sending shrapnel across an ocean.

Like the weight of my backpack stuffed with civilian clothes, I carried the memory of that twelfth night back in February as I put the beginnings of an August sunset behind me when I entered Butler, Pennsylvania, but my escape from Đông Bích had failed once again.

17

SANDBURN
APRIL 1975
RICHMOND, VIRGINIA

Nixon had went and got himself all impeached. Wallace had went and got himself shot. Ford had went and let the fucking communists take over Vietnam. The klutz shoulda at least given those bastards a going away present, some 'round-the-clock B-52 raids for the rest of April. A little Easter arc light on paddy country.

The world was completely fucked up as far as I was concerned, but I had done pretty good for myself. I was makin' close to twenty grand. At least that's what I told the boys at the IRS. For a twenty-six-year-old, I had learned how to cozy up to a tax loophole real good. In spite of how pissed off my old man was about my droppin' out of the University of Virginia after a couple of semesters, I found that real estate was where I could make some real money, which beat the hell out of those piddly-ass GI Bill checks I got for school. Better yet, I was able to shove it all in my dad's damn face. Proved the fucker wrong. I had succeeded without college, and that felt real good, but not as good as the night I punched him out.

My father was a first-class son of a bitch. Ever since that night when I was drunk enough to stand up to the prick, he stopped givin' me shit, but he was still a son of a bitch. My fists couldn't cure him of being such an asshole. Ever since then, he kind of ignored me.

My mom will probably never figure out the reason for this. Always been a nice lady, but she never had much of a clue about anything outside the kitchen. Mom always made Thanksgiving and Christmas great when it came to food, but the social shit hasn't been too much fun since me and my old man had our knock-down-drag-out fight a couple of years back. That's why I made up a bullshit excuse to get out of Easter dinner. Of course, my father knew the real reason, but as usual, my mom believed my lame story. Damn, was she ever gullible, which sure was great back in high school when I needed to get away with somethin'. There always has been a lot of lying goin' on in our house. Bullshit was the order of the day. I was pretty good at it, even with my father, but since he didn't trust no one, I was screwed no matter how good my bullshit was.

My mom, on the other hand, she'd have trusted Satan because he'd have smiled and swore on the Bible that he was tellin' the gospel truth. Sweet lady but double dumb. Guess my father liked his women that way. Hell, that S.O.B. liked the ladies just as long as they was breathin'. He had his minimum standards.

Being as I was twenty-six years old and had done a tour of duty in Vietnam, I had no use for no Easter egg crap, much less dinner with that asshole. I wasn't no little kid no more. Andrea, a lady I'd met recently, knew that, so I figured being with her on Easter would be a lot better. Actually, I was horny. Damn, did she have some fine knockers. Oh, yeah. Definitely built. What a bod. When she laid her invite for Easter dinner on me, I hopped on it as fast as I would've hopped on her. It definitely sounded like she finally wanted to let me give her a cheap thrill. She was turnin' me into an optimist. Unlike all the other ladies that fell for my bullshit lines, there was something different about her, something that kept me comin' back.

We first met 'round about Christmas time, and although this may be hard to believe, she hadn't let me jump her bones yet. This was strange since I got looks, a good job, and a red Pontiac Firebird. One of these things usually could get me laid, and without no commitment and all that other crap that some ladies think they gotta have. I didn't even care every time my drinking buddies told me that I was definitely pussy whipped. Naturally, I denied it since these guys were a bunch of dumb asses. There was something that made her different. I suppose there was a shitload of other things about her besides her fine body. Maybe that was why I still called her the day after Easter, even though she still wouldn't let me get into her pants. But I sure was horny.

Naturally, I gave my drinking buddies all the details of our night of passion. After the fourth round, which I didn't have to buy, they were slapping me on the back with each new line of bullshit I fed them. They weren't as nice as my mom but just as damn gullible. By the fifth round of drinks, they were cheering every time I said, "And then she..."

By the time we closed down the bar, I had them convinced that I was the world's greatest lover and had sex with her six ways to Sunday. In the morning I not only woke up with a serious hangover, but I also woke up just as horny as I'd been the day before. I guess Andrea was worth it, but figuring out why would take me a while.

18

CHARLIE'S SISTER
APRIL 1975
DÔNG BÍCH (1)

Uncle Ho was right. When the Americans grew tired of their war of aggression in our beloved Viêt Nam, they returned to the comfort of their own country. Without the assistance of the Americans, Saigon's puppet army ran like terrified dogs from our comrades from the north and from the brave fighters of our own National Liberation Front. When word reached us that the Presidential Palace in Saigon had fallen, there was much joy among those of us of the Q16 Company who had survived to celebrate our country's great victory.

Sadly, there were only a few of us who remained from the old days, the time before my brother Tuan's death at the hands of the American war criminals. He had been a soldier of the Revolution, and for his many great acts of unselfish courage, his reward was a single bullet in the back of his head. My dearest brother was one of many from our National Liberation Front's Q16 Company who willingly sacrificed their lives. Of the one hundred and twelve brave comrades in the Q16 from the time before the Year of the Monkey, there were only seventeen of us who survived to see this glorious victory, which cost our family so dearly.

The earth of Dông Bích owned the bones of our family: my mother who would never know her grandson, now a year old; my father who was forced to teach his children the ways of war; and my brother who left his sister too soon. At this important time in the history of our nation, the fire of my joy was tempered by my sadness and longing. The foreigners were gone, yet so too was my family, who joined my ancestors too soon. The great victory that Uncle Ho promised had finally arrived, yet in our success, the rich, red soil that we loved so dearly had become drenched with an awful, crimson color. Stained with the blood of peasant soldiers, the earth could no longer sing; and the clouds could only shed tears on our land.

I am the earth and the clouds.

19

O'BRIEN
MAY 1975
TUCSON, ARIZONA

For my students, high school seniors drooling with anticipation for graduation night, Alfred, Lord Tennyson's words were merely hurdles that I had cruelly placed in front of them. Written several days prior to his death at the age of eighty-one, the meaning of the sixteen lines of "Crossing the Bar" were a mystery to the majority of the thirty-four students who wanted me to simplify their lives, something I typically resisted. Tennyson spoke to me, a twenty-eight-year-old English teacher, but his eloquent insight ricocheted like a pinball off the bulletin board at the back of the room, missing all but two students as it escaped through a partially opened window and into May's triple-digit afternoon air.

Having taught high school English for almost three years, I had learned a number of valuable lessons, many of them being repeats from my Marine Corps days. Ingrained in me at an early age by my parents and nurtured during my twelve year sentence in Catholic school, tenacity was both revered and honed by the Marine Corps drill instructors who reminded us that *giving up* was what the enemy was supposed to do. Eventually, most of the students would surrender to my stubborn will; it was only a question of when they would raise the white flag.

Oddly enough, the valedictorian of slouchers and ditchers, a lanky boy who grimaced when I called him Anthony and who always reeked of his lunch time cigarette, had volunteered to read Tennyson's four stanzas orally, not because he was enthralled with nineteenth-century English poetry, but rather because he liked the number of syllables in the word *graduation*. Tired of the consequences of his grade of *F*, he had finally decided to trade all that in for a *D*. Sixty percent seemed like a good number for an eighteen-year-old who firmly believed in the art of sliding by, also known as *physics and the high school senior.*

In spite of Tennyson's gracious assistance by offering both rhythm and rhyme, the boy read the poem with a jerky motion resembling the same lack of grace typical of the early stages of learning how to drive a stick shift. My auditory learners didn't stand a chance of understanding this poem, much less appreciating its beauty. Whispering a silent prayer, I petitioned God for two requests: forgive the boy and offer my apologies to Tennyson for allowing the slaughter of his poem. I didn't receive an immediate response from God, but the boy, who had settled back into his slouch mode, raised his hand and asked, "So when's class over, Mr. O'Brien?"

I chuckled and then replied in a mildly sarcastic tone which he failed to detect. "For whom the bell tolls, it tolls for thee in twenty-two minutes. Actually, when I'm done...John Donne, that is."

On our John-Donne days, he had been a ditcher; the fifth period bell had not tolled for him because leaving campus with his girlfriend seemed like the best thing to do. He had listened to his hormones and had heard none of John Donne's poetry, so his eyes were vacant as he said, "Oh." His *Oh* was nothing more than a synonym for *Huh?*

"That was a joke...a two-for-one special."

"Oh, I get it," he replied, fooling only himself, but everyone who had passed the test on metaphysical poetry the previous week knew that his words were as empty as a ditcher's notebook.

Feeling a twinge of remorse for my sarcasm, I told him that I appreciated that he had volunteered to read Tennyson's poem. Wearing a content grin, he nodded his response, now certain that he finally had a chance, although only a slight one, of passing my class.

Then, I said, "It's my turn to read." With no objections from an audience fearful of being chosen to volunteer to read the poem, I began reading "Crossing the Bar:"

> Sunset and evening star,
> And one clear call for me!
> And may there be no moaning of the bar,
> When I put out to sea,
> But such a tide as moving seems asleep,
> Too full for sound and foam,
> When that which drew from out the
> boundless deep
> Turns again home.
> Twilight and evening bell,
> And after that the dark!
> And may there be no sadness of farewell,
> When I embark;
> For though from our bourne of Time and Place
> The flood may bear me far,
> I hope to see my Pilot face to face
> When I have crossed the bar.

Before I elicited any observations from my students, I explained several key terms. "Tennyson's *bar* is not a pick-up joint where Victorian people drink until everyone becomes good looking, but rather a bar is a sand bank at the opening of a harbor. Now, look in the seventh line. He uses the word '*that*' to mean *the soul*, and finally, in the last stanza, the word '*bourne*' means *boundary* or *destination*. This poem speaks to the reader on several levels. Does anyone know what Tennyson offers to the auditory folks?"

"Rhythm and rhyme...rhythm and rhyme."

"Good observation, but I'd like you to raise your hand next time. Remember this isn't Jeopardy, but I must admit you're quick."

Pleased with himself, Bob, a teenage Columbus in search of adult approval, interjected, "I'm as quick as an angry rattlesnake...that's a metaphor...no, it's a simile. Right?"

Although I had known Bob for eight months, it seemed apparent that he hadn't changed much in the past twelve years. With mocking eyes rolling and heads shaking back and forth, the body language of most of the students spoke with clarity. This silent mantra had become a daily ditto for more years than they wanted to remember. Many of his classmates had carried a lunch box to first grade with Bob the year President Kennedy had been shot. They had known him through all his name changes: Bobby, Robby, Robert, Rob and finally Bob.

Bob and his fellow classmates were eager for graduation for a number of reasons. At the beginning of June, they could bid him *adieu* and *adios* with the hope that he'd fall off the edge of the earth or at least be held prisoner by Rod Serling in a *Twilight Zone* rerun. Over the years, as the poster child for Simon and Garfunkel's famous song "I'm a rock, I'm an island," Bob, wearing the armor of Don Quixote, fought tirelessly to prove that John Donne had been incorrect with his assertion that "No man is an island, entire of itself."

He knew the words and understood the metaphor just long enough to receive a ninety-five percent on the exam the previous week. As far as Bob was concerned, what did Donne know; he was Mr. Thee-Thy-Thou, the metaphysical metaphor man, the archaic someone who, although rarely understood by the intellectually lazy, had never been the target of mockery.

Bob, however, failed to realize that Donne had fallen out of favor with the literary world for several hundred years. At least John Donne, a child of antiquity, never had to sit in a classroom with people who believed that there was permanent open season on dorks; unfortunately for Bob, he had been their prey since the days before he had grown in his two front teeth. Being a twentieth century dork hadn't been easy, so Bob, like his peers, oozed with anticipation for that magical night in early June. Finally, he would be able to escape, or so he thought.

I had gained some insight that Bob had yet to discover: we never escape our ghosts which, like our shadows, only change shape during the day and offer the nocturnal illusion that they are gone, yet with each new day, they return, following us into the next night and all the other nights that await us. Bob, a master at the art of acing an exam, had yet to learn that we can run, but we can't hide—one of the lessons that the not so subtle Nam had forgotten to ask if I were interested in learning.

I was the Nam for my students, offering unrequested lessons. They were just grunts in search of their flight dates; graduation would be their Silver Bird away from their tours of duty, twelve years of public education. It was late May, and they were all getting short, just like everyone in the Nam did, one way or another.

The bell rang as usual, and my fifth period students escaped the confines of my classroom, disappearing into their adolescent world, a place with no need for English teachers, poets (whether metaphysical or Victorian), and most definitely, the welcome mat wasn't out for John Donne and his *bell* metaphors.

Although the students were gone, Donne's images from his "Meditation XVII" lingered, and I wondered about Bob, who struck me as a latter-day Trent Sandburn. The similarities were striking, both being angry and wounded pariahs, naysayers to Donne's belief that "No man is an island." Transported back in time, would Bob have been just one more Trent Sandburn carrying an M16 and a full magazine of rage? Probably, and that was the tragedy. Unfortunately, they both seemed to have chosen to squander their opportunities to celebrate life. I wanted to kick their butts for wasting oxygen, for existing while Corporal Webster and all the other men in our squad had to, as Donne put it, get "translated into a better language."

I wanted to scream, but only shook my head back and forth, finally letting out a deep sigh. Peering down, the words of Donne leapt up from the page: "*All mankind is of one author, and is one volume.*"

Did you hear that, Sandburn? Santos, Reyes, Corporal Webster, yeah, the entire squad, and even the Fuckin' New Guys are part of one volume.

"*When one man dies, one chapter is not torn out of the book, but translated into a better language, and every chapter must be so translated. God employs several translators. Some pieces are translated by age, some by sickness, some by war, some by justice.*"

My eyes raced on through sentences saturated with the

profound until I reached the final sentence in the excerpt: *"Any man's death diminishes me, because I am involved in mankind, and therefore never send to know for whom the bell tolls; it tolls for thee."*

Did Private Hesse and the other cherries know that they were getting short in the Nam. Did they hear their death knell, or did the steady spattering rhythm of February's drizzle drown out the tolling of so many bells come too early. God, You employ several translators, so why didn't You lay off at least one of them on that horrible night back in '68. But instead, You sent our squad a telegram written in Latin: *"Nunc lento sonitu dicunt, Morieris."* You didn't send a copy to me, so I, the only person in the squad who had studied Latin, couldn't warn the men. Why did you let Charlie be Your translator. Didn't You know that the politicians told us that You were on our side. Don't You watch the news. Why didn't You send me a copy of that telegram so that I could have at least put it into English for them: *"Now this bell, tolling softly for another, says to me, Thou must die."*

My questions have no question marks because I don't expect a reply from You, God. I disconnected my phone that night out by Dông Bích since You weren't home when I called for help.

20

SANDBURN
WINTER 1980
RICHMOND, VIRGINIA

Jimmy Carter. That man was a genuine embarrassment, especially since he was a son of the South. He called it the New South, but I knew there was only one South, the Old South, the South of great patriots like Robert E. Lee and Jefferson Davis. Stars and bars for goddamn ever. It was hard to have to admit, but there was times when I had to play the New South game. Real estate had become a tricky business with all them new laws about equal opportunity, which the Washington bleeding hearts called fair housing.

The rules of the game had changed, so I learned to smile at the coloreds when I'd sell 'em a house, and if they wanted me to call 'em African-Americans, well, their money was green. At the end of the day, we both knew that they was just niggers no matter how hard the boys up in Washington wanted to pretend otherwise. Actually, some of them African-Americans seemed to be pretty nice folks, but I still wasn't ready to sell one of 'em a house in my neighborhood. A man can only take so much, so about the time we finally sent Jimmy packin' back to Plains, Georgia, I got out of residential real estate and moved up into commercial real estate.

Two good things happened back in November. The voters stood up for America by votin' Reagan in, and my wife Andrea finally decided to give birth to a son. Having two daughters was real nice, but a man's gotta have a son to carry on the family name. Alyssa, three, and Missy, a two-year-old bundle of energy, were my princesses, but they'd never grow up to be my huntin' buddies. They would be Virginia ladies if I had anything to say about it. Of course, their mother agreed with me, which she usually did, and so our marriage was workin' out good so far. The only problem we had was that every once in a while she came up with these strange notions about gettin' herself a job. She always started out the same way: "When the kids are both in school…"

I'd always reply, "Children need their mother."

Before she could add anything to her *"But I think that…,"* I'd explain that there was no need, especially since I was bringin' in good money. "You're the wife and mother." She began to just stare at me as I proved my point to her by explaining, "The job of the mother is to bring up children so they grow up all respectful, and the job of the wife is to love her husband. Like the song says, stand by your man. If you think about it, you have two jobs, so why would you even want another one?"

Back about the time Missy was almost two, my wife began to nod and then walk away when I told her this stuff. It didn't bother me then since it meant we wouldn't have a big fight. Those I hated. When I was growing up, there were lots of fights in my house. They were always kinda one-sided since my mother couldn't get a word in edgewise. Even if she had, my old man wouldn't of heard a damn thing she said.

Their fights were always the same. She'd go and get brave and say somethin'. Of course, he didn't like that, and then he'd start his rantin' and ravin' shit. He was crazy. I mean fucking crazy when he'd get goin'. He'd always slam the door as he headed out to a bar to get wasted, and she'd always be a cryin', sobbin' away. Me and my sister had to put up with this crap until she went and got pregnant and I joined the Marines to escape the fuckin' crazy house. Naturally, my dad was ready to kill the guy who knocked up my sister, but my mom convinced him that the baby needed a father. He went along with the marriage idea, but my sister got herself divorced a couple of years later. My dad reminded my mom that my sister's shotgun wedding was her idea. He was good at remembering that kinda stuff.

When I joined the Marines, he thought I was bein' patriotic and tryin' to be like him. He had been in the Army during World War II, but he didn't see no action since he was a clerk or somethin' like that. Since he had been a doggy, I figured that I'd piss him off if I joined the Marines. That didn't work. He was all thrilled that I was servin' my country, so the branch of service didn't seem to matter to him.

My mother was another story. She wasn't real happy when I told her about me joinin' the Marines, but I figured she'd get over it. She'd have three years for that. Besides, when my old man put the word on her, the conversation was over. The world sure has changed as far as women are concerned. Period. End of fucking story. I was still waiting for my wife to get over her crazy ideas about her gettin' a job. Trent, Jr. didn't need no working-mom. He needed his mother full-time, and my mind was made up. My wife, although she was a pretty good woman, would just have to get used to it or be miserable.

As it turned out, we both ended up miserable. Trent, Jr. died in his sleep on February 16, 1981. Died in his goddamn sleep. The doctor called it SIDS. I just called it *fucked*, but life wasn't through fucking with me. Two years later, Andrea decided to be a bitch and leave me for some asshole 'cause she liked the way he treated her, so I went and became real damn good friends with Jim Beam, especially on Sunday nights after I returned Alyssa and Missy to the woman I thought was the love of my life. I've always hated being wrong. Fuck. Now, I've learned to hate Sunday nights even more.

21

O'BRIEN
8 MAY 1981
TUCSON, ARIZONA

Loving the Blues but hating the bar scene complicated things, especially, since Blues bands didn't do house calls. As dive bars go, the Cajun Roadhouse was at the top of the class; the ceiling was a patchwork of license plates and the walls wore a wide array of stolen road signs. The ambiance reflected the *It's-Midnight-And-I'm-Really-Drunk-On-My-Ass-But-Can-Drive* genre; however, it was only 10 p.m.—two-beers time—so the ceiling and the walls had yet to appear appropriate.

Ten o'clock was the perfect time in a bar; most patrons had sipped their way to loosening up and getting in touch with that spontaneous kid who had been held at bay all week long. But not everyone on a Friday night sips their mixed drinks or their beer; there are always those who chug their beers or slam down their shots on the way to getting in touch with their inner badass. By 11 p.m., more than a few people were wearing the six-shots grin and pretending to be happy.

Although I had been hesitant about being at the bar—just too crowded and too noisy for my liking—the band, playing with wild abandon to the third power, made it a little easier to be there. Their music turned out to be closer to Bob Seger-style Rock than the Blues, which was okay with me, since it had me tapping my foot and mimicking the keyboard player's every move. Having arrived at the bar unattached, I noticed three single women at a table who were not only poster children for musically induced hyperactivity but were on the right side of the looks scale. It seemed obvious that the dance floor was where their hearts were, but no one had asked them to dance. My eyes shouted, '*Oh, yes!,*' so after polishing off my first bottle of beer, my feet listened, and without hesitation, I strolled up and asked a blonde in her mid twenties if she wanted to dance. With a quick glance of her cobalt blue eyes, she replied, "No."

I was taken aback for a moment because her body had been shouting, '*I want to dance*', but it seemed that she hadn't been listening. Rather than give her the *What-the-hell-are-you-doing-here-then?* speech, I shifted gears to plan B. Undeterred, I smiled and replied, "Maybe another time." I turned toward the woman seated next to her, and my thirty-four-year-old heart was sixteen in the instant that our eyes met. Her friend's lack of interest in dancing with me had been a gift.

After several dances to rowdy music—the slow dance would have to wait—I walked her back to her table. Before I could thank her, she extended her hand and said, "I'm Kate, and these are my friends Norma and Janice. You already met Janice."

She smiled impishly and invited me to join them. "I'm Michael...Michael O'Brien, and I'll take you up on your offer."

Being outnumbered had usually been a negative experience in my life; three-to-one odds, and Kate and her two friends were not only much better looking than the NVA, they were definitely much friendlier. I bought a round of girly drinks for the trio of friends, but stuck with my Budweiser. In spite of the blaring music, I made a tenacious attempt at conversation. As it turned out, I discovered that my earlier rejection by Janice had nothing to do with me; being blonde, beautiful, and blue-eyed had been a two-edged sword; she had just been laid off from her job as a legal secretary—sleeping with her boss hadn't been such a good idea.

Kate and Norma, on the other hand, led much more vanilla lives as a kindergarten teachers; they got their hugs from five-year-olds who have a natural affinity for hugs and questions like *why*. Kate's gentle smile could win over any five-year-old, not to mention a thirty-four-year-old English teacher. What had I done to deserve this? The fire mission from Cupid was right on target. Kate's chestnut hair, full and flowing just past her shoulders, and the sparkle in her deep blue eyes made me a dozen shades of helpless. The band pumped out several songs with lyrics of angst and suffering, a modern musical version of the Buddha's first Nobel Truth—life means suffering—but, as I sat there mesmerized, the only lyrics that raced through my head were those of the Kinks: *"Girl, you really got me goin'. You got me so I don't know what I'm doin'. Yeah, you really got me now."*

After the first dance, I was about a mile past smitten. As we danced, her body swayed with confidence and rhythmic sensuality that was nothing short of delicious; however, it was the one-two punch of her broad smile and her eyes, ocean blue and sparkling, that captured me. Oh, to be five again, spending all day in Miss Kate Gallagher's class.

Although I typically wore happy feet when a rock-n-roll band was playing, I didn't complain when the band took their first break, which meant that yelling wouldn't be necessary to hold a conversation with Kate. Her friends were definitely attractive, but Kate, with her long chestnut-colored hair, was stunning, the heart-pounding variety. Passionate and intelligent, two qualities I valued in a woman, and Kate was flush with both characteristics. I was Columbus and Kate was the Indies; I was hungry to discover more about this woman who had captured my heart.

Some ambushes are better than others. The English teacher had met the kindergarten teacher, and the lesson was all about chemistry. Having taught for five years, Kate's enthusiasm and passion for teaching had not diminished, as is the case for some teachers. Listening to the excitement in her voice, it became readily apparent that her love of her students and her commitment to teaching were based on her love of life. My intuition, which had served me well in Vietnam, was usually on target, and it screamed that Kate was a keeper. And our first slow dance was confirmation. Our bodies knew. When we returned to the table, her friends were smiling.

I ordered another beer and left to go to the restroom. As I was returning, I noticed Kate was saying something to a man in his early twenties and was vehemently shaking her head back and forth. As I approached the table, he kicked my empty chair, threw his arms into the air and slurred, "Fuck you, bitch!"

Now standing an arm's length away from him, my right fist ached to knock his face to New Mexico or even Texas, but I said, as calmly as I could, "Excuse me, but you're talking to a lady. If she doesn't want to talk to you, back off." He was somewhere close to that third sheet to wind. Even a drunk should have some manners, but his mama had forgotten that part of the bringing up thing. Generally, women cringe at the thought of being anywhere near a fight, especially if they're the focus of the brawl. While maintaining eye contact on Mr. Tough Guy, I sensed that Kate and her friends were wishing this were nothing more than a bad dream, but a fight was brewing.

Rather than move away from the table and find another bottle of beer to chug, the unwelcome inebriated man was bobbing as he got in touch with his inner-stupid-drunk. "Who the fuck you think you are...yeah, you think you can kick my ass or somethin'? Fuck you and your..."

"Whoa!" Although he had at least thirty pounds on me, I remained calm, but it was becoming more difficult with each insult he was hurling. Without raising my forearms into the fighting position, my fists remained clenched. Vietnam had taught me to always be prepared and never underestimate the adversary. "I don't think you want this to get out of hand. Your friends over there need to take you home." As he turned away when I mentioned his friends, I motioned to Kate and her friends to leave. The evening had lost its special magic. By the time he turned back toward me, Kate and her friends had left the bar.

"Your girlfriends are all gone, so they won't be watchin' me kick your fuckin' ass. You wanna take it outside?"

Adrenaline was surging through me as I struggled to reply in a calm voice, "Not really. You don't wanta fuck with me right about now. You fucked up a perfectly good evening. You're drunk, so I'm gonna let it slide. I'm outta a here."

Just then, one of the bartenders walked up and stood between us and said, "Is there a problem here?" There was nothing warm and fuzzy in his voice, and his credentials, a scowl and a barrel chest, convinced us that a brawl would be a poor idea.

We both shook our heads, and the bartender replied, "We don't need no shit in here. Got a problem...take it outside."

I turned and walked to the door. The evening that had started out so well was disintegrating quickly. Kate was gone, and seeing her again was a ten-foot question mark. When I reached the parking lot, I looked to my left and saw Kate and her friends getting in their car. The gods of love were smiling on me: there was still an opportunity to get her phone number.

As I turned toward her car, two men in their mid-twenties, wearing baseball caps, backwards, of course, began walking toward me, but the drunk from the bar confrontation was not with these men. About ten feet away, the taller of the two—6'3" or so—slurring as he yelled, "You need your ass kicked!" The shorter man, about my height at 5'10", nodded, agreeing completely with his friend that my ass needed to be rearranged. I stopped immediately, preparing for the worst—two-to-one odds and no bartender to play the role of the UN. I had come to dance, but it was quickly becoming clear that the night would end in an ass whooping, and it wouldn't be mine. It had been more than a decade since I had been called on to dance with violence; the past had snuck up on me and was claiming me once again. A fight had not been on my agenda, but if they pushed it, I'd accommodate them.

Standing at the ready, I took a deep breath, shaking my head side to side. "I don't need any trouble. I..."

Just as I was about to finish explaining why fighting me would not be the brightest idea for them to pursue, I was grabbed around the neck from behind by a third man. In an instant, my automatic reaction from my Marine Corps training, which had served me well at least once during my two tours in Vietnam, took over. I was speed shifting in the fight-or-flight gears, and a tsunami of adrenaline was rushing through me.

Reaching up with my right arm, I hooked my attacker's right elbow with my right arm. Before he realized what had happened, I flipped him over my right shoulder and sent him crashing to the pavement. He had only a second to feel stunned at the reversal of his fortunes; with him on his back, I slammed my knee into his stomach and simultaneously crushed his nose with my fist. He was screaming, slurring his profanities as blood was pouring out of his broken nose. It was obvious that having an over-supply of the stupid gene hadn't helped his situation, but being obnoxious and drunk, combined with having bad manners when dealing with women, with Kate in particular, had created the perfect storm that guaranteed that the evening would not end well for him.

"FUCK!" The commentary from his friends was succinct. They stopped several feet from me. I stood up and moved back several feet from their friend who was lying on the parking lot pavement, wailing and moaning, still wondering what had happened.

"Take your dumb-ass friend home. I don't think you want to fuck with me! I'm not pissed off yet...I said, *'not yet'*. I'm outta here. Quit while you're behind." I rubbed the knuckles of my right hand, which were covered in blood. Behind me, the two friends did what they should have done in the first place; they helped their injured friend up and drove off.

Kate's car was pulling away, and with that, the opportunity to get to know her evaporated. I would have traded one ass-whooping of an obnoxious drunk for Kate's phone number any day. Maybe it wasn't in the cards.

A week later, while I was shopping at the Safeway, Kate literally bumped into me as I was wrestling with a cereal purchase decision: Chex or Raisin Bran. Just like in the song, my heart skipped a beat, and I dropped both boxes of cereal into my basket. Somehow breakfast just didn't seem to matter. The sparkle in her eyes owned me as we both walked toward the check-out line; then, I walked her to her car, where she gave me her phone number and a hug, the *you-make-my-heart-flutter kind*.

The soreness in my right hand faded away, and a broad smile ran wild across my face. Being wanted—desired—was a delicious feeling indeed.

22

TUAN
THE PRESENT
HEAVEN

I am no longer the man I was before the ambush, so I realize that I cannot give my sister relief from her suffering because she has her own path to travel. She is tethered to her pain, her anger, her loss, her past; it is like a heavy stone around her neck as she struggles to cross a deep river. She has been cursing the river for being too deep, when she only needs to release the stone before it drowns her in her ancient sorrow.

Dear sister, by releasing your anger and hatred of the French and the Americans, you will allow the river's current to carry you on your journey to experience nirvana, yet after many years you still harbor hatred toward the French and the Americans for coming to our beautiful land. You killed many to rid our beautiful Viêt Nam of the foreign occupiers, and yet you allow hatred and anger to occupy your heart. Liberation from the foreign armies happened seven years after my death, but the true liberation has yet to occur for you because you still suffer, because you remain a young child who misses her mother, because you still hate the American Marines, because you are convinced they are responsible for my death.

My dear sister, does the sun actually move from east to west because a farmer sees it rise in the east and set in the west? Knowing what actually happened to me that night during Têt

74

will only bring clarity to your mind, but your mind does not only need clarity; your mind needs to become calm and your heart needs to heal itself. If you saw a man trying to hold on to the wind, would you think him to be a fool? Let your resentment and anger be the wind that rustles through the tress but doesn't make a home in your heart. Empty your heart so you can fill it with the joy of knowing your children. Empty your heart of yesterday, of yesteryear. The war of liberation is over; the life of liberation can begin now or whenever you wish. Your brother Tuan, smiling gently, loves you.

23

O'BRIEN
10 FEBRUARY 1982
5ᵀᴴ STREET AND WILMOT

Hesse knows that without his foot, which isn't where it's supposed be, he's up shit creek without a paddle, so he ponders his situation...I'm permanently fucked and the good fairy, the cavalry, and Jesus aren't dumb enough to come and save my ass, but Doc Reyes thinks he's the Mexican miracle man and I just want to find my foot and, oh, yeah, what they told us about "the more you sweat in peace, the less you bleed in war" is bullshit, 'cause I sweated my ass off back at Camp Pendleton, but my artery ain't being too cooperative spurtin' blood like an oil well gusher, and on the bright side, I'll get to go home early, but bein' dead, well, never been there before so maybe it won't be as bad as not getting any dates 'cause I'm missin' a foot...I don't take it personal that Reyes doesn't have time to waste, but I'm dead, which is what happens to eighteen-year-old Marines who let the Việt Cong lob grenades at them, especially the kind that hit their mark and sever limbs and, well, you get the picture...I just wanted to find my foot, but that was a waste time even though I begged God and promised Him I'd be good if He'd just help me find my damn foot.

President Reagan was turning seventy-one, and I was supposed to be turning left at the intersection of 5ᵗʰ Street and Wilmot Road where I had waited for the left turn signal to send me on my way; however, Hesse, a 1968 hitchhiker from Dông Bích, decided to be a passenger in my Toyota truck.

Enough with you popping into my life and screwing with my head, 'cause I'm just trying to drive down the road and be alive which you just can't accept, so...

The sound of horns honking went on in a parallel Universe where people get tickets when they are on autopilot while driving.

Someone was a pounding on my window, and the veins in his neck were bulging as he screamed, "What the fuck is your problem, buddy? You on drugs or somethin'? Jesus Christ!"

Tell that loud mouth asshole that a one-footed dead Marine will kick his sorry ass if he doesn't get back in his damn car.

I ejected Hesse out of my truck and made my overdue left turn. I was heading north but feeling like my life was going south. Dông Bích had become a suburb of Tucson. Charlie was coming.

24

O'BRIEN
VALENTINE'S DAY 1982
THE RINCON MOUNTAINS

Women have certain expectations, and Kate, being a fairly typical woman when it came to romance, was less than happy when I didn't show up on the most sacred of all romantic holidays. Beyond no roses, beyond no candle-lit dinner at an overpriced restaurant, beyond my failure at providing all the other clichéd demonstrations of love, beyond it all, I had committed the unpardonable sin: I was AWOL on Valentine's Day.

I needed her to be somebody she was incapable of being. How could I expect Kate, a twenty-five-year-old without a clue about war, to understand what the 12th of February meant to me? Of course, she knew I had served two tours in the Nam, but how could I expect her to realize how difficult the anniversary of the night out by Dông Bích—and the days around it—were. The rat called war tenaciously continued to gnaw at my heart, and I wished she could understand its unrelenting power in my post-Vietnam life. I was hungry for her to be able to hear beyond the words, to be able to empathize, yet this was no more than my pipe dream.

In all my years, I had never met a woman like her, but that wasn't enough. No matter the depth of her love for me, she had never heard the sound of incoming mortar fire or the final gasp of a dying grunt who just wanted to be nineteen. Kate was beautiful; God, my eyes loved it whenever she answered the door. Penetrating, deep-blue eyes and a smile that sent me into the sighing mode—that was Kate.

In spite of her beauty, intelligence, and a compassionate heart, I was in the Rincon Mountains staring at a fuzzy, waning moon and had been doing so for the past two nights. To the west was Tucson and Valentine's Day love, but Kate and I would not be part of it. The ache in my heart could have produced a double album of the Blues, and my head overflowed with too many painful memories of the Nam for me to even pretend that love was in the air. The acrid smell of that February's morning ambush hung heavy in my memory, made fresh by the tricks of a calendar.

Anniversaries are supposed to be special, and it seems men have a unique gene that causes them to sometimes forget those special days. For a combat vet, anniversaries of the time in hell are too easily remembered. Not surprisingly, the 12th of February, the fourteenth anniversary of the ambush at Dông Bích, affected me in such a negative manner. Kate wasn't a *fucking bitch*, yet those were the last words she heard from me as I slammed the door behind me the last time I saw her.

She would forgive me—it was in her gentle nature to do so—but I wasn't sure if I could forgive myself for treating her that way. Our relationship had always been about respect, and yet I had violated that basic tenet of our relationship. My anger began to subside several hours after I had left, but then the guilt began to gnaw at my heart, reminding me of a long-buried feeling which I thought, mistakenly, I had resolved by visiting all but one of the families of the men who had been killed the night of the ambush at Dông Bích.

I was so wrong, and the cold February air wrapped itself around me as I shivered under a waning moon, staring unsympathetically down at me as regret raced through my mind. In the stillness, the chill of the air was enveloping me, but I would shiver through it, yet an emptiness that I had successfully evaded for years was slipping through my barbed wire defenses. The overwhelming sense of loss from that night back in 1968 had not been resolved, regardless of my long-held belief that I had moved beyond the tragedy of the ambush; Kate, unfortunately, had become collateral damage several days earlier when she said, "Michael, I don't know why you're getting so upset. All that stuff happened fourteen years ago. It's time to get over it."

Forgiveness was not part of the nocturnal landscape as I bellowed my anger into the western sky, to the woman I had wanted to marry. Now the landscape of my life was only painted with doubt, anger, guilt, loneliness, and the chill of the February night air, one that was all too familiar. Alone on a mountain, I slept with my well-seasoned pain, a companion I knew all too well.

25

O'BRIEN
SPRING 1982
TUCSON, ARIZONA

The bottle of Merlot emptied too quickly; no sipping of red wine, just the slurring of syllables as I babbled my monologue of pain at the furniture in my all too quiet house. I was certain that it was over. Yes, finally over and done. I was wrong. The first tear rolled down my right cheek. The ambush was on. Kate wasn't supposed to affect me this way. I thought everything was under control since we had decided it would be better if we went our separate ways. After all, we had parted amicably; of course, that was the mature thing to do. My head understood this, but my heart need to be in the ER.

It was an empty Saturday night, and I didn't want to have anything to do with *mature*. Red wine became my sodium pentathol. I had resisted the truth for months, but tonight all my delusions about being okay with the break-up stood naked in front of me. I was baffled as to why I had fooled myself into believing that I was just fine with *our* decision. Insight—the accurate type—and red wine don't dance together well; time and sobriety would provide those answers. The last Saturday night in April would be about overdue tears and a step forward—one that I didn't understand at the time—but not before I spilled the last few ounces of a second bottle of red wine on what had been a bland, beige carpet in my living room. "Fuck!" reverberated around the house which I had wanted to become a home, *our home*.

Shaking my head from side to side, I sighed and clenched my teeth. Then more tears streamed down both cheeks as the short-lived sighing gave way to a slurred chorus of *goddamn-its*, all bellowed for the neighbors to hear. Slumped over as I sat next to the wine-stained carpet, I stared with glazed-over eyes, mumbling at the basketball-sized stain on the carpet as though it were a sentient being capable of making sense of my slurred words.

"Out, out, damn spot. Lady Macbeth, your life sucked too, but I didn't fuckin' kill anybody like you did. Well…at least not recently. Just got all scared about gettin' married."

In an attempt to stand, I immediately fell back. With the carpet as my resting place, I turned my head toward the carpet stain, which began fading away with the hum of an unnoticed ceiling fan becoming the soundtrack for the end of the wrong kind of Saturday night. Another gone-wrong night, but at least nobody got killed on this one; however, Kate's leaving hurt just the same: the sound of her voice slowly becoming a fading memory, floating away into yesterday.

Rusty red dirt. Plum colored pool of blood. A single, afternoon cloud with a fancy name that I'll never know glides casually above my tired eyes, bluer than this final sky made so special because of circumstances not of my choosing. I bet Charlie is happy…VC one, me zero. Colleen, I'm sorry, so sorry. I wanted you to be proud of me, but I messed up and let Charlie get a bead on me. That final cloud isn't exactly what I want for my eyes. They really want to be seeing you. Colleen, all I can do is remember. God, do my dying eyes want you Colleen…Colleen. The unnoticed hum of the rotor blades of the medevac chopper becoming the soundtrack of a gone-wrong afternoon in a killing place called the Nam.

Aspirin worked its magic, and my hangover became nothing more than a memory, but the dream about MacAndrews lingered, unlike most dreams that evaporate by the morning's second cup of coffee. For breakfast, I had a perspective omelette.

And in Morristown, New Jersey, with its Norman Rockwell quaintness, a thirteen-year-old boy wants *his* dad: not a picture of a Marine in dress blues, not the patriotic colors of that triangled flag, and not the stories about a hero. But in the Year of the Monkey, a lucky headshot had been in the script for a Fuckin' New Guy who just wanted to read his first letter from his pregnant wife Colleen.

26

O'BRIEN
SUMMER 1982
TUCSON, ARIZONA

A virgin margarita will work its magic on taste buds, but I wasn't concerned with my taste buds or quenching my thirst— my margaritas would be nothing less than the sluttiest whores as far as margaritas go. The fifth one helped to make everything clear, or at least, the tequila made it easy to believe that my conclusions were accurate. The chapter called *Kate* was over: definitely *no más*; I had moved on, yet this mumbled mantra rang hollow as I stumbled ever so slowly toward the acceptance of my loss. Elisabeth Kubler-Ross had been my dance partner for months. Like so many people who are grieving a loss, I had surrendered one more time to alcohol, which made my delusions so much more believable in the same way that tequila could easily turn a moderately good looking woman into a stunning beautiful one. Unfortunately, the morning would only provide a hang over and visual regret.

As it turned out, the woman beside me in bed in the morning was beautiful—the liquor had not lied—but I didn't care. Her name didn't matter; after all, she and my margaritas were nothing more than my drugs of choice. The smell of empty goin'-through-the-motions sex was replaced by the aroma of the omelette with bacon, *jalapenos*, green *chiles*, and pepper jack cheese that I placed in front of her as she sipped her coffee. She smiled her thank-you, probably believing that I was interested in seeing her again. Without thinking, I had mixed up four eggs rather than two and tossed in the rest of the ingredients, not because I gave a damn about her, but because accidents happen, just like shit happens. I humored her, allowing her the luxury of her delusions during breakfast, but that all came to an abrupt halt when I said, "It's been real. I'm done playing house."

All she saw was a vacant stare as I escorted her to her car. As she opened the car door, she turned and made one last attempt at eliciting an explanation for my lack of interest.

In a monotone, I replied, "You're a big girl, and well...I really don't give a shit right now."

Rolling down her window as she backed out of my driveway, she shouted, "Fuck you, asshole. You were a shitty lay anyway!"

I ignored her evaluation of my sexual prowess; after all, she was nothing more than a diversion, something to do while the pain of my break-up with Kate figured out where it wanted to hang its proverbial hat.

My friends were even beginning to tire of my wallowing in my pain. My life had become a Country-Western song, one sung poorly. I had bought into the belief that I had an inalienable right to wallow in my sorrow; it was somewhere in a rough draft of the Constitution. After four months of my lamentations, my friends, one at a time, and not always gently, began to explain to me that it was time for me to get the hell out of the swamp. Their *time-to-move-on* phrase sounded painfully familiar to me; moreover, the last person who had muttered those words was no longer part of my life, but friends are different—when they spoke, my heart listened. Although my friends were right, my journey to acceptance had its own calendar.

The next night, tears were streaming down my cheeks, but this time their origin had nothing to do with a woman and a failed love but rather were the result a perfect storm of events in my life. The planets had aligned themselves perfectly to bring out all the pain of loss that I had been feeling, some of it admitted, some denied, but all uncomfortably real and most of it buried much too long as it remained dormant below the surface. In my perfect world Kate would be in my life to encourage and support me during this difficult time, but Kate was my past-tense woman; she only danced in my memory.

St. John of the Cross had written about the dark night of the soul; I lived my version of the experience throughout most of the summer of '82. Oddly, the sunlight appeared at the end of the summer when I met a homeless Nam vet who had been sitting near a dumpster behind a Frys' supermarket; he was smiling, and God had painted his gentle eyes with a brown not found on the color palette. My pain melted away on that muggy August day.

Here was a another person who had lived through the same hell that I had known, and his daily situation was so much more bleak than mine; after all, I had the luxury of feeling sorry for myself in my house with its air conditioning and a thirty-pound felt roof; he had a piece of cardboard the size of my dishwasher to shelter him from the rain. I had the luxury of tears under a real roof; Lenny, my new-found friend, only had the protection of just-found cardboard, yet when I inquired about the source of his optimistic view of life, he succinctly said, "Hell, no one's shootin' at me, so life's pretty good." He smiled as he handed me a fresh perspective. The Universe had saved me in the Nam, and it had done it one more time, sending me Lenny, the shopping center Buddha.

Margaritas ceased being an integral part of my life. I eventually thanked Lenny for helping me to realize that coping had only gotten me through the night; I needed to start dealing with the Nam; I had discovered that coping, like pleasure pretending to be happiness, is limited in its capacity. Facing my long buried pain, I finally began to realize that courage and I needed to become reacquainted. Short-term solutions seemed to fall short; substance was the ingredient I needed in my life. I wasn't sure if the nine guys who had died in the middle of February of '68 really cared about my new awareness, but I felt nervously good that I had set the margarita glass down for the last time. It would be different this time; alcohol would be placed on the shelf of my memory to gather dust.

Sobriety turned out to be its own reward; greater clarity about my future was my bonus. I took a sabbatical leave from teaching and began investigating the idea of becoming a Catholic priest.

27

O'BRIEN
THANKSGIVING 1982
CONROE, TEXAS

Corporal Izaiah Webster's grandmother, an east Texas Maya Angelou sans the formal education, owned a presence that elicited respect and a "*Ma'am*" from those in Conroe who forgot, just for a moment, that she was blacker than a no-moon night. In her younger days there was no waddle in her walk, of course, but no sassy strut, just a confidence in the way she held herself; it was part of the Webster DNA, a cherished quality her eldest grandson would never pass on. The Nam took care of that when Charlie pruned that branch off the family tree.

1968, the year his grandmother turned sixty, was the year her grandson's birthdays became obsolete. Fortunately, she possessed a perfect blend of a stoic nature and a steadfast faith like that of the early Christian martyrs just before feeding time in the Coliseum. She had a basketful of reasons to justify dwelling on the past, yet being bitter or feeling hatred because of the racial injustice she had experienced and witnessed was not part of her character; however, that had not always been the case.

As a twelve-year-old, she became consumed with hating white people for several months after the lynching of a black teenage boy in Center, Texas. In the Texas of 1920, a young black girl knew it was wise to hide her anger when she overheard a group of men at the general store laughing about the lynching.

Eventually, when she confided in her mother about why she was so angry, her mother simply said, "It's not that these peoples is white that's the problem. They's ignorant folk who pretends they know Jesus. These here same church-goin' people woulda crucified our Lord and Savior back in them olden days. Jesus said, 'Father, forgive them for they know not what they do.' Jesus was talkin' all 'bout ignorance. I know it be difficult, but your mama never said the road to salvation would be smooth."

Adolescents are prone to ignoring parental admonitions and advice, and she was not atypical, yet her mother's logic made sense. After some preteen pondering, she made a life-long commitment to combating ignorance. She refused to be seduced by the easy path of hating the ignorant and the hateful, but rather she would choose a road less traveled, focusing her life on the importance of learning and love.

Jesus and Mrs. Webster's mother had been right, so at the age of seventy-four, her broad smile, minus one incisor, continued to bear witness to her tenacious refusal to allow her heart to become cluttered with bitterness even when shots had rung out back in '68, sending Doctor King and her Izaiah to "dwell in the house of the Lord forever." She didn't understand the ways of the Lord. Two gentle souls, one thirty-nine, the other only nineteen, were too young. She was ready, so why would the Lord not take her. "*Take me, Lord*" was her mantra for most of '68. And in early June, her heart ached and grew weary once again upon hearing the news of Robert Kennedy's assassination. It seemed that her God had taken a year-long vacation during 1968, thus allowing open season on the men she loved. Her well of faith was deep, so it sustained her, and the "*Amens*" she shouted on Sunday continued to echo through her week.

The Holy Scripture did not lie; this she knew. "The Lord is my shepherd." Oh, yes, this was true. "Yea, though I walk through the valley of the shadow of death, I will fear no evil: for thou art with me," but for some unknown reason, it was in the Father's plan to let the Grim Reaper guide the five-round burst from an SKS rifle that cut down her Izaiah on the side of a trail as the cold February rain splashed randomly, mixing in with a puddle of his useless blood.

For this erudite woman of words, she might as well have been a stroke victim hopelessly searching for words to articulate the burning ache in her heart that day back in mid February of '68 when her sobbing daughter mustered the courage to share the terrible news. Of course, she consoled her daughter, but this woman of words only uttered, "Your mama's here," holding her and wiping the tears from the face of one more mother who had become collateral damage of a firefight on a rainy night.

The Marine Corps gave the family a flag folded in a triangle; the Websters of Conroe, Texas, like so many other Texas families, ended up on the wrong end of the trade. Corporal Webster's grandmother didn't want a hero planted in east Texas dirt, but she was an Amen lady who loved words almost as much as she loved her Jesus, so she took comfort in the knowledge that one of the meanings for *Amen* was *let it be*. And she did; she believed fervently, accepting that God had a plan, one she didn't understand nor like, because there would always be a vacant seat at her Thanksgiving table but never a vacant spot in her heart for her grandson Izaiah.

The flight from Tucson to Houston took more than fourteen years, yet Corporal Izaiah Webster was still nineteen, forever nineteen. One final bit of unfinished business awaited me in Conroe, Texas before I would venture off to the seminary and the life of a Benedictine monk. My resumé read: Marine mortarman and forward observer; high school English teacher; almost husband; retired wine and tequila sponge; and soon-to-be-celibate monk; however, the job that mattered the most wasn't really a job; it was a responsibility, a debt, to offer comfort and some closure to the families of the men who had been killed on that horrific night during Tét of '68. Corporal Izaiah Webster was the final person on my list of the nine Marines killed out by Dông Bích. By meeting Webster's family, my fourteen-year odyssey would be completed.

Fortunately, early on I had recognized that survivor's guilt served no positive purpose in my life, yet a lingering pain remained. Dwelling on the reason why I had survived the Dông Bích ambush while nine others hadn't was nothing more than useless speculation, which I could ask God about on Judgment Day. I could wait. Rather than be a poster child for narcissism by focusing on how badly I felt about the deaths that occurred back in 1968, I had resolved that I would honor the memory of each of my fallen Marine brothers by visiting their families and by appreciating the generous gift God had mysteriously given me: the gift of life. Unknown to me was God's purpose; more than a decade had passed since the ambush out by Đông Bích, and the answer still eluded me. All I knew was that I was alive and nine other men from the squad had stopped needing birthday cakes, and their families celebrated holidays with an unwanted guest called grief.

The Thanksgiving Day traffic on I-45 North was light as I approached the outskirts of Conroe, Texas. As a former forward observer, I appreciated accurate directions, and Webster's grandmother's directions were simple; furthermore, Conroe's layout wasn't complicated, especially in the southeastern part of town where the street signs played the numbers-meet-the-alphabet game and sidewalks were just a pipe dream. I parked across the street because several cars were parked in front of the Webster home, a modest white clapboard house with a front porch swing waiting patiently to be made useful. As I approached the porch, I sighed deeply—twice.

Webster screams just as he pops a second red star cluster into the rainy sky, the signal to the folks back at the hill that we're being overrun. He knows that the reaction force won't make it here in time. He desperately wants to be wrong, but he's a busy pragmatist yelling something at me, but bursts of automatic weapons fire and the explosion of a Chicom grenade and the terrified screaming for Doc Reyes own the night. His inaudible words, becoming past tense and useless, float away through the black, wet night air. Webster crawls toward me, sloshing through the muddy soup, and I finally can hear him as he screams, "FUCK!" A burst from an SKS rifle and a half dozen rounds randomly tear into his back. These bullets don't care. They just do what bullets do—go from point A to point B, and Webster is point B. In that instant he knows if Heaven truly exists and if all those shouted hallelujahs mattered. Just a few feet from me, a rain-drenched Việt Cong soldier is standing over the soon-to-be-going-home body of Webster, and I know I am in hell. A wet, cold, lonely hell where Lucifer is called Charlie. But

Mrs. Webster, I want you to know how brave your grandson was. Such a good Marine, and I need to just focus on the positive. Leave the facts back at the hotel.

My speech—oh, how good it sounded in the laboratory of my mind—well, it just evaporated. Images of Webster's last moments had refused to stay on the shelf of unwanted memories, collecting dust. Anxiety was owning the moment, so I took another deep breath as I stood positioned to ring the doorbell. Before I allowed fear to sneak back into the picture, I rang the doorbell. After all, no one was shooting at me, so my fear was nothing more than an illusion. Corporal Webster would have concurred with my perspective and would have added, "If bullets are flyin' your way, you should be scared...if not, it's just bullshit in your head." Did Webster have time to be scared the night he died, or was he just too busy being a Marine squad leader at his best? Sadly, in the early morning rain out by Dông Bích, being at his best wasn't good enough.

The front door opened, and Corporal Webster's family was about to discover what kind of a Marine he had been. Wearing a crescent smile and a face full of wonderment, a girl, probably in third or fourth grade, stood, staring up at me. "Mister, you be one of them Jehovah's Witness folks? Maybe you lost or somethin'?"

Smiling, I resisted chuckling. In her world, her questions made sense. What was a white man doing ringing her grandmother's doorbell on Thanksgiving or any other day, for that matter. Like the street layout in Conroe, knowing your place wasn't complicated either: *they* don't come over here and *we* don't go over there. But I was from Tucson; I extended my right hand, shaking the girl's hand. "Nice to meet you, young lady." Upon hearing my greeting, she had determined that I most definitely wasn't from around these parts—I sounded different, but not scary different; she was still smiling, and question marks danced in her brown, third-grader eyes. I continued, "And, no, I'm not a Jehovah's Witness and I'm not lost. My name..."

Before I was able to finish my introduction, Webster's grandmother, a thin woman wearing her Sunday-go-meeting dress sans the accompanying hat, entered the living room, wiping her hands on her apron and smiling broadly enough to make a depressed person sing. A medley of aromas—perfectly seasoned turkey, grandma's special stuffing, pumpkin pie, east Texas style—escaped the crowded kitchen, roaming aimlessly through the living room, lingering and teasing the senses.

"Child, this gentleman is Mr. O'Brien. He's come all the way from Arizona to share Thanksgiving with us."

Moving toward her, I extended my right hand, but she would have nothing to do with my formal greeting. Her arms enveloped me, hugging me the way grandmothers do. I was Izaiah's friend, and she would have it no other way. She took one step back, and gazing directly into my eyes, reached up and touched my cheek and softly said, "Welcome."

In that moment, I felt the tender and generous love of a stranger, our sole connection being the death of Izaiah Webster: grandson for her, a friend for me. It was a perfect dance of healing, but one delayed too long. This woman who loved words was unaware of the power of the one simple word she had uttered: *welcome*. I felt like my coming home alive mattered to someone, something that I hadn't always believed or felt before. I hoped that I would be able to reciprocate by offering her and the Webster family some solace and closure. I had survived the ambush for a reason, and maybe this was part of that reason.

With the afternoon meal behind us, four generations of Webster's caravanned with me to visit Corporal Webster's gravesite at the Conroe Memorial Park Cemetery, which was on the outskirts of town, only about a mile away. Tucked away near the center of the cemetery and shaded by a tall, loblolly pine tree, Corporal Webster's final resting place awaited us. Staring nonchalantly at me, a gray, granite headstone stood at attention as I approached a part of Texas I wished never existed, but it did. Standing there with Webster's grandmother beside me, I peered at his tombstone:

Corporal Izaiah Webster
United States Marine Corps
Born 1-15-1949
Died 2-12-1968
The flower fadeth: but the word
of our God shall stand forever.
Isaiah 40:8

Instinctively, with a pride that our drill instructors had masterfully instilled in us during boot camp, I saluted crisply but in slow motion, honoring Webster, my friend and fallen brothe-in-arms. He had been planted in east Texas dirt, and I was doing the saluting under an overcast, late afternoon sky, but his grandmother, wearing her stoicism like a flak jacket, found a way to make sense of it all. Long before her grandson's tombstone wore the words of Isaiah 40:8, those words had been etched on her heart, and she was thankful that she had found solace. Her mother had been right: the road to the Promised Land would not always be smooth.

Webster's grandmother grasped my hand as she turned toward me. "Michael O'Brien, The Lord sent you to us. You are our good Samaritan, and we thank you. I will keep you in my prayers...you seem to be carrying a heavy burden. Remember, the Lord is your shepherd and you shall not want."

Her healing words lingered, seeping into the deep recesses of my wound. I had survived Dông Bích, but I was just beginning to discover how to travel beyond survival and taste the banquet called life.

The next morning, before leaving for the airport in Houston, I returned to the Webster home to give Corporal Webster's grandmother a bouquet of flowers to thank her for her hospitality. For a widow who had suffered the loss of her daughter to cancer and her grandson to war, she possessed a spirit that enabled her to continue smiling in spite of her personal losses. In character, upon opening the door, she greeted me with a smile, one that also radiated from her eyes. She invited me in for coffee. "I have a plane to catch, so I have to turn down your coffee, but I can stay for a few minutes."

I handed her the bouquet of flowers, but before I could explain why I had brought them, she was shuffling off to the kitchen to find a vase for them. Having thanked me several times, I finally shared the *why* behind the flowers.

"Ma'am, I hate war with a passion. During my two tours in Vietnam, I knew seventy-four men who were killed—all of this before I was twenty-one. I was experiencing what people in their eighties experience—everyone around you dying, but I was a teenager. That's just plain crazy. As you figured out yesterday, the War had a profound impact on me. Fortunately, there's some good news in all of this—I realized that we don't always let the people who matter to us know how much we appreciate them. I'm sure you've seen this at funerals, Ma'am. It's hard to understand why people say, "*Why didn't I?*" at a funeral rather than saying '*I love you*' when it matters, when they have the opportunity. Regrets and guilt don't do the deceased person any good. For this reason, I don't put flowers on a gravesite. Instead, I figure someone who is alive could use them a lot more, so, in short, Mrs. Webster, I appreciate you because of your compassion and class. Having met you, I understand why I liked and respected your grandson. He was an exemplary Marine who also had the respect of the men in his squad."

I paused for a moment before continuing. "Ma'am, on my way over here this morning, I stopped by Izaiah's grave and placed three joss sticks...incense sticks...by his headstone. The next time you visit your grandson, would you please light these three joss sticks. It'll be a way of honoring him. I'd appreciate that."

She smile and said, "Of course." She paused and sighed, and then she thanked me for my kind words, as she called them. Actually, I embellished a bit—I didn't want to explain about Sandburn being an asshole who hated her grandson. In fact, since lying was in full blossom, I bent the truth some more when I offered her the G-rated version of his last words—why did she have to ask—she didn't need to know that her Sunday school Izaiah, this up-and-coming wordsmith, had screamed *FUCK!* as his last word. "Something about Jesus...It was rainin' too hard, so I couldn't hear Izaiah real well. But I do know he didn't suffer at the end."

It was time for me to leave; and she needed to believe my story, so I obliged and didn't even feel any guilt as I walked toward the front door, passing by a wall with several framed photographs of Corporal Webster at various ages and individual pictures of Jesus, John Kennedy, Robert Kennedy, and Martin Luther King. Of all the important men in her life, her husband was the only one who had died of natural causes. In spite of this, she found time to focus on the good and share with me a not-so-fancy, but perfect, word: *Welcome*.

28

O'BRIEN
JANUARY 1983
TUCSON, ARIZONA

Jerusalem has its Wailing Wall, a sacred place for Jews to mourn the destruction of the Temple of Solomon. Back in '68 there was no Veterans' Memorial Wall, a monument to honor the fallen and a sacred place to grieve them. The idea for the Wall had yet to germinate in the mind of its architect Maya Lin, who was busy being a fourth-grader the year I returned from Vietnam. Lacking a wailing wall, I built my own—in many ways—to my detriment. My wall, like the one that had recently been dedicated in D.C., wore a list of names. Although not as extensive, the list of seventy-four names, all seared into my memory, was too long.

I was becoming aware that I had allowed my Wall to become as impenetrable as the polished, black granite of the Veterans' Memorial. I wanted to believe that time heals all wounds, but the veracity of this statement had a hollow ring. For twelve years, seventy-four names—an indelible litany of loss— lingered while I played the role of Odysseus searching for the land of catharsis.

The inquisitive fourth-grader from Athens, Ohio grew up and submitted a class project at Yale University, an idea that became better known to Vietnam War vets as the Wall. So, awaiting me in late November of 1982 were more than six dozen names, chiseled for the Ages. A chill hung in the D.C. air as I stared in silent reverence at the Grim Reaper's Southeast Asia shopping list. I wanted to scream, but that would have to wait. My anger and sadness rolled down my cheeks. Kneeling on one knee, I bowed my head and whispered a prayer: "Take care of these guys and help me to heal my pain...if You exist."

President Reagan and the rest of D.C. were operating on Eastern Standard Time, but I was on Nam Standard Time; unnoticed, the afternoon had morphed into dusk as I stood in front of the final name on my list: Angel "Doc" Reyes. "I miss you, Doc. You were one hell of a corpsman. Damn it. Why you?"

As I had done with the other seventy-three names, I stenciled his name on a piece of notebook paper, then lit and set three joss sticks down in front of his name. In a final act of respect, I stood at attention and presented Doc Reyes with a salute that would have made my drill instructor proud. A waft of incense smoke rose up, meandering aimlessly past his chiseled name. Did God really need one more Angel in Heaven? My misty eyes saw the answer staring back at me; and as I walked away from the ebony edifice, the sounds of Friday night traffic went on without me, and I hoped that this monument would bring a long overdue sense of closure, not just for me, but for all its visitors who had become collateral damage.

Six weeks had passed since my trip to Conroe and the Wall, and I hadn't shared the impact of my trip with anyone. Isolation had been the order of the day, everyday except Christmas. A mother's question about coming over for Christmas dinner has never truly been a question. Although I was present, I offered no details about my trip other than a generic, *"Fine."* I was as elusive about the details as a teenager is when asked about how school went. My mother knew me well, so she decided not to be Miss Marple. She just smiled and said, "Glad you had a good trip." But she knew there was a novel behind my terse *fine*.

I've never been a fan of New Year's resolutions; waiting for a holiday to make a positive commitment seemed a bit ridiculous, so I decided it was time for me to make one more attempt to reconnect with Kate. I needed to share the power of my Thanksgiving weekend trip with someone, and it was fitting that Kate should be that person. She had been collateral damage;

our relationship had been a casualty of my Nam experience, one that's never counted in the statistics. Believing that enough time had passed since our break up, I called her and she agreed to let me make her favorite dinner, baked salmon. Our candleless and wineless dinner was served with side dishes of mild tension and casual conversation.

After dinner, we moved to the living room where she found the end of my brown leather couch—No-Man's-Land between us. My mind began racing.

I've missed you so much, Kate. What are we doing apart? You're the woman I'd marry in a heartbeat. I'm sorry that I acted that way back on Valentine's Day. I'm so glad that you understand how much the war was messing with me...the anniversary of all those guys getting killed. I stopped drinking. I need to deal with my stuff, and booze just gets in the way. I'm so glad you understand and are willing to get back together. I've really missed making love with you, Kate. I'm so hungry to touch your soft skin and taste every delicious inch of your body. You are so special to me.

I crumpled up my wish list, tossing away a conversation that will happen about the same time Corporal Webster graduates from college. The intuition that served me well in the Nam was screaming in my ear: *She ain't interested, buddy!* Acquiescing, I shifted into edit mode, expecting nothing from her. *Us* was no longer a thread in the current tapestry of my life.

"So...tell me about your trip."

I wondered for a moment if she was just being polite, but then I didn't care if she were interested or not and replied, "I'll give you the brief version." A half an hour later, Kate, still listening and nodding, seemed to realize my need to share my experiences: meeting Corporal Webster's grandmother and my trip to the Memorial. The more I revealed, the clearer it became to her that my November trips were cathartic catalysts; however, only time would determine whether or not she wanted to be associated with my healing journey. Distance offers safety and predictability, and Kate was enamored with those two elements. Roses without thorns—that wasn't my style. After thirty-five years on planet Earth, I had discovered something a twenty-five-year old would have difficulty understanding: intimacy is messy, but it is real—*Velveteen Rabbit* real. She would discover that...someday, but this was the 4th of January, not *someday*.

Although it was just before nine, she looked at her watch several times, so I decided to show her the notebook with the stenciled names of the seventy-four men that I had known who had been killed during my two tours in Vietnam. At first I was hesitant, wondering if I'd break down emotionally, and vulnerable was something I didn't want to be, but when I showed her the last page—Angel J. Reyes—I swallowed hard and let out a deep sigh. The bluff had worked for seventy-three names. Scooting closer to me, Kate put her arms around me, patting my back—no lover's caressing hug this time. Pulling away, she said, "Michael, you know I'll always be there for you. I'm glad you went to the Wall in D.C. It's time to just get over it. If you really want to, you can."

Her half-smile and her civilian's wisdom had over extended their welcome, so I walked her to her car, telling her that I'd call her the next day.

As January dragged on, Kate's answering machine and I became well-acquainted; then, the three-messages-rule kicked in: 1983 was going to be a non-Kate year. And I wondered why the manners rule hadn't kicked in; it seemed to have gone the way of the eight track player. A simple *good-bye* would have sufficed, but obsolescence happens in the strangest places.

29

O'BRIEN
12 FEBRUARY 1983
TUCSON, ARIZONA

12 February 1983
Dear Mrs. Webster,
    Anniversaries are generally a time of celebration, but the 12th of February is one anniversary I have always dreaded. The memories of that day are harsh and tear at my soul—so much death, and for what? We all must meet our Maker, so we must accept death as part of life; however, when a young man dies in war, his dreams and opportunities die with him. To compound this tragedy, the lives of his family and friends are altered forever. With a single combat death, the hand of grief touches innumerable people. The Viêt Cong bullets that tore into your grandson Izaiah also tore into your heart and too many others in Conroe. The casualty count from the ambush where your grandson was killed was officially listed as 9 Killed In Action, 2 Wounded In Action, and 1 Missing In Action; however, these numbers only scratched the surface and paint a misleading picture.

After fifteen years, the families of the men who were killed that night are only left with memories, but never the opportunity to hug or laugh with these young men. Their gravestones are the only tangible things that remain. I am still struggling to come to terms with the events of the night Izaiah and his fellow Marines were killed. I don't think survivor's guilt is an issue for me any longer, but I sometimes feel so overwhelmed with grief that I want to scream—and I have on more than one occasion. Fortunately, just before I visited you on Thanksgiving, the Veterans' Memorial was dedicated in Washington, D.C. I say fortunately because this memorial has become an essential part of my on-going healing process.

After my visit with you at Thanksgiving, I realized that I needed to visit the Memorial, which I did last month; I just wish this monument had been built years earlier. There has been controversy concerning the design. The Memorial has become a political football which has been used by people who still want to debate the efficacy of the Vietnam War strategy. The Memorial should be about honoring the ultimate sacrifice made by more than 58,000 men and about healing the wounded hearts of all involved, whether as combatants or as grievers at a funeral. Those that voiced opposition to the Monument had an agenda and were more comfortable intellectualizing and politicizing rather than...

In mid-sentence, the Gestalt light was flashing—not out of character for an aha moment. My letter to Corporal Webster's grandmother was agenda driven also; quite simply, I was judging others. She didn't need to hear my views on war or the controversy concerning the design of the Memorial—intellectualizing and nothing more.

With this new awareness, I sat at my desk, stuck in pondering mode. I crumpled up my cathartic writing rant, successfully tossing it—on the first attempt—into a trash can at least ten feet away. *Swoosh.* While the clock kept busy being a good clock, the idea train had left the station without me. Then, with my paper looking like Nebraska after a January snow storm, I bought a ticket on the first plane leaving my head. Under the guise of being a letter to Mrs. Webster, my writing had been nothing more than head-tripping, an exercise in the intellectualization of my emotions. In the pain of remembrance, I had forgotten one of the major tenets of writing that I had pounded into the students in my English classes: be aware of your audience and write to it. Corporal Webster's grandmother deserved a focused and positive letter, one without a personal agenda. Having resolved that I would deal with my pain on my own time, the new words found a home on the paper that had stared blankly back at me for the past hour.

12 February 1983
Dear Mrs. Webster,

I hope all is well in your life. Life here in Tucson has been rather uneventful, which is fine with me. I left teaching last June, as I had mentioned when I visited you last Thanksgiving, and have yet to decide the direction my life will take. Teaching was my passion, but I'm not sure if that is my true calling. I am still searching. Enough about my life.

I need you to know how much I truly appreciated your hospitality. I admire the way you live your life, especially in spite of all the adversity you have experienced. You have a strength of character that is laudable; moreover, the way you put your faith into practice impresses me—actually, it touches me. You aren't a one-day-a-week Christian. I consider myself to be blessed to have met you. Izaiah was so fortunate to have you in his life, although it was cut short. I have a feeling that, had he had the opportunity, he might have become an English teacher. Had this been the case, I'm sure you would have been so proud of him. Most

Marines in Vietnam had nicknames, and your grandson was no exception; his was Dictionary— not exactly a typical nickname for a Marine in Vietnam. I liked him for several reasons: he was an excellent squad leader who won the respect of his men; both of us valued the importance of words; and finally, Izaiah was a decent person who possessed the wisdom to listen to his grandmother.

On my return flight to Tucson after my Thanksgiving visit with you, I had a most insightful conversation with a student who was returning to the University of Arizona. She was reading Man's Search For Meaning, and the title piqued my interest, which led to a thought-provoking discussion. I would like to share a quote from the book: "We can discover the meaning of life in three different ways: (1) by creating a work or doing a deed; (2) by experiencing something or encountering someone; and (3) by the attitude we take toward unavoidable suffering." I share this quote by Viktor Frankl with you because it made me think of you. The positive way you have responded to all aspects of life has helped me to grow and begin to regain the meaning that I have been searching for since Vietnam. By meeting you and by journeying to the Wall, I have begun to feel a healing spirit which has not been in my life for the past fifteen years. I greatly appreciate your compassion; you have taught me much. (Izaiah would have preferred 'plethora' over 'much'.) The saying about time healing all wounds is only partially accurate; I also needed you and my trip to the Memorial Wall to help me heal my heart. Thank you! Thank you!

I have enclosed a check for $1,000 in honor of your grandson's memory. Please use the money to assist a deserving student with college expenses or use it to purchase books for an elementary school library. I have also included a paper on which I *stenciled your grandson's name from the Wall. I also said a prayer for him. Corporal Izaiah Webster will always have a special place in my memory, as will you.*

With best wishes,
Michael O'Brien

For the first time in fifteen years, the 12th of February became a normal date on a calendar, still with significance, yet no longer the annual doorway into my personal hell. The Wall had taught me that remembering and healing were compatible.

The darkness that was the night of February 12, 1983 was nothing more than what happens when the sun decides to leave town, and that felt good. This anniversary went the way of the boogeyman; I had faced the monster, refusing to let it own me. My perspective was continuing to change for the better; a wise and gentle grandmother in Conroe, Texas had helped me to discover that which she had known all along—that *Amen* means *let it be.*

30

O'BRIEN
VALENTINE'S DAY 1983
MOUNT WRIGHTSON

The panoramic view that reached across the Mexican border forty miles to the south was breathtaking, and the air at 9,000 feet would bring clarity, so I continued my day-long trek to the summit of Mount Wrightson. The chill in Arizona's February air was refreshing, making the final thousand feet of my ascent tolerable.

Shortly after 1 p.m., the summit was mine. I plopped myself down by a boulder and took several well-deserved swigs of water. Above me, the early afternoon sun was inching its way west, preparing to tour California. A light breeze brushed across my sweaty face, and I felt refreshed and alive. Then, the memory train pulled into the station where calendars are obsolete, and Kate stepped off the train. As I sighed, back then became now, Mount Wrightson became my bedroom, and love was not a four-letter word.

Holding each other, knowing that the evening will morph into the morning, we snuggle as my hands roam her soft skin, the tips of my fingers softly, rhythmically caressing every sensuous pore. Kate's body, hungry for my touch and anxious for my kisses, moves closer as her breasts begin the heaving cadence of desire. Behind the shear fabric of her dress, now edging up her thighs, her nipples are less than subtle about her hunger for my touch, for my kisses, and...

"God, I miss her."

Like all ambushes, the Kate-ambush was quite unexpected; after all, time is supposed to heal all wounds. But then I realized that my reminiscence was not about a wound, but rather, it was a fond memory, a chapter in my life where I had allowed love in and had shared love. For many years, the Nam had killed that part of my soul, but Kate had brought it back to life. My new chapter would also be about love, a spiritual love. The sensuality of our embraces would become memories; I would be trading making love with Kate Gallagher for a life of prayer, a life of making peace with the Nam. It would be different, but it would be perfect; Kate would always have a special place in my heart, made better for having known her.

I smiled with my eyes, and as I stared out across southern Arizona's powder blue skyscape, I knew that my life was a gift and that I had been blessed.

31

CHARLIE'S SISTER
SUMMER 1990
DÔNG BÍCH (1)

Khiem knew that he was dying. His cancer would soon send him to join his ancestors, but before death took him, he asked to speak with me, so I went to his small hut on the outskirts of our hamlet. We were all part of the village family, but I was no longer especially close with him although that had not always been the case.

Something had changed during the Year of the Monkey, around the time of our Tết holiday offensive when he and my brother had both fought against the Americans and their puppets. Khiem, the man who had trained my brother Tuan in guerrilla tactics when he first joined the Q16 Company, had become distant after my brother's death. I never understood why he had changed, but Khiem was a good soldier who had fought with great courage, which was the responsibility of all cadres.

He had been wounded several times, the worst being the scaring on his face from napalm. We were only now realizing that the Americans' chemicals, which they had sprayed over our beloved land, were the cause of much sickness. Their Agent Orange, as they called it, would kill him when all their bombs, artillery and bullets could not. We drove the foreigners from our beloved Việt Nam, but their killing had lingered, taunting us even today, fifteen years after our great victory over the puppet regime and the Americans.

Although I didn't know why Khiem wished to see me, I decided to visit him because he had lost his three children and his wife to an American artillery barrage. He would soon be with them, but he needed someone now. As I thought about what happened to his family, my heart began seething with great anger.

Why did the Americans have to come to our land? They traveled across a great ocean to bring us suffering. They succeeded at this, but they were doomed from the start. They could never conquer us. They failed to understand that the spirit of the Vietnamese people has always been too great for all foreign invaders. Even before I was born, the Japanese and the French needed to be taught this same lesson about our willingness to resist to the death. The fact that I am without my parents and my brother Tuan is proof of this. We are like the bamboo. The Americans and the French had cut down three stalks, yet they were unaware of the pervasiveness and indestructibility of the bamboo's taproot system. They owned much wealth, but they also possessed great ignorance.

When I entered Khiem's hut, Phan, a young boy who was ten or eleven, told me that Khiem was sleeping. His gaunt face looked peaceful as he slept, so I told the boy I would return later in the afternoon.

Upon my return, Phan informed me that Khiem was still tired but wanted to talk with me. I sat on the earthen floor next to Khiem who was too weak to sit up on his bamboo mat. Struggling to speak, he forged on, recounting the events that had occurred the day the American Marines had killed my brother. After talking proudly about Tuan's ability as a sniper—his shot had killed the first American Marine as they had approached our village—Khiem began talking about the night ambush itself. "The Americans were so...surprised when we appeared so close without being heard. Our tunnels made it so simple. It was...a great victory."

He stopped for a moment to regain his strength before continuing, "We sent eight or nine of them home and we...." He paused, and behind his tired eyes there was only the drizzling rain and the blackness of that night so many years ago. A single tear rolled off his cheek as he sighed. As he struggled to continue, his lips were trembling. His speech was becoming more labored, but he refused to stop. Heaving, he sighed deeply, and there was a rasp in his voice. "Your brother...your brother...I'm the..." Exhausted, Khiem mumbled something, but the sounds coming from him had ceased to be words. He was sleeping once again, so I decided to return in the morning. Maybe then I would learn why he had asked to see me. The answer would wait.

During the night, Khiem visited his ancestors and my brother Tuan. I lit three joss sticks to honor a comrade who had fought the Americans for almost ten years. As the afternoon rain soaked into the red clay of our village, I was sad for Khiem, but my heart ached for Tuan. I wondered if I would ever stop hating the Americans for what they had done to my brother Tuan.

32

SANDBURN
SUMMER 1990
WASHINGTON, D.C.

Some years back, well, maybe seven or eight, I got a call from my past. It was that damn O'Brien, who, it seemed, hadn't forgotten that I had saved his life. In the heat of battle I hadn't gotten to choose whose life it would be, and he was one guy that wouldn't have been on my list. The Nam was strange that way, so it seemed that I was stuck with his gratitude, somethin' I didn't have much need for.

When he asked me how I was doin', I said, "Great, great, just great!" Sounding enthusiastic was a real important part of my success in real estate, so it was only natural for me to tell him this lie with such enthusiasm. That made it sound authentic, which always helped. I had learned a long time ago that people really weren't interested in the truth when they asked how you were doin'. *Great* sounded better than the truth, so O'Brien got himself a long distance line of bullshit.

There was no way I was going to tell him about Trent Jr. or about my fucking bitch of an ex-wife and how she left me for an asshole who helped her spend my child support money. I hated that bastard-ass boyfriend for what he did just about as much as I hated O'Brien back in '68, but I realized that Andrea's lover boy was a bigger asshole than O'Brien. In fact, there were two asshole worse than O'Brien—my old man and the shithead who was banging my ex, and both pricks lived in Richmond. At least O'Brien wasn't anywhere near Virginia, but before the phone conversation was over, I learned that that would change soon. The *soon* part I didn't like, but the good news was that his bein' in my part of the world wouldn't be permanent.

"You're goin' to the Memorial in D.C., and you want to know if I want to go there with you?" I should have told him what I was thinking—*"no fucking way"*—but I didn't.

"I'm real busy with work…doin' real good in real estate, the commercial side of it. I've got a couple of kids. They sure grow up real fast. Don't see them as much as I should."

"That's good you take such an interest in your kids. I don't have any of my own. Marriage hasn't been in the cards for me."

Getting him side-tracked was pretty easy, but the small-talk was gettin' old real damn fast. What the hell. It was his nickel, and I'd been in the Nam with him, so I figured I could put up with him a little longer. Then I realized that I'd screwed up when he said, "Boys or girls?" and I didn't reply. He then asked, "One of each?"

All I could see was Trent Jr.'s face starin' at me. Why couldn't O'Brien just mind his own fucking business? He hadn't changed much since that day at Dông Bích. He still thought it was his job to stick his goddamn nose where it didn't fuckin' belong. This time he hadn't even realized that he was ruinin' my day. Back in the Nam, he did it on purpose. He must've gone to college and majored in being a nosy son of a bitch, the subconscious type. Either way, he was a son of a bitch. Nothing had really changed.

I was too pissed off to say anything, so there was nothing but silence.

"Are you there?"

"Yeah, must've been a bad connection or somethin'." I paused a moment and then continued, "Two girls."

"How old?"

"O'Brien, hey, I'd love to chat, but my girls just walked in the door, and I gotta play dad. Could you hold on a second?" On the other end, O'Brien heard me say, "Help your sister. Don't be mean to her."

I wasn't sure if he bought my act, but I didn't give a shit. I just knew that talking to him was somewhere towards the bottom of my list of fun things to do. "O'Brien, you're gonna to have to do the Washington thing on your own. Life's pretty hectic here. Don't really have no time for tourist stuff. Thanks for calling. Better get to my two little princesses. Bye."

After I hung up the phone, I walked into the kitchen and opened a cupboard above the oven. I sat down at the kitchen table with a half empty bottle of Jim Beam that begged to be poured into a glass brimmin' with ice. Each time I filled the glass, the pile of ice cubes shrank until there weren't none. By that time, I had stopped caring that there were no ice cubes left to greet my friend Mr. Beam. The only thing that mattered was the smell of whiskey, which I loved, and this night was no damn exception.

Sundays had become too goddamn predictable, especially Sunday nights, which I hated, and tonight was made worse because of O'Brien's damn phone call. I hated O'Brien for sticking his nose where it didn't fuckin' belong, but at the top of my list, even higher up than my prick of an old man or my ex, bitch that she was, and her lover-boy asshole, was God. I hated Him the most for what He'd gone and done to me. A man shouldn't have to lose his son. Not fucking fair.

Eventually, I stopped hating God some time last year. I guess it just seemed to take too much damn energy. I even started goin' to church, but not every Sunday. That was for choir people and ministers, those kinda folks—definitely not me. My daughters, especially Missy, talked me into goin' to church. Alyssa, who was about thirteen then, tagged along because she thought the boys in the youth group were cute. That was the explanation that Missy gave me about her older sister.

I wasn't sure if she noticed that I enjoyed church because of the abundant supply of single ladies. The preacher's sermons were interesting enough to keep me awake most of the time, but there was somethin' about women all dressed up in their Sunday's best that I just couldn't resist. I figured that some of them dressed up to impress God while others were tryin' to make a favorable impression on an eligible bachelor like me. Plenty did. Sometimes it would take a chorus of *Amens* to bring me back from my day dreaming about my hand slidin' up the smooth thigh of one of God's finest creatures. I wanted to pay attention to the minister, but God had done such a damn good job creating these lovely ladies that I couldn't help but appreciate them. After a couple of months, *them* became just *her*.

She was such a fine specimen of womanhood—really hot— and I considered myself most fortunate that our paths had met. Actually, our paths had crossed earlier, but that was when all I was interested in was looking for a one-night-stand and a bottle of whiskey, absolutely nothin' more. Angela had been Missy's teacher several years back, but I had never talked to her at any of the parent conferences since my ex was always there playin' the part of custodial parent to a tee.

Once we started dating, Angela shocked me a bit by tellin' me that she had noticed me back then. I was the guy who always showed up but only looked at the students' work that she had displayed on the classroom walls. Angela, better known as Miss Johnson to her fourth-grade students, always had one of Missy's poems plastered on the back bulletin board, right in the center. Back then I figured she just grabbed something, anything, and it didn't matter much to her what ended up on the wall.

After we had been going out for a couple of months, I found that Angela actually had liked Missy's poems; she even thought they were pretty damn good. I liked that, but it also pissed me off findin' this shit out, since Missy never showed me none of her poems. Not that I've ever cared much for poetry and all that deep meaning crap, but I was losing out since she wasn't gonna stay a kid forever. After all, I was her dad, but that was back when I was doin' some serious-ass drinking, so she probably figured that I didn't give a shit about her poems and stuff.

But all of that changed, and so did her poetry. Being a typical fourth-grader back then, her poems always rhymed. But Missy gave that up for some Jap kinda poetry called *haiku*. She started showing me her poems about the time she found out that Angela and I were seeing each other. Even though they were short, I understood her *haikus* about as good as I understood why she didn't make a stink about Angela being in my life. I guess Angela had made a good impression as her teacher. Whatever the reason, I was glad that neither of my girls gave us any crap.

The first haiku poem that she read to me kind of caught me off guard, which is somethin' I've never been real fond of. The Nam taught that real good.

"Dad, Miss Johnson helped me with this one, but only the last line. All the other ones I did all by myself. It only has three whole lines, so you really have to listen."

I smiled, and she proceeded to read: "The baby is gone...The clouds are in the dark sky...Raining down my tears." I wanted to give her a hug, but I've never been real good at that kinda shit. All I could do was stare. One of those thousand-yard stares straight out of the Nam. Angela had been right about Missy's poetry, and as I sat there, I wished she had read me one of those damn rhyming poems about a tree or somethin', not a haiku that even I could understand.

All in all though, life had been fairly copasetic over the last year. Referring to my ex-wife as *that fucking bitch* had been replaced by a less toxic term, *the girls' mother*. Occasionally, I'd been tempted to use my original term of endearment for their mother, but Angela and a good Sunday sermon usually got me back on the straight-and-narrow fairly fast. I'd a lot of practice being a sinner, so being a good Christian was difficult sometimes. The day I finally went to the Vietnam Memorial was one of them times.

O'Brien had been right, but I still had a hard time admittin' that. Going to the Wall with a buddy from the Nam was the right way to face that black granite with all those damn names, especially for the first time. I didn't know what I was thinkin', but I figured it was the right time to finally do this. I hopped in my car and headed north to D.C. even though I knew that the Capitol would be swarmin' with tourists even with it bein' Thursday. Turned out that my brain wasn't workin' too damn good. Although I had been going to church for over a year and was tryin' to hate less, I fell back into my old ways once I parked and began wading through all those tourists who were wearin' dumb-ass expressions and carryin' cameras around their necks.

My dislike for tourists increased as I got closer to the Memorial, which I couldn't see at first. It was like the people who designed it were tryin' to hide it from view. I just followed the sign that pointed me away from the street until it snuck up on my right. It was black and shiny when the sun hit it just right. It was much too crowded for my tastes, so I stared at it from a distance, kind of hopin' that the summer crowd would do a disappearing act. They didn't.

As I walked towards it, I stopped and took a deep breath of D.C.'s hot, sticky air. When my heart started pounding up a storm, it felt like I was back in the Nam, back in Indian Country, one feeling I wasn't interested in relivin'. I just wanted to do an about-face and get the hell out of Dodge City, but I didn't. Instead, I just stood there, frozen. Finally, I reached up and wiped the sweat off my face. My legs began to move. All those names on that granite slab were drawin' me closer. As I followed the slope of the walkway, I shuffled sideways, staring at lists of names that were taller than me. The names kept comin'. The tourists were there, but for a while I only saw my reflection in the huge, black wall of stone. Then, as I continued walking through the crowd, I began to notice sentimental items like pictures, Zippo lighters, insignias, a pack of Camels, a candle, and, of course, all sorts of flowers sittin' at the base of this wall that seemed to be overpowering people. I didn't understand it.

What really amazed me was how many grown men were cryin'. Obviously, they were Nam vets, but they were cryin' and huggin' each other. What the hell had happened to those bad-asses who never let anyone see them shed a tear back in the Nam? Maybe my minister had an answer to this one, but I sure as hell didn't have a clue.

I was beginning to feel uncomfortable starin' at this strange sight. It baffled me, so I headed toward an information booth. There I discovered that they could tell me the location of a casualty's name on the Wall. I've never been one for a stroll down memory lane, especially the Nam version of it. My ex-wife had found this out the hard way when she made the mistake of askin' me why I wouldn't talk to her about Vietnam. Just because she was Mrs. Sandburn, she hadn't earned the right to know that kind of shit. Nosy ladies and the Nam just didn't mix. When she wouldn't leave it alone, I flipped out on her. Broke lots of shit, lamps and stuff. Screamed at her, used all sorts of language that a drill instructor would envy. I think that was the first time I referred to her as a fucking bitch. That was also the first time I let Jim Beam into our marriage. The rest was history.

I guess I hadn't learned nothing from my ex-wife's mistake about bein' too curious. I asked the man in the booth to check some names for me. It took him about five minutes to look up the panel location of the five names on my list. As he handed it back to me, he said, "Welcome home." Although his white hair made him appear too old to be a Nam vet, I knew he had served over there. His *"Welcome home"* gave him away. I broke a half smile and said, "Yeah, Thanks."

Walking away, I peered down at the list which really should have been twice as long, but I had never learned the names of the cherries in our squad who got themselves blown away out by Dông Bích, so I was out of luck as far as finding the Fuckin' New Guys on the Wall. I never really got to know 'em, so it really didn't fuckin' matter.

Baptisto Santos was the first name on the list, but his name was lined out, so I headed back to the information booth to find out why the hell Santos's name had been crossed out. I was informed that he was not in their registry of casualties. All I knew was that he had been listed as an MIA since they never found his body the day after the ambush. We figured the NVA or the Cong had captured him that night, but survivin' being captured would have been pretty damn difficult. Maybe Santos had been tough enough. The shit he learned on the Papago reservation back in Arizona probably came in handy.

Although life with the gooks must have been pretty damn horrible for Santos, at least he didn't end up with a bullet hole in the head the way the rest of the squad did. I didn't like Corporal Webster much, but even he didn't deserve that kinda shit. What they did to Nellis was the worst, 'cause he was only nine days short. Nine days and a wake up, but they cancelled that.

My head felt like it was going to fuckin' explode. All I could feel was hate. Nothin' else. My minister wouldn't much go for that, but I really didn't give a damn. I looked down at my list, and hate seemed to fit the bill. *Fucking pricks* were the only words, the best words, to describe Victor Charlie. Those damn VC assholes, but I hated Jane Fucking Fonda, now more than ever before, for betrayin' us.

Before I could hate anyone else, I bumped into a middle-aged woman who was tryin' to take a picture of the panel of names in front of her. Not in the mood to apologize for ruinin' her picture, I just muttered, "Fuck." I didn't notice the expression on her face, but I wasn't interested. At that moment, she wasn't a potential real estate client, and even if she had been, I was too damn pissed to give a shit what she thought of my behavior.

About twenty feet away, I stopped in front of the panel that held the names of three of the men on my list. Webster's name was on the next panel over. Looking up to the top row of names, I scanned each line carefully until I came upon A. B. Nellis's name. It had taken me all these years to discover that A. B. was really Alexander. The longer I stared at his name, the more pissed I got for what the gooks did to him, so I browsed through the other names chiseled into the smooth, black granite wall in front of me. When I spotted the name of Angel Reyes, I kinda lost it. Actually cried harder than a man should ever have to cry, that is if he's gonna cry at all. It ambushed me, and I couldn't stop it. Damn, he was a fuckin' Mexican. I was crying for a damn Mexican, somethin' I thought I'd never do. I didn't understand what was happenin' to me, and that scared me shitless. All I could do was gawk at his name and mumble, "Doc, you was a corpsman. Why the fuck did they have to kill your ass?"

I wanted an answer that made some sense, an answer that would stop my tears, but I knew that Reyes couldn't do diddly squat for me. Finding the names of the rest of the squad would have to wait. Maybe another time, but not today. I crumpled up my list, threw it on the grass behind me, and walked quickly away to my car. All I wanted at that moment was to put some serious distance between me and that ugly, black wall.

I had never liked O'Brien much because he had a knack for stickin' his nose where it didn't belong. As I drove down I-95, I realized that by going to the Wall, I had been just like O'Brien. Once back in Richmond, Jim Beam and I staggered down memory lane, somethin' I hadn't done since I had met Angela the previous year. In my head I knew that boozin' it up wouldn't make Reyes and the others any less dead, but knowin' this didn't make me feel any less shitty. By getting drunk, I had screwed up big-time. I was a failure—just like my old man said—but Angela threw me a curve ball when she just held me as I babbled, "I know I'm a fuck-up for being stupid and goin' to the Wall." She didn't ask me anything. She only replied, "You're not a failure. You're just hurting…nothing more."

I was too damn drunk to understand what she meant by her comment, but her hug felt real good.

33

O'BRIEN
AUGUST 1990
ST. DAVID, ARIZONA

My mother's beautifully flowing handwriting was always recognizable. Whenever the art of perfectly curving and slanting the letters of the alphabet had been mastered, the odds were excellent that the honing of these skills had occurred during the indelibly-stamped early years of a Catholic education. The pride that she felt for her Irish Catholic roots extended well beyond her Catholic education, her Church, and her Emerald Isle; I was her greatest source of pride—that's the way she put it when I was ordained as a priest, a Benedictine monk.

She was good about letting me know how proud she was of my choices—becoming an English teacher and serving in the Marine Corps—but she was at least three galaxies away from being elated when she discovered back in the summer of '67 that I had volunteered to return to Vietnam for a second tour. So, her rosary mantras went into overdrive, which, of course, gave me an unfair advantage over the NVA and Việt Cong who had toiled tenaciously to send me home early in a body bag.

Maybe God had been seduced by the sound of my mother's never-ending litany of Hail Marys wafting through the clouds, or maybe the NVA and their friends were just lousy shots. Fate, of course, could be thrown into the mix, but the reason for my survival was irrelevant to me; all that mattered was that I had been blessed with the gift of life, and my mother fortunately never had to read—with trembling hands—the feared letter about "*A proud nation...*" with its unread, officially-typed paragraphs splotched with a mother's unwanted tears. There's something less sterile and matter-of-fact about graceful handwriting—a concept the Department of Defense neglected to realize while they were being consumed with the math of victory. After all, typing over 58,000 letters was much more efficient—not to mention, more cost-effective.

She always used over-sized manila envelopes to forward any of my mail that had gone to her address, so I knew not to expect one of those motherly update letters; instead, I pulled out an envelope with a return address that read: Thomas MacAndrews Jr., 263 E Cory Rd, Morristown, NJ 07960. The road to Dông Bích had a return address. With trepidation owning that uncertain moment, I opened the envelope and began reading:

August 13, 1990
Dear Father O'Brien,

My name is Tom MacAndrews, Jr., and you knew my father so I hope you don't mind that I'm writing you. I spoke with your mother on the phone, and she was kind enough to offer to forward my letter to you. My mom is so grateful that you came to Morristown to meet her after you got out of the Marines. She really appreciated you coming all that way to tell her and my grandparents about my dad even though you didn't know him really well. My mom remarried when I was seven. She said a boy needs a father, and my stepdad turned out to be okay although we didn't get along at first. But no one can ever take the place of my real dad. I never got the chance to get to know him or to do all those father and son things that most of my friends just take for granted. What's really sad for my mom is that she was notified of my dad's death on Valentine's Day. Bad enough that she was a pregnant widow at 18. Fortunately, my grandparents were very helpful,

plus people like you helped her through her trying time. So, I just thought I should let you know how much my mom and I appreciate that you were there for her during her darkest hours. Also, I want you to know that I'm going to make my father proud. I not only graduated from college in May, but I've just joined the Marine Corps. I'll be leaving for Officer Candidate School next week. I'm hoping he's smiling down on me from Heaven. Like the Marine Corps Hymn says, "The streets of Heaven are guarded by United States Marines." Thank you for your kindness toward our family.
Gratefully,
Tom MacAndrews, Jr.

P.S. Please say a special prayer to keep me safe. I'm willing to put my life on the line for my country and die for it if necessary, but I just don't want my mom to have to experience what she went through when my dad was killed.

Moved by the young MacAndrew's letter, I wrote an immediate response.

22 August 1990
Dear Tom,
    I appreciate your kind words. Although I did not have the opportunity to really get to know your father because of his untimely death, I'm sure he would be proud of you; moreover, it is easy to understand why he married your mother. I pay tribute to her. You are proof of her great capacity as a parent, especially under her extremely difficult circumstances.
    I'm certain that your father would be proud of you for your academic achievement and for your decision to become an officer in the United States Marine Corps to serve our country. You said that you would willingly give your life for our country,

but I hope and will pray that your family never experiences that sacrifice. I have learned over the years that it is just as honorable to live a meaningful life for our country. I'm sure you have much to offer to make America a better place. I would like to share one final lesson that I have learned due to my experience in war. Surviving combat, while others died, is a two-edged sword which I carried with me when I returned from Vietnam. Sitting around feeling bad about surviving did not bring the dead back; in short, it didn't serve a positive purpose for anyone. I decided to focus on the present and that allowed me to have a different perspective—surviving was a gift, one I didn't understand, but an opportunity for me to live my life fully and with meaning. For me, life—and what I have chosen to do with it—has become a perpetual, living eulogy to my fellow brothers-in-arms who died in Vietnam; how I live my life has become my way of honoring the memories of those men, your father being one of them.

May God watch over you and your mother; I'm sure your proud father is smiling down on you from Heaven. You will always be in my thoughts and prayers.
SEMPER FI,
Father Michael O'Brien, OSB

The drums of war were calling to another generation. If the naval blockade against Iraq failed, we would be at war once again. Hopefully, MacAndrews Jr. and combat would be strangers, and Fate would ignore him and see him as though he were a clumsy, skinny kid that no one wants to pick for dodge ball. I could only write the letter and pray, so I left the rest up to God, hoping that He would remember that He already had one Thomas MacAndrews, USMC. There were enough United States Marines guarding the streets of Heaven.

34

CHARLIE'S SISTER
12 FEBRUARY 1994
DÔNG BÍCH (1)

In the distance, the rich ribbons of color painted across the western sky were signaling the end of another day. The rice fields around our village would soon be empty, and my two sons and my husband would share our evening meal. My students would tell their parents about the lessons that I had taught them.

As we were finishing our meal of *cà ri gà*, my husband's favorite chicken curry dish, Bao, our eldest son told me that he liked the meal. Then, he peered toward a table where several joss sticks lay burning in a dish in front of a small and tattered picture of Tuan. Wafts of incense smoke lingered above this altar that had served as a place for remembrance, but that was for graying grandmothers, but I was not one, and I possessed too many memories painted with sadness. I only hungered for an older brother to share a meal where the aroma of my chicken curry hung in the air, but instead, there was the altar with incense smoke hovering above Tuan's photograph: remembrance and nothing more.

Bao's lips wore silence, yet his eyes spoke loudly, shouting for answers to questions that would come someday, but I had always been willing to wait. Children, even if they are grown, never wait for the perfect time to ask their difficult questions. He had been a curious yet respectful son for twenty years, so he had never asked any details about his uncle Tuan's death. I looked to my husband who nodded, and I sighed deeply as I prepared to go down a difficult path, one I had avoided for years.

As we are finishing our meal, our eldest son asks, "Would you please tell me about my uncle? I know he died in the war against the Americans, but I want to know what type of man he was. Was he a good brother to you? I know my questions are difficult for you, mother. Please forgive me." His dark eyes are hungry to know about Tuan, so I reply, "My son, you deserve to know about your uncle"

I tell him about how fortunate I was to have him as a brother, but also my son must know of his courage as a soldier who died to unify our beloved Viêt Nam. I turn to the small altar a few feet away, and my eyes well up with tears as I realize that my son's face is that of Tuan, with the same high cheek bones, dark and penetrating yet gentle eyes, and hair as black as the night that surrounds our simple home, and I love my son, but he is reminding me of my brother, and tears are rolling down my cheeks as I only see Khiem, my brother's friend, telling me that my brother has been killed, and Khiem's sadness is so great that he is unable look at me.

The ambush of the American Marines has sent eight of them back to their mothers, but the Marines have stolen Tuan's life. I ache for a special kind of magic that only children know, but I know it does not exist for me. I only have memories of a brother who was a hero of the Revolution, but my tears scream that I want a brother, not a hero, but the Americans had to meddle in our lives and come to our land, so my tears will speak to my son more eloquently than my words, but as I sit, looking into my son's wondering eyes, sadness drenches me, and I fight to hold in my anger so it won't explode like a booby-trap, with the metal shards of my grief cutting into my sons who do not really know their mother, only her agony, her longing for a family stolen.

My son Bao left the table with his head full of unanswered questions. I wondered if I would ever be able to tell him about his uncle Tuan, who would not be proud of me for lacking the courage to be a good mother. I had lost my mother, my father, and Tuan; and now I was losing my sons. Will they forgive me?

35

SANDBURN
DECEMBER 1994
RICHMOND, VIRGINIA

Angela must have really loved me. She let me talk her into leaving her world as an elementary school teacher, not because she was sick of the little darlings, but because she wanted to start a family. Finally, at the end of '93 my daughters got to play big sister when Angela gave birth to eight pounds, three ounces worth of James Trent Sandburn. He was not only the cutest baby in the whole city of Richmond, he was turning out to be pretty damn smart also. I have to admit that he got both his looks and his smarts from his mother. They both have the bluest, big ol' eyes.

A few years down the road, the ladies won't be able to resist James, or J. T., as his sisters liked to call him. Right now though, he was the main topic of our annual Christmas letter that Angela was composin'. I could write up a real estate offer, but I was smart enough to know that a school teacher was the right person for this job. Definitely, not man's work. As far back as I can remember, I've hated writing letters, even when I was in the Marines and letters were so damn important. If I had never went and got married, nobody outside of Richmond would've had any idea what I was up to.

I must've really loved Angela. I even let her talk me into sendin' O'Brien a Christmas card. He had gone and become a

Catholic priest. A damn priest. That seemed a bit odd to me, but I had never quite understood what made that guy tick, so I just signed the card that Angela handed to me.

When we got a card from him, it sat up on the mantle with all the others. We got our first card from him back in '91, the year we got married. I still go to church, but I've never liked Christmas cards with a religious message, and, of course, what else could I expect from a Catholic priest with a name like O'Brien. He didn't know how to stop thanking me for savin' his damn life back in the Nam. It wasn't '68 no more, so I couldn't understand why he had to keep harpin' on that. I just started ignorin' it. When Angela would ask if he had written anything in his card, I always bullshitted her and said, "He only signed it."

I think she knew I was feedin' her a crock, but she never bugged me about it. I liked that about her. I also liked that I only had to run off a stack of these annual Christmas letters at the office. Once Angela had signed all our names to each card, one of my girls, usually Missy, would volunteer to stuff each envelope with a letter and a card. Because she had recently gotten her driver's license, she also volunteered to drop off the stack of about two hundred cards at the post office. Away the cards went, even one to my priest 'buddy' in Arizona.

December 1994
Dear Friends and Family,

This is that special time of year, a time of celebration of the birth of our Savior. Trent and I, along with Alyssa and Missy, eagerly look forward to the celebration of our first real Christmas with our precious James who just celebrated his first birthday on the 3rd of December. Now that he is old enough to enjoy Christmas, we are all excited. Trent has told me that Santa Claus will bring many gifts to James because he wasn't naughty but was nice. Actually, nice is a word that doesn't fully describe how we all feel about our new addition. He is truly a gift from God, and we thank Him daily for James who has ventured out into the world of walking. We are so glad that we had a video camera to record these moments. Someday we will look back with joy on these precious times. We all know how quickly children grow up.

Alyssa and Missy are proof of this. Trent often says that just yesterday his daughters were little girls, but now they are both in high school. Alyssa is about ready to graduate in June; college is in her plans, but she's not sure yet where she'll be attending. Missy, who is a junior, plays on the girls' varsity volleyball team. Her coach thinks that she may have a future in volleyball.

Trent, of course, is as busy as ever with his commercial real estate business and with numerous civic organizations. I know that he can't wait to take James deer hunting with him. I just hope he doesn't think our James is ready now that he's learned how to walk. As you can tell, in spite of the rigors of being a mommy, I haven't lost my sense of humor. Our son keeps me busy, busier than those fourth graders ever did. This thirty-something is glad she didn't wait much longer to have a child.

All in all, this year has been a joyful one, with an occasional bump in the road. The Sandburn family is looking forward to the future. May you and yours have a joyous Christmas and a wonderful and prosperous New Year.
Best wishes,
Trent, Angela, Alyssa, Missy, and James

36

SANDBURN
MAY 2000
RICHMOND, VIRGINIA

Alyssa was living with a guy who had one of those dot-com jobs that everyone wished they had. I didn't have much use for him, but at least he had a job that paid real good. On the bright side, unlike me, both Alyssa and Missy finished college. Missy amazed everyone by graduating a semester early, and she did it with honors. Actually, I wasn't that shocked since being a cut above the crowd was standard operating procedure for her. James, who will turn seven in December, just finished first grade. Although I didn't understand why Alyssa picked assholes that acted like jerks to her, I figured that I was the luckiest dad alive since I had the three best kids in the world.

Add Angela to the mix, and I considered myself damn fortunate. Angela was the best mother a kid could hope for, so I had a hard time trying to understand why she insisted on goin' back to her job as an elementary school teacher. I was makin' over a hundred grand a year, which meant life was treatin' us real good, so we really didn't need her teacher salary.

This was one road I had no intention of or interest in traveling down again. Back when my daughters were little, I had to hassle with their mother about the same bullshit. Angela's way of dealing with this subject was a lot different than my ex who stopped arguing with me when I put my foot down. The current

Mrs. Trent Sandburn, well, she looked me square in the eyes and reminded me that she was a forty-one-year-old woman with a master's degree. I didn't have no problem with that just so long as everything ran smooth. Plus it was kinda nice have a fine lookin' lady in the house.

I figured she was just gonna give me a glare or two, but she definitely wasn't finished with me. As I stood there stunned, I was informed that she had done just fine for herself as a single lady or *single person* as she put it. Because she had always made it real simple for me to be in love with her, I ignored her first outburst. Probably that time of the month. I was wrong. She brought up the topic every damn chance she had. One time was too many times as far as I was concerned, but Angela got all pigheaded and wasn't interested in givin' up her crazy ass-idea. Well, Mr. Stubborn had met Mrs. Damn Stubborn.

After about a month of her being all assertive, as she put it, we had ourselves a knock-down-drag-out fight about her foolish notion. The yelling match lasted a full ten rounds, and then we got to eat dinner together, which was a shitload of fun. Since she started arguing with me just before she finished cooking dinner, it was lukewarm at best when we finally sat down to eat. She was far from lukewarm. In fact, she was too pissed off at me to even fake it with any pleasant conversation. I thought that was real inconsiderate of her since I had put in a long day at work. I really hated eating a cold steak. She was just like that steak— cold as hell in the bedroom. Went and hunkered down on the edge of her side of the bed.

A man's got his needs, but she didn't seem to give a rat's ass anymore. A married man deserves to have sex available on a regular basis, but she seemed to have forgotten that. She was making it real difficult on me, so I began stayin' at the office later, usually about eight or nine. This didn't help my sex life one damn bit, but I was so pissed at her for bein' stubborn that I really didn't give a shit no more. The only bad part about stayin' out late was that I didn't see my son James much, especially when I went out to a bar for a few drinks. I didn't try to pick up no ladies, but my wife was still pissed off since I had been drinking. I never got drunk, just had a couple of drinks to take the edge off. She didn't see it that way though. Things between us were going downhill fast, and I was startin' to not give a damn what happened. To be honest, I really missed her cookin'. Angela was good lookin', smart, and a great cook, but I think that it was the smart part that caused all our problems.

Andrea and Angela were different in a couple of ways. When Andrea left me for another man, she didn't have the balls to face me and tell me to my pissed-off face. She left a note on the fuckin' kitchen counter. What a fuckin' bitch. A goddamn note. Said she was sorry that things hadn't worked out, etcetera. All the usual bullshit that a chicken-shit bitch would say. Angela, on the other hand, didn't leave a note. She actually told me face to face on the day she left.

She didn't even slam the door or use any foul language. I did the door slammin'. Slammed it so hard the glasses in the china cabinet shook. I cussed her out and used enough bad language for the both of us, but I waited till James was in the car since the one thing we agreed about was that all our fightin' wasn't good for James. It hurt real damn bad that she was leavin' with my son, but I figured she just needed some time away at her mom's up in northern Maryland.

Even though I was really pissed, I knew she wasn't feedin' me no line of bullshit when she said she wanted us to get together in about a week so we could talk. She had never lied before. Maybe that was why I was willin' to try to get all our problems squared away. I didn't want to lose either Angela or James. I'd already lost one son and that really sucked big time, and I could still remember those shitty Sunday nights after I had to return my girls to their damn mother. That really kicked me in the balls, so I was even willin' to quit drinking again. I had done that before. They were worth it. I just hoped that her mom could knock some damn sense into Angela's pretty little head.

Angela's mom never got the chance, and James never made it to second grade in the fall. Just outside Frederick, Maryland, some motherfuckin' asshole decided to run a damn red light and killed 'em both. God let Angela suffer for a day, just long enough for me to waste my time begging Him to let her live. I even promised God that I'd let her work, and I'd quit cussin' so much and quit drinking for good. This damn time, I actually meant it, but God was too damn busy to listen, or maybe He just didn't give a shit, or maybe He was fuckin' with me for my shit from the Nam.

Our damn pastor came to our house to remind me that there was no room for hate in a Christian's life. He brought his Christian message of forgiveness and told me that Angela was in Heaven with our son James. His words of comfort for what he called, *"my time of sorrow,"* just didn't cut it. Sorrow was a word that didn't quite measure up to how shitty I felt. Fuckin' pissed was how I felt. The pastor hadn't lost his world, so how the fuck could the son of a bitch know about my feelings? I had absolutely no comfort, only hate, memories, a stack of *what-ifs*, and permanent visitation rights at the cemetery. So, whenever I got drunk, I wanted to kill the fuckin' bastard who destroyed my life. When I was sober, I didn't want him dead because I realized that his bein' a paraplegic in prison would fuck up his day even more.

37

SANDBURN
31 DECEMBER 2000
RICHMOND, VIRGINIA

No Christmas cards this year. Not ever. I'll never send another one of those fucking things out as long as I live. Each time that damn mailman filled my mail box with a stack of Christmas cards, I just tossed them into the trash with all the other damn junk mail. There was one exception, the card from O'Brien which I set aside, unopened, in my desk drawer. One damn Christmas card, and I didn't even care what he had to say. I hadn't been in the mood for any religious messages ever since that bastard in Maryland killed Angela and James.

The last time I had been to church was for the funeral. I didn't want their damn sympathy or their fuckin' prayers. I didn't feel no better when the minister told us that Angela and James were in a better place. I wanted to jump up and scream, "If it's such a fuckin' wonderful place, why are you still hangin' around here, Pastor?" I wanted my wife and son back, but no one, not that fucking sanctimonious minister, not God sittin' on His almighty ass on some damn cloud, no one could come through for me. All their damn flowers and cards didn't change a fuckin' thing.

The only thing that helped, at least for a while, was a good stiff drink of whiskey. I knew Angela wouldn't approve of this. Like the preacher said, my wife and son were in Heaven, and there's no need for booze up there. Me, on the other hand, I was stuck here, and Richmond definitely wasn't a better place. Even the minister would have to agree on that, but he was such a tight ass that he'd be afraid to drink some serious whiskey. Didn't have no need for his First Church of the Nazarene. I'd found me a new church, the First Fuckin' Church of Jim Beam, with worship services every damn night.

If it was legal for people in Heaven to be pissed off, I figured that Angela was real damn mad at me for all my drinkin'. I had turned into a fuck-up, but she would have forgiven me and told me that I wasn't a *fuck-up*...I was just *fucking up*. She wasn't real big on the *F*-word, so I guess she'd have said *failing* instead, just like that time when I came back from the Wall and got wasted. I never really understood exactly what she meant by her little play on words, but I did know that she was real big on forgivin' me whenever I was a jerk. I was making it real damn difficult for her to forgive me for all my shit, but at least I stayed sober durin' the day. I didn't want to screw up my business since I was tryin' to sell it. I wanted the hell out. No more fucking real estate for me. No more Richmond. I didn't know where I wanted to be or what I wanted to do, but things had to change. That was for damn certain.

Up in the Big Apple, all them people went crazy as shit at midnight. Down here in Richmond, all sorts of folks acted just as stupid, hollerin' and makin' lots of commotion. They were celebratin' up a storm as if something special had just happened. Me, hell, I had nothing to get excited about except that the worst fuckin' year of my life was officially over, at least on the calendar. I was stuck in 2000, and no damn official celebration was going to make that year disappear, so I drove out to the cemetery to visit Angela and James.

Being drunk on my ass didn't help my drivin', but it made me feel better, until I got to their graves. There wasn't much moonlight out, just enough for me to read their tombstones, but I didn't need no help from no moon. I slurred the words...*Angela Marie Sandburn, Beloved wife and mother who is with her son in Heaven, Born 5 March 1960, Died 27 May 2000. James Trent Sandburn, Beloved son who is with his mother in Heaven, Born 3 December 1993, Died 26 May 2000.*

Standing there, I peered down and saw one more grave, baby Trent's. I looked up at what was just a sliver of a moon. It didn't seem to give a shit as I screamed, "You'll have to do for now, moon. I'm pissed...real pissed. Can't seem to see God sittin' on a big old cloud tonight, but you tell Him that He screwed up big-time. He wasn't supposed to take the people I love. He's fucked up my life royal. What did I ever do to deserve all this shit? Tell me. Fuck it!"

The moon just sat there starin' back at me. Three tombstones stared up at me. I didn't even feel bad when I threw my empty bottle of Jim Beam against someone else's tombstone. My heart was just as empty as the whiskey bottle and just as shattered. That's what my daughter, the poet, would have said. I didn't need no damn poetry to describe the goddamn emptiness that was eatin' me alive. Only four damn words. *Happy Fucking New Year!*

38

TUAN
THE PRESENT
HEAVEN

My sister, drowning in her own tears, is a blind woman because she cannot see the world through her tears. Life is difficult; she is Vietnamese, so she knows this all too well, but she has yet to realize her many blessings. She curses the darkness of the night sky, but forgets that the blackness is what makes her see the shining stars and their beauty. The little girl's smile has run away from her face, which is now nothing more than a barren field of sadness, a parched landscape, one vacant of all joy.

My dear sister, you have been living your life as though the yin exists without the yang. In your blindness, you have been fooling yourself and not realizing the many blessings that have touched your life. You were attacked and almost violated by an American Marine, yet another Marine saved you from being raped. Sadly, you have been spending your years hating one Marine and forgetting to be thankful that the other one protected you just as I would have. I hope that one day you will realize this, and you will find peace.

39

O'BRIEN
25 MAY 2001
SOUTHEAST OF TUCSON, ARIZONA

Outside the window of my office, the Sonoran Desert beamed a smile back at me. Gyrating at the whim of the wind, the branches of several Palo Verde and mesquite trees bounced and swayed obediently in the six o'clock air. It was rabbit-scurrying time, the p.m. version. On the inside, separated by two-foot-thick, mud-adobe walls, it was Mozart time, which always followed a CD's worth of Gregorian Chant, or as a Southern Baptist might call it, the Vatican's attempt at gospel music in a foreign language. I was fairly certain that God was proficient in Latin and capable of enjoying this foreign music.

I, too, possessed some expertise in the dead language, which rarely came in handy since the Church had given it up as the official liturgical language when I had been in high school. In some ways, being a Catholic priest had become easier; not needing to learn Latin was one of these, but the journey to salvation for a priest at the beginning of the new millennium was, in some ways, more difficult than my struggle to come to terms with my war experience.

Turning on the computer, I logged on so I could read my email. Having taken care of a pair of necessary replies, I decided to browse the Internet. I called this my free time, but that was a misnomer. When I decided to become a priest in the early '80s I had come to realize that all time was God's time. The young Catholic version of myself would have felt a surge of guilt for such an indulgence, but I had come to believe that God was not a neurotic nickel-and-dimer but rather a generous God who would survive if I surfed the Internet, so I typed in the search box, "*Casualties War.*"

As a soon-to-be-setting sun painted a mosaic of light and shadow on the mountains to the north, I scrolled through forty sites on the computer but returned to one that had captured my attention: *War Casualties by Category*. Each table of statistics told me something I had always known; Marines, especially those under twenty years of age, had paid a heavy toll during the Vietnam War. As I moved on to each new category, I repeated the ritual of staring and nodding, absorbing words and numbers that quickly became tracer rounds that hit their mark. Not much had changed over the years; I had walked into another ambush.

Outside, the wind still toyed with the mesquite and the Palo Verde, and the adios sun splashed the western sky with its goodnight colors as tears rolled down my cheeks. God's grandeur went on without me. The only thing that existed was the drizzling rain and a peekaboo moon in a February night sky in a place called the Nam, on the outskirts of a hamlet called Đông Bích (1). The desert wind knew none of this, yet I did.

Shaking my head back and forth, almost in an act of denial, I pleaded with God to stop my tears but with no success. I gawked at the computer monitor and its list of numbers that seemed to have triggered a response from that night in 1968. A. B. Nellis didn't fit into the statistical categories very neatly. He was a twenty-three-year-old corporal with less than two weeks left in the Nam. The only category he fell into was the *unlucky* one.

Nellis was bush savvy, but that didn't seem to matter. His actions seemed meaningless; the only thing that seemed to matter was the burst from the RPD light-machine gun that tore into his too-busy-to-be-scared face, hurling chunks of it haphazardly through the rain-soaked night. What had been a lucky headshot for the Việt Cong had been an unlucky headshot for Nellis. When they were finished with us, they no longer needed automatic weapons fire; they walked among us and systematically fired a single bullet into to the head of each member of our squad, just in case. Without a head for a target, they fired their *just-in-case* round into the crotch of Nellis. His father, a retired Marine who lived in San Diego, had seen horrific casualties during the epic fighting and the breakout at the Frozen Chosin Reservoir during the Korean War, but the part of him that was a father, the part that remembered holding his baby boy in his arms back in '45, wished he had left the coffin closed. No one had ever seen him cry until that day when the Marine Corps traded a flag folded neatly into an orderly triangle for his son.

When I visited his family during the summer that I returned from the Nam, his mother told me that her husband had returned to his former stoic ways. Their boy was gone and tears were useless, but I could tell in the sadness that lurked in her eyes that she would eventually find time for her own tears. Her husband, on the other hand, could only manage to scold his wife for asking if I wanted a glass for the can of beer that he had offered me. "Honey, the Sergeant is a Marine, and a Marine don't need no glass for his beer."

Neither his wife nor I disagreed with him. With beads of sweat rolling slowly down the can as it sat untouched on the coffee table in their living room, the tick-tock of a grandfather clock marked its steady cadence in the uncomfortable silence which I struggled to break, but my words seemed so awkward and contrived. I looked at his mother and said, "He was a good man." Then, peering at his father, who only nodded and stared at the carpet, I offered, "He was a good Marine."

Instantly, Nellis' father fired back, "A damn good Marine!"

His father was right. *Damn good* were two tombstone words that fit A. B. Nellis impeccably.

May's silent wind finally stopped bullying the mesquite and the Palo Verde trees outside my window, and the allegros and andantes of Mozart's *"Eine kleine Nachtmusik"* reverberated though my room, through me. And I knew that God had been listening, but I wanted more than He seemed willing to offer.

Turning toward a crucifix that hung on the wall above the window, I muttered Horatio's famous good-bye words to his friend Hamlet: "Good night, sweet prince, and flights of angels sing thee to thy rest!" Pausing for a moment, I continued, "A. B. Nellis, *Adieu.*"

40

SANDBURN
MAY 2001
LAND OF ENCHANTMENT

There I was out in Indian Country, but not the Nam kind, where the NVA were crawling all over the damn place, but this was the back-in-the-World version. It wasn't quite as desolate as I had imagined, but it sure as hell wasn't Virginia with all its gorgeous green. All that I loved about Virginia couldn't keep me back home, not even my daughters. I just had to get the hell out of there. Too many memories of Angela and James, so I escaped to Indian Country.

Sometime in the beginning of May, I drove off into the sunset, never lookin' at a road map until I was in New Mexico, driving south on Interstate 25 rather than west on I-40. I had been driving continuously since I'd checked out of a Motel 6 in some shithole town outside of Little Rock. Interstate 40 was supposed to take me to Flagstaff, but in Albuquerque I must've taken an exit that sent me south on Interstate 25.

I realized I'd screwed up when I pulled into a rest stop just after I saw a sign that said that Las Cruces was 140 miles away. Unfamiliar with such a place, I looked at my road map to see how far Las Cruces was from Flagstaff and discovered my fuck-up. With my eyes feeling like they were gonna fall out of my head, I decided to catch a few hours of sleep at the rest stop. Unfortunately, the *few* turned into six, so I decided that back tracking was out of the question. I barreled south on I-25 until I got my first speedin' ticket, that is, my first one in New Mexico. The officer had already heard all the same lines of shit I fed him, so he gave me a ticket for goin' 92 miles per hour. I knew what he wanted to hear, so I told him, "Sorry, sir, I'll slow it down."

When he disappeared in my rearview mirror, I cranked it up. My Porsche was built for speed, not for the damn speed limit. I got my second speedin' ticket in a speed trap just outside of Truth or Consequences. I was only doin' a little over fifty, but the town needed my money. I didn't even waste my time sayin' anything to this particular cop. I just looked straight ahead, took his ticket and placed it on the passenger's seat with the other one. He said, "Have a nice day," but I knew he didn't mean it, so I didn't reply as I drove away through a town I never expected to visit. With Truth or Consequence shrinking behind me, I added littering to my list of New Mexico crimes. Knowing that there would be no sequel to my New Mexico road trip, I didn't even bother rippin' up the tickets before I tossed them out the window.

No matter how many miles I put between me and Truth or Consequences, I couldn't get Doc Reyes's damn face out of my mind. Why did that town have to ambush me with a chicken shit speed trap? I didn't need no Nam memories to fuck with me. I had a shitload from Virginia. Definitely didn't need no more, but there he was—big as life—and I couldn't make him go the hell away, even by screamin' at him. Nothin' worked. At first, he was there in front of me, smilin' as he handed out toothbrushes to the gook villagers, but then he had no face, only what was left of it after the VC shot him in the head. Lots of blood and no face, but it was Doc. His face became the highway in front of me, all the way south until just outside of Las Cruces, and then he finally disappeared. Thank God!

All the way from Richmond, though Virginia, Tennessee, Arkansas, Oklahoma, the Texas Panhandle and New Mexico, I hadn't been at all fazed by the speed limit, but, when I looked down at the speedometer, I took my foot off the gas pedal until I had slowed down to about 70 miles per hour. The eight speeding tickets I had accumulated on my cross-country trek hadn't been able to slow me down, but just north of Las Cruces, just before

I'd make my right turn to Arizona, I slowed down and pulled off to the side on a desolate stretch of Interstate 10.

As I sat there, it hit me like a B-52 raid—Arc Light in the desert. I finally understood why a Mexican from a shitty little town in a God-awful state could affect me the way Doc had, both at the Wall and on the highway. In the Nam we had called him Doc, but to me, he had been nothing more than a wetback, a damn beaner. In the middle of the New Mexico desert, I realized that we had called him Doc because of what he did. As a corpsman, he patched up wounded grunts while everyone else was lookin' for cover and tryin' to stay alive. He never made a big deal about what he did. Maybe that was why it took me so damn long to appreciate what he had done for us in the Nam.

As I was about to pull back on to the highway, I adjusted my rearview mirror. I saw no on-coming traffic, only the face of a fifty-two-year-old who didn't give a damn about his graying hair. In that instant, my face disappeared, and I saw his face again, the one he had before the bullet hole fucked it up it forever. Doc Reyes would never see age twenty or the New Mexico desert that was starin' back at me. I peeled out, hit my fist on the dashboard, and turned up the music on the radio to the blare-level in hopes of makin' his face disappear. It finally did, but Angela's took its place all the way to just past the damn Arizona border.

Behind me, I left a state that I had learned to hate. It had been mistakenly called "the land of enchantment", but for me it had been nothing more than a gauntlet of fuckin' pain, and ahead of me stretched more than a hundred miles of desert, Southern Arizona style. My ultimate destination, the Tohono O'odham Reservation, Papago land awaited me, but no one there had a damn clue that Trent Sandburn was on his way there.

41

SANDBURN
29 MAY 2001
SOUTHERN ARIZONA

When I rolled into downtown Tucson at about noon, the temperature almost matched my speed on Interstate 10. There wasn't much to see except for some mountains as I got close to Tucson, so it made sense to do over 90. I wasn't sure where the Arizona Highway Patrol boys had been, probably resting after the Memorial Day weekend, but they definitely missed out on givin' me a ticket. I had gotten away with speeding, which was just fine with me.

After a two-margarita-lunch minus the lunch, I decided to head out to the reservation. When the bartender asked me where I wanted to go on the reservation, I shrugged, so he tried to be nice. "You realize it goes on forever...maybe a hundred miles or so? You could get lost out there if you don't know where you're goin'."

Having explained that I wanted to find one of their government offices, something official, he replied, "Any one in particular?"

When I shook my head, he said, "If it don't make no difference to you, then I wouldn't waste my time goin' way out by Three Points or Sells. Like I said, the Tohono O'odham's got themselves one hell of a big reservation, so I'd save me some time and head down I-19 to San Xavier del Bac. You can't miss it. It's a mission, a regular tourist spot. They got another reservation there, so someone should be able to help you out...and if you're in the mood, they also got a casino nearby."

I pulled a twenty-dollar bill from my wallet and tossed it in the direction of the bartender. I was out the door and into the God-awful, mid-afternoon heat by the time he had said his third *thank-you*.

One thing had not changed since the Nam. Recon first. Then go in. His tip was well worth the twenty bucks. Within a half hour, I parked my dusty car in front of the mission. It was easy to see why tourists brought their cameras. Even a klutz could take a great picture of the mission. I wasn't no tourist, and I wasn't packing no camera, so I took one quick look and headed inside the church.

Oddly, this was the first time I had been inside a church since the funeral of both Angela and James. It had been almost a year to the day since I buried them back in Richmond. Too much had changed in my life, so I found myself in, of all places, a Catholic church with a Mexican name on an Indian reservation. God was definitely messin' with me.

There were too damn many statues and candles for me, so I was relieved when I found a priest who had just finished talkin' to a couple of old ladies. He was friendlier than I expected a priest to be. All that prayin' and hearin' those confessions had to make them depressed. Staying holy all the time, especially without no sex, would make anybody depressed. But I wasn't interested in why he didn't mind smilin', so I cut to the chase. "Padre...is that what you go by?"

"Only in the movies."

He had a sense of humor. Since I wasn't there for his comedy routine, I politely responded, "Only in the movies. That's good. I think you missed your calling." He smiled and asked how he could help me. I asked for a pen, which he had to go to another room to get. I wrote a check, folded it, and as I handed it to him, I said, "Do me a favor and make sure this gets used for somethin' good on the Papago Reservation." He had a look on his face that made me think he was gonna say somethin' like, "Bless you, my son." Luckily for both of us, he didn't, but rather he thanked me and asked if I wanted to light a candle.

"What for?" Before he could reply, I had turned and was out the door. As I pulled away from the San Xavier Mission, my rearview mirror had two things in it, a ton of dust and a padre with a check, which he obviously had looked at. I wasn't sure what brought him outside into my cloud of dust. The amount of the check probably got him away from his candles, but the two words that I had written on the memo line kept him standing there in the parking lot. Maybe his God would tell him the meaning of those two words. *Dông Bích.*

42

SANDBURN
30-31 MAY 2001
ST. DAVID, ARIZONA

I hadn't learned squat from my New Mexico tickets, so I blew right by Benson, Arizona without even noticing it or the exit that was supposed to take me down to St. David and the monastery where O'Brien did his monk thing. When I realized my fuck up, I made an illegal U-turn and headed back to Benson, a place that was pretending to be a town. They would've been arrested for impersonating a real town, or at least they would've been laughed out of the State of Virginia.

I putted along for almost a mile down their joke of a main drag, not because there was anything to see, but because I wasn't in the mood for no speed-trap ambush. I hadn't turned over no new leaf. I just had to be somewhere. When I finally got off Benson's main drag, I figured my Porsche with its 450 horsepower engine would most certainly thank me when I finally turned south and headed away from Benson, but the highway to St. David wasn't no interstate. That was for damn sure. They must have called it a highway so people would feel like they would get somewhere fast. Actually, it was nothin' more than a two-lane country road that liked to wind just enough to piss off the folks that were in a hurry. Naturally, my Porsche 911 Turbo wasn't fazed at all when it came to passin' the vehicles that bought into the 50-miles-per-hour speed limit. It was built to top out at almost 190 miles per hour, and it did zero to 100 in 9.2 seconds, which I had fun with on my little cross county trip to see O'Brien.

Before some DJ could play two country songs all the way through, I ended up doin' some serious slowin' down, thanks to the town of St. David that, in comparison, made Benson look like a regular city. It was so damn small that it didn't deserve to even have a name, but whoever came up with the name probably just liked the idea of bein' a dot on a road atlas. Must've had one of them there identity crises that folks have nowadays.

I had either blown right by the monastery where O'Brien lived or it was hidden away. In any case, I pulled into a Mom-and-Pop café. The waitress, who was still lookin' pretty good at about forty, smiled at me with one of those my-boy-friend's-out-of-town smiles. Although she had a nice set of tits, I only wanted the dinner special, with coffee and directions—not dessert.

After she poured my coffee, she set the near-empty pot next to me on the counter and asked, "Need anything else today?"

When I nodded my *yes*, her eyes got all sparkly, the way ladies' eyes get when a man's about to ask 'em out. "I'm lookin' for a monastery that's supposed to be around here. You know where it's at?" With my question, she instantly lost her smile, but she politely replied, "You must be Catholic? Most folks around here are Mormon."

Uninterested in playing a game of Twenty Questions, I replied with a dose of sarcasm. "Love to chat, but I was hopin' for some directions…possibly before sunset." When she abruptly turned and walked away, I figured that I had pissed the bitch off. When she returned with a plate of the St. David Sunset Special and plopped it down in front of me, I knew she hadn't appreciated my comment.

Unexpectedly, she returned to offer me directions and a refill of some of the worst coffee I had ever tasted, even more disgusting than the shit the Marine Corps pawned off as coffee back in my Marine Corps days. I said *no thanks* to the coffee and *thanks* for the directions. "Keep headin' south about ten miles. If you end up in Tombstone, you've gone too far. It's on the left side of the highway…can't miss it."

When she handed me the check, I gave her a hundred dollar

bill. She pointed to a sign on the wall behind her about their policy of accepting no bills larger than a twenty. "You have anything smaller?" Feeling a slight twinge of guilt for givin' her a hard time earlier, I said, "Nope, but what the hell, keep the change." I turned and opened the door, leaving her and the six other customers to their own bewilderment. I wasn't sure what her eyes were doin', but her mouth probably had dropped to the floor. Obviously, no one in this one-horse town had ever given her a ninety-three dollar tip.

As I was opening my car door, she ran up to me. "I feel so guilty for…" Not only was I uninterested in what made her feel guilty, but also the road to the monastery was callin' me, so I interrupted her guilt trip. I refused to let her return any of the tip, but she butted in that she had given me wrong directions to the monastery because of my earlier, sarcastic comment. She was right. Ten miles down the highway was a lot different than three miles, which was where the monastery really was. "And it's on the right side. Sorry."

Before I could offer a half-hearted *thank-you* and finally get the hell out of there, she slipped a small piece of paper into my hand. I didn't look at it, but I knew. She had that I-wanna-fuck-you twinkle in her eye. As I started up the engine and began to close the door, she smiled her original smile and said, "Drop by any time." She waved, but I said nothin' and just backed out. I had shit to do, and she just stood in her little gravel parking lot, wondering when I'd call her. I glanced at the paper she had given me, and then I tossed it out the window. I had gone from being a big tipper to being a litterbug in an instant.

Just as she had said, the monastery was three miles down the road and on the right, nestled peacefully in a pecan grove. In the distance was a church that looked similar in some ways to the one out on the reservation. Sitting at the entrance to the monastery grounds and not quite ready to enter what was beginning to feel like a hot LZ, I wondered if O'Brien would even recognize me, or if he would be like the padre out on the reservation and invite me to light some damn candles. Maybe that was why I never got along with O'Brien in the Nam.

We came from real different worlds even though we were both white. Catholics with their weird-ass rituals and their candles and statues and shit were too fucking weird for me. A lot like the gooks and their incense sticks and all their Buddha statue shit. The more I thought about talking to O'Brien, who I hadn't seen in over thirty-three years, the more I knew that I needed a swig or two of good ol' Jim Beam, which I had fortunately brought along. I hated admitting it, but I was still feelin' nervous after my third swig of bourbon, so I drove away, leavin' O'Brien and his damn monastery behind me.

Sports cars were built for speed and handling, not for sleepin'. Mine was no exception, so I woke up feeling not so rested the next morning. I should've headed down the highway a little ways and slept in Tombstone, but instead I opted for the end of a dirt road near a pecan orchard. The night sky got my attention because there were so damn many stars. It reminded me of how dark the damn nights were in the Nam, which made the stars really stand out. While I was looking up there, I got myself ambushed when I started thinkin' about Angela and James, who I had buried just about a year earlier.

Although Richmond was a couple of thousand miles away, the distance didn't seem to matter much. Even out here in Arizona, my heart was as empty as the sky was clear. All I was able to do was stare straight ahead after awhile. I wasn't even interested in screamin' at God. It wasn't worth it any longer. I knew He had no miracles up His damn sleeve for me. No way was He interested in returnin' the dearly departed. They were gone forever because I had pissed Him off, and He wanted me to suffer. Taking Angela, James, and Trent, Jr. was His way of messin' with me. So, I finished off most of the bottle of Jim Beam. Nothin' changed, but it helped me to sleep, or more accurately, pass out.

When the sun woke me up around six, I took a serious leak and stretched, which felt great, but my head didn't. A couple of swigs of whiskey didn't help much, but they sure tasted good. I was hungry, so I headed back into St. David to my favorite little café, but the waitress from the night before wasn't workin' the morning shift. Probably got lucky with another customer.

Even though I was suffering from a hangover, I avoided havin' their shitty coffee with my St. David Sunrise Special, half of which I left on the plate. Three aspirins, the best part of the meal, were on the house. My reputation as a big tipper seemed to have preceded me. The breakfast crowd and my waitress, in particular, weren't disappointed. I wasn't being generous. I just didn't have no small bills, only hundreds. Without asking for the check, I dropped a hundred dollar bill on the counter and was out the door. These small town folks got entertained real easy, but that was their last damn show compliments of me.

As I approached the monastery, I convinced myself not to hesitate at the entrance as I had the day before. I had driven all the way from Richmond to take care of some seriously overdue business. It was put up or shut up time. It was finally time for me and O'Brien to meet. As I turned into the entrance of the monastery grounds, I wished I hadn't finished off the bottle of Jim Beam before heading to the café for my very forgettable breakfast. The church, which stared directly at the entrance, was set back about a hundred yards from the highway. I spotted a small building to the left as I drove towards the church. It was a bookstore, and someone was inside, so I pulled up and parked.

A lady inside the bookstore looked out at me but didn't seem at all impressed with my red 2002 Porsche 911 Turbo like the waitress at the café had been. I also didn't expect that the lady would be offerin' me her phone number since this was a monastery and all. Besides that, I looked like hell since I hadn't shaved since leavin' Richmond, and I damn sure must have smelled like booze. She must have been in a forgivin' mood or somethin'. Besides being real pleasant, which kind of shocked me, she was helpful, explaining that Father O'Brien would be available shortly after the 8 a.m. Mass. On autopilot, I thanked her and returned to my car.

I opened the glove compartment and reached in, pulling out a .357 Magnum and three rounds of ammunition, which I randomly loaded in the cylinder. When I slammed the cylinder shut, I spun it. Then, I wrapped it in a windbreaker. I was ready, so I walked toward the church and morning Mass. O'Brien's sermon would keep me awake, probably. No doubt some pious bullshit would be flowin' out of the motherfucker's mouth. Maybe he'd recognize me, but probably not. One thing was certain. The time had finally come, and I wouldn't be lightin' no fuckin' candles.

43

O'BRIEN
31 MAY 2001
HOLY TRINITY MONASTERY

Even with the passage of thirty-three years, certain faces never evaporate from memory, especially the face of the man who saved my life out by Dông Bích. Images from that night, the ambush gone terribly wrong, have refused to die. Illumination rounds popping overhead, miniature parachutes swaying rhythmically through the rainy night sky, floating nonchalantly to the ground like the electric company's version of the 101st Airborne; that's all they did until they burned out and died after landing all around us and the Viêt Cong. Then, just in time, another illumination round would pop in the rain-soaked February sky, the world of light and shadow replacing the rain-drenched, deadly darkness. Even a nearly full moon got smart and was hiding behind some clouds.

Of all the possible memories from that night, how odd it was that this quiet image had parked itself front and center when I spotted him sitting in the last pew of the church. I stopped in mid-sentence, but only momentarily. Although I had lost my focus, I finished my homily based on "Luke 15". When Mass ended, I exited as usual to the sacristy. When I returned to the church sanctuary, it was empty except for an elderly woman who was frenetically praying the rosary aloud, just in case God was deaf. Walking down the center aisle, I offered her an unsolicited smile, which went unnoticed. As I passed by her, the pace of her Hail Mary mantra seemed to accelerate as did my stride as I approached the vestibule and finally the hand-hewn door that led to a courtyard which guarded the entrance to the monastery church.

I squinted as the early-morning sun hurled a blast of light at me when I swung open the door. Behind me, I left the captive coolness of the sanctuary and its almost silence as I stepped into Southern Arizona's nine o'clock summer heat. Sitting on a bench several feet away was Sandburn, the man who had saved my life back when neither of us owned any gray hair. Those days were eight presidents ago, and so much more than our thinning and graying hair had changed since that time when two Marines, a nineteen-year-old and a twenty-one-year-old, only wanted one thing: get out of Dông Bích alive. It didn't matter to either of us at the time whether it was luck, fate, karma, or prayer that was our ticket back to our battalion hill. *Survival* had quickly leapfrogged past *victory* on our shortlist of immediate priorities. *Tomorrow* had become much more than just the next day in my diary, more than another mundane sunrise.

We had escaped a bullet in the head from the Viêt Cong of the Q16 Company, but over the years I had felt a mixture of feelings about my surviving the ambush when eight had not. My joy at escaping with only a bayonet wound had been overshadowed for years by a sense of guilt, which I understood to be illogical, but the sorrow that overwhelmed me had taken up residence in my heart, not my head. My initial visit to the Wall back in 1982 had helped me to begin to exorcise my sense of guilt for having survived while Reyes, Webster, and the others had not. I had left a river of tears at the Wall, but that was only the beginning.

In 1982 I was a cherry at the healing thing, and since then, whenever I have felt confident that I was a short-timer in my tour of duty in my grief process for the squad, I have been ambushed. Even as a priest, I have sparred with God when this has happened. I have frequently wondered if I have caused God, renowned for His patience, to reconsider remaining so.

Sandburn stood up, and as we stared silently at one another, I pondered for an instant what God was up to. I moved toward

Sandburn, whose vacant eyes peered past me, and reaching out to shake his hand, I said, "Welcome home."

He only mustered up a lethargic, "Yeah." Closed-for-business signs hung in his empty eyes that stared past me, and through his five-o'clock shadow that was several days old, there was no smile to be found, not even an attempt at a courtesy smile. Following my suggestion, we sat on the bench behind Sandburn. For at least a minute there was no other sound except for the rustling of leaves as a light breeze floated through the pecan grove a short distance away. His silence provided no clear clues to the mystery of his appearance at the monastery, but his thousand-yard stare did. He would have to provide me with the particulars, but it seemed apparent that all wasn't well in Richmond.

Finally, he mumbled in a voice lacking any emotion, "*I Heard the Owl Call My Name*...that's the book Missy read. I hate that fucking book and Chukut...Goddamn his dream."

His logic had taken a left turn without me, so I replied, "I taught that novel when I was an English teacher, so I'm not shocked that you might not like the book. Tough topic. It's not for everyone...but what's up with you hating Santos because of his dream? I'm lost."

Then, Sandburn slowly began to detail how he had not taken Santos's dream about the owl—*chukut*—seriously just before Tét. When I agreed with Sandburn that it was eerie that Santos's dark premonition had been accurate, he offered no response but only stared down at the concrete patio slab. The meandering crack and the caravan of ants that snaked across the patio floor didn't exist for Sandburn. At that moment, only owls and the dead dressed his landscape. Then, he muttered, "Even after the ambush, I thought it was just a bunch of bullshit...but then...a couple of months after my daughter tells me about that book she read, my...my..."

Unable to continue, he gulped and sighed deeply. He leaned forward, cupping his face in the palm of his hands. I wanted him to tell me that his wife had divorced him, but I sensed that something more ominous had occurred in his life. Although feeling uncomfortable, I decided to take an indirect approach, so I asked, "I was wondering why I didn't get a Christmas card from you last Christmas. We weren't real tight in the Nam, so you might not believe this, but I actually look forward to it each year. You saved my life, and I'll never forget that. So...what's going on with you? No one comes out to Arizona this time of the year for the weather. I'm here to listen."

Sandburn sat up straight, let out a deep sigh and began rubbing his temples. Behind his eyes, lay a cache of pain. Then, as he peered toward the church, his eyes began to well up with tears that he had successfully held in check until he said, "My wife and son...they both...died...A car accident a year ago." Streaming down his cheeks, tears, like the first drops of a summer shower, splattered randomly on the concrete slab. Upon regaining his composure after taking several deep breaths, he continued, "Should've figured it out when my daughter told me about that damn owl book. At first I just listened politely as she told me the story, but later on I started feelin' a little weirded out when I remembered Santos's dream...and then both my son and my wife went and got themselves killed. Definitely fucked up my life."

Verbalizing seemed to the perfect prescription for his malady, but his pain reached to his core. He continued to explain about how his life hadn't been the same since the accident, how their deaths had sent him into a tailspin. He informed me then of the loss of Trent, Jr., his first son who had died back in '81. He blamed the demise of his first marriage on that traumatic event. It was apparent that Angela, his second wife, had profoundly influenced his life in a positive way; however, his logic, seen through the prism of grief, caused him to be consumed with a deep sense of guilt because he saw himself as being responsible for sending her out on the road the day of the accident.

Having wrestled with similar demons, I wanted to interrupt and explain that he was suffering from survivor's guilt, but I resisted the temptation because my psychological interpretation, although probably accurate, was irrelevant to his world of sorrow. The words of solace offered in "Isaiah 43," which seemed to fit Sandburn's angst, floated through my mind like a cloud offering shade on a hot day: *When you pass through rivers, they will not sweep you away; walk through fire and you will not be scorched, through flames and they will not burn you.*

For I am the Lord your God, your deliverer".

But for Sandburn, at that moment, God lived in distant clouds, and His words were nothing more than empty promises for the mindless proverbial sheep. Sandburn's isolation and sorrow had reunited us after more than three decades, so I owed the man who saved my life the courtesy of listening and offering my compassion. After all, that was a key part of my job description as a priest. Ultimately, his catharsis needed to come from his own words, not mine.

He still avoiding looking at me, as he sighed and muttered, "That fucking owl." He paused and then continued, "It followed me home from the Nam. Should've known when Missy told me, but I screwed up by not figuring it out until it was too late to stop God from payin' me back for what happened that night out by…" The rest of his words remained parked in his throat.

"Paying you back? For what?" He offered no answers to my questions, so we both sat in silence, I with my ignorance and he with his agony. Finally, the word-train pulled out of the station. Sandburn spoke only two words. "*Dông Bích.*"

At first, I thought he was experiencing a multiple dose of survivor guilt, but as his story unfolded, I began to grasp why he thought God had taken a personal interest in reeking havoc on his life. In a monotone voice, he began detailing how he had taken the ten-to-two watch that night, but while Santos slept, he snuck away, drank some whiskey and then fell asleep, which meant that he had left the PRC 25 radio unattended. To make matters worse, that also meant that no one at their listening post at the top of the hill was using the night-vision scope to scan the ambush area.

Sandburn didn't wake up until more than halfway through his watch when the Việt Cong had begun their ambush of those of us who were lower down, along the trail. Once he awoke, he spotted the VC who were firing at us from an array of spider holes to the north and south of us. He didn't want Santos to know that he had been asleep at his listening post, so he remained hidden in the thick shrubbery that covered most of the hill.

After about ten minutes, he observed Santos crawling to the east side of the hill, which seemed odd since the firefight was going on at the hill's western base. It appeared that Santos wasn't going to place any bets on the squad's survival, but then, when an artillery barrage began pounding a target in the rainy darkness several hundred meters southeast of the hill, Sandburn drew a very different conclusion. Sandburn had left the night-vision scope back where Santos had been originally, so he could only guess that, with the help of the night-vision scope, Santos had spotted a force of NVA trying to infiltrate into the "rocket belt" through the rice paddies that stretched across the corridor between the hamlets of Phuóc Ninh (6) and Phuóc Ninh (7), which were almost a klick southeast of their listening post on the hill. A series of secondary explosions made it clear that Santos had caught elements of a North Vietnamese rocket battalion in the open and had called in a fire mission to Hill 10.

Feeling a twinge of guilt and a dose of bravado, compliments of the whiskey that was coursing through his veins, Sandburn finally decided to join the fight, especially when he realized that the Viêt Cong ambush was succeeding. He fired several short bursts from his M16 at the Viêt Cong below him, but as he was slamming a new magazine of ammo into his rifle, he stopped abruptly. His heart began pounding faster than it ever had. Fear swept through him like a raging fire, causing him to tremble uncontrollably.

Above him, recently fired illumination rounds continued lighting up the night sky, but the shrapnel-bearing HE mortar fire from the 81s back on Hill 10 had ceased. Sandburn, understanding the value of mortars, quickly realized that, without the aid of mortar fire to suppress the heavy volume of fire coming from the Viêt Cong, who seemed to be everywhere, the squad would be doomed.

Both the deteriorating situation below him and the stuporous effects of the whiskey convinced him that being alive made more sense than being heroic, so he crawled east, away from the fighting and toward the area where he had last seen Santos. Sprinting to Santos's position was his first choice, but he knew he would have become a silhouetted target because the sky was lit up from the illumination rounds that kept popping overhead. As he crawled closer to Santos's position, Sandburn heard the resumption of another mortar barrage with the distinct thud sound the accompanied the explosion of each round, but it ended after only ten rounds. As Sandburn crawled within several meters of Santos, the din of the firefight ended abruptly, giving way to the sound of sporadic bursts of small-arms fire. Santos, arched low and carrying his radio and M16, jogged up the hill and back toward the VC ambush.

With the absence of tracer rounds being fired in Santos's direction, Sandburn knew that the Viêt Cong weren't aware of either of them, but all of that changed the instant Santos began firing his M16 at the VC below. Santos even managed to lob several grenades at the Viêt Cong who had spotted his M16's muzzle flashes and had responded by pouring out a heavy volume of fire, some of it coming from a light machine gun.

Sandburn caught sight of several Viêt Cong as they attempted to out flank Santos from the southern slope of the hill, but a wall of mortar fire from Hill 10 kept them at bay long enough for Santos to make his exit to the east. With the illuminated sky behind him, Santos, no longer wearing his helmet, sprinted past an unseen Sandburn who was lying prone under a bush. With speed and luck, Santos would escape the hill and reach the rice paddies, the last yet tenuous leg on his two-thousand-meter journey back to the safety of Hill 10.

Not far from where Santos had just dashed past Sandburn, his speed met the butt of an NVA rifle, the impact thrusting his head back, dropping him hard to the ground. As the last illumination round popped overhead, Sandburn first heard Santos's moans and then watched while several NVA appeared to be discussing what to do with Santos. When they bound his hands behind his back and blindfolded him, it became apparent that the bullet-in-the-head faction had lost to the POW faction.

Because the unexpected jolt from the rifle butt had knocked him to the rain-drenched ground, two of the NVA kicked Santos until he struggled to his feet, at which point one of the soldiers removed Santos's radio and picked up his M16, which lay near him. Then, another soldier yelled what appeared to be orders at Santos, prodding him forward with the muzzle of his AK-47 shoved into the small his back. Into the darkness, a half-dozen NVA soldiers and Santos disappeared.

The appearance of the NVA complicated Sandburn's

situation; evading capture had become doubly difficult with the Việt Cong behind him and the NVA in front of him. To compound his dilemma, all friendly mortar fire had ceased. Sandburn was on his own, with his only allies: the drizzling rain and the darkness.

With his heart sprinting double-time, Sandburn left the concealment at the top of the hill, cautiously maneuvering his way down its slippery slopes toward a footpath at the base, where he halted immediately upon hearing the first of eight separate gunshots coming from the ambush site, which was a little more than a hundred meters to the west. Realizing the significance of those distinct sounds, he hurled himself to the ground, hiding behind a scruffy bush about five meters from the trail, where he lay trembling until he saw the vague outline of someone coming toward him slowly. Getting caught would have meant a bullet to the forehead, and Sandburn would do anything to avoid the same fate of the rest of squad.

When the man, who was carrying an SKS rifle in his left hand, passed by him, Sandburn saw that he was also carrying someone over his right shoulder. Sandburn waited for a minute or so before resuming his escape to the east. He had only gone a few feet before he quickly dove for cover by the side of the trail. Another person, this one crouching and moving at a faster pace than the first, passed by so closely that Sandburn wished he had never joined the Marines.

Even if he succeeded in slipping by the two Việt Cong who had just passed by him, he still had to evade any of the NVA that were lurking between his position and Hill 10. His mind vacillated between his possible options, and his heart pounded a double-time cadence. As he lay there snuggling up with his indecision, the two Việt Cong, who had just passed by separately, returned, but this time they were walking together. The Việt Cong soldier who was carrying the SKS rifle was in front of the other man who only had a pistol in his hand, and neither were carrying anyone over their shoulders. Sandburn, waiting long enough for them to be out of earshot, sprang to his feet and began jogging east on the muddy footpath. Just as the trail began to dip into a small ravine, a single pistol shot rang through the rainy darkness.

As Sandburn's story unfolded, I felt like I was being sucked into a giant black hole, the doorway to Hell. Sandburn had pulled the linchpin, yet I continued to listen as most of what I believed about that night out by Dông Bích was unraveling. With each new revelation, I was sorely tempted to take a momentary break from being a priest, just long enough to be Sergeant O'Brien again.

I had to remind myself more than once that Christ admonished those who judged others. As I sat there in the patio outside the monastery church, I realized that pulpit Christianity was so much simpler than patio Christianity. I wanted to hate him for drinking booze and falling asleep, but that wouldn't bring Nellis, Reyes, or any of the others back. I wanted to hate Sandburn, but that wasn't in my contract with God, so I struggled to listen as Sandburn said, "Right after I heard that single gun shot, I saw somebody lying off to the side of the path in the brush. It was you."

I sat dumbfounded until two words stumbled from my lips, "Me? Me?" He shrugged and replied in a lethargic tone, "All I know is you were muddy and soakin' wet. You were unconscious and were wounded, so I threw you over my shoulder and carried you until we ran into the reaction force from Hill 10. Other than that, I don't have nothin' else to tell you except that it was kinda weird that you weren't wearin' no poncho. That made no sense since it was so damn rainy that night." Sandburn paused and then added, "And…how the hell did you end up where I found you? Don't make no sense."

"You got me. So, why are you telling me these things now?"

"Guess 'cause I've gotta. God's been messin' with me big time. Payback's a motherfucker…and when it comes from God…well, He don't take no damn prisoners. When He let that bastard kill my wife and kid last year, that was the final damn straw. Hell, getting fucked up doesn't even help. There ain't enough damn Jim Beam in Kentucky…that's how bad it's gotten."

Sandburn stood up and continued, speaking in a sarcastic tone, "Tell you what, padre…why don't you light me a few of those magic candles. That's what you folks do, right?"

Although bewildered by his comment, I nodded and said

reassuringly, "Sure, but my job description also includes listening and giving a damn...even though it's real hard right now."

Staring down, he replied, "What about forgiving? That's a big deal with you Catholic types. Right? You conveniently forgot to mention that, padre."

I thought for a moment and then stood up, looking directly at him and replied, "I haven't achieved sainthood, so I'm still working on a few things. Right now, forgiveness...well, I don't know how good I'd be at it. But I can tell you that forgiveness is God's specialty. He's a pro at it since He's had a ton of practice...been doing it for a long time. Today during Mass, I spoke about the message of forgiveness. The Pharisees complained to each other because Jesus welcomed and ate with sinners; Jesus responded with a parable about the shepherd who lost one of his sheep but left the rest of the flock to find the missing sheep. Upon finding the sheep, he rejoiced with his neighbors. Then Jesus provided the *Cliff-Notes* version so that even the Pharisees would get it. 'In the same way, I tell you, there will be greater joy in Heaven over one sinner who repents than over ninety-nine righteous people who do not need to repent.' God is all about forgiveness. Pure and simple. End of story. All the rest is ornamental. Give God a chance. Give yourself a chance. Sandburn, you survived that night for a reason."

Sandburn looked directly at me for the first time, but his catatonic gaze made it clear that he remained unconvinced by my comments. "Your God ain't my God then. There's no way God would forgive me for Dông Bích. What He did to my family is proof enough for me."

Sandburn backed away from me before I could respond to him. Unwrapping a bundled up windbreaker, which he grasped with his left hand, he pulled out a .357 Magnum, quickly spinning the cylinder and pointing the barrel at his right temple. Before I could say or do anything, he squeezed the trigger.

Sandburn's vacant eyes drifted past me as he stood motionlessly, a statue frozen in failure, frozen in that Dông Bích night. Just as he was about to pull the trigger again, I took one step toward him slowly and said, "Sandburn, you don't have to do this. I need you to give me your weapon. Everything can work out. Just let me…"

Remaining expressionless, Sandburn replied in a slow-motion, monotone voice, "Fuck you, O'Brien. Everything that mattered to me is fucking gone."

"What about your girls? They need their father. Right?"

"They're grown-up girls. Don't need me no more, so stay the fuck out of my business."

"Can't do that, Sandburn. You know me better than that." Then, pretending to be calm, I firmly asked him to hand me his weapon as I began inching cautiously towards him. He pulled the .357 from the glistening sweat that rolled from his temple and then, cupping the handle with both hands, pointed it at my face. Speaking in a steely monotone, he said, "Back off, padre, unless you want to meet your fucking maker before lunch. I ain't fuckin' around. Go light some damn candles or somethin', but get the fuck back."

I immediately sucked in a deep breath of air in hopes of drowning the fear that had just sent my heart rate sprinting. As I sighed deeply, I hoped that the rosary lady in church had gotten God's attention so He would hear my silent petition for help.

More than two years of combat had taught me much that I abhorred, but one of the valuable lessons was that fear lost its debilitating grip when I acted upon it rather than pondering my situation. Survival in the Nam was all about being reactive and letting adrenaline run the show. Knowing this didn't make it any easier for me to start walking toward Sandburn and his .357 Magnum, which was now pointed squarely at my chest. Silently, Sandburn squeezed the trigger, but I won this round of Russian roulette. The chamber of the .357 still held one bullet, waiting patiently. I reached up with both hands and coaxed the revolver out of Sandburn's clutch. His arms dropped limply to his side as he shook his head back and forth. His eyes welled up and a single tear slid down his cheek.

Before I had a chance to do anything else, Sandburn shoved me to one side and sprinted away from me. As I turned, he had already reached his car, which was parked in front of the bookshop. Killing the monastery's silence when he revved up his Porsche, he slammed it into reverse. His red sports car, enveloped in a cloud of dust, roared out of the parking lot but failed to slow down as he turned left on to the highway which bordered the monastery grounds.

A gentle breeze pushed Sandburn's good-bye dust cloud west across the parking lot until it died in the nearby pecan grove. The odor of burning rubber from his tires lingered long enough for the wind to whisk it away. In the distance, the angry voice of his Porsche receded as it headed back toward St. David.

I entered the coolness of the church. Rosary Lady, who had just finished up her praying, walked by me as I was lighting a candle for Sandburn. She stopped to smile and say hello, but her mouth fell open and astonishment rolled across her Medicare face when she saw Sandburn's .357 Magnum. I left her standing there with her rosary beads and her bewilderment. Behind me, the flame in Sandburn's candle danced, bobbing and weaving in the cool darkness.

44

RICHMOND TIMES-DISPATCH
3 JUNE 2001
RICHMOND, VIRGINIA

Sandburn, Trent Jefferson, age 52, passed away outside of St. David, Arizona on May 31, 2001. Born April 27, 1949 in Richmond, he attended local public schools, and upon graduation from high school, Trent enlisted for three years in the United States Marine Corps, serving his country in combat as an infantryman in the Republic of South Vietnam during 1967 and 1968. During his service in Vietnam, he received a Purple Heart and the Silver Star for saving the life of one of his fellow Marines during the Tết Offensive. He was honorably discharged with the rank of Sergeant. He studied briefly at the University of Virginia but left to pursue a real estate career which spanned three decades. For the last twenty years, he concentrated his energy on developing a highly successful commercial real estate business. He was recognized as the Richmond Realtor of the Year in 1998, and he additionally received the Virginia

Commercial Realtor Award in 1998. He was a life member of the American Legion and also was a member of the First Church of the Nazarene. He served on a variety of local boards including the Boys and Girls Club of Richmond. A life-long member of the Republican Party, he served as a precinct committeeman and was also the vice chairman of the Richmond Committee To Elect Dole. As a lifetime member of the National Rifle Association, he was an avid sportsman and hunter. Sandburn was not only a successful businessman. Sandburn was a family man, the loving father of two grown daughters, Alyssa, 24, and Missy, 23. Sandburn is survived by his mother Susan Sandburn, his sister Marcia Bolinger and her two children Thomas and Krystal. Sandburn was predeceased by Jefferson Sandburn, his father, and also by Angela, his loving wife, and his two sons, Trent, Jr., and James Trent. The community and his many friends, as well as his loving family, will truly miss Trent Sandburn, whose life was taken tragically in an automobile accident in Arizona while visiting with Father Michael O'Brien, a fellow Marine whose life he saved during the Vietnam War.

A memorial service honoring the life of Trent Sandburn will be held Wednesday June 6 at 11:00 a.m. at the First Church of the Nazarene here in Richmond, VA. Interment will follow the service with full military honors at the Hollywood Cemetery. Sandburn's daughters have suggested that in lieu of flowers, friends can make donations in his memory to the Tohono O'odham Educational Fund, in care of Fr. Michael O'Brien, Holy Trinity Monastery, St. David, AZ 85630.

45

O'BRIEN
6 JUNE 2001
RICHMOND, VIRGINIA

A funeral is always a family gathering, a time for good-byes, usually laced with doses of guilt. Unlike most people—the friends of the deceased in particular—God would never put much stock in an obituary, which, after all, is nothing more than a resumé about the dead. Death, especially for the unprepared, is always a bad career move, even with the best of resumés.

Weddings and funerals never seem to start on time. Sandburn's funeral was no exception; it started a little late, maybe ten minutes or so, but it was a safe bet that he didn't care one way or another, since for him, it wasn't 11:10 a.m. Eastern Standard Time but some sort of permanent *now* in the Dead Standard Time Zone.

Life offers some interesting *quid pro quos*. Over the years my eyesight had diminished a bit, yet, at the same time, my insight had become keener. As I sat in my appointed pew at the front of the sanctuary of the First Church of the Nazarene, I only hoped that I possessed the necessary insight for the task of eulogizing a man who had become an enigma since his startling revelations at the monastery the previous week.

Missy, Sandburn's youngest daughter, had called me shortly after her father's death. Because the car accident that killed her father had occurred just outside St. David, she figured I was aware of his death, which was not the case—local news not being an integral part of a monastic life—but her primary mission was to find out if I would be interested in giving a eulogy. She made this request for several reasons. Two or three years earlier, her father had told her about how he had saved my life during the war, the reason for the Silver Star that was displayed prominently on the wall in his study. Upon learning of her father's car accident on the highway just outside of St. David, she discovered a note that Sandburn had left by the phone on the desk in his study, which explained that he was going to Arizona to take care of some business. It continued, asking that she set up an in-lieu-of-flowers fund in the event of his death, and ending the note with both my name and the address of the monastery, for anyone who wished to contribute to the fund.

When she phoned and shared this information, I didn't tell her about her father's .357 Magnum or the two times he had squeezed the trigger. I didn't need to; something in her voice, which seemed to resonate, told me that she had insight. Although this twenty-three-year-old woman was perceptive, all her wisdom could not mask a child's sadness, born of longing—at least for now. On the other hand, her older sister Alyssa lived in a different world, wanting to believe that her father's note was nothing more than a tragic premonition that had come true. Just like the Nam, each of Sandburn's daughters did what they had to do to get through their dark night.

Pipe organ music, both sacred and solemn, rolled through the church as the funeral procession, lead by Sandburn's two daughters, his mother and his sister, moved slowly toward the front of the sanctuary. The flag-draped casket, escorted by a contingent of Marines in their dress blue uniforms, trailed closely behind his immediate family, who upon reaching the front of the church, turned to their left, filing into the first pew and sitting there, wrapped in their summer sorrow.

When our procession of Marine pallbearers halted, they parked Sandburn's flag-draped casket front and center. A pew full of family members turned toward his coffin; their stunned silence quickly evaporated and was replaced by the sobbing of Sandburn's mother. As the Marines peeled off, half to the pew to the left and half to the one on the right, Missy was hugging her grandmother. Alyssa and Sandburn's sister just stared straight ahead in reflection or remembrance, but most probably in numbness.

Sitting in my appointed seat in the row behind Sandburn's family, I asked God for guidance with my eulogy. Although I hadn't procrastinated, as had frequently been the case in college, I had been unable to write Sandburn's eulogy, at least an appropriate one considering the circumstances. Although I had become privy to the truth that lay hidden beneath Sandburn's canopy of lies, it was not part of my job description to judge the man or to tell the world of his flaws. I was hard pressed to understand what purpose this would serve. He had already served a self-inflicted life sentence for everything that he caused out by Dông Bích.

As a nineteen-year-old Marine, both arrogant and ignorant, Sandburn, like so many, had failed to grasp that the Universe has a reputation for never allowing even the shrewdest person to get away with anything. As I sat there, I realized that Sandburn had never gained this essential insight about life's journey. The ghosts of our past mistakes haunt us while we remain prisoners to ignorance, foolishly believing we pulled a fast one, got away clean, but we can remain fools for only so long.

The pain usually helps us to recognize our ignorance blended with arrogance, after which, the choice of whether or not to change is ours. The Universe, with an endless supply of roads for us to travel, offers an equal number of forks, and at each one Robert Frost presents his insightful poem about "the road less traveled," yet many are too busy to listen. I wondered whether Sandburn was one of them, or had he finally found the peace that he desperately sought yet which seemed to elude him. Fortunately for Sandburn, his eternity rested in God's hands.

At the midpoint in the service, the minister motioned for me to come up to the pulpit. Carrying a folded sheet of paper containing three scriptural readings that I had scribbled down at the hotel, I shuffled out of the pew and walked to the pulpit, and once there, turned and faced a church brimming over with mourners. As I surveyed this sea of sadness, I pondered for a moment what, besides the obvious, was our common bond. The answer eluded me until I silently read over several lines that I had jotted down from the "Book of Job." A theme emerged with this epiphany, and so I began my by-the-seat-of-my-pants eulogy, first by introducing myself as both a Catholic priest and a Marine who had served with Sandburn in Vietnam, and then, by reading the final lines from Chapter 3 of "The Book of Job."

> *Why should a man be born to wander blindly,*
> *hedged in by God on every side?*
> *Every terror that haunted me has caught up with me,*
> *and all that I feared has come upon me.*
> *There is no peace of mind nor quiet for me;*
> *I chafe in torment and have no rest.*

Having quoted this passage, a fitting prologue to my eulogy, I explained to the mourners that I had chosen these words for several reasons. Most people possess at least a cursory familiarity with the story of Job, a man with a lifetime of bad days. Job's angst had many similarities to the grief the congregation of mourners was experiencing in varying degrees. I leaned forward and began my eulogy:

> *"Grief is a strange and frequently misunderstood creature that visits us all. Life, by its very nature, will guarantee each one of us the opportunity to experience loss, but God in his infinite mercy and wisdom has created us with the capacity to heal. As is witnessed in the story of Job, God does not leave us out in the cold to fend for ourselves.*
> *It is essential for us to note that grief does not discriminate; it just shows up, unannounced and unwelcome, on the doorstep of our everyday lives. When we answer the knock at the door, grief hands us a puzzle; if we stop our complaining about how unfair life has become and finally put the pieces together, we will see, with refreshing clarity, a picture, whereas only fragments or pieces existed at the onset of our loss.*

Grief, however, is not a one-time visitor, for it is like General MacArthur, and we are the Philippines. Upon its next visit, grief hands us, the reticent, one more unwanted puzzle: this one often being even more complex than the previous one. Our healing process does not begin until we connect the first two pieces in this puzzle; this enigma, we call grief. But there are days or even weeks when we feel too immobilized to lift a single piece, much less muster up the motivation to search for its matching piece. We pout and scowl or even argue with God, as did Job, who had a good case to argue that life wasn't fair. Unfortunately for the lazy, the pieces in the puzzle that grief gives us are not easily intimidated by our whining; they will not be manipulated into connecting themselves. The pieces of the grief puzzle just wait.

One of the pieces that many of us wrestle with is guilt. Let me speak from personal experience as someone from an Irish Catholic background. It is said that we have cornered the market on guilt, but there seems to be an ample supply remaining for the rest of humanity. Before I give guilt a bad name, let me make several qualifications first. Not unlike a glass of fine bourbon, guilt can be beneficial. A shot of good Irish whiskey can warm the soul on a chilly winter's evening. Guilt also serves an important purpose; it signals that our conscience is alive and well.

Unfortunately though, too many Irishmen have overindulged with their whiskey, drinking enough to warm the souls of ten men. Likewise, I've known of Irishmen, I having been one of them, who become consumed by guilt, wallowing in enough guilt to wake up the consciences of ten sinners.

So, why do I speak of guilt? Simply, because guilt is woven through the fabric of our lives, and in particular, it is an essential element in the grief process. I would like each person in this congregation to look inwardly and determine the nature of the guilt that you might possess. For many in this gathering, the guilt that you own has to do with your failure to let Trent Sandburn know how much you cared about him. Were you one of the complacent people who took it for granted that his hourglass had a forever supply of sand? Maybe your guilt was born in a cruel comment, one that you meant to apologize for, but fate disrupted your plans made useless by a car accident on a winding road in the Arizona desert. Are you an individual who is experiencing survivor's guilt? Whatever the brand of guilt, we all are experiencing one of the steps in the grief process, which, if we listen to our intuition and ask for God's assistance, will ultimately help us to heal.

Let me, however, offer this word of caution about guilt; it can turn into a monster that will consume us, just as whiskey can be the cause of a person's ruin. Guilt was never meant to be held in, but rather we must have the courage to admit and experience it, and then reflect on it in the hope that we can learn a valuable lesson from it. If you are one of those who feels guilty for having taken Trent Sandburn for granted, then his death can teach you the importance of appreciating our loved ones each and every day. In our particular feelings of guilt there are lessons for us, but we must possess the courage to look closely so we can discover what they are. If we choose, however, to not examine this opportunity, we will have squandered a chance for growth. If we choose to wallow in our guilt, we will have discarded an opportunity to accept responsibility for a mistake.

Sadly, when we fail to move beyond the initial guilt, we tend to be consumed by it, and so we run until we discover that we can't hide from our conscience and our God, who is a merciful God, one who was willing to listen patiently to Job's complaints.

I find it interesting that the "Psalms," which are songs of praise, follow the complaint-filled "Book of Job." In every funeral, we tend to feel both the angst of Job and the joy of Solomon, but we must remember that by placing the deceased too high on a pedestal, we doom him to a fall from grace. Yes, it is natural to heap praise on this man whose body rests in this flag-draped casket, but let us be reminded by the words of "Psalm 150", the final psalm, that God is truly deserving of our praise because of his power and majesty: 'O praise the Lord. O praise God in his holy place, praise him in the vault of heaven, the vault of his power; praise him for his mighty works, praise him for his immeasurable greatness.'

Life is filled with lessons, which typically are not obvious at first. The people we meet along the way become our teachers although they usually are unaware of their role in our lives. Imagine the darkness of a moonless night. At first we might curse the darkness because we must stumble through the night, but upon looking up, the beauty of the stars becomes visible only because of the blackness of the night. Let us think about the people who have taught us during our journey through life. Let us remember the human side of Trent Sandburn.

When I think of the lessons that I learned from Trent Sandburn, one in particular stands out: forgiveness. Although he was unaware of his gift, Trent helped me to rediscover the importance of remembering to be compassionate, replacing my foolish acts of judgment with healing forgiveness, because this is Christ's essential message, which He put into painful practice upon the cross.

Let us offer our love and prayers to Trent's family in their time of sorrow. Please take a

*moment to close your eyes, picturing the Trent
Sandburn that you wish to remember. As we do
this, my firm faith in a merciful creator tells me
that he is at peace in God's loving embrace. Good-
bye, Trent Sandburn. Adieu."*

My difficult journey of forgiveness was only beginning. The
part of me that was a priest still wrestled with this issue, so the
part of me that remained a Marine Corps Sergeant stubbornly
refused to offer a salute and utter the words, "*Semper Fi.*" Missy
had pried a eulogy out of me, and that would be it.

At the end of the service, as we escorted the flag-draped
casket down the aisle, the sound of bagpipes playing *Amazing
Grace* reverberated throughout the church and out into
Richmond's sultry early afternoon air when the church doors
yawned open. Any tears that were shed went unnoticed by me as
the Marine honor guard rolled the casket to the hearse; my eyes
stared straight ahead, but I only saw the darkness and the cold
rain that soaked me on that February night in Dông Bích until a
blast of June's unfriendly, muggy heat slapped my face, hurling
me back to Richmond and the business at hand.

When the hearse was ready to leave, Missy motioned for me
to join her family in their limousine for the ride to the
Hollywood Cemetery, which was the final resting place for such
Confederate notables as Jeb Stuart and Stonewall Jackson; Trent
would certainly have no complaints about his new neighbors.
Stretching for several blocks down Monument Avenue, the
procession of cars traveled slowly, rolling past two-and three-
storied row houses and dogwood trees. At some point our
journey took us past the campus of Virginia Commonwealth
University, which Sandburn's daughters seemed to ignore as
though it didn't exist. The cemetery, with its grand statues and
mausoleum, beckoned us.

Sandburn, having spent the previous ten years of his life at
his fashionable, red-brick row house on Grove Avenue in the
Fan District, was about to down-size and take up residence in a
much quieter neighborhood, one with a view of the James River
and Belle Isle. Our caravan of mourners meandered through the
cemetery on a narrow road bounded on both sides by giant shad

trees, which had stood for more than a century as sentinels for many of Virginia's honored dead. The hearse finally halted where a flat, green blanket of grass began its gradual ascent toward a distant knoll capped with a statue of a soldier on a horse. Trent Sandburn's casket was finally home.

Following the burial, we drove several miles to the Sandburn residence on Grove Avenue. On the way to the cemetery, the trees along our route seemed to have stood still, yet they whizzed by our limousine as we approached the reception that was being held at Sandburn's house. When we opened the front door, the aroma from platters of home-cooked food drew us in. Several members of the hospitality committee from the First Church of the Nazarene had taken over Trent's house prior to our arrival and were scurrying about in an attempt to make everything right for the reception.

When one of them, a silver-haired woman who had learned to avoid the wrinkles of time, saw Trent's two daughters, she strode gracefully towards them. Stopping in front of Alyssa, she extended both her hands, gently clasping Alyssa's right hand as she said, "I'm so sorry for the untimely loss of your father." Then, looking at Missy, she continued offering her condolences. "He was such a fine man."

Alyssa nodded and replied, "Yes, he was." Missy, mustering up a polite smile, only said, "Thank you, Mrs. Tyler."

Even as Missy was introducing me, Mrs. Tyler's hand remained cupped around Alyssa's hand, but she finally released it to shake my hand. Mrs. Tyler politely excused herself a moment later, but before returning to the kitchen, she made a pair of comments. "So you were in Vietnam with Trent." She paused only briefly, so I sensed that she wasn't expecting a response. In her parting words, she used a word that I had always detested. If I were a word in search of a best friend, I would never choose or even associate with this word: *interesting*. Its meaning was so bland, so nebulous, and therefore, safe. Then she added, "Interesting eulogy, Father O'Brien. Nice meeting you." As she turned and disappeared into the kitchen, the opportunity to understand the meaning behind her comments walked away.

For the next hour or so, I nibbled on baked ham, potato salad, and a freshly baked roll. Southern cooking was alive and well;

had Southern ladies fed the Union Army some of their home cooking, General Sherman would have surrendered some time in the middle of dessert. Although I was hungry, I nibbled at the food on my plate, not because I was dieting, but rather because I never had the opportunity to sit down and focus on eating. The steady stream of Trent's acquaintances who chatted with me made it impossible for me to enjoy an uninterrupted mouthful of potato salad or a piece of honey baked ham. Talking with my mouth full was out; funeral reception talk was in. Although southern hospitality was ricocheting though out the house, this gathering lacked the raucous spontaneity of an Irish wake. Eventually, I gave up my attempt at eating and set my partially finished plate down on a coffee table that was cluttered with abandoned plastic cups.

I began to look for an escape route after the tenth, "So you were in Vietnam with Trent." Besides tiring of the repetition of my response, I began to experience haunting memories from the past. Thirty-three years earlier, I heard similar words when people discovered that I had served in Vietnam. At first, I naively believed that they were interested in what I had to say, but I quickly discovered that their questions about the war were cloaked in their own political agendas. I sensed that I was nothing more than a vehicle to help reinforce their particular political belief about America's conflict in Southeast Asia. In those early months after I had returned from the Nam, no one ever asked about how the war had affected me. Feeling used, I deleted that part of my life from any conversations I had when I met someone new.

Unfortunately, in the living room on Grove Avenue, I was discovering that the passage of time apparently had no effect on the way most people dealt with the Vietnam experience. The abstract intellectualizing that Søren Kierkegaard had described nearly a century and a half earlier was flourishing in twenty-first century Richmond. I was vexed by why the Vietnam War, even after three decades, still seemed to turn so many people, even these mourners fresh from a burial, into armchair generals.

Fortunately, Missy became the chopper that extracted me from a hot LZ, well, maybe a warm LZ. Missy made quick business of the middle-aged man who was in the midst of his explanation about how airpower was the solution to a total victory in Vietnam. I wanted to offer my observations on the topic, but I sensed that his opinions were buried in stone. I was only a Catholic priest, not a modern Michelangelo with a chisel, so I smiled and politely excused myself and walked with Missy to her father's office, which was at the end of a hallway.

Dark wood-paneled walls stared back at me as we entered his office, which reeked of organization. Several feet behind his dark oak desk, a bookcase was home to books that stood at attention, never daring to lean. The order that seemed to be an integral part of Sandburn's life was even apparent on the wall in front of his desk, where various framed awards and certificates of achievement, organized chronologically, were perfectly aligned in three rows. Opposite his desk were two prominent features: a double-hung sash window and to the right of it, a Confederate flag, stretching defiantly for approximately four feet. Directly below it, a bronze statue of Jeb Stuart rested neatly in the center of the top of a bookcase, which was no more than three feet tall.

Across the room, the wall next to his desk was naked except for a single, picture hook. On his desk was a picture frame that was twice as tall as the other certificate-sized frames on the other walls. It remained face down until Missy turned it over.

Sandburn, in a moment of self-delusion, had framed and proudly hung up his Silver Star and the Marine Corps's letter of commendation, but the empty wall and the picture frame with its face buried in shame spoke volumes of how Sandburn must have felt just before he began his road trip to Arizona the prior week .

Looking at her father's medal for just a moment, Missy then began to read the letter of commendation aloud:

> *"The President of the United States takes pleasure in presenting the Silver Star Medal to Lance Corporal Trent J. Sandburn, United States Marine Corps, for service as set forth in the following citation: For heroic achievement in connection with a night ambush against the enemy in the Republic of South Vietnam while serving as a rifleman with Charley Company, First Battalion, Seventh Marine Regiment, First*

Marine Division. In the early morning hours of 12 February 1968, during a night ambush on the outskirts of the hamlet of Dông Bích (1), seven miles southwest of Da Nang, Sandburn's squad was attacked by a platoon of Việt Cong from the Q16 Company. The enemy force sprung an ambush from spider holes and poured relentless automatic weapons fire into the Marine squad, which despite being outnumbered by three-to-one odds, fought bravely, upholding the time-tested tradition of the Marine Corps. As the battle raged, the Việt Cong forces gained the upper hand with their superior firepower, which included numerous Chicom grenades being tossed from the spider holes that were on two sides of the beleaguered squad. Sent to an adjacent hill with a starlight night scope, Lance Corporal Sandburn demonstrated initiative when he utilized his position to call in accurate mortar fire on the Việt Cong platoon although he was not a forward observer. He also put himself in danger when he unselfishly exposed his position by pouring a heavy volume of small-arms fire into the enemy below him. While the battle raged below, he had the wherewithal to use his night scope to notice that a company-sized force of North Vietnamese Regulars was attempting to slip in to the east of Dông Bích and set up its 122 mm rockets for an attack on the airbase at Da Nang. Thinking quickly, the Lance Corporal accurately called in the position of the enemy force. Thanks to his quick thinking and his ability to remain calm even during the heat of battle, artillery from Hill 10 was able to inflict numerous casualties on the North Vietnamese who were forced to beat a hasty retreat, leaving more than twenty of their dead behind and failing to initiate their rocket attack on Da

Nang. Aware that his own squad still needed his assistance, he called in mortar fire on the Việt Cong who were attempting to out-flank his position. Having done this, he, without regard for his own safety, began his descent to help the wounded in his squad. As he moved quickly down the hill, he encountered the enemy on several occasions, but they failed to stop him although he received a blow to the head from the butt of a rifle. Before he could reach the squad, the enemy roamed the ambush site, executing any of the surviving Marines. Realizing the futility of remaining, Lance Corporal Sandburn, carrying a wounded Marine out of the area, evaded the Việt Cong for more than a mile until he met up with a reaction force that had been sent to help his squad. Through his bold initiative and resolute determination, not only did he prevent great loss of life at the air facility in Da Nang, but he also saved the life of one of his fellow Marines. The Lance Corporal's courage, aggressive fighting spirit, and steadfast devotion to duty at great personal risk were in keeping with the highest traditions of the Marine Corps and the United States Naval Service. Lance Corporal Sandburn is authorized to wear the Combat "V" with his Silver Star Medal."

When she finished, I had no response, only a blank stare drifting out the window, between its mullions, through a muggy Richmond afternoon, across an ocean and into a rain-drenched night on the outskirts of Đông Bích. Would Missy have been capable of loving her father had she known that he had fallen asleep on watch after boozing it up earlier that night back in '68? Would she cherish his memory if she knew about her father's attempted rape of the young Vietnamese woman who lived in Đông Bích? Would Missy be able to forgive her father for living the lie presented in his Silver Star commendation letter? At some point, had Sandburn somehow mustered up the courage to accept responsibility for his actions and also share his dark past with someone other than me, or had he kept it buried until it reached up and choked the life out of him? Sadly for Sandburn and his family, it seemed obvious that his feelings of guilt had consumed and overwhelmed him, and so this twenty-three-year-old daughter spent a summer day burying a father.

I returned from my journey through time and space when Missy shook my arm gently and said, "Father O'Brien." Having apologized for drifting off, I peered down at the medal and the letter of commendation, which she held in her hands. The angry part of me that was still wrestling with the issue of forgiving Sandburn wanted to announce to the world that his medal and everything that it stood for was a fraud, a lie. Once again I was painfully reminded of my own human frailties; yes, Christianity was so much simpler from a pulpit. I also reminded myself that there would be nothing honorable about sharing the truth with Sandburn's daughter unless I were free of an ulterior motive. Because anger had hunkered down in my emotional landscape, regardless of how much praying I did to purge myself of it, I knew that my anger toward Sandburn could taint the motive for my telling of the truth about the night of the ambush.

Intellectually, I understood the absurdity of having anger toward a dead man, but Sandburn's revelations at the monastery the previous week had forced me to revisit memories and see faces that were too young to die, but they died just the same. Since Sandburn's confession, my nights, filled with the ghosts of our gone-wrong ambush, were less than restful. My heart would be sprinting when I would wake up to escape my nightmare, and as the beads of sweat rolled down my face, all I felt was anger toward Sandburn for being so selfish and stupid. I had urges to punch his face in with my priestly knuckles; forgiveness, the centerpiece of Christianity, would be difficult, but I had faith that eventually the combination of time and prayer would help me to free myself of the anger I harbored toward Sandburn. As I looked at Missy, a daughter in mourning, I wondered one last time what good would come from my revealing the truth about Dông Bích, and so I decided to let the truth about that night be buried with Sandburn.

Missy turned the picture frame over and set it back on her father's uncluttered desk. Then, she removed the back from it and detached Sandburn's Silver Star. She turned back toward me and extended her medal-filled hand in my direction. "Here…I want you to have this. I think that is what my father would really want." Once again I was speechless as I held her father's medal in my hand. Realizing that there was no response in the pipeline, she continued, "Father O'Brien, I've read the letter of commendation many times, first as a proud young daughter and now with insight that I would prefer not to have."

She opened the middle drawer of her father's desk and retrieved a piece of paper, which she showed me. Having scanned over it, I realized what she meant by her comment about insight. For the third time since I had entered Sandburn's office, I was without words; Missy, who on the other hand was not, continued, "During the past year…ever since the accident that killed Angela and my brother, well, he was really depressed. I was very worried about him, especially when he sold his business and bought a brand new Porsche."

Missy paused for a moment as she stood silently, staring off into the land of questions. Then she continued, "When I read this note, I had a strong sense that something bad was going to happen. My sister's a lot like our grandmother. Neither one has a clue. They both think my dad's note was just a strange coincidence, but when I was listening to your eulogy, I realized that my dad's accident probably wasn't one. The way you kept emphasizing the theme of guilt, and then you talked about how my father was also teaching you a lesson about forgiveness…forgiveness for what? It all made sense to me when you told us not to put him on a pedestal. I don't know what happened in Vietnam, and right now I don't think I want to know, but I think it has a lot to do with this medal. Otherwise, why would he have taken it off the wall? So, please take his medal…I think you are more suited to do what's right with it."

A gentle smile rolled across her face, but her smile could not mask the sadness in the eyes of a child whose father had fallen from grace. Leaning over, I hugged the little girl who was desperately longing for the embrace of her never-to-come-home father.

46

CHARLIE'S SISTER
6 JUNE 2001
DÔNG BÍCH (1)

An Toán, my first grandson, joined our family five years ago, and he changed my life. It had been a lifetime since I had felt such joy, but An Toán changed all that. I had begun to smile again. But today, while we were eating, I looked into his eyes, filled with childhood innocence, and I was torn as my memories of yesteryear floated through me.

Tuan and I are laughing as he chases me...I run to the well and an old lady is yelling at us to go away...she isn't laughing when I run into her as I'm trying to escape from my brother...her bucket of water drops, splashing, and tipping over...she is flapping her arms in the air...and we are laughing uncontrollably as we run away...and we hope she doesn't tell our mother...but we know our mother won't be mad for very long...she is a good mother...she brushes my hair and tells me that I'm smart and beautiful...and she always kisses Tuan and me and tells us that she loves us before we go to sleep each night...and our father, although he is tired from the long hours he spends in the rice paddies, always seems to smile when he is around her...but when we are running away from the old lady with the flapping arms, Tuan runs into a French soldier who is standing outside our hut...he is not like our father...the soldier doesn't like to smile...he yells at Tuan, but his language is strange, yet we know he isn't happy with us...children get in the way in a war...it seems that no one is happy with us today...then another soldier is clutching our mother's arm and is pulling her from our hut...Tuan and I stop laughing, but our mother looks down into our nervous eyes as she passes by us and tells us in a calm mother's voice not to worry...and as the French soldiers march her away with her hands bound behind her back, I wonder why they want to take her away from us...they have mothers somewhere else, so why do they want us not to have ours...and after several days, our father, who isn't smiling, tells us that our mother has gone to visit our ancestors, but how can she do that after she has told us not to worry...our ancestors have their own mothers, but Tuan and I only want ours...so no one brushes my hair, and our father is too tired at night to tell us all the things that a mother says to her children...and Tuan and I want our mother's hug, but the soldiers stole that, and our father begins to disappear in the middle of the night when he thinks we are asleep, but I need someone to brush my hair so I can run away to dreamland where Tuan and I can still run and be silly and laugh when the old lady with the flapping arms yells at us, but even in my dream world, the French soldiers visit us, and I don't believe my mother when she tells us not to worry.

The innocent eyes of An Toán reminded me of my brother Tuan when he was about five, the last time we saw our mother. We were so fortunate to have An Toán as our grandson, but my memories continued to haunt me. I was sad for my husband because I had pushed him away for so many years, yet he still loved me. The answers that I sought ran away, and the ache in my heart ran as deep as the bamboo taproot. My brother Tuan would know how to help me find peace, but he was gone.

And then I looked anew into those five-year-old eyes, and began to truly see my grandson for the first time. A smile rolled across my face, and I was certain that Tuan's eyes were smiling with that twinkle, that childlike sparkle that I had known so many years ago in the time before the French, in the time when a brother and a sister chased each other and laughed about the old lady and her flapping arms.

47

O'BRIEN
7 JUNE 2001
35,000 FEET

I shut my eyes, and before I knew it, our 747 was landing in Truth or Consequences, New Mexico, which was tucked neatly in a valley that was greener than an outsider would expect for this section of the country. To the east and stretching down toward the muddy and meandering Rio Grande, a ridgeline waited patiently for the view to change; eventually, the town with the odd name would disappear, but the ridgeline would continue to celebrate birthdays. In the opposite direction, rolling hills that tried but failed to look picturesque lay just beyond Interstate 25, a black ribbon that worked at mimicking the Rio Grande's journey south to the border with Mexico.

Like most business loops, Truth or Consequences had an ample supply of motels with permanent vacancy signs, and of course, cafés that offered *home cooked* meals because tourists and truckers always feel a little homesick. A feed store, a body shop, a trailer park, a post office building sporting a fully functioning flagpole, and of course, several gas stations, each one offering over-priced gas. As far as small towns are concerned, *typical* would accurately describe the town that proudly sent Angel Reyes off to war.

Although his mother took pleasure in referring to him as her Angel, Reyes gobbled up the name Doc when he became a corpsman. At first he liked his new name because, like a typical teenager, he wanted to develop his own identity, so he left his heavenly name back in New Mexico for safe keeping with his mother since she was so fond of it. Several months into his tour in the Nam, Reyes started to talk about becoming a doctor, or a Mexican Dr. Kildare, as he put it. Although he had only been in the field with the grunts for four months when he had his career epiphany, he told me that he liked the idea of helping people when they were sick or hurt. He had been a *'B'* student in high school, but he realized that medical schools wouldn't be paying attention to him unless he performed at the *'A'* level at the University of New Mexico.

Motivated to succeed, he had only one obstacle: Victor Charlie and his buddies from up North. But he knew they didn't stand a chance for several reasons. Besides the fact that his sister Anna, who died at birth, was his personal guardian angel, Reyes also had two *nannas*, four *tías*, and one *mamá* praying for him on a daily basis. Father Flores, who helped Reyes learn his altar boy version of Latin, had promised to keep him in his prayers. Just in case, Reyes wore two medals, one of Saint Christopher and the other of the Virgin of Guadalupe. He needed all available help since he had a knack for disregarding his own safety during firefights, but that was what made him so special and so respected by the grunts in Charley Company.

Our plane rolls up to the Dairy Queen, and Mrs. Reyes, who doesn't look a day over forty, is sitting in the parking lot in her son's 1950 Ford. She smiles and steps out of the car to greet me. "It's so nice of you to drop in for a visit. My Angel will be so happy to see you. We can drive over to the clinic. He will be very busy, but he will make time to spend a few moments with you before you have to leave. He always speaks so highly of you. You seem to be such a nice young man." Feeling a bit embarrassed, I could only muster up a polite, "Thank you." On the way to her son's clinic, we pass the Hacienda Mexican Restaurant, the Sierra Food and Mercantile, and the Café Rio before we finally turn left and travel several blocks until we reach a concrete block building, which begs for a fresh coat of paint. From the car, I can see Reyes, who has gone to medical school at the University of Arizona and has become a bona fide doctor, talking to one of the scores of patients that fill a large waiting room. I have entered the priesthood, a profession that wasn't even on my top-ten list back in '68 whereas Reyes, the corpsman with a life-long dream, has attained his goal. His mother's eyes sparkle with pride as she escorts me inside to see her son who has his back to us as he speaks with a patient, a little girl with sniffles and two missing front teeth.

When Reyes turns around, his mother begins trembling and sobbing. Standing there frozen, only able to stare, all I want to do is scream like a banshee and dash into the summer heat, back up to the main drag, past all the buildings with their Spanish names, and finally back to the Dairy Queen where I'd order a triple shot of bourbon. Then, I'd wait impatiently for my 747 to taxi down Main Street and extricate me from Truth or Consequences, but Mrs. Reyes is weeping uncontrollably in the waiting room of her son's clinic, and Doc wears a face without a smile, and there is a neat bullet hole in his forehead. In that instant, the heat of the New Mexico summer vanishes along with his mother and her useless tears.

The drizzling rain, only letting up momentarily, splatters off leaves, ponchos, and helmets. Going unnoticed, the lazy-day sound of the pitter-patter of the raindrops gets lost in the chaos of the thud of exploding mortars rounds and grenades, the crackling of small-arms fire, the staccato bursts from the light machine guns. All the sounds of the night ambush competing to be heard. As I'm screaming on the PRC 25 radio, making a firing adjustment that will bring mortar rounds almost on top of our position, the radio ceases to transmit. I'm screaming useless information at the handset. Before my radio operator realizes that his radio has been shot dead, he stops firing his M16, not to fix the radio, but to bleed from his sucking chest wound. Leaving Sartoretti and his flesh wound, Reyes crawls several yards through the mud and over to my radioman Ethridge, who is desperately gasping for air as he drowns on his own blood. Without a radio to call in more mortars, I become just one more rifleman, so I grab my M16 and squeeze off several quick bursts, spraying the area in front of us, where a Viêt Cong machine gun is set up and is pouring in a heavy volume of deadly fire. A silent God sits in the clouds and has taken a siesta. Doc Reyes, praying with all his might, begs for more bandages, bulky ones to soak up blood by the pint, but one last bandage will have to suffice for Ethridge's wound. Before he can place it on Ethridge's bloody chest, Reyes slumps forward, sprawling like one half of a giant cross across my radioman's chest. With his mouth agape, his face buried in the mud, and his back riddled with bullet holes, Reyes lies there, no longer hearing Ethridge's gurgling sounds or his gasps for air. A Việt Cong soldier catches sight of him but not of me. Raindrops splatter in Ethridge's eyes as he peers up into the barrel of the VC's SKS rifle, and in that final instant of lonely terror, in the time it takes one raindrop to slide off his face and drown into the mud, he knows the miracle train won't be pulling into his station. He's lost the dead-man's game. A single bullet enters his forehead neatly, but the blast blows out the back of his skull. With vacant eyes staring up into the rainy blackness, Ethridge stops gasping for air.

I gasped as I was jolted out of my nightmare at 35,000 feet.

48

O'BRIEN
7 JUNE 2001
HOLY TRINITY MONASTERY

Although I felt exhausted because I was operating on East Coast time, I could only muster up occasional yawns as I lay in my bed waiting to nod out. I adjusted my pillow at least a dozen times, eleven more than I should have. If I had still been a smoker, I would have ripped open a new pack of cigarettes. Rather than revisit a repugnant habit that I had abandoned in my twenties, I left my room and walked outside, where the night air was beginning to cool down. A slight breeze rustled through the mesquite and the Palo Verde trees that faithfully stood guard next to my room, which served as an office as well as sleeping quarters. The Spartan lifestyle of the Marine Corps had prepared me well for the monastic life.

A gentle blanket of light from the full moon made it simple for me to stroll over to the Church. As I approached it, I turned and headed toward the bench where Sandburn and I had spoken a week earlier. When I reached it, I stood for a moment and then sat down and sighed. The disinterested moon hovered overhead as I let my mind roam aimlessly. Why had Trent Sandburn confided in me, sharing all of his revelations about the night of the ambush? Had his Porsche become a surrogate for his .357 Magnum once his game of Russian roulette had failed? Could I forgive him for his actions out by Dông Bích? I could, but *would*

I? Why had he put me, his nemesis from the Nam, in charge of his In-Lieu-of-Flowers Fund? Why had he called it the Tohono O'odham Education Fund? After surviving captivity with the NVA, did Baptisto Santos return to the reservation? The questions flowed like a monsoon flash flood, but eventually I wondered about Sandburn's daughters and how they would deal with his death.

Being familiar with the dynamics of the grief process, I began to wonder when Missy, who was not only insightful but had presented such a strong persona on the day that she buried her father, would begin to let down her guard, allowing herself the luxury of a daughter's tears. Odd as it might sound, an insightful nature can become an obstacle for some individuals when they experience a loss.

During my twenties, and even into my thirties, I was the poster child for coping with loss. I understood my pain, but I never allowed myself to express it; I coped with my losses, but I never dealt with the underlying feelings. Several years into my teaching about Søren Kierkegaard's concept of existentialism, I finally began to realize that I had misused my insight by intellectualizing, playing the role of Kierkegaard's abstract intellectual well enough to walk off with an Oscar. I only hoped that Missy would not delude herself as I had done but rather would somehow find the courage to wrestle with the messy emotional demons that were guaranteed to plague her. I peered up at the moon, which was inching its way across the western sky, and asked God, "Please give Missy Sandburn a full moon on her journey through the night."

Although I considered adding on a request for droopy eyelids, I nixed the request since I figured that divine intervention wasn't necessary. I knew that I would eventually feel drowsy enough to fall asleep. Sitting there, my mind drifted off, but this time to Morristown, New Jersey and the doorstep of Colleen MacAndrews, the eighteen-year-old bride and widow of Tom MacAndrews, who managed to get himself killed on his fourth day in the Nam.

As fate would have it, MacAndrews made the mistake of being the recipient of a lucky headshot from a Viêt Cong sniper. As he lay on the rust-colored trail in a puddle of his young and useless blood, he faded out of consciousness despite the desperate pleas from Doc to hang in there long enough for the medevac chopper to arrive and take him away. A typically invincible teenager, he hadn't planned on getting killed. He had planned on writing a reply to every letter his wife would send, but his wife's first letter from the World didn't arrive until he had been dead for five days. He had plans for a non-Motel-6 honeymoon with his new bride when they'd meet in Hawaii for R&R halfway through his thirteen-month tour of duty. Unfortunately for him, the halfway point of his actual tour turned out to be only two days.

The one thing that turned out as MacAndrews had planned was the birth of Thomas, Jr. Unfortunately, he would only know a father through the stories told by his widowed mother, yet he would know the pain of seeing the name of Thomas S. MacAndrews etched in a black granite wall.

The Norman Rockwell quaintness that was Morristown in the summer of '68 did not exist for me for the several hours that I spent trying to console Colleen MacAndrews. There was a part of me that almost didn't stop by her house. Because I thought that my visit might dredge up feelings of loss that she was trying to lay to rest, I reconsidered not stopping to see her, but ultimately, I rang the doorbell, and as it turned out, neither she nor her family had any regrets. Fortunately, my misgivings were unnecessary, but I'd always wondered how life turned out for both Colleen MacAndrews and her son. Although I had resolved to return someday, the time had not yet come, but it would.

Sighing, I looked high into the western sky and beyond the bold brightness of the moon. I only wanted to see the black skyscape with its silver-dollar moon and feel the coolness of the subtle night breezes whispering in the pecan grove, but it had been a Dông Bích night, where the ghosts of '68 had neglected to read the calendar.

49

TUAN
THE PRESENT
HEAVEN

I want to tell her the truth about that night, but my sister has her own journey, which is perfect yet painful. Her suffering is hers. The Buddha's teachings are there for her. Someday she will open her eyes, but first she must open her heart and allow the fresh and healing breeze of compassion and forgiveness to enter and cleanse her of the anger that holds her prisoner to her past. Her suffering will float away on this gentle breeze just as the incense smoke from joss sticks drifts away, as it did when the American Marine lit the three joss sticks on that afternoon just before I was killed. My death was so freeing because I chose compassion over both hate and political dogma when I realized that the Marine I was about to stab with my bayonet wasn't wearing a poncho, and so, I diverted my rifle's thrust. It was in that instant that I decided to carry the American Marine to safety because this man had saved my sister from harm. Had I left him there, he surely would have been shot by Khiem or by another fighter in the Q 16 Company.

Knowing the truth of that night will not open her heart, too long overgrown with the weeds of sorrow and suffering. And even if I could tell her about the last moments of my life, it would change nothing. I would remain her dead brother, and she would find someone else to hate for robbing her of her only brother. My sister's anger and anguish has been a distraction that has clouded her eyes, preventing her from realizing the foolishness of her ways. Because she assumes that the Americans stole my life, she has harbored hatred toward them, and so she stumbles through life, suffering and not truly living. There is such sad irony in the way her story has played out because she has allowed her anger to steal from her the one thing that was taken from me: *life*.

When Khiem fired the shot that sent a bullet tearing into the back of my skull, there was nothing else for me to do but die and enter a new life, one filled with bliss. Unfortunately, my sister has chosen to squander the gift of life that she has. She breathes, but in many ways she is dead to life. My act of compassion toward the Marine who saved her from being raped was both a death sentence and a gift that freed me from my own hatred. I could have just as easily thrust my bayonet into his chest when we overran the American Marines, but I realized who he was and appreciated what he had done. Carrying him down trail could be considered foolish, but it was the right action, and the Buddha says that we must live by right action regardless of the consequences.

The beauty of my current existence is that I do not harbor any resentment toward Khiem for what he did. There is no need for hate and anger because compassion brings serenity. Holding on to his secret only created suffering for him in his own life.

My dear sister, you will have to find peace in your own way and in your own time. Just as was the case in my own life, gentle compassion will be the key that unlocks the door to your heart, allowing you to set yourself free of your suffering. You are beginning to understand that your grandson is part of the answer.

50

O'BRIEN
11 JUNE 2001
INTERSTATE 10 WEST

I had set the cruise control at 75 miles per hour as I headed west on I-10. The traffic, although sparse for an interstate, went unnoticed, as did the array of mountain ranges that squatter in the distance. Had I bothered looking to the south, Elephant Head and the formidable, 9,453-foot Mount Wrightson would have reminded me of my hiking days, which had been sandwiched between the Nam and my life as a priest. A pair of mountain ranges lay north of the highway; the first one to come into sight was the Rincon Range, stretching in a north-south direction until it intersected with the Catalina Mountains, which, as the natural northern boundary for Tucson, extended to the west for at least twelve miles.

My hiking boots had known all three ranges, each one rugged yet serene. The first time that I had ascended to the summit of Mount Wrightson, I met two scary creatures. One, a black bear that I encountered about halfway up, sized me up and decided that I didn't fit the bill for his noon meal. On the narrow trail just below the tree line, I passed a man who was packing a pistol and a pair of steely eyes. Hoping that he wasn't an Arizona version of Robert DeNiro's psychopathic character from *Taxi Driver* who had somehow escaped his celluloid confinement, I stepped up my pace to put distance between him and me. Ahead of me, a steep and unmerciful trail, wound through the final thousand feet of a treeless rock outcropping, which offered no shade, only pain. Ignoring the burning in the sinews of my thighs, I refused to stop to rest until the pistol-packin' hiker had vanished at a bend in the trail.

Finally, having reached the summit but too drained to celebrate my accomplishment, I flung my backpack to the ground as I plopped my exhausted and sweaty body down on a small boulder and drank several gulps of warm but refreshing water. Like the Spanish conquistadors who had roamed this area in search of gold, my eyes gobbled up the panoramic view that stretched to the south for fifty miles into the distant haze that blanketed northern Mexico, but all that lay before me vanished in an instant like a desert mirage.

The vulnerability and the raw fear that had rushed through me when I encountered the man on the trail was a jolting reminder of my Nam experience. The elevator from 8,000 feet had sent me crashing to the rice paddies at sea level. The rarely challenged aphorism, "Time heals all wounds," tumbled down the slopes of Mount Wrightson that day. The Nam, like a hungry pitbull, had sunk its teeth in and had no intention of letting go.

Although eight years hadn't been enough time for me to purge my demons, I had assumed that some semblance of normalcy in my life was just around the bend. Following in the tragic and myopic tradition of the best and the brightest of Kennedy and Johnson advisors who believed that there was light at the end of their metaphorical tunnel, I conned myself into believing that, on my search for emotional closure, the tunnel was short and the glimmer of light was close at hand.

In retrospect, I discovered that I had deluded myself; as it turned out, my own emotional maze, my trauma tunnel system, was deeper and more complex than I dared believe. In many ways, it mirrored the Viêt Cong's skillfully camouflaged Cu Chi tunnel system that meandered undetected for countless miles in a subterranean world. As I descended from the mountain, I grudgingly accepted the difficult role of a tunnel rat, always aware that both light and danger were around every bend. Realizing that eight years above ground hadn't worked, I wondered if the aphorism concerning the power of time on the healing process was only applicable underground.

The Rincon Mountains proved to be less exciting with only an occasional rattlesnake crossing my path. Whenever I was hungry for serenity, I drove to the eastern end of Speedway Boulevard, parked my car, and hiked up Douglas Springs Trail, which meandered for seven or eight miles over several rolling ridgelines, until there was nothing but the sound of a gentle wind, God's voice.

As I would roam aimlessly further away from a distant and disappearing Tucson, the stillness would swallow me up, making it increasingly difficult for me to want to return to my life in the city. Obligation to something, usually my job, always brought me out of the mountains and back to the mundane pettiness of everyday life. Fortunately, the sense of calm that swept over me while I wandered through the Rincon helped me to look inwardly with honesty.

As I peered back at a distant Tucson, the solitude of the wilderness enabled me to recognize my responsibility for any emotional games that I had brought with me. Isolated from the trivial and surrounded only by what Gerard Manley Hopkins called *"God's grandeur,"* I was forced to live in the present moment. I eventually discovered that I wasn't really a backpacker, but rather a solitary pilgrim with no excuses. Once out of the mountains, the implementation of this insight proved to be difficult, but my tenacious nature served me well as I struggled to live in the Zen Time Zone.

51

O'BRIEN
11 JUNE 2001
INTERSTATE 19

Oblivious to the Valencia Road exit that would have sent me due west on a straight shot to the San Xavier del Bac Mission, I remained on I-10 and headed northwest until I realized my error. At the first possible opportunity, I found an exit that took me south on Interstate 19. After several miles, I pulled onto the correct off-ramp for my visit to the mission, which was within sight of the freeway. San Xavier del Bac, with its whitewashed Spanish-colonial architecture made famous by Padre Kino, had been aptly dubbed the "white dove of the desert."

As a Tucson native, I was very familiar with the mission, but I had another connection with it as an adult, and in particular, as a priest. At a spiritual retreat during the early '90s, I had become acquainted with Father Luis Cebadilla, one of San Xavier's two priests. At 6'3" or 6'4", he was easy to spot at a distance. He was a humble man of deep religious convictions and was committed to the well-being of his parishioners. Father Luis had no patience for the pie-in-the-sky approach when it came to caring for his parishioners, most of whom were members of the Tohono O'odham Nation.

During the '80s, Father Cebadilla had been a staunch advocate of liberation theology, which tended to challenge American foreign policy goals in both Central and South

America. The murdered Archbishop Oscar Romero, a victim of the Central American violence during the early Reagan years, was the spiritual Michael Jordan for Father Luis. Likewise, I shared his admiration for Archbishop Romero, the champion of social justice. What intrigued me most about my friend was his balanced approach to life: beyond his tireless commitment to social justice, another dimension lay; he was a pilgrim on a spiritual journey, enthusiastically yet patiently seeking spiritual growth much as Thomas Merton had. Being a Catholic priest was not just a day-job for him.

Upon entering the sanctuary, I spotted him near the altar. When he noticed me, he smiled his signature broad smile and strolled toward me. As far as he was concerned, a handshake was meant for sealing a business deal, so, still smiling, he wrapped his arms around me.

"So nice to see you, but did the monastery throw you out, or did they let you out for the day?" As we walked toward the vestibule of the church, I chuckled at his refreshing sense of humor, a characteristic that he 'blamed' on his father.

"The Grand Inquisitor hasn't figured out a way to excommunicate me yet, so I'm still down at St. David living the wild and crazy monastic life. Prayer, work, prayer, with an extra dose of prayer for good measure. You know the drill, Padre. You just get more social interaction." We laughed in unison at our shared priest-humor.

"So...what actually brings you out to my neck of the desert?" An impish smile rolled across his face as he quipped, "The slot machines at the casino?"

I had an urge to perpetuate this banter with a comment about giving up gambling for Lent, but I resisted since I was operating under time constraints. "I was hoping you'd be able to help me out with a task that I was saddled with about a week ago." He nodded, and I continued to detail my request. "I'm sure you know the workings of the tribal government. Who should I contact to set up an educational scholarship fund?"

"Don't worry, O'Brien. I know just the person." He jotted down the name and phone number of his contact and then handed it to me. "Out of curiosity, how did a monk get hooked into the business of setting up a scholarship fund? That's not part of your job description. Remember, it's prayer, work, prayer."

"I'll give you the brief version. At least I'll make a valiant stab at it. It all started back in Vietnam. A member of my squad, that was virtually wiped out, asked his family to have one of those in-lieu-of-flowers accounts set up in the event of his death. Just after he visited me about a week and a half ago, he died in a car accident near the monastery. He was doing at least a hundred when he rolled his Porsche."

Before I could finish my story, Father Luis interjected an unexpected question. "Porsche? A red Porsche?"

Baffled by his lucky guess about the car's color, I replied, "Are you psychic or something?"

"Not really, but about a week and a half ago, a man in his early fifties showed up here and handed me a check for ten thousand dollars. Told me to make sure it went for something useful for people on the reservation. If my memory serves me correctly, he was about six feet tall...some gray hair, and he needed a shave. One other thing...he drove off in a new looking, red sports car . He just handed me the check and disappeared from sight as fast as he'd appeared."

In an almost inaudible voice, I muttered, "Trent Sandburn."

Father Luis, although befuddled, paused for only a moment to utter, "Hmm," before continuing, "That's the name. Trent Sandburn. That was one strange afternoon. Besides giving me a check for ten thousand dollars, which was just a bit peculiar, I remember his response when I asked if he wanted to light a candle. *'What for?'* was his reply."

As I stood in the coolness of the mission, the image of the candle, which I had lit for Trent back at the monastery, floated through my mind. Like the candle's flickering flame that refused to stand still, the answer to the enigma that was Trent Sandburn defiantly refused to stand at attention so I could see it with clarity. The combination of time and my tenacious nature would hopefully generate the answer, but for now, there were only two certainties: Trent Sandburn was dead but definitely not gone.

52

O'BRIEN
16 JUNE 2001
TOHONO O'ODHAM NATION

No strokes of ruby-red or sapphire-blue splashed across the eastern sky. The morning would have to make do with baby colors; on a blanket of powder blue, varying shades of pastel-pink drifted subtly like ethereal ribbons, outstretched until, like a halo, they owned the morning sky. Behind me lay a quickly forgotten, forty-mile stretch of I-10 that brought me to Tucson's Westside, the corridor to the Tohono O'odham Nation.

Just outside the city limits, the Ajo Highway, a two-lane road with a number, meandered in a westerly direction across Pima County. No one drove the posted speed limit of 55 miles per hour; occasionally, a clunker rolling along at five miles per hour under the speed limit would raise the blood pressure of the at-least-15-miles-per-hour-over drivers, who braved the odds as they passed. Of course, they failed to notice the eighteen memorial crosses that decorated the first eighty miles of the highway.

Barely visible, the final vestige of the morning's sunrise lingered long enough for me to take notice before disappearing behind me as I approached Three Points, which was about twenty minutes west of Tucson. Even with the help of a sign that warned traffic to slow down to 45 miles per hour, the complete tour of the town lasted only a half-minute or so. Just west of

Three Points, a cotton farm hugged the highway, and beyond it to the north lay the Roskruge Mountains, which were tall enough to be noticed but were strictly minor league when compared to the Rincons or the Santa Catalina Mountains. Continuing southwest on Highway 86 for a few more miles, I finally entered the Tohono O'odham Nation. As I approached the exit to Highway 386, which leads to Kitt Peak Observatory, I spotted the Baboquivari Mountains, a range that stretches to the Mexican border and forms most of the eastern boundary of the Tohono O'odham Nation. Nestled in the center of the range and easily visible in the distance is Waw Kiwulik, better known to outsiders as Baboquivari Peak, which is the sacred home of I'itoi, the god of creation.

The seemingly endless highway continued to stretch west but couldn't resist the temptation to veer to the southwest until it became fickle and began heading northwest as it ran through the town of Sells. Although a traffic sign slowed me down, Sells didn't provide me with a reason to do anything but glance from side to side, once. Sells, an island of blandness in a verdant sea of desert trees and cacti, didn't stand a chance against the competition.

To make matters worse, the highway in the vicinity of Sells was lined on both sides by a forest of tall desert grasses speckled with a kaleidoscope of summer colors: bright orange, yellow, white and purple. Like a sidewalk for the wind, the blanket of green swayed at the whim of the traffic racing by. Even the thick clumps of grass, crowned with either brown or beige cattails, easily drew me away from the blackish-gray monotony of the road and its yellow stripes. Just beyond the grass dappled with wildflowers was a wide enough array of desert plants to hold a convention. The Palo Verde and mesquite trees, some of them at least twenty feet tall and many infested with mistletoe that hung like giant hornets' nests, towered over the creosote bushes and teddy bear cholla cacti. Interspersed among the taller jumping chollas and the majestic saguaros were a few lonely ocotillos, each one enthusiastically raising its lanky arms to the sky like Amen-shouters at a Bible-belt revival meeting. On either side of the road, rust-colored hills flecked with splashes of green stared back at me. Occasionally, through the desert's green blanket, peaks sprouted up, boldly brandishing a volcanic appearance, and my eyes didn't have to wander far in any direction before spotting a mountain range with its layers of muted colors: shades of green, lavender, and blue.

Just before I was to turn north on Tribal Route 15, the flashing lights of an SUV jolted me back to my road reality. The tribal police seemed to have more pressing business elsewhere, so they were uninterested in pulling me over for driving five miles per hour over the speed limit. I had long since stopped noticing whether there were any Border Patrol vehicles hidden at strategic points along the highway. Just as I had done with Three Points and Sells, I had blotted them out. Had I continued gobbling up the scenery, I easily might have missed the turn off at the Gu Achi Trading Post and would have eventually ended up in town of Ajo, which means garlic in Spanish. On the bright side, I would have been safe from vampires there. I easily spotted the sign that pointed north to Santa Rosa, the home of Baptisto Santos, so the Ajo scenario never materialized.

As I turned north on Tribal Route 15, the sight of one more memorial cross greeted me immediately, and just beyond it gang graffiti sprawled across several road signs. The lyrics of Simon and Garfunkel's "Sounds of Silence" reverberated though my mind. Simon and Garfunkel's prophets had moved west to the Sonoran Desert to scribble their message of alienation and pain, not on the subway walls and tenement halls of the song, but on the road signs on a quiet section of an Arizona road, one that originated in Dông Bích more than thirty-three years earlier.

Along the final twelve miles to Santos's village, I spotted what appeared to be a towering, white chess pawn that seemed suited for the chess-playing needs of King Kong or Godzilla. This odd-shaped object, so aesthetically out of place, turned out to be the largest water tower I had ever seen. When I passed by it, the white change to beige, and it began to resemble the world's tallest mushroom. Whatever it was, I left it behind as I pulled into Santa Rosa.

53

O'BRIEN
16 JUNE 2001
BAPTISTO SANTOS'S HOUSE

Although I had gained confidence over the years, my stomach began to experience the nervous feeling that had been all too common when I had to do an oral presentation during my high school days. I pulled up in front of a simple, rectangular-shaped house with a pitched roof, which was typical of the housing design that the Bureau of Indian Affairs provided on most reservations in Arizona.

As I walked past a white Ford pickup, probably from the late '80s, I sucked in an extra dose of calming air. Would we recognize each other after more than three decades? What would we say to each other since so much had changed? Santos and I were the sole survivors of that life-altering night out by Dông Bích, so there would be no turning back for me. I knocked twice, and Santos, sporting the expected gray, shoulder-length hair, opened the door and smiled gently as he leaned forward to embrace me.

"It's been a long time, O'Brien. Too damn long."

Leaving the June heat and my apprehension behind, I nodded and followed him inside. Before sitting down in his living room, he offered me a cold soda. "Sure, I'll take a Coke."

Upon returning with my soda, he headed toward a dark-brown couch and then motioned to me to sit in an over-stuffed chair opposite it. A collage of framed photographs, the pieces in the puzzle of his past, covered much of the wall behind him. The spectrum of pictures, mainly black and whites, ranged from school and Marine Corps to family. Clustered together, off to one side, were three group photos: one of the 1966 graduating class of the Phoenix Indian School, and two others, both from his time in the Marine Corps. An array of family photographs filled up the rest of the wall. Captured in color, his wife, children, and grandchildren smiled politely across the room. The Santos tradition of serving in the military was apparent from four black-and-white pictures of relatives who had served during World War II and the Korean War. The wall behind Santos spoke volumes, but I was eager to discover how his life had unfolded since the night of his capture thirty-three years earlier.

Taking a sip from his Sprite, he then rested it on his lap. Wearing just a hint of a smile, he chuckled as he shook his head back and forth and said, "A priest. You went from calling in fire missions to hearing confessions."

We both smiled. "One thing's for sure...you haven't lost your sense of humor. Actually, it wasn't quite that simple. I went to the U of A, and I got a teaching job in Tucson. A lot of the time, I felt like a salesman who got stuck with the job of selling C-rations to the troopies in the Nam. Have you ever tried to sell a teenager on the importance of semicolons, metaphors, five-act tragedies, and research papers...all their favorites? It was a challenge. Most of the time, I felt like I was a dentist pullin' teeth...actually, just some of the time. But I haven't worked in the good old knowledge factory since the early '80s. Right now, I'm living outside of St. David at a monastery, and I love it there."

"So...you pretty much stayed in the Tucson area. I didn't travel too far from home either, except for the year I lived in Casa Grande."

An uncomfortable feeling rolled through me, but with a sigh I admitted that I hadn't tried to find out if he had survived the Nam. I was uncertain about his Missing In Action status. Fear won that round, and grief loitered, unwanted, dancing mockingly in my heart back in the summer of '68. The hippies had their summer of love; I would've settled for the summer of nothing, a summer sans tears. And so, I settled for just not knowing, but there was a smidgen of long-shot hope that Santos had somehow made it out of the Nam alive. In typical fashion, Santos just said, "Don't feel bad." The smile on my face paled in comparison to the smile in my heart. Karma had done its job well.

"I finally mustered up the courage to look you up, but it seems my timing was off. You were in Casa Grande when I came out here to find you...but you were gone and no one knew exactly where. Just said you had gone to the city to find work."

"I tried Phoenix at first, but without any luck. Finally I found a job in Casa Grande. It sure wasn't very friendly up there."

Then, living up to his trademark honesty, he admitted that, after moving up to Casa Grande about a year after he finished his enlistment in '71, he was one pissed-off Indian, as he put it. Without exception, whenever he'd enter a bar, he'd instigate a fight within ten minutes. Although being drunk was not a prerequisite, alcohol had not been a stranger in his life.

A few inches shorter than I, Santos, who had a wiry build and was only 5'7", had starred as a point guard in high school and was fearless, or maybe stupid, as he later realized. But back in the early '70s, he had taken great pride in the fact that he had only lost once, a fight against three cowboys and their two-by-four. The third cowboy and his piece of lumber were just too much for him that night, but the other two gave up chewing tobacco for a day or two. He drank and brawled his way through the 1970s and into the early '80s. In retrospect, he had discovered that the culprit for his behavior wasn't his youth, but rather it was the intense anger that had consumed him.

"I can relate to everything you've said about anger. I didn't get into fights...well, maybe one, but I was jam-packed with anger for a long time. It wasn't pretty."

Santos, nodding his concurrence, added. "It's so easy to be dumb when you're young. Honestly, being young just made it easier to stay that way. I was one angry Indian back then. I never want my life to be like that again. It was a fucking nightmare. I just thank the Man up stairs that my wife stayed with me. She's a special woman. I'm so..." Having realized that he'd used "*fucking*" to describe his years of anger, Santos, feeling embarrassed, hesitated and then continued, "Sorry about my language, but I forgot for a moment that you're a priest now. I only knew you as a Marine, and you do remember how we used to talk back then."

"Santos, don't sweat it. Fucking nightmare sounds like a pretty good way to describe that time in your life." Then, speaking in a voice that seemed to resonate with solemnity, I said, "For your penance, do fifty push-ups the Marine Corps way, maggot." With this juxtaposition of two never-to-be-forgotten mantras, we simultaneously burst into laughter. For a moment, O'Brien, the priest and Santos, the former POW, found it irresistible to act like a pair of adolescent boys. Hopefully, God, well-known to every student of a Catholic catechism for being all-knowing and all-powerful, also possessed a sense of humor.

After our laughter morphed into a pair of impish smiles, I returned to the issue of anger, which had played a prominent role in each of our lives. "When you spoke of your anger...well, that reminded me of something. When I was an English teacher, I used to hate it when students had unrealistic expectations of me. Misspell a word...no way. Whenever they asked a question in class, I felt like I had to always have the answer. The myth of perfection...that's what life was like as an English teacher. In many ways, being a priest is the same way. You had your expectation of me as a priest, and we had a good laugh about it. I even do it to myself even though I know that being a priest doesn't equate to being perfect. Intellectually, I know this, but still I buy into the myth. For example, over the past several weeks, I've been wrestling with some anger. Let's not mince words...fucking pissed is better way to describe what I've been feeling."

Santos leaned forward. "Pissed off? Life not so good at the monastery?"

Wondering if I should explain, I hesitated. Ever since I had contacted Santos several days earlier, I vacillated about broaching the subject of Sandburn, which had never come up during our phone conversation. At first, it seemed sensible to believe that the events of the night of his capture had certainly guaranteed that Santos still retained vivid and negative memories of Sandburn. This, however, was merely conjecture since I wasn't certain if Santos knew that Sandburn had fallen asleep on watch and then had been cowering and watching as the NVA took him away. Although, in several ways, Sandburn was a sleeping dog that I should have let lie, I followed my instinct about Santos. "Sandburn. You remember him?" Of course he did. I felt about three miles past stupid the instant my question rolled off my lips.

Speaking softly, as was usual for Santos, he replied in an unwavering voice, "Oh yeah. I'll never forget that guy. He was an asshole, but just so long as he didn't get in my way, well...I didn't much care if he wanted to be an idiot. I will tell you though...I came damn close to ripping his throat out once. You probably don't remember that time I was telling you and Nellis about the dream I had a little bit before Tết."

Before he could continue, I interrupted, "Don't know why, but I never forgot that night you told us your dream."

Santos continued, "I didn't care that he didn't believe my dream, but when he decided to call me *Chukut*, that pissed me off. Had I just gotten a Dear-John letter, I probably would have jumped him and rearranged his face. Yeah, I remember him, especially since we had watch together the night the NVA captured me. Speaking of that...who survived the ambush? Webster? Nellis? Any of the new guys? I'm figuring Sandburn didn't make it since I didn't notice him at all once the firefight began. So, who made it?"

I wanted to plead the Fifth, start a new paragraph, and come down with an instant and expedient bout of dementia; anything but answer his questions. But there would be no *deus ex machina* solution for me; the Greek gods had signed off on this one. Wrapped in my discomfort, I was on my own as I stared past Santos. I was drawn to what seemed to be a recent family portrait; each of his three children looked older than any of the men in our squad. Even Nellis, who at twenty-three was affectionately known as "Pops", was a baby-san compared to the Santos children. I remained mesmerized until Santos repeated my name twice. I apologized and then said with a sadness in my voice, "You and I and Sandburn...no one else...that's it, but..."

Wearing an unwanted expression that straddled shock and

resignation, Santos responded, "That's it?" A part of me felt relieved that Santos had interjected his question before I could explain that, due to Sandburn's recent death, we were the only surviving members of our ill-fated squad.

Almost inaudibly, I uttered, "Yeah." Then, without intention on our part, the dead got their moment of silence. As Santos, with his hands cupped over his mouth, sighed deeply, his gaze rolled across the room, beyond the living room wall and into a montage of memories made fresh. It was as if he were staring into a kaleidoscope of the terror of that night. Behind his stare, the acrid smell of smoke swirled about as the concussion of grenade and mortar rounds echoed in his ears; shivering from the chilly February rain, he scurried from one position to another as tracer rounds sliced up the blackness all around him. Like a pulsating strobe light from below Dante's Ninth Circle of Hell, the forever-young faces of Webster, Nellis, Reyes, and all the others flashed through the landscape of his mind, and then the sound of single gunshots rang out in his head.

When Santos sighed again, he looked toward me and said, "I had hoped for something better, maybe that's why I never made it to the Wall in D.C....didn't want to see their names...had to hold onto some hope that more guys had made it out alive. Damn."

The room was filled only with the erratic, humming sound of an oscillating fan. For a minute or two, my words were trapped like fogged-in planes waiting patiently on the tarmac. Finally, I said, "All we knew back in the Nam was that you were MIA. I made it to the Wall. That's how I found out that had you survived. That was back in the early '80s, but it took me forever to finally get in touch with you. I'm not exactly sure why, but...I think I was scared. Of what?...I don't know." I wanted to ask Santos about his life as a prisoner of war, but I was leery of broaching the subject, so I asked, "Do you want to know about Sandburn?"

Not quite sure what to make of my question, Santos ignored it and asked his own question. "I'm kinda curious. How did you track me down...and why did you, after all these years, finally try to find me?"

"Sandburn. He's the catalyst, so I guess I'll tell you his

rather bizarre tale."

Santos nodded for me to go ahead, so I began to peel away each layer of Sandburn's story. Santos's eyebrows scrunched up each time I revealed a new detail about the night of the ambush. Behind his contorted expressions lay both anger and bewilderment. He seemed especially baffled when I told him of Sandburn's behavior just before his death. Initially, this answer seemed too pat, but Santos deduced that guilt was the motivating force behind Sandburn's gift of a ten thousand dollar check he had given to Father Cebadilla at San Xavier del Bac. Santos, who had learned to be pragmatic during his life as a prisoner of war, concluded that, regardless of Sandburn's motive, some good would come from the initial gift and the money that the in-lieu-of-flowers fund would generate.

Finally, after at least a half an hour, I drew the story to a close by saying, "We're it, Santos. I don't have a clue why we survived, but I sense there's a reason for that. When I used to be an English teacher, I taught *Hamlet*. There's one line in the play that definitely fits: 'there's a special providence in the fall of a sparrow.' Maybe someday, we'll understand the reason you and I made it out of the Nam alive. Life is so clear in a rearview mirror." Santos shook his head in agreement as I continued, "I discovered that God has always guided me during my entire life...although it took me many years to finally come to this realization."

As I looked across at Santos, he leaned forward in what turned out to be a gesture of trust. "I'm glad I'm not a kid any more. Growing up has helped me just like it helped you. When I was younger, I would have killed Sandburn if I had found out about him sleeping on watch. Don't get me wrong...just like you, I'm pissed off at that son of a bitch, but he's dead, and I'm too old for any more violence...had my share of it. Maybe some good can come from the scholarship money he left."

"I sure hope so. Something positive has to come from that night." While speaking those words, I realized that I had left Sandburn's Silver Star in the car. I excused myself and quickly retrieved the medal. Upon returning, I handed it to a perplexed Santos and said, "Based on what Sandburn told me, if there's anyone who deserves a medal for that night, you do."

Without any hesitation, Santos leaned forward and handed it back to me. The man whose living room was crowded almost to the point of clutter with sports trophies was not in the least bit interested in receiving any recognition for his heroism the night of the ambush. We both knew that receiving a medal didn't prove anything. The way we saw it, we didn't need an officer to tell us if we had been good Marines or if we had exhibited courage. Santos summed it up with a self-deprecating response. "Just doin' my job. All in a day's work."

He was right, but the question of what to do with the Silver Star lingered; it was a medal without a home, but that was quickly solved when a rain cloud of inspiration drenched Santos with a desert epiphany, which he then shared with me. The medal, tainted by Sandburn's lie, belonged to no one individual, but rather to those who had sacrificed their lives that night out by Dông Bích. The solution to our dilemma was close by, so we drove east across the floodplain that surrounded Santa Rosa until we arrived at a sacred Tohono O'odham site, which they called A'al Hihi'añ, the Children's Shrine.

When Santos explained the origin of the site, it became apparent why he had chosen this place for the Silver Star. According to Tohono O'odham tradition, four children were sacrificed at this spot to prevent a great flood from destroying their land. The people, believing that their children were their most valuable possession, offered them in sacrifice, and thus, they succeeded in saving their world. Consequently, the tradition of placing gifts at the shrine sprung up.

Unlike the giant water tower that stood guard on the outskirts of Santa Rosa, the Children's Shrine was subtle and simple; in the realm of monuments, words like ostentatious or ornate simply didn't fit this small mound of rocks, maybe two feet tall, which was surrounded by a semi-circle of dead ocotillo branches which reached up to the sky.

We approached the cairn and stopped. As we stood there, I peered down at the Silver Star that rested in the sweaty palm of my hand. Santos, carrying an eagle's feather in his right hand, brushed it across the medal, and then, turning the medal over, he repeated the ritual. Having done this, he motioned to me to set the Silver Star down on the mound of rocks in front of us. "It's our custom to leave a gift of value just as our ancestors did so they could save the world. I think this is the right gift to leave, but first I needed to purify it, as is our custom."

A gentle wind whistled through the ocotillo stalks as Santos and I stood with our eyes transfixed on the medal; it had finally found a fitting home.

When we returned to his house, Santos, without any coaxing on my part, volunteered to share his experience as a POW. "The first night was the worst. Not the physical part but the psychological part. You recall that first day in boot camp, right? The shock of something so different happening so abruptly. Just like the night of the ambush. One minute I'm hauling ass off the hill...the next, I'm flat on my back. My whole world got turned upside-down the instant the NVA knocked me down with his rifle butt. I had a headache that wouldn't quit, but that was the least of my worries."

Because the NVA were well aware that a reaction force was on its way to the ambush site, they understood the urgency of leaving the area immediately. The NVA frequently lingered in the area of a night ambush, anticipating a reaction force, which they also would ambush; a two-for-one special.

For whatever reason, the NVA's sole interest was escaping with their prisoner, a radioman. For prisoners, survival could depend on the whim of the captors. A prisoner like Santos might be perceived as having some value because he was a radio operator. The NVA might have believed that, with some unfriendly persuasion, Santos might provide them with radio codes or other valuable information. Whatever their rationale, Santos was grateful that they found him valuable enough to keep alive. Unfortunately for the NVA, Santos turned out to be uncooperative, which he suffered for until his escape.

Santos, who had filed away these traumatic experiences under *ancient history*, continued his narrative with uncommon clarity. Written indelibly in his memory and seared there forever, the events from thirty-three years ago rolled off his tongue like they had happened yesterday. "Running with my hands tied behind my back...at night and in the rain...that really sucks. Running down the hill, I tripped and fell twice. One of the NVA kicked me in the ribs the first time, and I broke my nose the second time I fell. Trying to breath with a bunch of blood streaming out of my nose, well, you can figure out how much fun that was."

The initial events of his capture had happened at a breakneck pace, probably in the first five or ten minutes. Once they descended from the hill behind Dông Bích, they started heading south through rice paddy country, but they didn't get far before they heard the reaction force as it headed in Santos's direction. The half dozen NVA knew they were outnumbered, so they crouched like granite statues behind a rice paddy dike. The NVA had taken away Santos's poncho, so he was shivering from the drizzling rain, and being drenched from lying in the paddy water further exacerbated his condition.

When the reaction force approached within forty or fifty meters of the NVA and Santos, he rolled over on his back and attempted to draw the attention of the reaction force by kicking the water frenetically. By flailing his legs in the rice paddy water, Santos succeeded, but only partially. Both the NVA and the reaction force responded: the Marine squad fired several bursts from their M16s and tossed several grenades in the vicinity of the noise, and an NVA soldier next to Santos punched him in the ear. For good measure, the NVA who was next to him also stuck his bayonet under Santos's jaw, pressing it almost to the point of breaking the skin. "That convinced me, at least for the time being, to not make any more noise."

Once the reaction force had passed by them and was a safe distance away, one of the NVA soldiers unbound Santos's hands. A surge of compassion hadn't transformed him, but rather his motivation was pragmatic. One of Santos's captors had sustained a leg wound from one of the grenades that had been hurled their way, so the NVA, keenly aware of the importance of leaving the immediate area post haste, 'volunteered' the services of Santos, who instantly became the NVA's version of a medevac chopper.

"We kept heading south...fast. The good news was that I didn't have my hands tied any more, but doing a fireman's carry for several thousand meters wasn't much fun. Looking back on that night, I hate to admit it but those NVA had great fire discipline, and they could sure haul ass."

Although mesmerized by his story, I nodded and interjected,

"You're preaching to the choir. The NVA were tough customers. No ifs, ands, or buts about that."

"So, we headed towards Phuóc Ninh (6) and eventually ended up in the western part of Charlie Ridge. We did some serious humpin' though some rugged-ass mountains before all was said and done. I finally ended up in Laos, but I was stuck with these guys for a while before I ended up there."

"Wow. Did you return with all the other POWs in '73?"

"Actually, it was in '68, about six months after I was captured...early August. Being a prisoner was bad news, so I knew I couldn't wait around for the politicians to get me released. My first attempt back in the rice paddies didn't work too good, but that didn't stop me from finally being successful. Even when I finally escaped, it took me just about a week of evasion before I slipped out of Laos and got spotted by a chopper. Crazy world when your goal is to get yourself to Vietnam, especially when you know what it's like there."

Santos gobbled up his opportunity to give a voice to his traumatic experience which he had buried three decades earlier. For the most part, Santos was subdued and soft-spoken as he spent at least another two hours detailing the events that had helped to define his adult life. On two occasions, he felt compelled to pause to regain his composure. In both cases, he revealed how his NVA captors had demonstrated their capacity for sadistic behavior.

The incident that seemed to affect him the most was one that dealt with another POW, a Green Beret who had been a prisoner for more than a year. It took Santos more than a decade of barroom brawls in Southern Arizona for his epiphany to occur; responsible for breaking more noses and jaws than he could remember, Santos needed surrogates to satisfy his need for revenge against a particularly malicious NVA officer. *Loathing* and *revulsion*, SAT-words for college boys, fell a thousand miles short of describing the depth of hatred Santos harbored for this particular officer. Hate, a succinct one-syllable feeling, had coursed through his veins for almost a dozen years.

Leaving the Nam had turned out to be more difficult than he'd expected: twelve years of rage finally had ceased when he released his grip on the throat of a stunned cowboy. Baffled yet thankful, the cowboy struggled to his feet, wiped away the blood that covered his nose and mouth, and, feeling a surge of foolish bravado, taunted Santos who slammed the bar door behind him.

Later that night, surrounded by his childhood friends, the mesquite and saguaro, Santos—realizing how close he'd come to killing the man in the bar—became a coyote, howling from deep within his anguished heart. Twelve years of hate had taken its toll; having known nothing else for so long, exhausted, he finally ached for peace. To his surprise, both I'itoi and his Catholic God had been listening after all, hearing his cries for help and seeing his tears that soaked into the desert soil. As Santos lay there, curled up in the fetal position, a cool and gentle breeze floated through the desert darkness.

The sultry mountain jungle knew no cool and gentle breezes. Even though the other prisoner, a twenty-seven-year-old Captain from Little Rock, Arkansas, had conscientiously prayed for a miracle, God seemed to ignore his requests. Initially, he prayed for his freedom, but as he drifted into a downward spiral due to malaria and dysentery, he began to settle for a mundane miracle: fresh water for the main course and a cool wisp of air for dessert. Hidden beneath a dense canopy which seemed to shield God from his Baptist prayers, the Captain lay, waiting for the inevitable.

No longer an asset, the Captain had become expendable, so the officer, who Santos reviled, hatched the idea of breaking the seriously-ill Green Beret's arms and legs and then placing him within a few meters of one of the NVA bunkers. Incapable of escape, he eventually became the focal point of an ethical dilemma for the Marine platoon that attacked the entrenched NVA position. In the end, the Marines chose to open fire on the helpless Green Beret so he wouldn't have to watch as a napalm canister, an unfriendly gift from a Marine jet, tumbled gracefully towards him. For him, death had become as certain as a sunset; the only part of the equation that remained was the method.

Santos watched from a near-by bunker as a single rifle shot to the forehead freed the Captain from his final terror. In that instant, the Green Beret had escaped the Nam and had been relieved of all his pain, but that was not the case for Santos. After so many years, Santos finally stopped hating the NVA officer who received his karma compliments of Dow Chemical, but the memory of that day had seared his heart.

Even with hands cupped over his eyes, he could not hide the tears which streamed down his face. Santos struggled to sob silently, and then he muttered in an apologetic tone, "Sorry, I didn't mean..."

I interrupted to offer him reassurance. "Don't worry about it, Santos." I thought about telling him that we both knew that the desert needs rain, and that God gives the desert the summer rains just as He gives us tears to help us heal our wounds. This metaphor remained parked in my mind; Santos needed my support more than he needed a poetic perspective. Although he wiped his eyes with the palms of his hands, a stubborn layer of tears lingered, but a subtle smile inched across his face. He sighed and continued his story.

I felt honored that Santos had invited me on his painful journey through a dark landscape, where the magic of memory can destroy or purify. As I listened intently, it became apparent that the essential core of Santos, the gift of tenacity that he had received from his parents and grandparents, had sustained him through his ordeal as a prisoner of war. What impressed me even more about this man of character was his willingness to continue his struggle upon his return home. Although his early years back in the World were wrought with self-destructive behaviors, his tenacious nature bought him the necessary time to gain the wisdom that seemed to permeate his current life.

The characteristically bright afternoon light began to soften as it always did with the first hint of the daily changing of the guard. As the afternoon's good-bye began to stretch across a soon-to-be-mottled sky, we said our good-byes; we both knew that they would not be our last.

My recent life had turned into a line from a famous Willie Nelson song: "On the road again." Such a lifestyle would have been more befitting of a much younger version of me. The events of the past seventeen days had monkey-wrenched my monastic life, but I hoped for an understanding God who realized the importance of two Marines being there for each other; *esprit de corps* was more than just a catchy phrase.

Leaving Route 15 behind, I headed east and shortly passed a

sign that read: Quijotoa, which means *mountain shaped like a carrying basket.* I chuckled as I thought about how large that sign would have been if the English-only people had their way. Then I recalled Santos telling me about his second month in the Nam, the time before he had become a radio operator. Although, at the time, he didn't admit that he was terrified, the older Santos found it easy to admit and found some humor in his solution to his Fuckin' New Guy fear. On every day patrol, night ambush, or operation, Santos brought what he referred to as his life insurance policy, which consisted of two bandoliers of M16 ammo, three clips of .45 caliber rounds, four fragmentation grenades, and twenty-four M79 rounds, with each round packing the explosive power of a grenade.

I burst into laughter once again as I recalled Santos's observation: "Didn't think about it at the time, but one lucky shot from a sniper and I would've blown up." For a moment, my sense of humor was back, but it quickly evaporated when I spotted a cumulus cloud hanging like a giant white ornament in the distant eastern sky. The billowy plume which decorated the late afternoon sky was just one more cloud for the casual observer, but for me it was the smoke from a bombing run on a ridgeline in a place called the Nam.

Unwelcome, yet still there, images of Santos's POW experience ping-ponged through my mind as the mountains, with their various coats of purple, glided by unnoticed, while the cruise control ran the show. The mesquite, Palo Verde, and a litany of cacti—ranging from the smallest hedgehog cactus to the towering and stately saguaro—raced by, but the only landscape that existed for me were the mountains of Vietnam, NVA turf.

Santos, rain-soaked and shivering, begins to slow down as he and the six NVA begin their ascent into the safety of Charlie Ridge. Burdened by the weight of the wounded NVA, Santos begins to stumble. Thoughts race through his mind. Will they hit him again if he falls or slows down? Don't they care that the blood from his broken nose is making his breathing even more labored? In his last lucid moment before numbness washes through his mind, he reminds himself that his nose and the blood that's trickling from it don't matter to these his captors. Getting back to their base camp at the western end of Charlie Ridge is all that matters. His heart is pounding too fast for him to think; mental clarity, yesterday's luxury, is gone, so Santos, huffing and puffing, reaches deep inside to find the strength to keep moving, not because he wants to, but because they have automatic weapons. Then, in the darkness and the steady drizzle, his pain evaporates. The burning in the sinews of his shins and thighs disappears. The aching in the small of his back and the tightness in the back of his neck disappear; the blood seeping down his throat from his broken nose disappears; the throbbing pain, pounding its unwelcome rhythm on his forehead disappears, and the double-time thumping of his heavy heart disappears.

The sound of the wind rushes by Santos as he soars, his wings spread as he glides above the rice paddies and on to the South China Sea. In a magical instant, the Pacific is only a pond on the way to the world of the Desert People, the land of the mesquite and the saguaro, the sacred place where I'itoi dwells. The summer scent of monsoon rain dances though the air as Waw Kiwulik, I'itoi's cloud-draped home, draws Santos on, until he finally swoops down onto the sacred peak. Santos is home.

I had left my laughter back at Quijotoa; leaving Baptisto Santos back at Santa Rosa was proving to be difficult if not impossible. I wanted peace, but my wishes didn't seem to matter. I wanted to believe that I was a Catholic priest driving east on Highway 86; I was wrong. I was a boxer, standing long enough in a ring to be clobbered with an uppercut that lifted me off my feet, sending me crashing to the canvas. The summer rains were starting early for me as I rushed back to the safety of the monastery at St. David. Gulping hard, I wiped away the tears that were rolling down my face. I sighed and wanted to be an eagle, gliding effortlessly above the fray.

Highway 86 had become nothing more than a gauntlet where yesteryear's memories ambushed me without mercy. I longed for the simpler life, the monastic life during the month of May, in that simpler time before Sandburn had decided to complicate the lives of those around him once again. Having never had an affinity for taking the easy route, I opted not to hate him, but I owed Sandburn a heavy barrage of anger.

54

CHARLIE'S SISTER
15 JULY 2001
THE DREAM

Closing my eyes, the lessons that I would teach in the morning marched across my mind. There was much excellence in my teaching because I loved my students, but I still felt an emptiness; and tonight, there was a great uneasiness in my chest. My husband was right; I needed rest.

In the distance, the blurry figure of a man standing in front of a mirror the size of an elephant...in the background, a rainbow with stripes of purple, white, and green...my hair is black and flowing down my back, and the gray is only a memory...flowers line the path as I approach the man...many of these flowers I've never seen before, but oddly, they seem familiar in a way that I don't understand...the long-stems of common yarrow are capped with a clump of tiny white flowers...the green, purple and pink colors of basil stare up at me, and its pungent, spicy aroma draws me close, yet I also feel repulsion as I speed up my pace to escape the source of this feeling...and in the distance the man is now standing behind a wheel with eight spokes and is looking through it, but I still can't recognize the image, his face, so I continue walking hesitantly toward him...more flowers along the path...on the opposite side of the path is a clump of Birdsfoot Trefoil flowers, standing knee-high and sporting yellow flower-heads with red streaks...a smoky scent wafts across the path from a single stalk of Dogsbane, crowned with a lavender blossom...then, mixed together in a rainbow of colors, mimic orchids and snapdragons, followed by yellow and orange marigolds with their pungent scent which surround the path...moving further along, a bunch of white, lavender and pink Mourning Bride flowers, standing waist-high, brush against me as I pass by...and the path disappears into a field of Whin flowers, yellow as far as I can see, and I stumble and fall...and, then, standing in front of me is my brother Tuan...behind him are three paths that cut through the Whin flowers, and a wheel with eight spokes is just behind him...even farther back, the mirror stares at me, but I can only see the frame around it...and hovering in the air above the wheel is a blind man with a cane, a potter kneading clay, a small house with six shuttered windows and a closed door, a woman with an arrow in her eye, and two people carrying a corpse on a stretcher...as Tuan smiles, my mother and my father appear from behind the wheel...all are smiling...each is holding a burning joss stick in one hand and a flower in the other...my mother offers me her joss stick and a flowering reed...my father presents me with his joss stick and a lavender water willow flower...my brother Tuan hands me his joss stick and branch of allspice...the aroma of the flowers mixes with the intoxicating scent of the burning joss sticks...the incense smoke bending and swaying aimlessly around me, enveloping us...looking down, I see an unopened white lotus flower resting in my hands, and on the ground is a small shovel, and it smiles at me...next to it sits a small alabaster jar...stooping down, I reach to touch it, but it moves away from me with each attempt...a tear rolls off my cheek and lands on the jar...I reach out and touch it.

Awake in the blackness that surrounded me, the images of my dream raced through my mind and my heart pounded rapidly, shattering the stillness. Next to me, my husband, such a good man, was in his own dream world; and An Toán, my grandson, slept soundly, unlike my brother and I had during our wars of liberation. The fight was worth it—for my sons, for my grandson, for all the children of our beloved Việt Nam.

55

O'BRIEN
17 JULY 2001
HOLY TRINITY MONASTERY

A Richmond postmark. Why was Missy Sandburn writing me? The answer to my question was completely unexpected. Like so many children of Vietnam War veterans, Missy was hungry to know about her father's war experience. He had buried himself in his career, working tirelessly to achieve a dual agenda: acquire financial success and hide the war's impact on him; however, his daughter's intuition told her that he only wore a mask of normalcy. With keen clarity, children often see through the disguises worn by their parents. Missy had observed her father deluding himself for years; unlike him, she recognized his emotional pain, which was always lurking, looking for a way out. Rather than accept his responsibility for his actions out by Dông Bích, Trent Sandburn had myopically chosen a well-traveled path, opting for a lifetime mortgage of avoidance and guilt .

Unfortunately, if Truth and Jim Beam were hitchhiking on the road of life, Trent Sandburn would have picked up Jim Beam and peeled out, leaving Truth in the dust. Missy, on the other hand, had decided early in her childhood that the sins of her father were one part of her inheritance that she didn't want. She was eager to know her *real* father, flawed as he had been. Missy had discovered the importance of something that her father had failed to grasp: acceptance. Her years of practicing forgiveness were being put to a test; the circumstances around her father's death were serving as a crucible, challenging her ability to forgive her father's ultimate flaw. Sensing the origin of his pain—or some aspect of it—to be rooted in the events surrounding the February ambush back in '68, Missy was eager, but with a dose of trepidation, to embrace the off-the-pedestal truth about her father.

With his interment, Missy Sandburn had buried the myth of the man. There were two things Missy knew for certain: she didn't have a spare, perfect father to love, and she refused to be a slave to resentment. Her road to forgiveness and acceptance would be fraught with potholes, but the journey would be worth it because she, unlike her father, refused to live a life of lies. Even at her young age, she understood that she couldn't go on a journey without getting bugs spattered on her windshield. Jack Kerouac, watch out for the young woman from Richmond, riding along the healing highway that will take her down the road to Dông Bích, but finally home.

July 10, 2001
Dear Father O'Brien,

I hope all is going well in your life. It is difficult to accept that my father is gone. Maybe someday my heart will heal, but for now that day seems far off. My sister and I would like to thank you for coming to our father's funeral and presenting the eulogy. I also hope that you found a place for my father's Silver Star. Recently, I have been wondering about the night of the ambush which earned my father his medal. My father had difficulty coming to terms with or admitting the truth. Too much of his life was based on a lie. I want to know exactly what happened the night of the ambush. Hopefully, it will help me to understand my father better. (I need to learn to accept the real person he was.) Maybe what you tell me won't help, but hopefully it will. Although I want you to provide me with the details of that

night, I fully understand that you may not want to share your memories, which I would completely respect. However, if you would be willing to share with me the events of that night, I would be indebted to you.
Thank you,
Missy Sandburn

Upon reading Missy's letter, I realized that Trent Sandburn—most certainly with a heavy dose of spousal influence—had achieved genuine success in one arena of his life. I set her letter down on my desk and shifted into pondering mode.

Although she hungered to know the truth about the night out by Dông Bích, I doubted if she would be prepared for the gruesome reality of the events that make up combat. Were Missy my daughter, would I be willing to spill the indelible, blood-red ink of combat's reality on the parchment of her innocence? She was naïve about how her request would alter her life. She had never danced with death, feeling its cold breath, or listened to the ambush soundtrack, a cacophony laced with staccato bursts of small arms fire, the thud of Chicom grenades, and the desperate screams of teenage boys who ached to be men but would never know that luxury. Did I even want to meander down a memory lane that wove its way past the village of Dông Bích? Was the sacrifice worth it for me? Was stumbling through 1968 something I wanted to do? I was a monk, so why would I want to put on my flak jacket and helmet again? Too many booby-traps awaited.

My question-fest failed to generate any definitive answers but only served to send me traipsing through my stream of consciousness. I was nothing more than a supplicant genuflecting at the altar of the past. The 17th of July 2001 existed only on a calendar on my wall. Faster than the sniper's bullet that had dropped MacAndrews cold, the Pacific Ocean faded away behind me.

Tempered by the light of the full moon, the early morning darkness shrouding me...the steady drizzling rain chilling me, drenching my utilities...the pitter-patter of the raindrops on the leaves, on our ponchos, on our helmets, finally stopping...back at Dông Bích, my poncho provides cover for the leftover ashes of three joss sticks...I'd give anything for a spare poncho right now...my radio operator Ethridge is sleeping Nam-style, one noise away from being awake, so I do the radio check with Sandburn, and the rain starts up again, heavier than before...Sandburn's overdue...there's no reply...in the midst of my second attempt, the thud of a Viêt Cong grenade, quickly followed by the loud blast from a Claymore mine, shattering the steady monotone sound of the endless rain...thousands of sharp pellets exploding through the rainy darkness like so many ambassadors of death with full intention of serving their master...the blast misses Nellis and Hesse who are crouching in a shallow ravine nearly fifteen meters south of the trail...under cover of darkness, the Viêt Cong have turned the Claymore mine around...and Nellis and Hesse are lucky for now...twenty meters to their right in the shallow ravine, Westlake's M60 machine gun begins spraying the brush on the north side of the trail with a steady stream of red tracer rounds...Jimmy Rappaport is learning quickly how to be the best A-gunner in the Nam, feeding the hungry machine gun with a steady supply of belts of 7.62 mm ammunition...he knows his life depends on it...and he's glad he remembered to bring his asbestos glove for changing the M60's barrel when it gets too hot...the other day when he forgot it, it didn't matter...tonight it does...Jimmy would love to be in Wiota, Iowa although its endless flatness is no place to write home about, but it's not here, so it can't be all that bad...but he has no time to ponder the geography of his existence...he only has time, for now, to feed the beast all the ammo it screams for...muzzle flashes from the M60 machine gun cut through the rainy nightscape and are joined by quick bursts of M16 rifle fire from the rest of the squad, all firing in the direction of a dozen muzzle flashes pouring in from the northwest, just across the trail...Ethridge's firepower from his M16 is needed more than his skills as a radio operator...he squeezes off a burst on full-automatic and quickly slams another magazine into his M16, firing several short bursts...I'm keying down on the handset of my PRC-25 radio, barking out my request for an immediate fire mission, illumination rounds first...I continue to scream into the handset of my radio for ten HE mortar rounds with its killing shrapnel...drop them twenty-five meters north of benchmark Cactus...left twenty meters and fire for effect...I need fast approval from the guys at the Fire Direction Center bunker and lots of dead Viêt Cong, not the usual five minute response...two minutes...shit...what the fuck are they waiting for...squeezing the handset...I need the rounds now, goddamn it...the loud thud of a Chicom grenade and then another...red-hot chunks of shrapnel are exploding and slicing through the rainy night air...corpsman up...someone is screaming...no crawling for Doc Reyes...crouching, he sprints toward the listening post...the volume of Viêt Cong fire is building to a crescendo and God lets the VC bullets miss Angel Reyes, His Angel...Hesse needing more than Doc can deliver...Hesse, crawling and flailing his arms through the muddy soup, searches desperately for his right foot...no miracle...no help from God...only blood spurting from his femoral artery...tossed from a spider trap a few meters south of the listening post, the Chicom grenade has hit its mark on Hesse's fifth day in the Nam...before Doc Reyes can apply a tourniquet to his leg, Erik Hesse surrenders to silence, his dead face is staring into the mud..."FUCK"...Doc Reyes grieves in Cliff-Notes' style...in the sky to the north, an illumination round pops and the rainy night sky quickly becomes a dance of light and shadows...Reyes is crawling back toward the rest of the squad...a burst of Viêt Cong machine gunfire fire tears into Jimmy Rappaport's neck and chest and Westlake wants to help his A-gunner but the Iowa farm boy is going to have to do his dying alone...Westlake's busy firing his machine gun, spraying the shadows that are quickly becoming silhouettes just north of the trail in front of him...Doc Reyes stops long enough to hear Rappaport begging for his mom, but she is in Wiota, Iowa waiting anxiously for him to come home, and Doc is only carrying bandages...he has left his miracles back at Hill 10...Rappaport is gagging on his too-young-to-die blood, and Doc Reyes is batting 0 for 2..."goddamn it all to hell"...as another illumination round pops in the sky, the light and the shadows swaying back and forth...Webster, spotting a silhouette directly in front of him, tosses a grenade and a Viêt Cong soldier, screaming in agony, tumbles to the ground...one less

SKS rifle firing at us...finally, the beautiful sound of the first of ten explosions...the distinct concussion of an 81 mm mortar round...music to our ears...finally, my fire mission is happening and the volume of Viêt Cong rifle and machine-gun fire that's in front of us is subsiding... "die motherfuckers"...on our left flank, Nellis is on his own, emptying his eleventh magazine of ammo into a group of five or six Viêt Cong who are within ten meters, firing as they charge Nellis...those of us that are still alive have fixed-bayonets for the inevitable...it's that time...and then two Chicom grenades explode...and behind Nellis, the Viêt Cong are lobbing grenades from two spider holes that are connected to their tunnel system...he's surrounded as a burst from an RPD light-machine gun tears into its mark, exploding most of Nellis' face, hurling shards of bone and chunks of blood-drenched flesh through the wet air, splashing and landing randomly in the muddy puddles made red by Viêt Cong success...always filled with question marks, his ocean-blue eyes, in an instant, gone, becoming nothing more than memories for his parents...with our left flank now vulnerable, Westlake, clutching his machine gun, sprays the area to his left as he stumbles through the stream of water in the gully while he moves closer to Webster who's just popped a second red-star cluster into the night sky, signaling that we are being overrun by the Viêt Cong...another Chicom grenade lands a few feet from Westlake...shrapnel tearing into his left arm and the back of his legs...he screams but doesn't stop firing...the ulna and radius bones in his forearm are shattered and his severed artery spurts bright red into the muddy ravine...Westlake will pass out before he lets his pain stop him from firing his M60...it's his job...quitting isn't...adrenaline and courage are coursing through his young veins, but that will not be enough...blood is soaking through his shredded utility shirt and trousers...the staccato bursts from his machine gun diminishing and fading away as his loss of blood sends him into unconsciousness as his Silver Bird touches down in a town called Eternity... "please remain sprawled out until the plane comes to a complete stop"...no call for Doc Reyes who is busy jamming a needle full of morphine into Sartoretti who doesn't have time to stop firing his M16 in spite of being hit by several pieces of shrapnel...flesh wounds don't rate any sympathy, and a

dozen Viêt Cong are attempting to break through the squad's
right flank so he slams another magazine of ammo into his rifle,
firing into the shadows...the bayonet at the end of his M16 rifle
is just moments away from tasting Viêt Cong blood...I squeeze
down on my radio handset...it's time for another mortar fire
mission...I want them to bracket us with another ten mortar
rounds since the Viêt Cong are all around us...if they're off, our
mortars will be landing on us...there is only silence on the
radio...it's been shot dead by Charlie...I slam the radio handset
down hard in disgust...Ethridge's M16 is silent, and he's
sprawled out on his back, trying desperately to breathe...the
finger-size holes in his poncho telegraph the bad news, and I pull
back his poncho...hoping, but only a sucking chest wound stares
back at me, so I scream for Doc Reyes who is crouching as he
sprints away from Sartoretti who is tenaciously defending our
right flank and keeping the VC at bay...without a working radio
to call in a fire mission, I become just one more grunt who's
firing an M16 in the direction of the muzzle flashes coming from
a light-machine gun twenty meters in front of me...then I squeeze
off several short bursts to the east and then back toward the
north...my rifle jams, so I grab my radio operator's M16 and
continue   firing...the   death   train   is   pulling   into   the
station...Ethridge will be on it, so he won't mind I've taken his
rifle...Sartoretti is on his own for now...just to my left, Webster
pauses long enough to toss two grenades toward the Viêt Cong's
spider holes south of us and on our left flank...another grenade
explosion, and he's back to firing his rifle, the crackling sound of
our M16s losing to the heavier volume of Viêt Cong rifle and
machine-gun fire...Doc Reyes, panting, is kneeling next to
Ethridge and applying the largest bandages he has to his sucking
chest wound...Ethridge is gasping, and the steady barrage of
raindrops just keeps rolling off his freckled face and the
oversized bandages soak up his blood like a thirsty vampire
that's fallen off the wagon and Reyes is cursing that he's out of
bandages..."fucking bandages"...he's too busy to notice the
bullets whizzing by, but they notice him...Doc Reyes slumps
forward, sprawling across Ethridge...his dead eyes staring into
the mud, and blood streams out of his open mouth...now,
standing over Ethridge, a Viêt Cong soldier, who is really the

conductor on the you're-shit-out-of-luck train, is pointing his rifle at him...and with a flood of adrenaline pushing out the last bit of desperate and useless hope from his body, Ethridge says good-bye to his irrelevant angst and surrenders to anxiety and then to the inevitable...he is a character in Satre's "No Exit" play...and raindrops splatter nonchalantly and then slide off Ethridge's face, and his eyes tacitly peer into a barrel of the rifle that will send him home to a full-military-honors, closed-casket funeral in Greenville, South Carolina...but he sees his dad walking in front of him on that hunting trip the time he shot his first buck and it felt good when he said, "good job, D. J.," but the conductor has no time for home movies so he punches his ticket, and the rain and the riot of noise halts abruptly for Ethridge but not for Webster, Sartoretti, and me...and maybe Sandburn and Santos on the hill...do the VC realize those guys are up there...crouching and firing our M16s, Webster and I start moving through the small ravine to get closer to Sartoretti who is out-numbered ten-to-one on our right flank...within ten meters of Sartoretti's position, a Viêt Cong soldier jumps into the ravine, lunging at Webster in a failed attempt at bayoneting him...Webster swings his rifle up, slamming the rifle butt into the Viêt Cong soldier's jaw, hurling his body back...Webster is stabbing him in the neck and chest several times in a frenzied motion until his screams end abruptly...wide open and haunting, his eyes, portraits of terror, stare into the early morning drizzle...Webster's bayonet is dripping with blood, crimson and fresh, as he is crawling through the mud, trying to catch up to me...he's yelling but I can't understand him...finally, I hear "FUCK" just before another Viêt Cong soldier fires down into the gully at Webster...the burst of rounds tearing into his back and neck...his struggle to stand up fails...staggering briefly, he stumbles and knows hope and birthdays are two words absent from the dictionary of his life...I look back and only see his vacant eyes, empty of all fear, empty of everything...falling face-down in the mud, leaving on that sweet chariot comin' to take him home...a Viêt Cong soldier is standing over Webster...I squeeze the trigger of my rifle, but my magazine is empty and the pounding of my heart is the loudest sound in the din of the fighting... "FUCK"...lunging toward the Viêt Cong soldier, I start to stumble in the mud, but I thrust my bayonet deep into his upper torso, twisting it...he gasps as I yank my rifle back, extracting my bayonet from his useless lungs, and he staggers, falling back, landing in the mud with his mouth agape in astonishment...before I can turn around to continue down the ravine to help out Sartoretti who's on his own and alive for now, at best, or dead, at worst, I spot a Việt Cong soldier a few feet away on my left...it's one more unwanted I'm-so-completely-fucked moment...he swings his rifle...my head, his target...a small silver-dollar moon, like a Buddhist monk meditating perfectly, just observing, staring down as the Việt Cong's rifle butt glides through the rainy night air...vanishing in an instant is the chaos of the ambush, laced with the blackness, the drizzling rain, the incessant crackling of rifle fire and the staccato bursts of their machine guns, the never-to-be-forgotten whizzing sound of all the bullets that somehow missed slicing through me, and the jarring thuds of grenades...but God isn't peering at a lengthy list of my transgressions and proceeding with an interrogation, or asking me why the hell I was a dumb ass for committing all those sins...no Saint Peter guarding the gate...no Marines guarding the streets of Heaven like the Marine Corps Hymn says...I'm either not dead or I'm deader than shit and there's no God...and as I take up residence in this land of question marks where time and space are standing on their heads, the frenetic firing floats away...then, in an instant, a surreal soundtrack...a single rifle shot...a second...a bayonet slices my side, but I feel nothing...I'm moving away from the chatter and some laughter...why is there laughter...another single shot rings out...then another...I tumble to the ground...then, four more single gunshots...and only silence in my limbo or maybe I've landed in hell, immobilized, powerless, and my youthful certitude is AWOL...but there's nothing dubious about an all too familiar sound that shatters the silence...one final, solitary shot...another insurance shot...it's a no-prisoners night...why can't they put a bullet in my skull...are the Việt Cong blind in this dream...am I in their dream...the ravine has faded away...my head is throbbing and the ambush's lingering acrid smell isn't in my world...I'm a six-year-old and the swing keeps going higher, and my face is brimming with a first-grader's smile...but the pain in my head keeps pounding mercilessly.

Puckering my lips, I shook my head back and forth, signaling my *no* vote on the full disclosure issue. In spite of my reticence, Missy Sandburn needed a reply; I would provide her with just *enough* truth. Because there is veracity in the aphorism about the devil being in the details, there would be an exorcism; I was going to purge the devil out of my narrative. Although lying was out of the question, there would be no capital letters in *truth*.

> *17 July 2001*
> *Dear Missy,*
>
> *I know this is a difficult time for you and your sister Alyssa. Both of you remain in my thoughts and prayers. I will try to shed some light on the events of the night of the ambush with you; however, much of what happened that night has faded over time. I can tell you that the fight lasted for about five or ten minutes, but it seemed longer at the time. I remember how cold I felt because I was soaked by the rain. Your father was on a small hill that overlooked the actual ambush site. He was with another Marine who was captured by the North Vietnamese—he later escaped. The rest of the squad—nine of us—were positioned near a trail just outside a small village called Dông Bích (1). We expected the North Vietnamese to possibly come down this trail, but they didn't. Instead, a Viêt Cong platoon—about 30 men—outnumbering us three to one, ambushed us. They used a tunnel system that brought them within ten meters of us. We were completely surrounded and were overrun. As a forward observer for mortars, I called in several fire missions to help us, but even that wasn't enough. When the fight was still raging, I was knocked unconscious. I remember nothing more about the ambush after that. I have no recollection of receiving a bayonet wound, but I had to be patched up for a minor slice from a Viêt Cong bayonet. Also I was later told that your father carried me away from the ambush site.*

I'm not sure if my information will help you, but I hope it will be of assistance. If there is anything else I can do for you, please feel free to ask. I shall keep both you and your sister in my prayers.
Sincerely,
Father O'Brien

56

O'BRIEN
28 AUGUST 2001
INTO THE TRADE WINDS

Father Jeremiah, the Prior of Holy Trinity Monastery, had listened intently to my request and then said, "Let us continue this conversation in a week...after you have prayed on this. The answer will be clear. Go in peace." Behind his gentle eyes, wisdom had hung its shingle and when he smiled, there was no pretense, only sincerity and compassion.

As a member of a Catholic religious order, the Olivetan Benedictines, I was required to pray the *Liturgy of the Hours*: *Lauds*, referred to as Morning Prayer; Vespers, Evening Prayer; and Compline, Night Prayer. Life in a monastery was all about prayer and work, and the Liturgy of the Hours guaranteed that the prayer portion of the equation would be met. Prayer, however, meant more than asking a spiritual sugar daddy for *stuff* from a myopic wish list.

Faith is about recognizing that God, possessing just a bit more wisdom and insight than the average short-sighted human being, will provide and guide us perfectly; upon acceptance of this premise, the need to ask God for *stuff* vanishes. I'm sure God just smiles when we petition Him; being accepting is part of His job description. *The Psalms*, which make up part of the *Liturgy of the Hours*, are all about praising God for the excellent job He's done with His creation of the Universe, and He pulled it off with only one day of rest—as if He'd need a break. Critical for one's spiritual development is a third type of prayer, which requires us to simply shut up and listen. God has manners; He prefers not to yell in order to be heard. He might be telling us to duck, but when we don't, we curse Him for permitting a tragedy to happen. Had we been listening, we would have heard Him and ducked. Both life in the monastery and my study of the Buddhist philosophy of life had helped me to finally realize the essential nature of quieting the mind. So I listened in silence with an open heart.

As usual, Prior Jeremiah was right; the answer floated through the muggy July air, arriving in a dream with several elements—I am staring at Salvador Dali's *The Persistence of Memory* painting, with its famous clocks, their faces hanging bent and limp, but Dali has added a pack of bloated rats that is gnawing at the feet of a young Vietnamese woman who is lighting three joss sticks, and the incense smoke is swirling past the clock which is hanging limply over a branch like a used bath towel.

Prior Jeremiah wished me well, recognizing that returning to Vietnam, to Dông Bích, was part of my spiritual journey, my life-long search for peace. I thanked him for his understanding and asked him to keep me in his prayers. He replied, "Of course. We'll see you in two weeks."

Below me, the Pacific Ocean; in front of me, a half-empty, plastic cup of Pepsi and a paperback copy of Viktor Frankl's *Man's Search For Meaning*. His profound insight about Man's existential dilemma resonated with me. Unlike so many existential thinkers, he possessed a positive perspective about life, in spite of the extreme suffering he had experienced in a concentration camp during World War II. One sentence stopped me: "Between stimulus and response, there is a space. In that space is our power to choose our response. In our response lies our growth and our freedom."

I folded the corner of the page, set the book down and looked out the window of the plane into the darkness that was beginning to give way ever so slowly to the breakfast sun. In retrospect, Vietnam—the Nam—had been my *stimulus* that Frankl had written of, and the thirty-three years that followed made up that space where I had been choosing my response to life.

My combat experiences had impacted me profoundly—there was no glory to savor and relish—yet I had made a commitment to beam a smile at least once a day, regardless of how I was feeling. A friend from my teaching days once asked why I was smiling at her when I had been feeling less than happy that day. "Because I can. Being in the war helped me to learn this." Bafflement was tattooed across her face, so I added, "The guys I knew that were killed over there can't smile...they can't do anything but be dead...young dead, but I can smile, so I do."

She replied, "Interesting," which meant she grasped my observation as much as she could without witnessing the nonchalant slaughterhouse called the Nam. She never had met Nellis or his grieving parents who had been robbed of an open casket funeral because the physics of bullets and bone ain't pretty.

The flight attendant asked if I wanted a refill of my Pepsi. I looked up and smiled. "No thanks, but do you know when we'll being landing in Ho Chi Minh City?"

"In about two hours...about 8 a.m. local time." She smiled and continued moving down the aisle. I opened my *Liturgy of the Hours* and began my required reading of Morning Prayer. The word *required* no longer elicited a rebellious response as it might have several decades earlier. At my ordination there were no guns pointed at my head; free will was alive and well.

Life in the monastery was focused on work and on prayer as essential vehicles for my spiritual journey; daily prayer, a priority, was done on a regular basis—food for the soul. Having finished my required reading of Lauds for Tuesday, I thumbed though several pages and was drawn to a passage from "The First Letter of Peter." "Do not repay wrong with wrong, or abuse with abuse; on the contrary, retaliate with blessings..." An image of Sandburn floated by, and I continued reading, "...but hold the Lord Christ in reverence in your hearts." I stopped to ponder Peter's message.

The Vietnamese man in his mid-forties, seated to my right since boarding in LA, evaporates and Trent Sandburn, looking not very dead, says, "This seat taken? Don't answer, Padre. I see you're reading a little bit of good ol' Saint Peter. Word on the street is he can be a tight-ass with the key. You know...the one for Heaven's gate. When I showed up, he acted like a bouncer at some exclusive night club, and just pointed toward the elevator, going down. Enough about me and the afterlife. How 'bout you, O'Brien? Learn anything about us at 35,000 feet? Yeah, us."

"Matter of fact, Sandburn, if I harbor any anger toward you, my heart would be filled with poison, and so I wouldn't have any room for anything else. Love, joy, compassion would be squeezed out. Although you are responsible for screwing up lots of folks' lives, yours included, I need to not be seduced by self-righteous indignation. I'll let God judge you...I'm too busy editing my own life, and I don't want to become another victim of the Dông Bích mess. You're hard to love and forgive, but I have to let go—for me, and besides, you're dead and I want to live in the present, and you're not in that novel, so do eternity without me. Amen."

I closed my eyes and Sandburn evaporated, no longer a piece in my puzzle—hopefully. Disliking him had never been difficult, and resenting him for drinking and passing out while on watch the night of the ambush was easier to do, but I had chosen a life where *easier* wasn't necessarily better. Webster's grandmother, without realizing it, had been my Socrates, teaching me the true meaning of Christianity: *forgiveness.* All the trappings were the dessert, and forgiveness was the main course, but the kid in me remembered gagging on the brussels sprouts that I had been forced to endure for my own good. In the realm of spirituality, forgiveness sometimes had the same overpowering aroma, causing us to want to gag. Amazingly, I eventually learned to appreciate brussels sprouts.

Time had afforded me the opportunity to gain a new culinary perspective, just as it had helped me to recognize the crucifixion of Jesus as more than a lousy way to treat an innocent man; the message emanating from the crucifixion was all about forgiveness, when anger would be an easier reaction. Jesus put it on the line—talk was not cheap on Mount Calvary—and philosophizing about forgiveness was nowhere to be found. Jesus practiced forgiveness, the lynchpin of Christianity, while under duress, to say the least. He was the real deal as a role model, so it was about time to follow His example.

The banging on the door is echoing in his eight-year-old ears, and little Dave Westlake doesn't care that Russia's Sputnik 1 satellite burned up and fell to earth yesterday. The apartment is cold. Chilly would be welcomed, but it's always cold in the winter. The police are yelling, but his dad is passed out which is good because then he can't hit him or his mom, but today is different for his mom who doesn't know how to slam the door behind her. Fear is her drug. Bourbon is his father's drug of choice, and the liquor commitment is strong. Until death do us part. And so the cops tire of waiting and kick the door open. "FUCK," rolls out of their mouths and in an hour or two or an eternity later, a lady puts her arm on Dave's shoulder and calls him a poor little dear, but he wants to tell her that his name is Dave Westlake and he needs to take care of his two brothers because he's the man of the house. His mom tells him this whenever his dad is passed out or not around, and that feels good, but he hates it because he just wants to be a kid like his friend down the street, and the cops tell him that his dad won't be around and mom went to Heaven yesterday when Sputnik was falling from the sky, and Dave Westlake, the eight-year-old man-of-the-house, waves good-bye to his brothers, and the three Westlake boys are scattered to the wind, and dad gets no Father's Day cards, just a death sentence compliments of the State of California, the Westlake brothers becoming ironic orphans, and hating his father has no magic in it for the eight-year-old boy who just wants to have a family like the ones on television, where they laugh, but he lives in San Francisco, not in television land, so he boards a bus when he's old enough to sign on the dotted line and finds his new family at the Marine Corps Recruit Depot in San Diego where he has three dads who yell at him but they don't kill his mother so he doesn't mind the yelling, and this quiet Marine lets his M60 machine gun do the talking, hopefully a one-sided conversation. He wears his stoicism like a badge of honor when he's squeezing the trigger in the middle of a firefight in the Nam, and maybe his dad is in front of him in the kill zone, or hopefully he has left his dad back in California, awaiting his final appeal, and when the Việt Cong have had enough of his killing conversation, they punctuate it with one final bullet. Did he and his mom finally meet down the road after the ambush at Đông Bích and maybe if his hatred for his dad owned him, did he hang out with him in Hell if it's a place and not a state of mind? I hope that he found a way to not let his father kill his heart, and I wish I had been able to find Westlake's brothers since surviving the Nam wasn't in the cards for him. Maybe someday I'll be able to find them. God willing.

Two dead Marines were tagging along on my trip. I had an entourage, yet I wasn't a movie star or anyone famous, just a Benedictine monk, one with a resumé that included skills that ranged from calling in deadly mortar fire on the Viêt Cong and the NVA to masterfully tricking high school seniors into appreciating *Hamlet* and semicolons. When I opened my eyes, the plane had landed in Tucson circa 1961, not 2001 Vietnam.

The plane is landing to pick up my parents and my older sister who is a high school junior, hoping that the cute guy in the back of her history class will ask her to the prom in May. But Thanksgiving has dropped off my list of favorite holidays when my mother sits me down two days prior to it and informs me that a drunk driver has killed both my dad and my sister, who dies before she ever discovers that genuine love offers much more than the love portrayed in the lyrics of the Everly Brothers' songs. In an instant, half of my family is gone, and my mother jumps on the grief train, heading into the sunset, only to reappear emotionally at the beginning of my senior year. I am thrilled to have her back; even a teenager needs a mother, but the two years she spends wrestling with her overwhelming sense of loss takes a toll.

Death is not like a perfect smart bomb; there's always collateral damage. The drunk driver car crashes through my heart, and I hear no music at the Senior Prom, but I hear the mesmerizing sound of the Marine Corps Hymn. Ignoring my advice that my dad would want her to remarry, my mom plays the widow's game, fondly remembering her Thomas; amazingly, over the years, while my dad has been elevated to the status of saint, my sister seems to have evaporated, morphing into a mirage in the desert of my mom's grief: my sister's death haunting my mom in silence. And so, this surviving son bends

God's ear, knowing that God is listening and hoping that Mrs. O'Brien, aka mom, is listening to the healing whisper of her God.

As the plane began its gradual descent, all members of my entourage evacuated the plane, scurrying off to their own realities—mine awaited me just below in a place I had known as *the Nam*, but hopefully, it would become *Vietnam*.

57

CHARLIE'S SISTER
28 AUGUST 2001
THE DREAM REDUX

The night air was muggier than usual, and my eyelids felt like stones.

I am looking into a mirror, one as large as I am, but I only see the images that surround it...the rainbow with purple, white and green bands...the large wheel with several people and a house floating above it...the array of flowers along the path...my parents and Tuan handing me their gifts of flowers and joss sticks...and looking down past the closed white lotus, I see the small shovel and the alabaster jar are resting at my sandaled feet...I look up and nothing remains, only my brother Tuan who is seated on an elephant and has a blossoming white lotus flower cupped in his hands...in my right hand is a red lotus flower and a blue one in the other hand...Tuan is smiling...and the melody of a lute kisses my ears and as I begin to smile, Tuan speaks...let the sweet sound of the lute not be a prisoner to your desire...its beauty can be a trap...experience its calming beauty and let its sound ride with the wind...like a cloud of wisdom, it cannot be held, only beheld...Tuan floats off the elephant and sits on the path and I follow his lead...he offers me a bowl of curds, a handful of white pepper, and puts a drop of ghi-wang medicine on my tongue...as I am eating the curd, he places a small bunch of durva grass in front of me...I smile and look into the mirror,

233

staring for a thousand years, and then I return from this journey into the mirror...I see my color has changed to a deep red...I am not concerned...and then all the images that were outside the mirror are inside it or the mirror expanded so nothing could be outside the mirror...and Tuan is smiling as he lights three joss sticks and it begins to rain but not on the joss sticks...the incense smoke from the joss sticks floats toward a bowl with clear water and I wash my brother Tuan's feet...and he removes my sandals and places the durva grass under my calloused feet...he washes them...and he reaches over and gently touches my face...I close my eyes for a moment or for a thousand years...I open them and Tuan is gone...and resting in my cupped hands is a blossoming white lotus.

As I lay awake, a rooster crowed, and I fought the magic of the dream world that makes dreams float away like afternoon clouds. Tuan had been gone for such a long time, and I was hungry to see and hear my brother. The dream was so real; it was as if he were in my world, and I began to realize the depth of my loss.

The ache in my heart was older than Tuan was when the American Marines killed him the night of the ambush. My children have lived through my years of pain. My anger and hatred of the foreigners for taking away my family have been the threads that have run through my life. I have become so tired of this pain which I know all too well. What would my brother Tuan say to me in these waking hours? There was much in the dream to think about. My brother appeared to me because of his love, which even death can't stop.

58

O'BRIEN
30 AUGUST 2001
DA NANG

The most appreciated change that had taken place in the city of Da Nang was that it had ceased to be a target for the 122 mm rockets of the North Vietnamese forces that had played a cat-and-mouse game with my battalion during my tour in 1967 and 1968. Our success at interdiction was always tempered by their occasional successes that lit up the night sky, a regular Fourth-of-July-fireworks spectacle. As a forward observer for 81 mm mortars, I had utilized my skills on numerous occasions to call in mortar barrages on Communist rocket sites in our tactical area of responsibility. Bob Dylan had called it right: "The times, they are a-changin'." And I was glad that I was bringing an idea and not my map with its grid coordinates; no fire mission this time, just a mission of compassion.

The idea for a clinic floated into to my life when I was sitting in silence by the serene pond on the monastery grounds. Bringing healthcare to Dông Bích was an idea that had hitched a ride on the wind as it wove through the leaves of the trees bordering the monastery pond. Although it seemed like a good idea, I was old enough to resist being seduced by arrogance, thinking that I knew what was in the best interest of the people of Dông Bích. As a student of history, I had internalized the critical lesson that many do-gooders fail to realize: those that will receive help from outside sources must be involved in the decision making process because they have insights that outsiders do not have. Providing a medical clinic was probably a good idea, but it was one that needed to be tweaked, and of course, they needed to take ownership of it.

After settling in at my hotel room and making arrangements for transportation for my six-mile trip to Hill 10—the end of the road—I strolled east from my hotel, past the Han Market and the Cham Museum, and finally crossed over the Han River. A half-hour later, I was standing in the sand of My Khe, better known to American servicemen as China Beach. Lost in a trance, I sat there absorbing its beauty; out past the waves that rhythmically rolled in, the Pacific Ocean stretched to the horizon and beyond until it got lonesome and cuddled up to California. Like the ebb and flow of the late afternoon waves, thoughts rolled through my mind.

Tomorrow will take care of itself. Faith, Padre. You're not going on a patrol to hostile territory. The odds of an ambush are as good as George Bush nominating a liberal to the Supreme Court, but do the people out there harbor any resentment of Americans, and the Marines in particular? Hope not, but I'll find out soon enough. How will they receive my idea? Deep breath. How much should I tell them about my motivation for this project? Do they need to know that I was a Marine? What about the ambush? Some of those folks out there that survived the war will have been in the platoon from the Việt Cong's Q16 Company. It could get uncomfortable to say the least, or hopefully they've moved on. Maybe they were part-time Việt Cong but are full-time Buddhists now. That would be good. I wonder if that girl that Sandburn tried to rape made it through the war. She's probably about fifty now. Kids...hmm? Wonder how her life turned out. Tomorrow will unfold, and then I have a week to get things set in motion. I'm glad I invested my winnings from Las Vegas back in '68. Playing roulette was a game that was very similar to the 'who was left standing in combat' game. Vegas was just the luck of the roll, nothing more, so the money really wasn't mine. It was dropped into my lap by God who probably had a bet with the Angel Gabriel about what I'd do with it. Someday I'll ask God which side of the bet He was on, but that can wait. For now, I'm glad the trust fund has done a lot of good in Conroe and on the Tohono O'odham Nation, and that Tom MacAndrews Jr. made good use of the money I sent his mom for his college education. He needed a secret Santa in his life. It's hard to believe the last time I was heading out to Dông Bích, Tom Jr. was still parked inside his mother's belly, in a widow's womb, but today he is Captain Thomas MacAndrews, Jr., United States Marine Corp, soon to be promoted to the rank of Major, and it will be great being there at Quantico for the ceremony on the 10th of September. I'll be exhausted from all the flying, but it will be worth it, and I'll visit the Wall and Arlington Cemetery the day before if there aren't any glitches in my plans. It'll be a long day since I had to book my flight to LA instead of Tucson. One more stop, but at least I'm flying on American, and it's their 8 a.m. flight, so, God willing, I'll return late on the 11th to the serenity of my beloved Holy Trinity Monastery. It will all be worth it. I sure hope my mom isn't worrying. She did too much of that the last time I was over here. Well, she did have a good reason, but it wasn't my time. Mom, let it be.

Behind me, the August sun was beginning its slow slide toward the mountains that stretched toward Laos, one of Vietnam's western neighbors. During the war, those mountains were a stronghold and a supply route for the North Vietnamese Army—definitely not a friendly place—but three decades later they were nothing more than border mountains, wild and beautiful: *National Geographic* country at its best.

Before heading back to the hotel and dinner, the South China Sea seduced me with its enticing Sirens' song of serenity and majesty. In a spontaneous moment, I stripped down to my boxer shorts and strolled toward the water; within a minute I was swimming away from the shoreline that was shrinking in the distance. The heat of the late afternoon sun warmed my back until I stopped, rolled over, and with out-stretched arms, floated like a bobbing cork with nothing better to do.

A pile of sheared sheep's wool, pretending to be a cloud in a children's book, glides across the azure canvas that all the people back on shore believe is the afternoon sky. The other side of the Universe becomes the horizon for me, and smiling, my eyes say adios, and my eyes only see pink, my new horizon, and my face and chest are warm with the lingering sun, and the refreshing coolness of the water bathes me as my out-stretched body sways in perfect rhythm in this watery womb. For the man-o'-war bird gliding effortlessly above me, I am the letter X in a bowl of alphabet soup, and the bird's chatter floats away, and in this ménage-à-trois moment where yesterday, tomorrow and now are all one and clocks are lost souls stumbling through the Universe in search of meaning but finding none in the land of O'Brien, and the laws of physics are sitting next to a geography book on a library shelf somewhere else and are useless in the only world that exists with this perfect tranquility, the kind that babies feel in the womb and, just maybe, this is what Heaven is, and if so, I'm sold on being good because this is the most blissful and serene experience I have ever had in my life. A Maslow peak experience, or at least rubbing shoulders with it, and now I'm thinking again, dropping an A-bomb on my perfect peace. No judgment, Padre, just observe and let it be, focusing on the breath, the breath, rhythmic breathing.

I opened my eyes; the sun had gone to dinner out near Laos, so I checked out of *Hotel Om,* where the Beatles were playing *Let It Be,* and swam back to the warm sands of China Beach. Riding the wind currents above me, a solitary man-o'-war bird—with its obsolete name—patiently perused the South China Sea's menu: as usual, it's fish night. But for me, the tranquility had been an unexpected treat, dessert before dinner.

59

O'BRIEN
31 AUGUST 2001
THE ROAD TO DÔNG BÍCH (1)

As we were turning right at the school, my driver asked, "How much further, Mr. Michael?"

"Maybe a kilometer...maybe a little more."

The Nam was so close. Yes, I had been in Da Nang, but I was heading out where geography stands on its head: the Nam, not so much a place as an experience, a state of mind—probably what Heaven and Hell are all about. Nothing profound had occurred in the Da Nang of yesteryear, other than getting on the beautiful Silver Bird and flying out alive—twice—having cheated the Grim Reaper; sitting upright and gawking at stewardesses beat the heck out of the green-plastic-bag routine, but it was definitely a second-class ticket for Webster and the other eight members of our squad who had been killed.

That fateful night out by Dông Bích had been a shit-city experience—yes, priests say, "Shit," especially when it's the right word, the perfect word—but I had also known another sixty-five men who had been killed during my twenty-six months in combat. Men in their late seventies don't even know numbers like these, but those numbers knew me. They stabbed me in the heart, and I needed a corpsman, but Doc Reyes was dead and permanently twenty, and now I was alone on the road to Hill 10 and then on to Dông Bích. My driver muttered something, but I forgot to tell him that I had turned right at 1968.

When the car stopped, I was still staring into yesterday. "Sorry...what did you say?"

He turned toward me, brimming a smile. "This Hill 10...yes, Hill 10. Is good, Mr. Michael?"

"Yes." I had left the need for conversation back at the hotel in Da Nang, so I sat in silence for a moment before I exited the car which had stopped where the road had given up and decided to let the rice paddies run the show—it was their turf for the next few miles until they snuggled up to the mountains, both to the west and to the south where Charlie Ridge sat, lording over rice fields and small villages as far as the eye could see.

The Blue Ridge Mountains...Charlie Ridge with a southern accent. J. D. Ethridge's parents were so proud—pride with a southern accent—definitely proud that he'd served his country. Southern stoic. When he did his duty for his God and his country, his mom was leery, but his dad was strong. That's what he'd call it, or maybe not knowing what to do with those feelings of grief except to drink a bottle of Bourbon one time too many and promise the Mrs. that he'd stop the drinkin', but promises are to be broken 'cause those are the lyrics to Southern songs of sorrow and sadness, and it's not about a pick-up truck this time, but about a boy who thought he was a man, or at least wanted that desperately so his daddy would slap his back, and they'd go hunting for squirrel or deer. It didn't matter, but instead they got to look at me, a Marine Sergeant who had escaped the wrath of the Việt Cong who didn't give a shit that Mr. and Mrs. Ethridge would have preferred to beat their son to the grave, but a sucking chest wound and a bullet to the head would make that quite impossible, and of course, the Ethridge family would only get the PG version of DJ's final exit off Shakespeare's stage, and I would serve them up the Henry V version. Oh, yes, 'from this day to the end of the world, but we in it shall be remembered, we few, we happy few, we band of brothers; for he today that sheds his blood with me shall be my brother,' but Đông Bích wasn't a 15th Century Agincourt, and Corporal Webster, in spite of his extensive vocabulary, was too busy to procure the perfect speech and be our Henry V, inspiring us to turn the tide in the wet and dreary darkness, in the muddy end-of-the-line on the outskirts of a village called Dông Bích. It was a need-to-know-night and Mr. and Mrs. Ethridge didn't need to know what I knew.

The ambush was shifting into second gear, and I wondered why I had left the serenity of the monastery; as the elevator to Hell obeyed the law of gravity, I wanted to scream but just plopped myself down on the red dirt in front of the car. Burying my face in my cupped hands, I sobbed, shaking my head back and forth. With the stealth of a North Vietnamese sapper— dropping in uninvited, leaving his gift, an exploding satchel charge, a ticket home in green body bag—my unresolved grief dropped in to say, *"Hi"* with the subtlety of a spoiled two-year-old in tantrum mode in a supermarket aisle.

The forty-minute walk through the rice paddies to Dông Bích would have to wait; I had already walked into a minefield, and the pages in my calendar were at the mercy of the winds of yesterday.

60

O'BRIEN
1 SEPTEMBER 2001
DÔNG BÍCH (1)

The village chief, a former officer in the Viêt Cong who was a frail but wiry man in his early sixties, walked with a limp and wore a stoic face yet was affable and gracious when we met, as was the custom with a guest. He invited me to his house, which was made of thatch and was smaller than a typical American living room. We sat, and his wife poured us some hot tea; she smiled at me with betel nut blackened teeth, but her eyes, like islands in a sea of wrinkles, sparkled.

For the next hour, I explained to the village chief why I had come to Dông Bích (1). I asked for input, which he offered, although it was minimal. He smiled and nodded his head as I told him that I wanted to build a health clinic. He then added that I should talk to the village's teacher, a woman in her early fifties who had been teaching since the war had ended, about my ideas for the school. I agreed to meet with her later, but first I wanted to visit the village pagoda.

After placing three joss sticks upright in the red clay soil by a small pagoda just south of the trail that led to Dông Bích (1), I lit them, and the incense smoke drifted aimlessly, swaying with the gentle, late morning breeze. I then placed a can of fruit in front of the joss sticks. Kneeling, I bowed my head and prayed, asking God to keep taking care of all who had died the night of the ambush. Thirty-three years had passed, but the dead never knew another birthday, only knowing the hero's funeral as its main attraction. I sighed and shook my head, wishing that a magic wand could have erased the events of that rainy night, but the Nam, like a gluttonous and rampaging vampire, could never quench its thirst for blood. No, the Nam was not the land of magic, but maybe it had sworn off its predilection for death and suffering. Hopefully.

Not far off was a tree line, the one that the sniper used to fire off the round that turned a pregnant, eighteen-year-old wife into a widow in an instant; however, the fatherless years of Thomas MacAndrews, Jr., lasted more than an instant. The sniper's bullet, like an obedient child, just did what it was told to do. Young Thomas MacAndrews, Jr., was like that bullet, but he was kinder to his mother than the snipers bullet had been.

Although I was uncertain if visiting the scene of the crime would prove to be cathartic, I felt compelled to venture to the grove of trees, but first I returned to the village when my guide and translator, a young man with an engaging smile, motioned to me, waving me in his direction. He introduced me to a woman, probably my age, wearing her gray hair up in bun; life had painted her face with serious brush strokes.

Having observed me placing and lighting three joss sticks at the pagoda just outside the village, she was jolted back to the 11th of February in 1968, a day that had been a hodgepodge of hate and compassion. She had lived in a tidy world where only black-and-white photographs hung in her memory, but I had arrived with my rifle butt for Sandburn's forehead and three joss sticks in the rain. She was anxious to know if I were the Marine who had *protected* her, putting a PG spin on Sandburn's attempted rape.

I nodded. "I'm so sorry about everything that happened that day." Although her eyes were empty of appreciation for my twenty-first century apology for the sins of '68, I decided to tell her about how difficult it had been for me to forgive Sandburn for causing so much suffering. "I didn't want to be owned by my anger towards what he did to you or the fact that he fell asleep because he was drunk…it was difficult, but I didn't want to be weighted down…forgiveness freed me…forgiveness changed my heart—the Buddha believed that compassion frees us from our suffering, and I want to be free of suffering. Besides, the man who attacked you is dead…he killed himself."

There was no magic in my words to change the event of that day; there was only pain and longing etched in her face as she told me about how she had informed her brother Tuan about me: how I had defended her, which she thought was out of character for an American, and how I had shown reverence for her Buddhist culture when I lit the joss sticks at the damaged pagoda just as it was beginning to rain.

"My brother thought it was very strange that an American Marine would act as you had. I was happy that I hadn't been dishonored, but he was enraged and so he and the other cadres decided to ambush your patrol."

Once again, God was reminding me that forgiving Sandburn was an ongoing process; there would be times when I'd be like an alcoholic falling off the wagon. I flunked *this* pop quiz from the Universe, but there would always be tomorrow for me to let go of my anger toward Sandburn, whose behavior seemed to have been the catalyst for the ambush by the Việt Cong. I shut my eyes and drew in a deep breath, exhaling slowly. *Be in the moment. Let go. He's dead.* I opened my eyes. She seemed to not even notice that I had floated away for a moment.

She continued, "We expected an American force to come from Hill 10. Under the best conditions, and if they ran, it would take them at least fifteen minutes to arrive. Because of the heavy rain and the darkness, we knew they would not arrive for at least thirty minutes, giving us ample time to set up another ambush. I had only helped gather weapons after the first ambush, but I wanted the opportunity to be involved in the ambush of the Marines who would be coming to save you but would die in the rain, and…"

The Universe's second pop quiz didn't go well either. I cleared my throat, and my heart was racing; her cavalier words about Marines coming to die lingered, and my confrontation gene screamed like a spoiled two-year-old hungry for attention. Fortunately, I took in a deep breath, letting go of my anger that would be no more than a momentary renter in my heart. And God was saying, "*So who said it would be easy?*"

Being a wounded resident of the land of oblivion, she continued, "Joining in this endeavor with my brother Tuan would be so gratifying, but this opportunity was lost because the commander of the Q16 Company decided against a second ambush. Then my disappointment turned to anger and great sadness when Khiem, my brother's friend, told me that my brother had been killed. Our victory that night was so hollow. That night, Khiem was a man of few words…horrible words, and he just walked away. I was alone."

She bit her lower lip as tears rolled down her cheeks. It was no longer 2001, and the heart that ached and longed for her brother belonged to an eighteen-year-old girl with long black hair. The translator looked back and forth, first at me for my reaction and then to the woman who was wiping her tears. Before I could move toward her to offer her a hug, my translator gently embraced her with his young and compassionate arms. He softly spoke several words to her, the meaning lost but the result was clear. When she apologized for crying, I replied, "That's okay. You have much to shed tears over. You may want to be alone right now, so I'll go for a walk. I have something I need to do." Reaching over, I squeezed her hand gently.

At heart-level, I placed my hands together in the prayer position and bowed, first to my guide and then toward the woman, who ached to come home to the happiness she had known as a child—but those memories had been nothing more than mirages in the vast desert of her grief. She sighed, and a slight smile snuck across her face.

She seemed ready to learn about my circuitous journey of healing that brought me back to her hamlet. I opted to share a brief version that began with my trip to Las Vegas, the source of the money that I would use to help Dông Bích. She was clearly moved when I told her about my odyssey to meet with the families of all the Marines in my squad who had been killed near her hamlet during the *Tết Offensive*. I would tell her more, and I hoped she would share her story with me, but first I had some unfinished business to attend to.

I turned and walked slowly past several huts as I headed toward the tree line, which bordered a rice paddy—no longer verdant, proof that the harvest was imminent. Like a celestial shepherd, a low-hanging cloud lingered overhead, keeping a watchful eye over the sea of golden rice stalks, swaying rhythmically in the light breeze. On the day the sniper sent MacAndrews home to his pregnant wife's young tears, these same paddies were a mosaic, pock marked with random bomb craters, and I was calling in a fire mission, having mortars drop a ten-round barrage on the sniper who summed up MacAndrews in a single and terminal word: target. He hadn't even been here long enough to hate this place.

Above me, the midday sun lingered behind a cloud, both as indifferent spectators, unconcerned that Shakespeare had it right—yes, "all the world is a stage, and all the men and women merely players; they have their exits and their entrances; and one man in his time plays many parts." This September sky may not have cared; it had not read John Donne's "Meditation XVII", but I had, and words of his seminal "No Man Is An Island" shouted to me as loudly and as joyfully as the Sunday Amen-shouters in Mrs. Webster church back in Conroe, Texas.

"No man is an island entire of itself; every man is a piece of the continent, a part of the main; if a clod be washed away by the sea, Europe is the less, as well as a promontory were, as well as any manner of thy friends or of thine own were; any man's death diminishes me, because I am involved in mankind. And therefore never send to know for whom the bell tolls; it tolls for thee..." Yes, I've played many parts. Why did MacAndrews and the others spend so little time on the stage? John Donne was so insightful, so Buddhist. Too bad Sandburn never figured out that we're all connected. "For whom the bell tolls; it tolls for..."

61

TUAN
THE PRESENT
HEAVEN

I am standing next to my sister who is shaking her head in disbelief as she kneels next to him, this man of God, who, in his youth, served a different master: death. Although he was not hateful, he plied his trade well, raining mortar rounds down on us, his enemies, with deadly accuracy.

My sister's eyes, veiled with tears, do not see me, but this American Marine from my youth sees me with a dying man's eyes, two candle flames flickering, swaying to the rhythm of life that still, for a transitory moment, courses through him. Unlike an obedient child sitting silently, his agony screams to be heard. And behind his eyes, as blue as the South China Sea, he knows that a breeze is sweeping across the rice fields, coming to snuff out—oh, so matter-of-factly—the flames that still dance in his eyes that are not prisoners of fear. The swan's song with its not-so-gentle melody belongs to him today; there is only the rhythm of his blood as it spurts and pulses, rushing away from his body, made useless by the explosion of an old booby trap, a mortar round, an ironic relic, a remembrance of our war of liberation, greedily reaching through the years for one more victim to add to the tally of death.

Abruptly, his screaming stops. Staring up at me, he asks calmly, *"Bạn bè? Thiên thần của cái chết?"*

And I reply to his question, "No, I'm not the Angel of Death. I am your friend."

His blood is draining quickly from his dying body; the reddish clay soil in the tree line becomes a sponge for his unfulfilled dreams, and even my sister's desperation can't stop his blood from spurting from what remains of his legs. The mortar round's success stares back at her.

His breathing is becoming more rapid as words from one of his prayers flows from his trembling lips. "Holy Mary, Mother of God, pray for us sinners, now and at our death. Amen."

Then, in perfect Vietnamese, he assures me that he is unafraid and is ready. "*Tôi đa sẵn sàng. Tôi không có sợ hãi.*" His ashen skin, becoming cool and clammy, hints about the next page in his journey, and he knows the ending of his story.

I am happy that he has no fear, but my sister wears a mask of confusion as she listens to his words, not understanding that she is not part of this conversation between two former brothers-in-arms. Bluer than the midday sky, his eyes see past the spectator clouds floating effortlessly, silently above my sister, but for him there are only the threads of the rich tapestry of his life, all being woven together.

And then, as the leaves above him in the tree line begin to rustle, his breathing becomes labored and he peers directly into her eyes and struggles as he says, "*Hòa Bình,*" rather than his American word: *peace.* He reaches up with his right hand and gently touches the tears that are streaming down her cheeks. As he gasps, searching for one more precious breath, his hand falls from her face, now painted with red streaks from the useless blood on his hand. With death's final brush stroke painting the perfect pallor on the canvas, his eyes, like empty pools, stare past it all. The circle of breath is finished.

My sister's tears fall, mixing with the blood of the American Marine whose blood is as red as that of any Việt Cong cadre. The strange, gaseous odor of death blends with the acrid smell from the explosion of the mortar round, both unwelcome guests, lingering in the September air. The late morning sun, curious about the commotion, slips from behind a cloud long enough to find out what the fuss is about. A finch bounces skillfully on a branch at the top of a bush a few feet away from the corpse of the man whose life I had saved, all because he had protected my sister from being raped.

Someday she'll discover the truth about what I did that night and how that brought about my own death. My body died that night in February in 1968, but her death was much worse—her heart died that night. The war has been over for many years, yet she has found no peace; she has been a prisoner of her pain and sorrow for too long. Maybe now, her tears for this man will help her to finally begin to live again and say good-bye to her suffering.

62

CHARLIE'S SISTER
1 SEPTEMBER 2001
DÔNG BÍCH (1)

After all these years, I discovered that he had survived the war, and I finally learned his name, this man who had saved me from being dishonored. He called himself Michael O'Brien, and he was a Catholic monk—no longer the American Marine who had come to my beloved Việt Nam to kill, but he returned with a different heart, a gentle and generous one. Why hadn't the Americans acted this way rather than trying to conquer our beautiful Việt Nam? They had been such fools.

I was grateful that he wanted to help out our school. He and I understood the importance of education because we were both teachers, although he had left teaching years ago to become a monk. I wondered what had motivated him to go in this direction. Maybe the war? I would never know.

Our village was fortunate also because he told us that he wanted to build a clinic if we had a need. I wondered why a priest would have wealth to do these things for us. His story seemed strange, but I had no reason not to believe him. He was quite matter-of-fact when he told me that he had won the money by gambling in Las Vegas when he had returned from the war. He said he had felt lucky. Our village was lucky also, finally, thirty-three years after the American Marines had destroyed most of it as revenge for our victorious ambush of Father Michael's squad. The image of my village in flames in the distance still burned brightly in my memory, and yet Father Michael's reappearance in our village was also a reminder that he had saved me, which was still bewildering to me.

I still had no love for the Americans because they had stolen my father and my brother Tuan from me, but this American was different. I didn't have to tell him of my animosity for the Americans. Because he saw the hate in my eyes and heard it in my voice, he asked his translator to ask me, "Have you forgiven the Marine who tried to dishonor you?"

"Never! To this day, I want him to die!"

Then he told me that the man who tried to rape me had killed himself, and he wondered if I would forgive the man now that he was dead.

The words for my reply raced through my head, but only silence dribbled from my lips. No answers to his uncomfortable question which had ambushed me. *Why should I forgive him or the American Marines who killed my brother Tuan...or anyone who destroyed our family? Tell me why, Father Michael! Why?*

Above us, the curious sun peered from behind a cloud, wondering if maybe I would answer Father Michael's questions. The sun and Father Michael knew, so he stopped waiting and then said, "At first I felt great anger towards the Marine who tried to dishonor you...for that, and also because his actions probably set in motion the ambush which caused the deaths of eight Marines, some of them my friends."

Before he could continue, my voice quivered as I said, "My brother was killed that same night. I have lived my life without him." I sighed, and Father Michael only stared, but behind his eyes I felt his compassion.

A minute or a year passed, and the warmth of the September sun felt good, but finally sharing my feelings about what happened to my brother also felt good in a strange way. There was a release, and my heart felt less heavy, so I asked him to continue telling me more about the Marine who tried to rape me and who also caused so many problems for the other American Marines. I learned that he had been drunk and had passed out when he was supposed to be on watch at the time the ambush began. Father Michael shocked me when he told me that he had hated him at first but had struggled for years to forgive him. He had realized that hating him only served to keep him living in the past, and although it was difficult, forgiving him had allowed him to live without the burden of carrying the past.

Finally, he said, "I won't tell you what to do, but I just wanted you to know what I did. The Buddha would ask you if you wanted to perpetuate your suffering. He'd tell you that forgiveness is an act of compassion, which will free you from your suffering. What would be your reply to the Buddha?"

"I..." My words were lost in the firestorm of my anguish that trickled down my cheeks. He reached over, touched my hand gently and said, "Would your brother want you to continue to suffer about something that happened so long ago?"

I was silent, and I could hear Tuan's voice. I had been married to hate and anger longer than I had been married to my husband, but I couldn't hate this priest who saved me the day the other American Marine tried to rape me, and more than thirty years later, he made it impossible for me to hate him just because he had been an American Marine. He understood the teachings of the Buddha, and he understood me. But his wisdom unearthed great anxiety. He had seen into the darkness of my sorrowful heart, clouded over by my ancient grief, and only told me of his struggle and asked questions; he knew that the answers were mine. Then, with a gentle look coming from those deep, blue American eyes, he placed his hands together just above his heart and bowed his head slightly.

Father Michael told me he needed to go somewhere but didn't explain what he was going to do. Then, he turned and began walking toward a grove of trees about a hundred meters southeast of our village. I wondered what drew him to those particular trees, so I followed, trailing about fifty meters behind. Just as he disappeared into the stand of trees, I yelled to him, "Chờ đợi," but he didn't wait.

Maybe he didn't hear me. Then, there was an explosion, a killing sound, all too familiar—it was probably a mortar round, a left-over booby trap, long forgotten. Immediately, dozens of startled birds shot out of the trees like shrapnel cutting through the blue September sky. My heart was racing as I ran toward the plume of smoke that was wafting out of the tree line. When I was eighteen, I would have smiled upon hearing this sound, but something had changed and I hated booby traps just this one time. As I approached the grove of trees, fear raced through my mind, and I wanted yesterday or tomorrow, anything but today.

I stopped and looked down; stunned, my mouth was agape for a brief moment, and then my fear shifted into rage as I screamed, "No!" My chest was heaving, and I was shaking my head in disbelief. Tears streamed down my cheeks as I dropped down, kneeling next to him. The shrapnel from the mortar round had blown off his right leg just below his knee and a bright red stream of blood was spurting from his severed artery. The mortar round's metal shards had shredded his other leg, and he lay in a pool of blood. His torso, arms and face were spattered with blood from dozens of smaller gashes. I was flailing my arms in the air in anger and frustration, screaming, "Why take this man? No!" The world was deaf to my pleas.

Screaming and moaning, the only language he knew, but then as his breathing became increasingly labored, he began mumbling in Vietnamese, but not to me. Then, with a deep sigh, he exhaled and looked up into my eyes with a gaze that was seared into my memory, and said, "*Hòa Bình.*" He was in agony, yet he found the strength to utter the Vietnamese words for *peace*. How odd. With great difficulty due to the gashes in his forearm, he lifted his right hand, touching my cheek the gentle way that a lover does, but his bloodied fingers were those of a dying man struggling to wipe away my tears; and as his gentle and trembling fingers slid down, finally falling off my chin, he muttered in Vietnamese, "*Xin vui lòng tha thứ.*"

He was busy dying, but he still found the words to ask me to forgive the other Marine who had tried to rape me. I thought he had realized that I would never do that when he asked me earlier to forgive. Never. Never. Never. But his face had no hate, no fear, and this man was the ultimate enigma for me. As my tears streamed down my blood-stained cheeks, the gentle look that he wore on his face faded away as he gasped, searching for one final breath of September's warm air.

And the stench of death clung to me as I threw up. Why did he have to die? My heart was exhausted from this war that never seemed go away.

63

O'BRIEN
THE PRESENT
HEAVEN

Being dead isn't quite what I thought it would be like—some obvious downsides, but not bad, all the same. No winged angels, no pearly gates, no billowing clouds, no white-bearded God. I won't even venture to explain it.

Floating through the cool air, held prisoner by the two-foot thick adobe walls of the monastery church, the lyrics of Pete Seeger's classic "Turn! Turn! Turn!" resonate with the mourners. An escort of nine Marines, attired in their dress blues with the traditional white formal cover, blue jacket, white trousers and spit-shined black shoes roll my casket to within a few feet of the altar. With impeccable, military precision, the Marines—three on either side of the casket—remove the American flag, folding it neatly into a triangle, and then hand it to another Marine, a Staff Sergeant wearing a saber, who leads the honor guard to their seats to the left. Two monks approach my casket, covering it with a white pall; and as another monk, Prior Jeremiah, sprinkles holy water on the casket, Pete Seeger's final lyrics—"A time for peace, I swear it's not too late"—evaporate. A bee, buzzing and swirling high above the coffin, swoops down, landing on the casket's white pall.

How odd that I tasted both a bit of Heaven and Hell in a place called Vietnam. As a young man I went there to kill—twice.

At the end of my life on Earth, I returned to Vietnam to die. Some might think that my return to the village of Dông Bích was my swan song because I knew that I was in the fifth act of the play that was my life, but I was unaware last week that the karma train had come to the end of the line in that stunningly beautiful and verdant land. Like a lurking Serengeti lion, patiently stalking the wildebeest, death waits for the perfect moment; it's fickle that way. "A time to kill, a time to heal." Going back was all about healing. "Turn! Turn! Turn!"...perfect choice. I wonder who picked the song.

Nine Marines, wearing their dress blue uniforms, sit smartly at attention in the front two rows, staring straight ahead as Prior Jeremiah motions for my friend Baptisto Santos, a Tohono O'odham man in his early fifties, to approach the pulpit to present a eulogy.

My funeral is the punctuation mark on the sentence that was my life, playing itself out perfectly, though some would say that it had been cut short. Of course, my mother would think it was cut short; I was her baby. A mother's worst nightmare—attending her child's funeral—and this is the second time for her. Tears on a September morning, but I know she is thankful for the fifty-four years she called me son. I was her Michael—the Marine, the English teacher, the priest. But now she is alone. She and Baptisto are lone survivors: one of a family, the other of an ambushed Marine squad.

Wearing a stoic face and standing erect behind the pulpit, Baptisto Santos, noticeably uncomfortable in his dark grey suit, first adjusts his solid-red tie and then the microphone; he clears his throat as he prepares to present his eulogy to the mourners who have come to bid me farewell.

The closest I ever had come to experiencing absolute bliss happened shortly before my death while floating on my back in the blue waters just off China Beach. That feeling of complete peace and timelessness foreshadowed this experience that the people at my funeral are referring to as Heaven. Pretending to be an afterlife geography expert, someone whispers, "He has gone to a better place," but my mother's tears are streaming down her cheeks and I must only observe. Can't be the consoling son, offering a hug and wiping away those tears. It seems that even being in Heaven has a downside, but the part of Heaven that I truly like is that time does not exist as it does on Earth, where it is September 10, 2001, yet now I truly experience the present. No calendars or clocks. Beautiful.

In the silence of the moment before he will eulogize me, Baptisto Santos peers down at his notes and expels a breath. He'd rather face an onslaught of North Vietnamese attackers than stand in front of several hundred mourners who fill the church to capacity and spill out into the courtyard, but he has checked his fear at the door; Marines take care of Marines, so Baptisto Santos, standing in front of a sea of sad faces, prepares to honor me, his friend, and I am touched.

It's deep-breath-time, my friend. Whatever you do, be succinct and don't put me on a pedestal. I'm not better than I actually was, just because I'm dead. I was just a man doing his duty, stumbling on the way to acceptance, and just trying to do the right thing. Don't use the four letter word—hero. Marines aren't heroes. The stuff we do is just part of the job description. Just tell my mom I was a good Marine; she'll love that. And give her a hug; she could sure use one.

In a soft-spoken voice and with measured words, he begins:

> *"My name is Baptisto Santos. We have all come together on this tenth day of September to mourn and honor the memory of Michael O'Brien. He and I served together with the 1st Battalion, 7th Marine Regiment in Vietnam back in 1968. I'm certain that he is in Heaven. He already did his time in Hell.*
>
> *We all knew Michael O'Brien but in different ways. For his mother, he was Michael, the son who made her proud because he made a positive difference. Mrs. O'Brien, I'm so sorry for your loss. For some, he was a friend who could be counted on. For his students, he was Mr. O'Brien who helped them to learn to think, to achieve their full potential. For others, he was Father Michael, who was a man of deep and genuine faith. For me, he was Sergeant O'Brien, who was one hell of a*

Marine, but more importantly, we were brothers-in-arms, and I'm proud to call him my friend.

I will be brief as possible. I was nervous when I came up here, but now I feel calm. I think his spirit is here right now, so I know he's listening in and wouldn't be happy with me if I went rambling on about him. I'll honor that, but there are a few things I want to share that most people aren't aware of. After he returned from his second tour of duty in July of '68, he visited the families of nine fellow Marines who were killed in an ambush that he and I and one other Marine survived. He wanted to help them to find some closure, some peace. He saw so much death during his two tours that he spent the rest of his life wrestling with his grief. He knew he had been given a gift, "the gift of life" as he called it, so he had to do something positive with his life. He wasn't about feeling guilty because he had survived. He believed that he could honor the memory of his fallen fellow Marines by living his life with meaning, so he became a teacher and a priest. He was all about service to others. In fact, his life ended while he was attempting to help the people in the village where the ambush took place back in 1968. Fate is strange. During his twenty-six months in combat, he was wounded twice, and he was awarded the Medal of Honor for an act of heroism during his first tour in Vietnam, but he didn't see himself as a hero. Because of the person he was, he never advertised the fact he had been awarded our nation's highest military honor. If asked about this, he would say that he was doing what needed to be done, taking care of his brothers, his fellow Marines. End of story. Small ego. Big heart. That pretty much sums up the life of this man who I'm honored to call friend. O'Brien, the English teacher in you will like the way I'll end this eulogy. Shakespeare wrote the perfect words for you:

"Now cracks a noble heart. Good night, sweet
prince; And flights of angels sing thee to thy rest."
Semper Fi, O'Brien."

Baptisto Santos sighs deeply, and a tear slides down his
face, splashing on his eulogy notes. With precision, he slowly
raises his right arm in a saluting motion until the tips of his
fingers rest just above his eyebrow. Taking another deep breath,
he glances toward the coffin, then looks up toward Heaven. In an
instant and without hesitation, his right arm cuts through the air
in the crisp fashion that is the signature of a Marine salute.

Not bad, Baptisto. Thank you for not trying to turn me into a
hero and putting me on a pedestal. The Heaven experience isn't
about egos. They're about as useful as a yacht would be in the
Sahara Desert. Life would have been so much better had I
realized that earlier on...at least I figured it out and lived it most
of the time. Good, you hugged my mom. Really appreciate that.
You're a good friend.

The funeral liturgy unfolds with precision; Prior Jeremiah, a
man in his element, offers opening prayers and proceeds through
the sacred liturgy. With trembling hands, Missy Sandburn, a
young woman in her early twenties yet a beleaguered passenger
on the grief train that chugged too slowly through her young life,
presents the Old Testament reading of Ecclesiastes' famous "For
everything its season", the original "Turn! Turn! Turn!" Upon
finishing his reading of the "Gospel of Luke", Prior Jeremiah
shifts perfectly, relating its message to my life, telling the
mourners, "Father O'Brien was prepared for death because he
lived his life fully and with no regrets." Then, a perfectly sung
"Ave Maria" accompanies my mom and Baptisto Santos as they
approach the altar with the bread and the wine for the offertory.
Upon completion of the consecration of the host, Prior Jeremiah
begins to distribute communion; simultaneously, the soulful
sound of bagpipes starts quietly; then, building to a crescendo, it
works its magic, capturing the congregation.

If I were there, not as guest of honor lying prone in my
coffin, I'd probably get choked up and shed a tear or two.
"Amazing Grace"—nice touch. My mom knows I loved that
song. Something in it that touched the depth of my being,

reached down and caressed my soul. It spoke to me on so many levels. "I was lost; now I'm found." Life's arduous journey was worth it. I hope Sandburn gets that same opportunity to find peace. I'm glad his two daughters came here today. His suicide only postponed his experiencing bliss. I never understood the whys behind his actions, even as far back as our time in the Nam. He was lost but will have to wait to be found. I hope he finds peace—next time around.

As communion ends, the bagpipe rendition of "Amazing Grace" tapers off and evaporates into the land of memories. Accompanied by two monks—Father Crispin and Father Paul—Prior Jeremiah strides slowly toward the casket where he offers prayers of commendation as Father Paul sprinkles holy water on the white-pall-covered coffin; then, as Prior Jeremiah petitions God to grant my soul entrance into Heaven, Father Crispin, holding a censer, moves around the casket, gently swinging the incense holder, creating wafts of smoke that linger while Prior Jeremiah removes the pall.

Prior Jeremiah, thanks for making the request with God. You and God are on the same page. It's not an issue, and Heaven isn't a place to enter…in the usual sense. You'll find out.

With incense smoke still lingering above my casket, nine Marines exit their seats and approach the coffin; with precision, six of them drape the casket with the American flag. Moving in unison, the funeral cortege, led by six Marines pallbearer s slowly escorts my coffin down the aisle through a sea of sad faces where there is no economy of grief to be found. Prior Jeremiah and the five fellow monks, followed by a the rest of the Marine honor guard, complete the retinue. As the funeral recession begins, the sound of bagpipes returns: this time the familiar sound of the "Marine Corps Hymn" accompanies my casketed exit from my beloved church, my sanctuary in the Southern Arizona desert.

Kate, now a woman in her mid-forties, is standing towards the back of the church. Annoyed by the buzzing of a bee, she swats it away; the mist in her eyes blurs her view of the flag-draped coffin as it passes by. She wants to be as sturdy as the church's massive adobe walls, but the Rolling Stones were right: "you can't always get what you want, but…you get what you need." Her husband squeezes her hand, offering support; for an instant, a slide show of yester-love flashes frenetically through her mind as she snuggles up to the possibilities, and then she feels the warm sweat of her husband's hand and not the long, lingering, gentle caresses and the lips of Michael O'Brien; the summer of love has been replaced by the summer of good-byes.

I'm so glad you were in my life, but my heart was too filled with the Nam, so your love got edged out. The 'us' that might have been was just one more casualty, collateral damage. Your husband will be your corpsman, and you will be fine. Anyway you look at it, a dead monk is about the most unavailable man around. It just wasn't meant to be. I was your Hamlet and you were my Ophelia. Kate, I love and appreciate you.

Once outside the church, the Marine escort moves slowly through a crowded courtyard of several hundred people; the entourage continues a few more feet and then turns left to make the final journey to the freshly dug gravesite, situated at the northern end of the monastery's cemetery, which is nestled between the church and a large pond and is surrounded by a mesquite bosque. It's a desert cemetery: green grass is AWOL.

Had I wanted a lush carpet of green, I'd have opted for burial at Arlington. This place is my home, at least for my body. It will be good for my mom to be able to visit. Yes, I am at home here.

Upon reaching the gravesite, the funeral cortege of no-nonsense monks and Marines waits while the mourners meander past the two dozen other tombstones that dot the small cemetery. My casket rests on the mechanical device that will lower me into the coolness of the desert's belly. As smartly as they had covered my coffin with the American flag, the six Marines remove it; their precision would make their drill instructors well up with pride—the few, the proud, the Marines. Having received the triangled flag from one of the Marines, the Staff Sergeant then turns crisply and steps toward my mother. Handing the flag to her, he says, "Mrs. O'Brien, please accept this flag from a grateful nation."

Knowing my mom, she wants to say, "Thanks, I'd rather have my son." But she knows I was on bonus time. The past thirty-three years had been gifts—this she knew, so she politely says, "Thank you."

He does an about-face movement, and then he and the contingent of Marines, except for the bugler, file away from the gravesite, leaving the casket to the monks and their rituals, their holy good-byes. Holy water sprinkles down, splashing like tiny raindrops on my casket as Prior Jeremiah petitions God once again, just in case He hadn't been listening the first time, to accept my soul, aka the faithfully departed, into Heaven. Then, more incense and its sacred scent to send me off.

As the Marine bugler places his bugle to his puckered lips and begins to play Taps, the final Marine Corps good-bye, my casket slowly begins its six-foot journey to the proverbial final resting place. With a clod of dirt in hand, my mother shuffles forward and tosses it into the open hole. Baptisto Santos is next, followed by several dozen other mourners who seek to be part of the process of bidding me adieu. Kate moves forward and tosses a single red rose into the hole.

Never understood why people wait to show love. Guess it's just part of the human condition. Hope all these mourners translate this into something concrete in their own lives. Hope they're not frugal with their love when it matters. Regret and guilt—who needs them.

As the last handful of dirt lands on my coffin with a mild thud, seven Marines' AR15 rifles point diagonally toward the September sky. The Staff Sergeant barks his command: "Fire!" The crack shatters the stillness. With the abrupt first volley, tears burst from my mother's sad eyes, blue in too many ways. She sobs, and Baptisto Santos wraps his arms around her and whispers in her ear.

Thank you. Thank you, my friend.

A second, less surprising volley rings out, and then the crack of a final volley: a twenty-one-gun salute as the punctuation mark on the final sentence in the novel that was my life on Earth.

I'd have given back my Medal of Honor in a heartbeat if that would have brought back the men who died out by Dông Bích that night back during Tết. They never had a chance at life that I had. Teenagers...what did they know?...how sad, but now they are at peace.

With the firing of the final shots of the twenty-one-gun salute, the Staff Sergeant and the eight other Marines march away, heading back toward the church. Prior Jeremiah and his monastic entourage follow. Within minutes, my gravesite, still uncovered, stares up at my mom who is clutching Baptisto Santos's left arm. Her lower lip is quivering as she mutters, "I love you, Michael." And she and Baptisto Santos walk away. Now she has a flag to go with the Medal of Honor, but she'd trade it all.

But not everyone has gone. Wearing flak jackets, helmets, jungle utilities and boots, Izaiah Webster and the others from the squad that died on the day of the ambush stand near my grave. Tom MacAndrews, A. B. Nellis, Erik Hesse, Jimmy Rappaport, Dave Westlake, J. D. Ethridge, John Sartoretti, and Angel "Doc" Reyes are standing by the hole that is my door to my new condition. A young Vietnamese man moves toward the circle of Marines; he stops and peers down at my casket, now partially covered with dry, Southern Arizona soil. He stands next to Webster. In unison, and with military precision, ten arms slowly slice the September air as they move in a saluting motion, first a slow, upward motion and then down.

Then, as the nine Marines and the Vietnamese man turn and begin to walk slowly away from my gravesite, I—now dressed as they are—walk toward them and stop. There is a gentleness in our eyes as we look at one another. The terror that was Dông Bích has been washed away and belongs to yesterday. Now we belong to eternity.

I slowly salute these men, and they return the salute. The final item on my bucket list is now crossed off. As I am about to turn and walk away, I look directly into the eyes of each man and say, "*...We few, we happy few, we band of brothers; for he today that sheds his blood with me shall be my brother...*"

As Shakespeare's fitting words evaporate in the afternoon air, my true honor guard vanishes, disappearing into their own individual eternities.

64

O'BRIEN
THE PRESENT
HEAVEN

A slight breeze cools the warm September air above me, and the ghosts of yesterday surround me, and I am at peace.

I am one with the earth, hard and overgrown with the desert weeds that don't know they're weeds because they checked their egos at the door; and the solitary bee, circling and then strafing the battalion of black ants that scurry with fervor and focused intention across the desert's skin in search of a mesquite leaf; and the carpet of lotus pads, cuddling up to the forest of reeds that hug the bank closest to the mesquite bosque; and the pond, offering a serene sanctuary for a family of ducks; and the pair of hungry Harris's hawks, hovering, floating effortlessly with outstretched wings in the midday air above the mesquite bosque and then rocketing toward the pecan orchard and their unsuspecting lunch, a cottontail rabbit that is on the wrong end of the food chain; and the billowy clouds, sliding slowly, silently across the powder-blue mural that is pretending to be the September skyscape; and I am one with this place, this oasis of serenity.

65

TUAN
THE PRESENT
HEAVEN

Standing motionless, my sister stares down at the red soil in front of the pagoda, but her dark eyes she sees none of this. Her eyes are the eyes of memory, and they only see the outstretched body of the man who had saved her so many years ago; his corpse is like a compass needle pointing north, and his useless eyes are staring into the western sky. The finch with a memory darts in front of her; and a cloud, who had a friend who saw it all, floats above, unnoticed; and the rice paddy, which rubbed up against the scene of the crime, sits fallow, waiting; and the October sun smiles above Dông Bích, above the pagoda, above my sister and her hands, now folded together at her heart as she bows her head slightly in reverence and appreciation; and incense smoke roams aimlessly, rising and swaying in the coolness that drapes the afternoon air; and drops of rain splatter haphazardly, exploding in the rust-colored dust.

Standing motionless, my sister stares down at the three joss sticks in the rain. And I know that my parents were right when they named her Lien; you are your namesake, the lotus—the white lotus.

And your journey is perfect.

ABOUT THE AUTHOR

Born in New York City, Peter M. Bourret, a proud grandfather and father, has lived in Tucson, Arizona for over sixty years, where he attended twelve years of Catholic school, graduating from Salpointe Catholic in 1965. After he served with the 1st Battalion, 7th Marine Regiment, 1st Marine Division as an 81 mm mortarman in Vietnam during 1967 and 1968, he studied at the University of Arizona, graduating in 1971, and received a Masters Degree from the U of A in 1974. During college, he volunteered with an adult education program for several years. Bourret taught in Tucson for his entire teaching career: social studies for seven years at Apollo Middle School; then English for eighteen years, seventeen at Sahuaro High School. Bourret is not only an author, but he was the subject of *Strands of Barbed Wire*, a documentary about his PTSD and his return trip to Vietnam in 1991; he also participated in *Vietnam Across America*, a documentary produced by his son Jeremy Bourret which examines PTSD and its legacy with Vietnam War combat veterans and their families. He was a candidate for the school board in Tucson in 1976 and is an avid hiker, who has traveled extensively, including two to Vietnam. During the Bosnian War in 1993, he brought humanitarian aid to Bosnian refugees.

During his retirement, Bourret has volunteered in the local public schools, teaching writing to second and tenth graders; he also has supported a school in Nicaragua with books; currently, he volunteers at the Southern Arizona VA Health Care System, teaching classes about PTSD to veterans who are experiencing PTSD symptoms. He has been a guest speaker on the topic of PTSD to nursing students at the VA; additionally, he speaks on this subject at the University of Arizona College of Nursing. He has been a hospice volunteer, focusing on the veteran population; additionally, he hosts a monthly coffee and chat with a group of Korean War and World War II veterans. For the past twenty-five years he has been a guest speaker in local high schools, teaching about the Vietnam War and PTSD; furthermore, he has presented poetry readings in high schools and libraries in Arizona and California. Bourret is a charter member of Detachment 1344 of the Marine Corps League and is a life member of Vietnam Veterans of America.

In July 2015, the author received a first place award from the National Veterans Creative Arts Festival for a prose piece titled "Perspective," and was invited to attend the Festival in Durham, N.C. In the same nationwide competition he received first place for "Alone with it on Veterans Day" in the personal experience category and was asked to present his prize-winning piece at the 2014 Festival in Milwaukee. *War: a memoir*, which deals with his PTSD, was published online by The Writers' Circle, Inc. in June of 2014. *The Physics of War: Poems of War and Healing*, his first book of poetry, was published in January of 2015; and *Land of Loud Noises and Vacant Stares*, his second book of poetry, was published in March of 2015. Although he has written extensively about war and its consequences, *Snowflakes from the Other Side of the Universe*, his most recent book of poetry, deals with aspects of the author's perspective on life. *Three Joss Sticks in the Rain* is his first novel. Currently retired, Bourret is in the process of writing his memoir. All of the author's books are available for purchase at amazon.com.

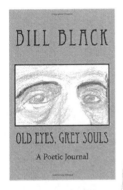

BILL BLACK

OLD EYES, GREY SOULS

A Poetic Journal

For books by Bill Black go to Amazon.com

Old Eyes, Grey Souls By Bill Black

Veterans are often heard to say "You wouldn't understand, you haven't been there." What are these images and memories that can be so misunderstood? Through poems that explore a veteran's soul, you are shown what these veterans wish families and friends could understand. Wars have colors, smells and images which can quickly and involuntarily be summoned. To remember brings pain but to forget betrays wounded and dead fellow soldiers. These small groups of tormented people shape our world even though most people never know them.

ISBN-13: 978-1500886325 **ISBN-10**: 1500886327

Regular Price: Book - $15.00

Cattlemen At The Cantina by Bill Black

Bill said, "These are collected poems from my shows and recordings of over two decades for those who want to see what the poems look like. Most have never been in print other than as a script in my pocket. I also give some notes on performing poetry shows. These poems have been edited and polished in shows and recording studios. They bring laughs, sighs, a few tears and moments you will want to share aloud. This collection is the majority of three CDs and audio book sets from 2002 to 2012."

ISBN-13: 978-1503223615

ISBN-10: 1503223612

Regular Price: Book - $16.00

A Cowboy Walked Into A Bar: The Monologue Show by Bill Black

Using his own poetry, Bill Black presents an entire theatrically-based monologue show. It was written and developed as an expanded show he presented to audiences in the Southwest. He then presents details on how a monologue show like this is created, including a short history of oral performance and a detailed analysis of this specific show. There is a selection of other performance poems he wrote during the same time he was developing the show. While many monologue shows have been developed, few writers have been as candid as Black on how the show is made to work. He brings over a half century of writing and performing experience into this play and its analysis.

ISBN-10: 1514798794   **ISBN-13:** 978-1514798799

Regular Price: Book - $19.50

Sea Song by Bill Black

Those raised by the sea are marked in ways beyond water stains and sun-colored skin. It is a life and culture that stays even when removed from the seaside. As Black moved away, memories of the shores never left him as he explored new places, people and stories. This is the fourth book of his story poems.

ISBN-10: 1534613994

ISBN-13: 978-1534613997

Regular Price: Book - $21.50

For more books by Peter M. Bourret go to Amazon.com

The Physics of War – Poems of War and Healing
By Peter M. Bourret
Bourret reaches deep within his personal war experience as a Marine and shares with the reader a glimpse of the true nature of war and its long-term consequences. His observations and insights will profoundly impact the way the reader views war.
ISBN-10: 1502471973
ISBN-13: 978-1502471970
Price: $15.00

Land of Loud Noises and Vacant Stares
By Peter M. Bourret
Bourret shares with the reader insights about the war experience - the profound impact of war on a twenty-year-old who discovered the horrors of war, letting the reader peek behind killing's curtain. This fasten-your-seat-belt experience will show what General Sherman meant when he referred to war as Hell, a view into PTSD and its insidious nature, the impact of war on the families at home, and the arduous healing process. Combat veterans will easily recognize the topics about which Bourret writes, and those who have never known the war experience will possess a better understanding of the phrase "Thank you for your service."
ISBN-10: 1507715315   **ISBN-13:** 978-1507715314
Price: $15.00

Snowflakes From The Other Side Of The Universe
By Peter M. Bourret

The author of *The Physics of War* and *The Land of Loud Noises and Vacant Stares* leaves the war behind and ventures into his perspectives on the tapestry of life. The reader is treated to a slideshow of the landscape of Bourret's journey, where aha moments, essential elements in the creation of a poem, percolate below the surface, waiting for the invisible connecting-of-the-dots process to finish; eventually, a poem is born. Meet his family of poems that were once like snowflakes from the other side of the Universe until he packed these snowflakes together like a five-year-old creating a snowman.
ISBN-10: 1515028844
ISBN-13: 978-1515028840
Price: 15.00

For books by Ray Keen go to Amazon.com

Love Poems For Cannibals
By Ray Keen

The reader finds poems of war in Vietnam, poems dealing with current spiritual issues, dysfunctional family relationships and feelings, portraits of great figures in contemporary human history presented with candor and wit, poems that rage against the omnipresence of human hypocrisy, and poems that present American/Western civilization under the glaring light of truth – with the single redemptive quality that this truth sings in these poems. A volume of contemporary poetry, **Love Poems for Cannibals** expresses the thoughts, feelings, quandaries and wonder of an American poet very much alive to the darkness and light of the 21st century.
ISBN-10: 1470182688   **ISBN-13:** 978-1470182687

The Private and Public Life of King Able

By Ray Keen
An old king, abandoned in his palace and clueless about his predicament, is being watched by men in masks. These men project an insidious clinical detachment. King Able, the only actor speaking in the play, cannot say anything to help or ameliorate his situation. His language of "self-comfort" is his mortal but unacknowledged enemy, an enemy of the truth.
ISBN-10: 149378577X   **ISBN-13:** 978-1493785773

PETER M. BOURRET

THREE JOSS STICKS IN THE RAIN

PETER M. BOURRET

pg— Ham O MF
P40 John Wayne —
Fighting Leathernecks
106 A O